THE
PRESIDENT
IS
MISSING

· THE ·
PRESIDENT
IS
MISSING

A Novel

BILL CLINTON

—

JAMES PATTERSON

LITTLE, BROWN AND COMPANY

ALFRED A. KNOPF

LARGE PRINT EDITION

Little, Brown and Company
Hachette Book Group
1290 Avenue of the Americas
New York, NY 10104
littlebrown.com

Alfred A. Knopf
Penguin Random House
1745 Broadway
New York, NY 10019
aaknopf.com

First edition: June 2018

Little, Brown and Company is a division of Hachette Book Group, Inc. The Little, Brown name and logo are trademarks of Hachette Book Group, Inc.

Alfred A. Knopf is a division of Penguin Random House LLC. Knopf, Borzoi Books, and the colophon are registered trademarks of Penguin Random House LLC.

The publisher is not responsible for websites (or their content) that are not owned by the publisher.

The Hachette Speakers Bureau provides a wide range of authors for speaking events. To find out more, go to hachettespeakersbureau.com or call (866) 376-6591.

The Penguin Random House Speakers Bureau represents a roster of speakers whose work is shaping national conversations. For more information, please visit prhspeakers.com or contact speakers@penguinrandomhouse.com.

ISBN 978-0-316-41269-8 (hc) / 978-0-316-41270-4 (large print)
LCCN 2018933152

10 9 8 7 6 5 4 3 2

LSC-H

Printed in the United States of America

Special thanks to Robert Barnett, our lawyer and our friend, who brought us together on this book, advised, cajoled, and occasionally cracked the whip.

Thanks as well to David Ellis, always patient, always wise, who stuck with us through the research, our first and second outlines, and the many, many drafts. This would not be the story it is without David's help and inspiration.

To Hillary Clinton, who has lived with and worked against this threat and the consequences of unheeded warnings, for her constant encouragement and reminders to keep it real.

To Sue Solie Patterson, who has learned the art of criticizing and encouraging, often in the same breath.

To Mary Jordan, who keeps her head screwed on while everyone around her is losing theirs.

To Deneen Howell and Michael O'Connor, who keep us all on contract, on schedule, and on the mark.

To Tina Flournoy and Steve Rinehart, for helping the novice partner hold up his end of the deal.

And to the men and women of the United States Secret Service and all others in law enforcement, the military, intelligence, and diplomacy, who devote their lives to keeping the rest of us safe and secure.

THURSDAY,
MAY 10

CHAPTER
1

❖

The House Select Committee will come to order..."

The sharks are circling, their nostrils twitching at the scent of blood. Thirteen of them, to be exact, eight from the opposition party and five from mine, sharks against whom I've been preparing defenses with lawyers and advisers. I've learned the hard way that no matter how prepared you are, there are few defenses that work against predators. At some point, there's nothing you can do but jump in and fight back.

Don't do it, my chief of staff, Carolyn Brock, pleaded again last night, as she has so many times. *You can't go anywhere near that committee hearing, sir. You have everything to lose and nothing to gain.*

You can't answer their questions, sir.

It will be the end of your presidency.

I scan the thirteen faces opposite me, seated in a long row, a modern-day Spanish Inquisition. The silver-haired man in the center, behind the nameplate MR. RHODES, clears his throat.

Lester Rhodes, the Speaker of the House, normally doesn't participate in committee hearings, but he has made an exception for this select committee, which he has stacked with members of Congress on his side of the aisle whose principal goal in life seems to be stopping my agenda and destroying me, politically and personally. Savagery in the quest for power is older than the Bible, but some of my opponents really hate my guts. They don't just want to run me out of office. They won't be satisfied unless I'm sent to prison, drawn and quartered, and erased from the history books. Hell, if they had their way, they'd probably burn down my house in North Carolina and spit on my wife's grave.

I uncurl the gooseneck stem of the microphone so that it is taut, fully extended, as close to me as possible. I don't want to lean forward to speak while the committee members sit up straight in their high-backed leather chairs like kings and queens on thrones. Leaning forward would make me look weak, subservient—a subliminal message that I'm at their mercy.

I am alone at my chair. No aides, no lawyers, no notes. The American people are not going to see me exchanging hushed whispers with an attorney, my hand over the microphone, removing it to testify that *I have no specific recollection of that, Congressman.* I'm not hiding. I shouldn't have to be here, and I sure as hell don't want to be here, but here I am. Just me. The president of the United States, facing a mob of accusers.

In the corner of the room, the triumvirate of my top aides sits in observation: the chief of staff, Carolyn Brock; Danny Akers, my oldest friend and White House counsel; and Jenny Brickman, my deputy chief of staff and senior political adviser. All of them stoic, stone-faced, worried. Not one of them wanted me to do this. It was their unanimous conclusion that I was making the biggest mistake of my presidency.

But I'm here. It's time. We'll see if they were right.

"Mr. President."

"Mr. Speaker." Technically, in this context, I should probably call him *Mr. Chairman,* but there are a lot of things I could call him that I won't.

This could begin any number of ways. A self-congratulatory speech by the Speaker disguised as a question. Some light introductory setup questions. But I've seen enough video of Lester Rhodes questioning witnesses before he was Speaker, back when he was a middling congressman on the House Oversight Committee, to know that he has a penchant for opening strong, going straight for the jugular, throwing off the witness. He knows—in fact, after 1988, when Michael Dukakis botched the first debate question about the death penalty, everyone knows—that if you blow the opener, nobody remembers anything else.

Will the Speaker follow that same plan of attack with a sitting president?

Of course he will.

"President Duncan," he begins. "Since when are we in the business of protecting terrorists?"

"We aren't," I say so quickly that I almost talk over him, because you can't give a question like that oxygen. "And we never will be. Not while I'm president."

"Are you sure about that?"

Did he really just say that? The heat rises to my face. Not one minute in, and he's already under my skin.

"Mr. Speaker," I say. "If I said it, I meant it. Let's be clear about that from the start. We are not in the business of protecting terrorists."

He pauses after that reminder. "Well, Mr. President, maybe we are parsing words here. Do you consider the Sons of Jihad to be a terrorist organization?"

"Of course." My aides said not to say *of course;* it can sound pompous and condescending unless it's delivered just right.

"And that group has received support from Russia, has it not?"

I nod. "Russia has given support to the SOJ from time to time, yes. We've condemned their support of the SOJ and other terrorist organizations."

"The Sons of Jihad has committed acts of terror on three different continents, is that correct?"

"That's an accurate summary, yes."

"They're responsible for the deaths of thousands of people?"

"Yes."

"Including Americans?"

"Yes."

"The explosions at the Bellwood Arms Hotel in Brussels that killed fifty-seven people, including a delegation of state legislators from California? The hacking of the air-traffic control system in the republic of Georgia that brought down three airplanes, one of them carrying the Georgian ambassador to the United States?"

"Yes," I say. "Both of those acts occurred before

I was president, but yes, the Sons of Jihad has claimed responsibility for both incidents—"

"Okay, then let's talk about *since* you've been president. Isn't it true that just a few months ago, the Sons of Jihad was responsible for hacking into Israeli military systems and publicly releasing classified information on Israeli covert operatives and troop movements?"

"Yes," I say. "That's true."

"And far closer to home, here in North America," he says. "Just last week. Friday, the fourth of May. Didn't the Sons of Jihad commit yet another act of terror when it hacked into the computers controlling Toronto's subway system and shut it down, causing a derailment that killed seventeen people, injured dozens more, and left thousands of people stranded in darkness for hours?"

He's right that the SOJ was responsible for that one, too. And his casualty count is accurate. But to the SOJ, that wasn't an act of terror.

That was a test run.

"Four of the people who died in Toronto were Americans, correct?"

"That's correct," I say. "The Sons of Jihad did not claim responsibility for that act, but we believe it was responsible."

He nods, looks at his notes. "The leader of the

Sons of Jihad, Mr. President. That's a man named Suliman Cindoruk, correct?"

Here we go.

"Yes, Suliman Cindoruk is the leader of the SOJ," I say.

"The most dangerous and prolific cyberterrorist in the world, correct?"

"I'd say so."

"A Turkish-born Muslim, is he not?"

"He's Turkish-born, but he's not Muslim," I say. "He is a secular extreme nationalist who opposes the influence of the West in central and southeastern Europe. The 'jihad' he's waging has nothing to do with religion."

"So you say."

"So says every intelligence assessment I've ever seen," I say. "You've read them, too, Mr. Speaker. If you want to turn this into an Islamophobic rant, go ahead, but it's not going to make our country any safer."

He manages to crack a wry smile. "At any rate, he's the most wanted terrorist in the world, isn't he?"

"We want to capture him," I say. "We want to capture any terrorist who tries to harm our country."

He pauses. He's debating whether to ask me again: *Are you sure about that?* If he does, it will take all the willpower I can summon not to knock over this table and take him by the throat.

"Just to be clear, then," he says. "The United States wants to capture Suliman Cindoruk."

"There's no need to clarify that," I snap. "There's never been any confusion about that. Never. We've been hunting Suliman Cindoruk for a decade. We won't stop until we catch him. Is that clear enough for you?"

"Well, Mr. President, with all due respect—"

"No," I interrupt. "When you begin a question by saying 'with all due respect,' it means you're about to say something that doesn't show *any* respect. You can think whatever you want, Mr. Speaker, but you *should* show respect—if not for me then for all the other people who dedicate their lives to stopping terrorism and keeping our country safe. We aren't perfect, and we never will be. But we will never stop doing our best."

Then I wave at him dismissively. "Go ahead and ask your question."

My pulse banging, I take a breath and glance at my trio of advisers. Jenny, my political adviser, is nodding; she has always wanted me to be more aggressive with our new Speaker of the House. Danny shows nothing. Carolyn, my levelheaded chief of staff, is leaning forward, elbows on her knees, her hands pitched in a temple under her chin. If they were Olympic judges, Jenny would give me a 9 for that outburst, but Carolyn would have me under a 5.

"I won't have my patriotism questioned, Mr. President," says my silver-haired adversary. "The American people have grave concerns about what happened in Algeria last week, and we haven't even gotten into that yet. The American people have every right to know whose side you're on."

"Whose *side* I'm on?" I come forward with a start, nearly knocking the base of the microphone off the table. "I'm on the side of the American people, *that's* whose side I'm on."

"Mr. Pres—"

"I'm on the side of the people who work around the clock to keep our country safe. The ones who aren't thinking about optics or which way the political winds are blowing. The ones who don't seek credit for their successes and can't defend themselves when they're criticized. That's whose side I'm on."

"President Duncan, I strongly support the men and women who fight every day to keep our nation safe," he says. "This isn't about them. This is about *you*, sir. This is no game we're playing here. I take no pleasure in this."

Under other circumstances, I'd laugh. Lester

Rhodes has been looking forward to the select committee hearing more than a college boy looks forward to his twenty-first birthday.

This whole thing is for show. Speaker Rhodes has engineered this committee so that there is only one real outcome—a finding of presidential misconduct sufficient to refer the matter to the House Judiciary Committee for impeachment proceedings. The eight members of Congress on his side are all in safe congressional districts, gerrymandered so cartoonishly that they could probably drop their pants in the middle of the hearing, start sucking their thumbs, and not only would they be reelected in two years, they would also run unopposed.

My aides are right. It doesn't matter if the evidence against me is strong, weak, or nonexistent. The die is already cast.

"Ask your questions," I say. "Let's get this charade over with."

Over in the corner, Danny Akers winces, whispering something to Carolyn, who nods in response but maintains her poker face. Danny doesn't like the *charade* comment, my attack on these hearings. He's told me more than once that what I did looks "bad, very bad," giving Congress a valid reason for inquiry.

He's not wrong about that. He just doesn't

know the full story. He doesn't have the security clearance to know what I know, what Carolyn knows. If he did, he'd have a different take. He'd know about the threat to our country, a threat like none we've ever faced.

A threat that led me to do some things I never thought I'd do.

"Mr. President, did you call Suliman Cindoruk on Sunday, April 29, of this year? Just over a week ago? Did you or did you not contact the most wanted terrorist in the world by phone?"

"Mr. Speaker," I say. "As I've said many times before, and as you should already know, not everything we do to keep our country safe can be disclosed publicly. The American people under-stand that keeping the nation safe and conduct-ing foreign affairs involve a lot of moving parts, a lot of complex transactions, and that some of what we do in my administration has to remain classified. Not because we *want* to keep things secret, but because we must. That's the point of executive privilege."

Rhodes would probably contest the applicabil-ity of executive privilege to classified material. But Danny Akers, my White House counsel, says I will win that fight, because we are dealing with my constitutional authority in foreign affairs.

Either way, my stomach clenches as I say these

words. But Danny said that if I don't invoke the privilege, I might waive it. And if I waive it, I have to answer the question of whether I placed a phone call to Suliman Cindoruk, the most wanted terrorist on the planet, two Sundays ago.

That is a question I will not answer.

"Well, Mr. President, I'm not sure the American people would consider that much of an answer."

Well, Mr. Speaker, I'm not sure the American people would consider you much of a Speaker, either, but then again, the American people didn't elect you Speaker, did they? You got eighty thousand measly votes in the third congressional district in Indiana. I got sixty-four million votes. But your buddies in your party made you their leader because you raised so much damn money for them and promised them my head mounted on a wall.

That probably wouldn't play so well on television.

"So you don't deny that you called Suliman Cindoruk on April 29—would that be accurate?"

"I've already answered your question."

"No, Mr. President, you haven't. You're aware that the French newspaper *Le Monde* published leaked phone records, along with statements from an anonymous source, indicating that you called and spoke with Suliman Cindoruk on

Sunday, April 29, of this year. You're aware of that?"

"I've read the article," I say.

"Do you deny it?"

"I give the same answer I gave before. I'm not discussing it. I'm not getting into a game of did-I-make-this-call-or-didn't-I. I don't confirm or deny or even discuss actions that I take to keep our country safe. Not when I'm required to keep them secret in the interest of national security."

"Well, Mr. President, if one of the largest newspapers in Europe is publishing it, I'm not sure it's much of a secret anymore."

"My answer is the same," I say. God, I sound like an ass. Worse yet, I sound like a lawyer.

"*Le Monde* reports that"—he holds up a paper—"'US president Jonathan Duncan arranged and participated in a phone call with Suliman Cindoruk, leader of the Sons of Jihad and among the most wanted terrorists in the world, seeking to find common ground between the terrorist organization and the West.' Do you deny that, Mr. President?"

I can't respond, and he knows it. He's batting me around like a kitten bats a ball of yarn.

"I've already given my answer," I say. "I'm not going to repeat myself."

"The White House never commented on that *Le Monde* report one way or the other."

"That's correct."

"Suliman Cindoruk did, though, didn't he? He released a video saying, 'The president can beg all he wants for mercy. The Americans will get no mercy from me.' Isn't that what he said?"

"That's what he said."

"In response, the White House released a statement. It said, 'The United States will not respond to the outrageous rants of a terrorist.'"

"That's right," I say. "We won't."

"Did you beg him for mercy, Mr. President?"

My political adviser, Jenny Brickman, is practically pulling her hair. She doesn't have security clearance, either, so she doesn't know the whole story, but her main concern is that she wants me to be seen as a fighter in this hearing. *If you can't fight back,* she said, *then don't go. You'll just be their political piñata.*

And she's right. Right now, it's Lester Rhodes's turn to put on the blindfold and whack a stick at me, hoping a bunch of classified information and political miscues will spill out of my torso.

"You're shaking your head no, Mr. President. Just to be clear: you are denying that you begged Suliman Cindoruk for mer—"

"The United States will never beg anyone for anything," I say.

"Okay, then, you deny Suliman Cindoruk's claim that you begged—"

"The United States," I repeat, "will never beg anyone for anything. Is that clear, Mr. Speaker? Would you like me to say it again?"

"Well, if you didn't beg him—"

"Next question," I say.

"Did you ask him nicely not to attack us?"

"Next question," I say again.

He pauses, looking over his notes. "My time is expiring," he says. "I have just a few more questions."

One down—almost down—but another twelve questioners to go, all prepped with their fresh one-liners and zingers and *gotcha* questions.

The Speaker is known just as much for his closing questions as he is for his openers. I already know what he's going to say anyway. And he already knows that I won't be able to answer.

"Mr. President," he says, "let's talk about Tuesday, the first of May. In Algeria."

Just over a week ago.

"On Tuesday, May the first," he says, "a group of pro-Ukraine, anti-Russia separatists assaulted a ranch in northern Algeria where Suliman Cindoruk was believed to be hiding. And in fact he was hiding there. They had located Cindoruk, and they moved on that ranch with the intention of killing him.

"But they were thwarted, Mr. President, by a team of Special Forces and CIA operatives from the United States. And Suliman Cindoruk escaped in the process."

I remain completely still.

"Did you order that counterattack, Mr. President?" he asks. "And if so, why? Why would an American president dispatch US forces to save the life of a terrorist?"

CHAPTER
2

❖

The chair recognizes the gentleman from Ohio: Mr. Kearns."

I pinch the bridge of my nose, fighting the fatigue setting in. I haven't slept but a handful of hours over the last week, and the mental gymnastics I have to perform while defending myself with one hand tied behind my back are wearing on me. But more than anything else, I'm annoyed. I have things to do. I don't have time for this.

I look to my left—the panel's right. Mike Kearns is the chairman of the House Judiciary Committee and Lester Rhodes's protégé. He likes to wear bow ties so we'll all know how intelligent he is. Personally, I've seen Post-it notes with more depth.

But the guy knows how to ask a question. He was a federal prosecutor for years before entering the political ring. The mounted heads on his wall include two pharmaceuticals CEOs and a former governor.

"Stopping terrorists is a matter of grave national security, Mr. President. You'd agree?"

"Absolutely."

"Then would you also agree that any American citizen who *interfered* with our ability to stop terrorists would be guilty of treason?"

"I would condemn that action," I say.

"Would it be an act of treason?"

"That's for lawyers and courts to decide."

We're both lawyers, but I made my point.

"Would it be an impeachable offense if it were the president who interfered with stopping terrorists?"

Gerald Ford once said that an impeachable offense is whatever a majority of the House of Representatives says it is.

"That's not up to me," I say.

He nods. "No, it's not. Earlier, you refused to say whether you ordered US Special Forces and CIA operatives to stop an attack on Suliman Cindoruk in Algeria."

"I said, Mr. Kearns, that some matters of national security cannot be discussed publicly."

"According to the *New York Times,* you acted on classified information indicating that this anti-Russia militia group had located Suliman Cindoruk and was about to kill him."

"I read that. I won't discuss it."

Sooner or later, every president faces decisions in which the right choice is bad politics, at least in the short term. If the stakes are high, you have to do what you think is right and hope the political tide will turn. It's the job you promised to do.

"Mr. President, are you familiar with title 18, section 798, of the United States Code?"

"I don't have the sections of the United States Code committed to memory, Mr. Kearns, but I believe you're referring to the Espionage Act."

"Indeed I am, Mr. President. It concerns the misuse of classified information. The relevant part says that it's a federal offense for anyone to deliberately use classified information in a manner prejudicial to the safety or interest of the United States. Does that sound right?"

"I'm sure your reading is accurate, Mr. Kearns."

"If a president deliberately used classified information to protect a terrorist bent on attacking us, would that fall under this statute?"

Not according to my White House counsel, who says that the section couldn't apply to the president, that it would be a novel reading of the

Espionage Act, and that a president can declassify any information he wants.

But that doesn't matter. Even if I were inclined to get into a semantic legal debate about the reach of a federal statute—and I'm not—they can impeach me for anything they want. It doesn't have to be a crime.

Everything I did was done to protect my country. I'd do it again. The problem is, I can't say any of that.

"All I can tell you is that I have always acted with the security of my country in mind. And I always will."

I see Carolyn in the corner, reading something on her phone, responding. I maintain eye contact in case I need to drop everything and act on it. Something from General Burke at CENTCOM? From the under secretary of defense? From the Imminent Threat Response Team? We have a lot of balls in the air right now, trying to monitor and defend against this threat. The other shoe could drop at any minute. We think—we hope—that we have another day, at least. But the only thing that is certain is that *nothing* is certain. We have to be ready any minute, right now, in case—

"Is calling the leaders of ISIS protecting our country?"

"What?" I say, returning my focus to the hearing. "What are you talking about? I've never called the leaders of ISIS. What does ISIS have to do with this?"

Before I've completed my answer, I realize what I've done. I wish I could reach out and grab the words and stuff them back in my mouth. But it's too late. He caught me when I was looking the other way.

"Oh," he says. "So when I ask you whether you've called the leaders of ISIS, you say no, unequivocally. But when the Speaker asks you whether you've called Suliman Cindoruk, your answer is to invoke 'executive privilege.' I think the American people can understand the difference."

I blow out air and look over at Carolyn Brock, who maintains that implacable expression, though I can imagine a hint of *I told ya so* in her narrowed eyes.

"Congressman Kearns, this is a matter of national security. It's not a game of *gotcha*. This is serious business. Whenever you're ready to ask a serious question, I'll be happy to answer."

"An American died in that fight in Algeria, Mr. President. An American, a CIA operative named Nathan Cromartie, died stopping that anti-Russia militia group from killing Suliman

Cindoruk. I think the American people consider *that* to be serious."

"Nathan Cromartie was a hero," I say. "We mourn his loss. I mourn his loss."

"You've heard his mother speak out on this," he says.

I have. We all have. After what happened in Algeria, we disclosed nothing publicly. We couldn't. But then the militia group published video of a dead American online, and it didn't take long before Clara Cromartie identified him as her son, Nathan. She outed him as a CIA operative, too. It was one gigantic shitstorm. The media rushed to her, and within hours she was demanding to know why her son had to die to protect a terrorist responsible for the deaths of hundreds of innocent people, including many Americans. In her grief and pain, she practically wrote the script for the select committee hearing.

"Don't you think you owe the Cromartie family answers, Mr. President?"

"Nathan Cromartie was a hero," I say again. "He was a patriot. And he understood as well as anyone that much of what we do in the interest of national security cannot be discussed publicly. I've spoken privately to Mrs. Cromartie, and I'm deeply sorry for what happened to her son. Beyond that, I won't comment. I can't, and I won't."

"Well, in hindsight, Mr. President," he says, "do you think maybe your policy of negotiating with terrorists hasn't worked out so well?"

"I don't negotiate with terrorists."

"Whatever you want to call it," he says. "Calling them. Hashing things out with them. Coddling them—"

"I don't coddle—"

The lights flicker overhead, two quick blinks of interruption. Some groans in response, and Carolyn Brock perks up, writing herself a mental note.

The congressman uses the pause to jump in for another question.

"You have made no secret, Mr. President, that you prefer dialogue over shows of force, that you'd rather talk things out with terrorists."

"No," I say, drawing out the word, my pulse throbbing in my temples, because that kind of oversimplification epitomizes everything that's wrong with our politics. "What I have said repeatedly is that if there is a way to peacefully resolve a situation, the peaceful way is the better way. Engaging is not surrendering. Are we here to have a foreign-policy debate, Congressman? I'd hate to interrupt this witch hunt with a substantive conversation."

I glance over to the corner of the room, where

Carolyn Brock winces, a rare break in her implacable expression.

"Engaging the enemy is one way to put it, Mr. President. Coddling is another way."

"I do not *coddle* our enemies," I say. "Nor do I renounce the use of force in dealing with them. Force is always an option, but I will not use it unless I deem it necessary. That might be hard to understand for some country-club, trust-fund baby who spent his life chugging beer bongs and paddling pledges in some secret-skull college fraternity and calling everybody by their initials, but I have met the enemy head-on on a battlefield. I will pause before I send our sons and daughters into battle, because I was *one* of those sons, and I know the risks."

Jenny is leaning forward, wanting more, always wanting me to expound on the details of my military service. *Tell them about your tour of duty. Tell them about your time as a POW. Tell them about your injuries, the torture.* It was an endless struggle during the campaign, one of the things about me that tested most favorably. If my advisers had their way, it would have been just about the only thing I ever discussed. But I never gave in. Some things you just don't talk about.

"Are you finished, Mr. Pres—"

"No, I'm not finished. I already explained all

this to House leadership, to the Speaker and others. I told you I couldn't have this hearing. You could have said, 'Okay, Mr. President, we are patriots, too, and we will respect what you're doing, even if you can't tell us everything that's going on.' But you didn't do that, did you? You couldn't resist the chance to haul me in and score points. So let me say to you publicly what I said to you privately. I will not answer your specific questions about conversations I've had or actions that I've taken, because they are dangerous. They are a *threat* to our national security. If I have to lose this office to protect this country, I will do it. But make no mistake. I have never taken a single action, or uttered a single word, without the safety and security of the United States foremost in my mind. And I never will."

My questioner is not the least bit deterred by the insults I've hurled. He is undoubtedly encouraged by the fact that his questions have now firmly found their place under my skin. He is looking at his notes again, at his flowchart of questions and follow-ups, while I try to calm myself.

"What's the toughest decision you've made this week, Mr. Kearns? Which bow tie to wear to the hearing? Which side to part your hair for that ridiculous comb-over that isn't fooling anybody?

"Lately I spend almost all my time trying to keep this country safe. That requires tough decisions. Sometimes those decisions have to be made when there are many unknowns. Sometimes all the options are flat-out shitty, and I have to choose the least flat-out-shitty one. Of course I wonder if I've made the right call and whether it will work out in the end. So I just do the best I can. And live with it.

"That means I also have to live with the criticism, even when it comes from an opportunistic political hack picking out one move on the chessboard without knowing what the rest of the game looks like, then turning that move inside out without having a single clue how much he might be endangering our nation.

"Mr. Kearns, I'd like to discuss all my actions with you, but there are national security considerations that just don't permit it. I know you know that, of course. But I also know it's hard to pass up an easy cheap shot."

In the corner, Danny Akers has his hands up, signaling for a time-out.

"Yeah, you know what? You're right, Danny. It's time. I'm done with this. This is over. We're done."

I lash out and whack the microphone off the table. I knock over my chair as I get to my feet.

"I get it, Carrie. It's a bad idea to testify. They'll tear me to pieces. I get it."

Carolyn Brock gets to her feet, straightens her suit. "Okay, everyone, thank you. Please give us the room now."

"The room" being the Roosevelt Room, across from the Oval Office. A good place to hold a meeting—or in this case, a mock committee hearing—because it contains both the portrait of Teddy Roosevelt on horseback as a Rough Rider and the Nobel Peace Prize he won for settling the war between Japan and Russia. There are no windows, and the doors are easy to secure.

Everyone stands. My press secretary pulls off his bow tie, a nice little detail he threw in to complete his role as Congressman Kearns. He looks at me with an apology, but I wave him off. He was just playing his role, trying to show me the worst-case scenario if I go forward with my decision to testify next week before the select committee.

One of my lawyers in the White House counsel's office, today playing the role of Lester Rhodes, all the way down to a silver wig that makes him look more like Anderson Cooper than the House Speaker, shoots me a sheepish look, too, and I give him the same reassurance.

As the room slowly empties, the adrenaline

drains from me, leaving me exhausted and discouraged. One thing they never tell you about this job is how much it's like your first roller-coaster ride—thrilling highs, lows lower than a snake's belly.

Then it's just me, staring at the Rough Rider portrait above the fireplace and hearing footsteps as Carolyn, Danny, and Jenny gingerly approach the wounded animal in the cage.

"'Least flat-out shitty' was my personal favorite," Danny says, deadpan.

Rachel always told me I swear too much. She said swearing shows a lack of creativity. I'm not so sure. When things get really tough, I can get pretty creative with my cussing.

Anyway, Carolyn and my other close aides know I'm using this mock session as therapy. If they really can't talk me out of testifying, at least they hope this will get the frustration, at its most colorful, out of my system, so I can focus on more presidential, profanity-free responses when it's showtime.

Jenny Brickman, with characteristic subtlety, says, "You'd have to be a complete horse's ass to testify next week."

I nod at Jenny and Danny. "I need Carrie," I say, the only one of them with the security clearance to speak with me right now.

They leave us.

"Anything new?" I ask Carolyn, just the two of us in the room now.

She shakes her head. "Nothing."

"It's still happening tomorrow?"

"As far as I know, Mr. President." She nods in the direction where Jenny and Danny just left. "They're right, you know. This hearing on Monday is a lose-lose."

"We're done talking about the hearing, Carrie. I agreed to do this mock session. I gave you one hour. Now we're done. We have more important things on our minds right now, don't we?"

"Yes, sir. The team is ready for the briefing, sir."

"I want to talk to Threat Response, then Burke, then the under secretary. In that order."

"Yes, sir."

"I'll be right there."

Carolyn leaves me. Alone in the room, I stare at the portrait of the first President Roosevelt and think. But I'm not thinking about the hearing on Monday.

I'm thinking about whether we'll still have a country on Monday.

CHAPTER
3

❖

As she emerges from the gate at Reagan National, she pauses a moment, ostensibly to look up at the signs for directions, but in fact she is enjoying the open-air space after the flight. She inhales deeply, pulls on the ginger candy in her mouth, the whimsical first movement of Violin Concerto no. 1, featuring Wilhelm Friedemann Herzog, playing softly in her earbuds.

Look happy, they tell you. Happiness, they say, is the optimal emotion to project when under surveillance, the least likely to arouse suspicion. People who are smiling, who are content and pleased, if not laughing and joking, don't look like a threat.

She prefers *sexy.* It's easier to pull off when

alone, and it's always seemed to work for her—the lopsided smile, the strut in her walk as she pulls her Bottega Veneta trolley behind her down the terminal. It's a role like any other, a coat she puts on when necessary and sheds as soon as she's done, but she can see it's working: the men trying for eye contact, checking the cleavage she's made sure to reveal, allowing just enough bounce in her girls to make it memorable. The women sizing up her entire five-foot-nine-inch frame with envy, from her knee-high chocolate leather boots to her flaming red hair, before checking their husbands to see what they think of the view.

She will be memorable, no doubt, the tall, leggy, busty redhead, hiding in plain sight.

She should be in the clear by now, walking through the terminal toward the taxis. If they recognized her, she would know by now. They wouldn't have let her get this far. But she is not free and clear just yet, and she doesn't let down her guard. Ever. *The moment you lose focus, you make a mistake,* said the man who put a rifle in her hands for the first time, some twenty-five years ago. *Dispassionate* and *logical* are the words she lives by. Always thinking, never showing.

The walk is agonizing, but she only shows it in her wincing eyes, concealed by Ferragamo sunglasses. Her mouth retains its confident smirk.

She makes it outside to the taxis, appreciating the fresh air but nauseated by the vehicle exhaust. Airport officials in uniforms are yelling at cab drivers and directing people into the cars. Parents are corralling whiny children and rolling luggage.

She moves into the center aisle and looks for the vehicle with the license plate she has committed to memory, the roadrunner decal on the car's side door. It's not here yet. She closes her eyes a moment and keeps time with the strings playing through her earbuds, the andante movement, her favorite, at first rueful and longing and then calming, almost meditative.

When her eyes open, the cab with the right license plate, with the roadrunner decal on the passenger door, has entered the queue of cars. She rolls her luggage over and gets inside. The overpowering odor of fast food brings her breakfast to her throat. She stifles it and sits back in the seat.

She kills the music as the concerto is entering its final, frenzied movement, the allegro assai. She removes her earbuds, feeling naked without the reassuring accompaniment of the violins and cellos.

"How is traffic today?" she asks in English, a midwestern accent.

The driver's eyes flash at her through the rearview mirror. The driver has surely been advised that she does not like people who fixate on her.

Don't stare at Bach.

"Pretty good today," he answers, measuring every word, uttering the *all-clear* code she was hoping to hear. She didn't expect any complications this early on, but you never know.

Now able to relax a moment, she crosses one leg and unzips her boot, then repeats with the other boot. She moans softly with the relief of freeing her feet from those boots and the four-inch lifts inside them. She stretches her toes and runs her thumb firmly under each arch, the closest she can come to a foot massage in the back of a cab.

With any luck, she won't need to be five feet nine inches for the rest of the trip; five feet five will do just fine. She unzips her carry-on, folds the Gucci boots inside it, and pulls out a pair of Nike court shoes.

As the car pulls into thick traffic, she looks out the window to her right, then glances to the left. She drops her head low, between her legs. When she reemerges, the red wig is in her lap, replaced with ink-black hair, pulled back mercilessly into a bun.

"You feel…more like yourself now?" asks the driver.

She doesn't reply. She steadies a cold stare for him, but he doesn't meet her eyes in the rearview mirror. He should know better.

Bach doesn't like small talk.

And it's been a long time since she's "felt like herself," as Americans would say. At most, she has an occasional window of relaxation. But the longer she stays in this line of work and the more times she reinvents herself—replacing one facade with another, sometimes lingering in shadow, sometimes hiding in plain sight—the less she remembers her true self or even the concept of having her own identity.

That will change soon, a vow she has made to herself.

Her wig and boots now changed out, her carry-on zipped up and resting next to her on the seat, she reaches down to the floor mat at her feet. Her fingers find the edges of the mat and lift, freeing it from its Velcro moorings.

Beneath it, a carpeted floorboard with latches. She pops the latches on each side and lifts open the door.

She sits up again, checking the speedometer

to make sure the driver isn't doing something stupid like speeding, to make sure that a police cruiser isn't happening by at this moment.

Then she bends down again, removing the hard-shell case from the floorboard compartment. She places her thumb on the seal. It takes only a moment for the thumbprint recognition to pop the seal open.

Not that the people who have hired her would have any reason to mess with her equipment, but better safe than sorry.

She opens the case for a quick inspection. "Hello, Anna," she whispers, the name she has given it. Anna Magdalena is a thing of beauty, a matte-black semiautomatic rifle capable of firing five rounds in less than two seconds, capable of assembly and disassembly in less than three minutes with nothing but a screwdriver. There are newer models on the market, of course, but Anna Magdalena has never let her down, from any distance. Dozens of people could confirm its accuracy—theoretically—including a prosecutor in Bogotá, Colombia, who until seven months ago had a head atop his body and the leader of a rebel army in Darfur who eighteen months ago suddenly spilled his brains into the lamb stew on his lap.

She has killed on every continent. She has

assassinated generals, activists, politicians, and businessmen. She is known only by her gender and the classical-music composer she favors. And by her 100 percent kill rate.

This will be your greatest challenge, Bach, said the man who hired her for this job.

No, she replied, correcting him. *This will be my greatest success.*

FRIDAY,
MAY 11

CHAPTER
4

❖

I wake with a start, staring into the darkness, fumbling for my phone. It's just past four in the morning. I text Carolyn. Anything?

Her response comes immediately; she's not asleep. Nothing sir.

I know better. Carolyn would've called me right away if something had happened. But she's become accustomed to these early morning communications ever since we discovered what we were up against.

I exhale and stretch my arms, letting out nervous energy. There's no way I'll go back to sleep. Today's the day.

I spend some time on the treadmill in the bedroom. I've never—not since my baseball days—lost the need to work up a good sweat, especially in this job. It's like a massage before the stress of the day. When Rachel's cancer returned, I had a treadmill installed in the bedroom so I could keep an eye on her even while exercising.

Today it's an easy stroll, not a run or even a brisk walk given my current physical condition, the relapse of my illness, which is the last thing I need right now.

I brush my teeth and check my toothbrush when I'm done. Nothing on it but the slushy remnants of the gel. I do a wide smile in the mirror and check my gums.

I strip off my clothes and turn around, look back at myself in the mirror. The bruising is mostly on my calves but is also on the backs of my upper thighs. It's getting worse.

After a shower, it's time to read the President's Daily Brief and hear about any late developments not covered in it. Then on to breakfast in the dining room. That was something Rachel and I used to do together. "The rest of the world can have you for the next sixteen hours," she used to say. "I get you for breakfast."

And usually dinner. We made the time, though when Rachel was alive, we didn't eat either meal in this dining room; we usually ate at the small table in the kitchen next door, a more intimate setting. Sometimes, when we really wanted to feel like normal people for a change, we'd cook for ourselves. Some of our best moments, in the time we shared here, were spent flipping pancakes or rolling pizza dough, just the two of us, as we did back home in North Carolina.

I cut through the hard-boiled egg with my fork and look absently out the window at Blair House, across from Lafayette Park, the hum of the television serving as white noise in the background. The television is new since Rachel.

I'm not sure why I bother with the news. It's all about the impeachment, the networks trying to bend every story to fit this narrative.

On MSNBC, a foreign-affairs correspondent is claiming that the Israeli government is transferring a high-profile Palestinian terrorist to another prison. *Could this be part of some "deal" the president has cut with Suliman Cindoruk? Some deal involving Israel and a prisoner trade?*

CBS News is saying that I'm considering filling a vacancy at Agriculture with a southern senator from the opposing party. *Is the president hoping to siphon off votes for removal by handing out cabinet appointments?*

I suppose if I turned on the Food Network right now, they'd be saying that when I let them visit the White House a month ago and told them my favorite vegetable is corn, I was secretly

BILL CLINTON AND JAMES PATTERSON

trying to curry favor with the senators from Iowa and Nebraska who are part of the bloc itching to remove me from office.

Fox News, over the banner TURMOIL IN THE WHITE HOUSE, claims that my staff is sharply split on whether I should testify, the yes-testify crew led by the White House chief of staff, Carolyn Brock, the don't-testify faction headed by the vice president, Katherine Brandt. *"Plans are already under way, as a contingency,"* says a reporter standing outside the White House right now, *"to claim that the House hearings are a partisan charade to give the president an excuse to change his mind and refuse to attend."*

On the *Today* show, a color-coded map shows the fifty-five senators in the opposing party as well as the senators from my party who are up for reelection and who might feel pressure to be part of the twelve defectors necessary to convict me at an impeachment trial.

CNN says that my staff and I are calling in senators as early as this morning to lock them down as not-guilty votes in the impeachment trial.

Good Morning America says that White House sources indicate that I've already decided not to run for reelection and that I will try to cut a deal with the House Speaker to spare me impeachment if I agree to a single term in office.

44

Where do they get this crap? I have to admit it's sensational. And sensational sells over factual every day.

Still, the wall-to-wall impeachment speculation has been hard on my staff, most of whom don't know what happened in Algeria or during my phone call to Suliman Cindoruk any more than Congress or the media or the American people do. But so far they've rallied while the White House is under assault, considering it a source of pride to stand together. They'll never know how much that means to me.

I punch a button on my phone. Rachel would kill me for having a phone at breakfast, too. "JoAnn, where's Jenny?"

"She's here, sir. Do you want her?"

"Please. Thank you."

Carolyn Brock walks in, the only person who would feel free to do so while I'm eating. I've never actually said that nobody else is allowed in. It's one of the many things a chief of staff does for you—streamlining, acting as a gatekeeper, being the hard-ass with staff so I don't have to think about such matters.

She is buttoned-up as always, a smart suit, dark hair pulled back, never letting her guard down while on camera. Her job, she has told me more than once, is not to make friends with the staff but to keep them organized, praise good work, and sweat the details so I can focus on the hard, big stuff.

But that's a dramatic understatement of her role. Nobody has a tougher job than the White House chief of staff. She does the little things, sure—the personnel issues and the scheduling. She's also right there with me on the big things. She has to do it all because she's also the go-to person for members of Congress, the cabinet, the interest groups, and the press. I don't have a better surrogate. She does all that and keeps her ego in check. Just try to pay her a compliment. She brushes it away like a piece of lint on her impeccable suit.

There was a time, not long ago, when people predicted that Carolyn Brock would one day be the Speaker of the House. She was a three-term congresswoman, a progressive who managed to win a conservative House district in southeastern Ohio and who moved swiftly up the ranks of House leadership. She was intelligent, personable, and telegenic, the political equivalent of a five-tool player. She became a hit on the fundraiser circuit and built alliances that allowed her to move to the coveted position as head of our party's political arm, the congressional campaign committee. She was barely forty years old and poised for the pinnacle of House leadership, if not higher office.

Then 2010 came. Everyone knew it was going to be a brutal midterm election for our party. And the other side fielded a strong candidate, a former governor's son. A week out, the race was a statistical tie.

Five days before the election, while blowing off steam with her two closest aides over a bottle of wine at midnight, Carolyn made a derogatory comment about her opponent, who'd just released an ad viciously attacking Carolyn's husband, a noted trial lawyer at the time. Her comment was caught on a live mike. Nobody knows who picked it up or how. Carolyn thought she was alone with her two aides in a closed restaurant.

She said her opponent was a "cocksucker." The audio made its way around the cable news networks and the Internet within hours.

She had options at that point. She could have denied it was her voice on that recording. Either of her aides, both of whom were women, could have assumed attribution for the comment. Or she could have said what was probably the truth—that she was tired and a bit tipsy and furious about the negative ad targeting her husband.

But she didn't do any of those things. She only said this: "I'm sorry my private conversation was overheard. If a man had said it, it wouldn't be an issue."

Personally, I loved her response. Today it might work. But back then, her support cratered with social conservatives, and she lost the race. With that *c* word forever glued to her name, she knew she'd probably never get another chance. Politics can be cruel in the way it treats its wounded.

Carolyn's loss became my gain. She started a political consulting firm, using her skills and brains to navigate victories for others around the country. When I decided to run for president, and I needed someone to run my campaign, I had only one person's name on my list.

"You should stop watching this garbage, sir," she says as some political consultant I've never heard of says on CNN that I'm committing a *serious tactical blunder* by refusing to comment on the phone call and letting the House Speaker *control the narrative.*

"By the way," I say, "did you know that you want me to testify before the select committee? That you're leading the pro-testify forces in the civil war going on in the White House?"

"I didn't realize that, no." She wanders over to

the wallpaper in the dining room, scenes of the Revolutionary War. Jackie Kennedy first put it up, a gift from a friend. Betty Ford didn't like it and took it down. President Carter put it back up. It's been up and down since. Rachel loved the wallpaper, so we put it back up.

"Have some coffee, Carrie. You're making me nervous."

"Good morning, Mr. President," says Jenny Brickman, my deputy chief of staff and senior political adviser. She ran my campaigns for governor and worked under Carolyn on my presidential run. She is petite in every way, with a mess of bleached blond hair and a mouth like a truck driver. She is my smiling knife. She will go to war for me, when I let her. She would not merely dissect my opponents. If I didn't rein her in, she would slice them open from chin to navel. She would rip them to pieces with all the restraint of a pit bull and slightly less charm.

Carolyn, after my victory, turned to policy. She still keeps an eye on politics, but her bigger role now is to get my agenda through Congress and push my foreign policy.

Jenny, on the other hand, just focuses on politics, on getting me reelected. And, unfortunately, on worrying about whether I will even make it through my first term.

"Our caucus in the House is holding steady right now," she says, having conferred with our side of House leadership. "They said they're eager to hear your side of the Algeria story."

I can't suppress a smirk. "It probably came out more like, 'Tell him to get his head out of his ass and defend himself.' Is that closer?"

"Nearly a direct quote, sir."

I'm not making it easy on my allies. They want to defend me, but my silence makes that nearly impossible. They deserve more, but I just can't give it to them yet.

"We'll have time for that," I say. We are under no illusions about the vote in the House. Lester has the majority, and his caucus is itching to push a button to impeach. If Lester calls for a vote on it, I'm toast.

But a strong defense in the House will make it much more likely that we'll prevail in the Senate, where Lester's party has fifty-five votes but needs a supermajority of sixty-seven for removal. If our caucus in the House holds together, it will be harder for our people in the Senate to defect.

"What we're hearing from our side in the Senate is similar," Jenny says. "Leader Jacoby is trying to lock down a caucus position of 'presumptive support'—her words—the idea being that removal is an extreme remedy and we should know more before such important decisions can be made. But they're not willing to do anything more than keep an open mind right now."

"Nobody's rushing to my defense."

"You aren't giving them a reason to, sir. You're letting Rhodes kick you in the balls and not fighting back. What I kept hearing was, 'Algeria looks bad, really, really bad. He better have a good explanation.'"

"Okay, well, that was enjoyable, Jenny. Next topic."

"If we could stay here for one more—"

"Next topic, Jenny. You got your ten minutes on impeachment, and I gave you an hour last night for that mock session. That's the end of impeachment talk for right now. I have other things on my mind. Now, is there anything else?"

"Yes, sir," Carolyn interjects. "The issues layout we were planning for the reelection? We should start it now with the issues we know the American people care about and support—the minimum wage, the assault weapons ban, and tuition credits. We need positive news to counter the negative. That will give us a counter-narrative—that in spite of all the political shenanigans, you're determined to move the country forward. Let them hold their Salem witch trial while you try to solve real problems for real people."

"It won't get drowned out in all this impeachment talk?"

"Senator Jacoby doesn't think so, sir. They're begging for a good issue to start rallying around."

"I heard the same thing in the House," says Jenny. "If you give them something to sink their teeth into, something they really care about, it will remind them how important it is to protect the presidency."

"They need a reminder," I say with a sigh.

"Frankly, sir, right now—yes, they do."

I hold up my hands. "Fine. Talk to me."

"Start with the minimum-wage increase, next week," says Carolyn. "Then an assault-weapons ban. Then tuition credits—"

"An assault-weapons ban has as much chance of passing the House as a resolution to rename Reagan National airport after me."

Carolyn tucks in her lips, nods. "That's correct, sir, it won't pass." We both know she's not pushing for an assault-weapons ban because we can pass it, at least in this Congress. She goes on. "But you do believe in it, and you have the credibility to fight for it. Then, when the opposition party kills it and the minimum-wage hike, both of which most Americans support, you will show them for who they are. And you'll jam up Senator Gordon."

Lawrence Gordon, a three-term senator from my side of the aisle who, like every senator, thinks he should be president. But unlike most of them, he's willing to consider running against a sitting president from his own party.

He's also on the wrong side of our party and our country on both these issues. He voted against a minimum-wage hike, and he likes the Second Amendment, at least as the NRA defines it, better than the First, Fourth, and Fifth Amendments combined. Jenny wants to take out his knees before he even considers lacing up his shoes.

"Gordon won't primary me," I say. "He doesn't have the balls."

"Nobody's watching the Algeria story more closely than Gordon," says Jenny.

I look at Carolyn. Jenny has sharp political instincts, but Carolyn has instincts plus institutional knowledge of DC from her time in Congress. She's also the smartest person I've ever met.

"I'm not afraid of Gordon primarying you," says Carolyn. "I'm afraid of him *thinking* about primarying you. Privately encouraging speculation. Allowing himself to be courted. Reading his name in the *Times* or on CNN. What's there to lose for him? It gives him a leg up down the road. He gets a nice ego stroke, too. Who's more popular than a challenger? He's like a backup quarterback—everyone loves him while he's sitting on the sidelines. Gordon will get nothing but a nice vanity tour out of it, but meanwhile, your credibility is undercut every second it happens. He looks bright and shiny; you look weak."

I nod. That all sounds right.

"I think we should float the minimum wage or the assault-weapons ban," she says. "We make Gordon come to us and ask us to sit on them. Then he owes us. And he knows if he screws us, we'll shove a legislative item or two up his keester."

"Remind me never to piss you off, Carolyn."

"The vice president is on board with this," says Jenny.

"Of course she is." Carolyn makes a face. She has a healthy suspicion of Kathy Brandt, who was my chief opponent for the nomination. She was the right choice for vice president, but that doesn't make her my closest ally. Either way, Kathy would make the same calculation in her own self-interest. If I'm removed from office, she becomes president, and she will almost immediately be running for election. She doesn't need Larry Gordon or anyone else getting any ideas.

"While I agree with your analysis of the problem," I say, "I think your proposed solution is too cute by half. I want to come out strong for both measures. But I won't back off for Gordon. We'll force the opposition's hand. It's the right thing to do, and win or lose, we'll be strong and they'll be wrong."

Jenny pipes up. "That's the person I voted for, sir. I think you should do it, but I still don't think it will be enough. You are seen as really weak right now, and I don't think *any* domestic policy move can fix it. The phone call to Suliman. The Algeria nightmare. You need a commander-in-chief moment. A rally-around-the-leader mo—"

"No," I say, reading her mind. "Jenny, I'm not ordering a military strike just to look tough."

"There are any number of safe targets, Mr. President. It's not like I'm asking you to invade France. How about one of the drone targets in the Middle East, but instead of a drone, escalate it to a full aerial—"

"No. The answer is no."

She puts her hands on her hips, shakes her head. "Your wife was right. You really are a shitty politician."

"But she meant it as a compliment."

"Mr. President, can I be blunt?" she says.

"You haven't been so far?"

She puts her hands out in front of her, as if trying to frame the issue for me, or maybe she's pleading with me. "You're going to be impeached," she says. "And if you don't do something to turn things around, something dramatic, the senators in your own party will jump ship. And I know you won't resign. It isn't in your DNA. Which means President Jonathan Lincoln Duncan will be remembered in history for one thing and one thing only. You'll be the first president forcibly removed from office."

CHAPTER
5

❖

After talking with Jenny and Carolyn, I head across the hall into my bedroom, where Deborah Lane is already opening her bag of goodies.

"Good morning, Mr. President," she says.

I pull down on my tie, unbutton my shirt. "Top of the morning, Doc."

She focuses on me, appraises me, and doesn't look happy. I seem to have that effect on a lot of people these days.

"You forgot to shave again," she says.

"I'll shave later." It's actually four days running now that I haven't shaved. When I was in college, at UNC, I had this superstitious routine—I didn't shave during finals week. It tended to shock people because, though the hair on my head is probably best described as light brown, my facial hair doesn't follow script: somehow, an orange pigment creeps in to give me a fiery auburn beard. And I can grow a beard fast; by the end of finals, everyone was calling me Paul Bunyan.

I never thought much about that after college. Until now.

"You look tired," she says. "How many hours did you sleep last night?"

"Two or three."

"That's not enough, Mr. President."

"I have a few balls in the air right now."

"Which you won't be able to juggle without sleep." She puts her stethoscope on my bare chest.

Dr. Deborah Lane is not my official doctor but a specialist in hematology at Georgetown. She grew up under apartheid in South Africa but fled to the United States for high school and never left. Her close-cropped hair is now completely gray. Her eyes are probing but kind.

For the last week, she's come to the White House every day because it's easier and less conspicuous if a professional-looking woman— albeit one with a not-very-well-disguised medical bag—visits the White House as opposed to the president visiting MedStar Georgetown University Hospital on a daily basis.

She puts the blood-pressure wrap on my arm. "How've you been feeling?"

"I have a gigantic pain in my ass," I say. "Can you look and see if the Speaker of the House is up there?"

She shoots me a look but doesn't laugh. Not even a smirk.

"Physically," I say, "I feel fine."

She shines a light inside my mouth. She looks closely at my torso, my abdomen, my arms and legs, turns me around and does the same on my other side.

"Bruising is worsening," she says.

"I know." It used to look like a rash. Now it looks more like someone has been pummeling the backs of my legs with hammers.

In my first term as governor of North Carolina, I was diagnosed with a blood disorder known as immune thrombocytopenia—ITP—which basically means a low platelet count. My blood doesn't always clot as well as it should. I announced it publicly at the time and told the truth—most of the time, the ITP isn't an issue. I was told to avoid activities that could lead to bleeding, which wasn't hard for a man in his forties. My baseball days were long over, and I was never much for bullfighting or knife juggling.

The disorder flared up twice during my time

as governor but left me alone during the campaign for the presidency. It reemerged when Rachel's cancer returned—my doctor is convinced that an overload of stress is a significant cause of relapse—but I treated it easily. It returned a week ago, when the bruising under the skin on my calves first started appearing. The rapid discoloration and spread of bruising tells both of us the same thing—this is the worst case I've had yet.

"Headaches?" Dr. Deb asks. "Dizziness? Fever?"

"No, no, and no."

"Fatigue?"

"From lack of sleep, sure."

"Nosebleeds?"

"No, ma'am."

"Blood in your teeth or gums?"

"Toothbrush is clean."

"Blood in your urine or stool?"

"No." It's hard to be humble when they play a song for you every time you enter the room, when the world financial markets hang on your every word, and when you command the world's greatest military arsenal, but if you need to knock yourself down a few pegs, try checking your stool for blood.

She steps back and hums to herself. "I'm going to draw blood again," she says. "I was very concerned by your count yesterday. You were under twenty thousand. I don't know how you talked me out of hospitalizing you right then and there."

"I talked you out of it," I say, "because I'm the president of the United States."

"I keep forgetting."

"I can do twenty thousand, Doc."

The normal range for platelets is between 150,000 and 450,000 per microliter. So nobody's throwing a parade for a count under 20,000, but it's still above the critical stage.

"You're taking your steroids?"

"Religiously."

She reaches into her bag, then gets to work rubbing alcohol on my arm with a swab. I'm not looking forward to the blood draw, because she's not great with needles. She's out of practice. At her high level of specialty, somebody else usually performs the rudimentary tasks. But I have to limit the number of people in this world who know about this. My ITP disorder may be public knowledge, but nobody needs to know how bad it is right now, *especially* right now. So she's a one-person show for the time being.

"Let's do a protein treatment," she says.

"What—now?"

"Yes, now."

"The last time I did that I couldn't string a sentence together for the better part of a day. That's a nonstarter, Doc. Not today."

She stops, the swab in her hand trailing down to my knuckles.

"Then a steroid infusion."

"No. The pills mess with my head enough."

Her head angles slightly as she considers her response. I'm not the usual patient, after all. Most patients do whatever their doctors tell them. Most patients are not leaders of the free world.

She goes back to prepping my arm, frowning deeply, until she has the needle poised. "Mr. President," she says in a tone I heard my grade-school teachers use, "you can tell anyone else in the world what to do. But you can't order your body around."

"Doc, I—"

"You're at risk of internal bleeding," she says. "Bleeding in the brain. You could have a stroke. Whatever it is you're dealing with, it can't be worth *that* risk."

She looks me in the eye. I don't respond. Which in itself is a response.

"It's something that bad?" she whispers. She shakes her head, waves her hand. "Don't. I—I know you can't tell me."

Yes, it's something that bad. And the attack could come an hour from now or later today. It could have happened twenty seconds ago, and Carolyn could be rushing in to tell me about it right now.

I can't be out of commission for even an hour, much less several. I can't risk it.

"It has to wait," I say. "A couple of days, probably."

A bit rattled by what she doesn't know, Deb just nods and plunges the needle into my arm.

"I'll double the steroids," I say, which means it will feel like I've drunk four beers instead of two. It's a line I have to straddle. I can't be out of commission, but I have to stay alive.

She finishes in silence, packing away the blood draw in her bag and getting ready to leave. "You have your job, and I have mine," she says. "I'll get the labs back within two hours. But we both know your count is cratering."

"Yes, we do."

She stops at the doorway and turns to me. "You don't have a couple of days, Mr. President," she says. "You might not even have one."

63

CHAPTER
6

❖

Today, and only today, they will celebrate.
He must give them that. His small team
has worked day and night, with purpose and devotion and with great success. Everyone needs a
break.

The wind off the river lifts his hair. He pulls
on his cigarette, the orange tip glowing in the
dim early evening air. He savors the view from
the penthouse terrace overlooking the river
Spree, the city bustling across the water—the
East Side Gallery, the entertainment center.
The Mercedes-Benz Arena is hosting a concert
tonight. He doesn't recognize the group's name,
but the muted sounds, audible even from across
the river, tell him that the music involves heavy
guitar and a thumping bass. This part of Berlin

has changed considerably since he was last here, a mere four years ago.

He turns back to look inside the penthouse, 160 square meters, with four bedrooms and a designer open-plan kitchen where his team is laughing and gesturing, pouring Champagne and probably already halfway drunk. The four of them, all geniuses in their own right, none of them over the age of twenty-five, some of them probably still virgins.

Elmurod, his stomach hanging over his belt, his beard unkempt, wearing an insipid blue hat that reads VET WWIII. Mahmad, already with his shirt off, showing off his decidedly unimpressive biceps in a mock bodybuilder pose. All four of them turn toward the door, and Elmurod goes to answer it. When the door opens, eight women walk in, all wearing teased-up hair and skintight dresses, all with bodies of centerfolds, all paid princely sums to show his team the night of their lives.

He steps carefully along the terrace, wary of the heat and pressure sensors—deactivated right now, of course—rigged to detonate the entire terrace should anything heavier than a bird land on it. It set him back nearly a million euros, these precautions.

But what's one million euros when you're about to earn a hundred million?

One of the prostitutes, an Asian who can't be over twenty, with boobs that can't be real, with a sudden interest in him that can't be sincere, approaches him as he walks back into the penthouse and slides the door shut.

"Wie lautet dein name?" she asks. *What is your name?*

He smiles. She is just flirting, playing a part. She doesn't care what he tells her.

But there are people who would pay anything, or do anything, to know the answer to her question. And just once, he'd like to let down his guard and answer the question truthfully.

I am Suliman Cindoruk, he'd like to say. *And I'm about to reboot the world.*

CHAPTER
7

❖

I close the folder on my desk after reviewing the various items that my White House counsel, Danny Akers, and his staff have prepared for me in consultation with the attorney general.

A draft executive order declaring martial law throughout the nation and a legal memorandum exploring the constitutionality of doing so.

Draft legislation for Congress and a draft executive order declaring the suspension of habeas corpus throughout the nation.

An executive order instituting price controls and rationing of various consumer goods along with authorizing legislation where needed.

I just pray that it doesn't come to this.

"Mr. President," says JoAnn, my secretary, "the Speaker of the House."

Lester Rhodes smiles politely at JoAnn and strides into the Oval Office, his hand outstretched. I'm already out from around my desk to greet him.

"Good morning, Mr. President," he says, shaking my hand and sizing me up, probably wondering why I have the scruffy beginnings of a beard.

"Mr. Speaker," I say. Usually I follow up with a *Thanks for coming* or *Good to see you,* but I can't summon pleasantries with this man. Rhodes, after all, was the architect of his party's reclamation of the House during midterm elections, based exclusively on the promise of "taking our country back" and that ridiculous "report card" on my performance that he blew up for all the candidates, grading me on foreign policy, the economy, a number of hot-button issues, with the tagline "Duncan is flunkin'."

He takes the couch, and I sit in the chair. He shoots his cuffs and settles in. He is dressed for the part of the powerful legislator: the slate-blue shirt with white collar and cuffs, the bright red tie perfectly dimpled, all the colors of the flag represented.

He still has that cocky glow of newly acquired power. He's only been Speaker for five months. He doesn't realize his limitations yet. That makes him more dangerous, not less.

"I asked myself why you invited me here," he goes on. "You know one of the story lines coming out of cable news is that we're cutting a deal, you and I. You agree not to seek reelection, and I call off the hearings."

I nod slowly. I heard that one, too.

"But I told my aides, I said, go back and watch those videos of the POWs who were captured in Desert Storm along with Corporal Jon Duncan. See how scared they were. How scared they *must* have been to denounce their own country on camera. And then, after you see that, ask yourself what the Iraqis must have done to Jon Duncan for being the only American POW from that unit who refused to go on camera. And after you've wrapped your mind around that, I told them, ask yourself if Jon Duncan is the sort of fellow who will back down from a fight with a bunch of congressmen."

Which means he still doesn't know why he's here.

"Lester," I say, "do you know why I never talk about that? What happened to me in Iraq?"

"I don't," he says. "Modesty, I suppose."

I shake my head. "No one in this town is modest. No, the reason I don't talk about that is that some things are more important than politics. Most rank-and-file congressmen never need to learn that lesson. But in order for the government to function, and for the good of the country, the Speaker of the House does. The sooner the better."

He opens his hands, signaling that he's ready for the punch line.

"Lester, how many times have I failed to discuss covert operations with the intelligence committees since I've been president? Or if it was particularly sensitive, with the Gang of Eight?"

The law says that I must make a finding before engaging in a covert action and must share that finding with the House and Senate Intelligence Committees—in advance of the action if possible. But if the matter is particularly sensitive, I can limit disclosure to the so-called Gang of Eight—the Speaker and House minority leader, the Senate majority and minority leaders, and the chairs and ranking members of the two intelligence committees.

"Mr. President, I've only been Speaker a few months. But in that time, as far as I understand it, you always have complied with your disclosure commitment."

"And your predecessor—I'm sure he told you that I always complied when he was Speaker as well."

"That's my understanding, yes," he agrees. "Which is why it's so troublesome that not even the Gang of Eight heard one word about Algeria."

"What's troublesome to me, Lester, is that you don't realize that I must have a good reason *why* I'm not disclosing this time."

His jaw clenches, some color rising to his pale face. "Even after the fact, Mr. President? You're allowed to act first, disclose later, if time is of the essence—but you're not even disclosing now, after that debacle in Algeria. After you allowed that monster to escape. You're breaking the law."

"Ask yourself why, Lester." I sit back in my chair. "Why would I do that? Knowing exactly how you'd react? Knowing that I'm handing you grounds for impeachment on a silver platter?"

"There can only be one answer, sir."

"Oh, really? And what's that one answer, Lester?"

"Well, if I may speak freely..."

"Hey, it's just us kids here."

"All right, then," he says with a sweeping nod. "The answer is that you don't *have* a good explanation for what you did. You're trying to negotiate some truce with that bastard terrorist, and you stopped that militia group from killing him so you could keep negotiating whatever peace-love-and-harmony deal you seem to think you can cut. And you almost got away with it. We never would have heard a word about Algeria. You'd have denied the whole thing."

He leans forward on his knees, looking me dead in the eye, his gaze so intense his eyes are almost watering. "But then that American boy got killed, and they got it on video for all the world to see. You got caught with your pants down. And *still* you won't tell us. Because you don't want anyone to know what you're doing until it's signed, sealed, and delivered." He jabs a finger at me. "Well, Congress will *not* be denied our oversight function on this. As long as I'm Speaker, no president will run off on his own and cut some deal with terrorists that they'll never honor anyway and leave us looking like the weak stepchild. As long as—"

"That's enough, Lester."

"—I'm Speaker, this country will—"

"Enough!" I get to my feet. After a moment, stunned, Lester stands as well.

"Get this straight," I say. "There are no cameras here. Don't pretend that you believe what you're saying. Don't pretend that you really think I wake up every morning whispering sweet nothings to terrorists. You and I both know that I'd take out that asshole right now if I thought it would serve the best interests of our nation. It's great political spin, Lester, I'll give you that— that garbage you're spewing about me wanting to 'make love, not war' with the Sons of Jihad. But do not walk into the Oval Office and pretend for one second that you actually believe it."

He blinks his eyes, out of his element here. He's not accustomed these days to someone raising his voice to him. But he remains silent because he knows I'm right.

"I'm doing you all kinds of favors here, Lester. I'm aiding and abetting you by remaining silent. Every second I say nothing, you get more fuel on your fire. You're beating the ever-loving crap out of me in public. And I'm sitting there saying, 'Thank you, sir, may I have another?' *Surely* you are smart enough to realize that if I'm going to violate every political instinct I possess and remain mute, there must be a pretty damn important reason why I'm doing that. There must be something vitally important at stake."

Lester holds his stare for as long as he can. Then his gaze drops down to the floor. He stuffs his hands in his pockets and rocks on his heels.

"Then tell me," he says. "Not Intelligence. Not the Gang of Eight. *Me.* If it's as important as you say, tell me what it is."

Lester Rhodes is the absolute *last* person to whom I would give all the details. But I can't let him know I think that.

"I can't. Lester, I can't. I'm asking you to trust me."

There was a time when that statement, from a

president to a House Speaker, would be enough. Those days are long in the rearview mirror.

"I can't agree to that, Mr. President."

An interesting word choice—*can't*, not *won't*. Lester is under so much pressure from his caucus, especially the fire-breathers who react to every sound bite on social media and talk radio, ginning up this whole thing. Whether it's true or not, whether he believes it or not, they've now created a caricature of me, and Speaker Lester Rhodes cannot let it be known that he decided to *trust* that caricature during this important moment.

"Think about the cyberattack in Toronto," I say. "The Sons of Jihad hasn't claimed responsibility for it. Think about that. Those guys always claim responsibility. Every attack they've ever done has come with a message to the West to stay away from their part of the world, central and southeastern Europe. Get our money out, our troops out. But not this time. Why, Lester?"

"You could tell me why," he says.

I motion for him to sit down, and I do the same.

"Your ears only," I say.

"Yes, sir."

"The answer is we don't know why. But my guess? Toronto was a test run. Proof that he had the goods. Probably to get his down payment for his real job."

I sit back and let that settle in. Lester has the sheepish look of a kid who realizes he's supposed to understand something but doesn't and doesn't want to admit it.

"Then why not kill him?" Lester asks. "Why rescue him from that attack in Algeria?"

I stare at Lester.

"My ears only," he says.

I can't give Lester all the details, but I can give him enough to nibble on.

"We weren't trying to rescue Suliman Cindoruk," I say. "We were trying to capture him."

"Then..." Lester opens his hands. "Why did you stop that militia group?"

"They didn't want to capture him, Lester. They wanted to *kill* him. They were going to fire shoulder-launched missiles into his house."

"So?" Lester shrugs. "A captured terrorist, a dead terrorist—what's the difference?"

"In this case, a huge difference," I say. "I need Suliman Cindoruk alive."

Lester looks at his hands, twists his wedding ring. Staying in listen mode, revealing nothing on his end.

"Our intel told us this militia group had found him. We didn't know more than that. All we could do was piggyback their operation in Algeria, try to stop them from a full-on attack, and catch Suliman ourselves. We stopped their attack, but Suliman got away in the melee. And yes, an American died. Something we wanted to remain covert and highly classified became viral on social media within hours."

Lester works that over, his eyes narrowed, head nodding.

"I don't think Suliman is working alone," I say. "I think he was hired. And I think Toronto was the warm-up, the trial run, the appetizer."

"And we are the main course," Lester whispers.

"Correct."

"A cyberattack," he mumbles. "Bigger than Toronto."

"Big enough to make Toronto look like a stubbed toe."

"Christ."

"I need Suliman alive because he may be the only person who can stop it. And he can identify who hired him and who else, if anyone, is working with him. But I don't want anyone to know what I know or what I think. I'm trying to do something that is incredibly difficult for the United States of America to do—fly under the radar."

A hint of realization comes to the Speaker's expression. He leans back against the couch like a man who's holding all the cards. "You're saying our hearings will interfere with what you're doing."

"Without a doubt."

"Then why did you agree to testify in the first place?"

"To buy time," I say. "You wanted to haul my entire national security team before your committee earlier this week. I couldn't have that. I offered myself up in exchange for the time extension."

"But now you need even more time. Beyond next Monday."

"Yes."

"And you want me to go back to my caucus and tell them we should give it to you."

"Yes."

"But I can't tell them why. I can't tell them any of what you told me. I just have to tell them that I decided to 'trust' you."

"You're their leader, Lester. So lead. Tell them you've decided that it's in the best interests of our nation that we temporarily hold off on the hearings."

His head drops, and he rubs his hands together, warming up for the speech that he probably recited into a mirror a dozen times before coming over here.

"Mr. President," he says, "I understand these

hearings are not something you want us to do. But just as you have your responsibilities, we have an oversight responsibility that serves as a check on executive power. I have members who elected me to ensure that we serve as that check. I can't go back to my caucus and tell them we are going to shirk our responsibility."

It was never going to matter what I said to him today. He's got a playbook, and he's following it. Patriotism was never going to factor in. If this guy ever had an unselfish thought, as my mama would say, it would die of loneliness.

But I'm not done trying.

"If this goes well," I say, "and we stop this terrorist attack, you will be standing right next to me. I will tell the world that the Speaker put aside partisan differences and did the right thing for his country. I will hold you up as an example of what is right in Washington, DC. You'll be Speaker for life."

He continues to nod, clears his throat. His foot, on the floor, has begun to tap.

"But if…" He can't bring himself to finish the sentence.

"If things go wrong? Then I'll take the blame. All of it."

"But *I* will be blamed, too," he says. "Because I stopped these hearings without giving my members, or the public, any reason at all. You can't promise me that I'll come out of this unscathed—"

"Lester, this is the job you signed up for. Whether you knew it or not, whether you like it or not. You're right. There are no promises here. No sure things. I am the commander in chief, looking you in the eye and telling you that the security of this country is in jeopardy and I need your help. Are you going to help me or not?"

It doesn't take him long. He works his jaw, looks at his hands. "Mr. President, I'd like to help you, but you have to understand, we have a responsib—"

"Damn it, Lester, put your country first!" I push myself out of my chair too fast, feeling wobbly, the anger consuming me. "I'm wasting my breath."

Lester rises from the couch, shoots his cuffs again, straightens his tie. "So we'll be seeing you on Monday?" As if nothing I said remotely registered with him. The only thing he cares about is returning to his caucus and telling them he stood up to me.

"You think you know what you're doing," I say, "but you don't have the slightest idea."

CHAPTER
8

❖

I stare at the door after Speaker Rhodes leaves. I'm not sure what I expected of him. Old-fashioned patriotism? A sense of responsibility, maybe? A bit of trust in the president?

Dream on. There is no trust anymore. In the current environment, there's no gain in it. All the incentives push people in the opposite directions.

So Rhodes will go to his corner, leading a charge he can't really control because his caucus twitches at each tweet. Some days, my side isn't much better. Participation in our democracy seems to be driven by the instant-gratification worlds of Twitter, Snapchat, Facebook, and the twenty-four-hour news cycle. We're using modern technology to revert to primitive kinds of human relations. The media knows what sells—conflict and division. It's also quick and easy. All too often anger works better than answers; resentment better than reason; emotion trumps evidence. A sanctimonious, sneering one-liner, no matter how bogus, is seen as straight talk, while a calm, well-argued response is seen as canned and phony. It reminds me of the old political joke: Why do you take such an instant dislike to people? It saves a lot of time.

What happened to factual, down-the-middle reporting? That's hard to even define anymore, as the line between fact and fiction, between truth and lies, gets murkier every day.

We can't survive without a free press, dedicated to preserving that fine line and secure enough to follow the facts where they lead. But the current environment imposes serious pressures on our journalists, at least those who cover politics, to do just the reverse—to exercise their own power and to, in the words of one wise columnist, "abnormalize" all politicians, even honest, able ones, often because of relatively insignificant issues.

Scholars call this false equivalency. It means that when you find a mountain to expose in one person or party, you have to pick a molehill on the other side and make it into a mountain to avoid being accused of bias. The built-up mole-hills also have large benefits: increased coverage on the evening news, millions of retweets, and more talk-show fodder. When the mountains and molehills all look the same, campaigns and governments devote too little time and energy debating the issues that matter most to our people. Even when we try to do that, we're often drowned out by the passion of the day.

There's a real cost to this. It breeds more frustration, polarization, paralysis, bad decisions, and missed opportunities. But with no incentive to actually accomplish something, more and more politicians just go with the flow, fanning the flames of anger and resentment, when they should be acting as the fire brigade. Everybody knows it's wrong, but the immediate rewards are so great we stagger on, just assuming that our Constitution, our public institutions, and the rule of law can endure each new assault without doing permanent damage to our freedoms and way of life.

I ran for president to change that vicious cycle. I hope I still can. But right now, I have to deal with the wolf at the door.

JoAnn walks in and says, "Danny and Alex are here."

JoAnn used to work for the governor I succeeded

in North Carolina. As he was leaving office and I was on my way in, she ran the transition with an efficiency that impressed me. Everyone was afraid of her. I was told not to hire her because she came from "them"—the opposing political party—but JoAnn told me, "Mr. Governor-Elect, I just got divorced, I have two kids in middle school, and I'm broke. I'm never late, I'm never sick, I can type faster'n you can spit, and if you're acting like a donkey's ass, I'll be the first to let you know it." She's been with me ever since. Her oldest just started in the Treasury Department.

"Mr. President," says Danny Akers, White House counsel. Danny and I were next-door neighbors in Wilkes County, North Carolina, growing up in a tiny town all of one square mile in area, nestled between a highway and a single traffic signal. We swam and fished and skateboarded and played ball and hunted together. We taught each other how to knot a tie and jump-start a car and string a pole and throw a breaking ball. We went through everything together— grade school through college at UNC. We even enlisted together, joining the Rangers as E-4s after college. The only thing we didn't experience together was Desert Storm: Danny wasn't assigned to Bravo Company, as I was, so he never saw action in Iraq.

While I was trying, unsuccessfully, to overcome my injuries from Desert Storm and play pro ball in Double A in Memphis, Danny was starting law school at UNC. He was the one who vouched for me to Rachel Carson, a 3L when I entered UNC Law.

"Mr. President." Alex Trimble—the barrel chest and buzz cut practically scream out "Secret Service" when you first look at him. He's not exactly a laugh a minute, but he's as straight and strong as they come, and he runs my security detail as efficiently as a military operation.

"Sit, sit." I should go back to my desk, but I sit on the couch.

"Mr. President," says Danny, "my memorandum on title 18, section 3056." He hands me the document. "You want the long or the short version?" he asks, knowing the answer already.

"Short." The last thing I feel like doing is reading legal-speak right now. I have no doubt the memo was prepared with precision. I always loved the battlefield of the courtroom as a prosecutor, but Danny was the scholar, combing over new Supreme Court opinions for fun, debating fine points of law, and prizing the written word. He left his law firm to be my counsel when I was governor of North Carolina. He was great at it until the then-president nominated him to the

US Court of Appeals for the Fourth Circuit. He loved that job and could have held it happily for life had I not been elected president and asked him to join me again.

"Just tell me what I can and can't do," I say.

Danny winks at me. "The statute says you can't decline protection. But there is precedent for temporarily refusing it as part of your right to personal privacy."

Alex Trimble is already leveling a stare at me. I've previously broached this topic with him, so this isn't coming completely out of the blue, but he was obviously hoping Danny would talk me out of it.

"Mr. President," Alex says, "with all due respect, you can't be serious."

"Serious as a heart attack."

"Now, of all times, sir—"

"It's decided," I say.

"We can do a loose perimeter," he says. "Or at least some advance work."

"No."

Alex clutches the arms of his chair, his mouth slightly agape.

"I need a minute with my White House counsel," I say to him.

"Mr. President, please don't—"

"Alex," I say. "I need a minute with Danny."

With a heavy sigh and a shake of the head, Alex leaves us.

Danny looks back at the door to ensure we're alone. Then he looks at me.

"Son, you've gone crazier'n a March hare," he says, a hint of the old twang in his voice as he invokes my mama's favorite saying. He knows them all as well as I do. Danny's parents were good, hardworking people, but they were away from home a lot. His dad put in a lot of overtime for a trucking company, and his mom worked the night shift at the local plant.

My father was a high school math teacher who died in a car crash when I was four. So when I was a kid, we lived on a grade school teacher's partial pension and what Mama earned waiting tables at Curly Ray's by Millers Creek. But she was always home at night, so she helped the Akerses out with Danny. She loved him like a second son; he spent as much time at our house as his own.

Normally when he triggers those memories, it brings a smile to my face. Instead, I lean forward and rub my hands together.

"Okay, you wanna tell me what's going on?" he tries. "You're starting to freak me out."

Join the club. I feel my guard slowly lowering, being alone with Danny. In this job, he and Rachel were always my ports in a storm.

I look up at him. "We're a long way from catching brookies at Garden Creek," I say.

"Good. Because you could never cast a line to save your life anyway."

Again, I don't smile.

"You're right where you're supposed to be, Mr. President," he says. "If the shit's hitting the fan, you're the guy I want in charge."

I let out air, nod my head.

"Hey." Danny gets up from his chair and sits down next to me on the couch. He lightly punches my knee. "Being in charge isn't being alone. I'm right here. Same place I've always been, no matter what your title is. Same place I'll always be."

"Yeah, I—I know." I look at him. "I know that."

"This isn't about the impeachment bullshit, is it? Because that'll work itself out. Lester Rhodes? That boy's so dumb he couldn't pour piss out of a boot if the directions were on the bottom."

He's pulling out all the stops, dusting off another of Mama Lil's greatest hits. He's trying to take me back to her, to her strength. After Daddy died, she cracked the whip as hard as any drill sergeant I'd later meet, smacking me in the head if she heard a double negative or an *ain't*, telling me I'd go to college or she'd tan my hide. She'd go to work early and come home in the afternoon with two Styrofoam cartons of food that would be dinner for Danny and me. I'd rub her feet while she checked our homework and interrogated us about our day at school. She always said, *You boys aren't rich enough to afford not to pay attention.*

"It's that other thing, isn't it?" says Danny. "That thing that you can't tell me, that's had you canceling half your schedule for the last two weeks? The reason that you've suddenly become so interested in martial law and habeas corpus and price controls? Whatever it is that's kept you quiet as falling snow about Suliman Cindoruk and Algeria while Lester Rhodes beats the snot out of you?"

"Yeah," I say. "It's that thing."

"Yeah." Danny clears his throat, drums his fingers. "Scale of 1 to 10," he says. "How bad?"

"A thousand."

"Jesus. And you have to go off leash? I gotta tell you, that sounds like a terrible idea."

It just might be. But it's the best one I have.

"You're scared," he says.

"Yeah. Yeah, I am."

We are quiet for a long moment.

"You know when the last time was I saw you this scared?"

"When Ohio put me over 270 electoral votes?"

"No."

"When I found out Bravo Company was deploying?"

"No, sir."

I look at him.

"When we were getting off that bus at Fort Benning," he says. "And Sergeant Melton was calling out, 'Where're the E-4s? Where're the goddamn frat-boy maggots?' We weren't off the damn bus yet, and the sergeant was already sharpening his knives for the college boys, who got to start at a higher pay and rank."

I chuckle. "I remember."

"Yeah. Never forget your first smoke session, right? I saw the look on your face when we were walking down the aisle of that bus. It was probably the same as the look on mine. Scared as a mouse in a snake pit. Do you remember what you did?"

"Piss my pants?"

Danny turns and looks at me squarely. "You don't remember, do you, Ranger?"

"I swear I don't."

"You stepped in front of me," he says.

"I did?"

"You sure as hell did. I'd been in the aisle seat, and you were by the window. So I was in front of you, in the aisle. But the moment the sergeant started going off about the E-4s, you elbowed your way in front of me so you'd be the first one off the bus to face him, not me. Scared as you were, that was your first instinct, to look out for me."

"Huh." I don't remember that.

Danny pats my leg. "So go ahead and be scared, President Duncan," he says. "You're still the one I want protecting us."

CHAPTER
9

❖

As the sun warms her face, as her earbuds fill her with the music of Wilhelm Friedemann Herzog performing the full set of Johann Sebastian's sonatas and partitas for solo violin, Bach decides that there are worse ways to spend time than sightseeing at the National Mall.

The Lincoln Memorial, with its Greek columns and imposing marble statue perched atop a seemingly endless staircase, is inappropriately magisterial, better suited for a deity than a president revered for his humility. But that contradiction is quintessentially American, typical of a nation that was built on the premise of freedom, liberty, and individual rights but that tramples freely on those principles abroad.

These thoughts pass only as observations;

geopolitical policy is not what drives her. And, like the country itself, this memorial, for all its irony, is no less magnificent.

The reflecting pool, shimmering in the mid-morning sun. The veterans' memorials, especially the Korean War memorial, move her in a way she hadn't expected.

But her favorite attraction was the one she visited earlier this morning—Ford's Theatre, the site of the most daring presidential assassination in the nation's history.

It is bright enough outside to force one to squint, which makes her oversize sunglasses a natural. She puts to good use the camera around her neck, making sure to capture multiple shots of everything—the Washington Monument, close-ups of Abe and FDR and Eleanor, inscriptions at the veterans' memorials—to cover herself in the unlikely event that anyone should happen to inquire how Isabella Mercado—the name on her passport—spent her day.

In her earbuds now are the soulful cries of the chorus, the dancing violins of the *Saint John Passion*, the dramatic confrontation between Pilate and Christ and the masses.

Weg, weg mit dem, kreuzige ihn!
Away, away with him, crucify him!

She closes her eyes, as she often does, losing herself in the music, imagining herself sitting inside the Saint Nicholas Church in Leipzig when the passion was first played, in 1724, wondering how the composer must have felt hearing his work come to life, observing its beauty wash over the congregants.

She was born in the wrong century.

When she opens her eyes, she sees a woman sitting on a bench, nursing her child. A flutter passes through her. She removes her earbuds and watches this woman, looking down as her infant feeds from her, a soft smile on the mother's face. That, Bach knows, is what they mean when they say "love."

She remembers love. She remembers her mother, the feeling of her more than a visual image, though the latter is buoyed by the two photographs she managed to escape with. She remembers her brother more clearly, though unfortunately it's hard to remember anything but the scowl on his face, the look of pure hatred in his eyes, the last time they saw each other. He has a wife and two daughters now. He is happy, she thinks. He has love, she hopes.

She pops another ginger candy in her mouth and hails a cab.

"M Street Southwest and Capitol Street Southwest," she says, probably sounding like a tourist, but that works just fine.

She stifles the nausea brought on by the greasy smell and the jerky movements of the cab. She puts her earbuds back in to prevent conversation with the chatty African driver. She pays in cash and breathes in fresh air for a few moments before proceeding to the restaurant.

A pub, it's called, serving all manner of slaughtered animals on massive plates with an assortment of fried vegetables. She is invited to TRY OUR NACHOS!—which, from what she can tell, consist of a plate of fried tortillas and processed cheese, a few token vegetables, and more meat from more slaughtered animals.

She doesn't eat animals. She wouldn't kill an animal. Animals never did anything to deserve it.

She sits on a stool fronting the window at a ledge intended for single customers, looking out over the street, massive vehicles lined up at a traffic light, scrolling advertisements on billboards for various beers and fast food and "auto loans" and clothing stores and movies. The streets are crowded with people. The restaurant is not; it is just now eleven in the morning, so the lunch rush, as they call it, has not yet begun. The menu offers almost nothing she could stomach. She orders a soft drink and soup and waits.

Overhead, clouds the color of ash have begun to appear throughout the sky. The newspaper said there is a 30 percent chance of rain.

Which means there is a 70 percent chance that she will complete her assignment tonight.

A man takes the seat next to her, to her left. She does not look at him. Face forward, her eyes glance only at the counter, waiting for the crossword puzzle to show.

A moment later, the man slaps down the newspaper, folded open to the crossword, and enters letters into the squares on the top horizontal line of the puzzle.

The letters say: C O N F I R M E D

Looking down at her map of the National Mall, she uses a ballpoint pen to write in the white space on top: *Freight elevator?*

The man, pretending to be considering another clue, taps his pencil on the word he already wrote.

The waiter arrives with her soft drink. She takes a long sip and savors the carbonation's settling effect on her roiling stomach. She writes, *Backup?*

He taps the same word again, confirming once more.

Then, in a "down" column on the crossword puzzle, he writes: Y O U H A V E I D

I have it, she writes. She adds, *If it rains, meet at 9?*

He writes, I T W O N T

She seethes, but she will say nothing and do nothing but wait.

Y E S A T N I N E, he writes in a lower horizontal column.

He gets up before the waiter can take his order, leaving the crossword puzzle on the counter next to her. She slides it over and opens the newspaper more fully, as if interested in one of the articles. The map and the newspaper will be destroyed and discarded in separate trash bins.

She is already looking forward to leaving tonight. She has little doubt that she will perform her task. The only thing she can't control is the weather.

She has never prayed in her life, but if she did, she would pray for no rain.

CHAPTER
10

❖

I t is 1:30 p.m. in the Situation Room, cool and soundproof and windowless.

"Montejo's going to declare martial law throughout Honduras tomorrow," says Brendan Mohan, my national security adviser. "He's already imprisoned most of his political rivals, but he'll step that up. There's a food shortage, so he'll probably institute price controls to keep the people calm for a few more days until he's in complete control. By our estimate, the Patriotas have an army two hundred thousand strong next door in Managua, awaiting word. If he doesn't step down—"

"He won't," says Vice President Kathy Brandt.

Mohan, a former general, does not appreciate the interruption but understands the chain of command. He shrugs his thick shoulders and turns in her direction.

"I agree, Madam Vice President, he won't. But he may not be able to hold the military. If he doesn't, he'll be overthrown. If he does, by our estimate, Honduras will be in civil war within a month."

I turn to Erica Beatty, the CIA director, a bookish, soft-spoken woman with dark, raccoonish eyes and cropped gray hair. She is a spook through and through, a lifer at the CIA. She was recruited out of college by the Agency and became a clandestine officer stationed in West Germany in the 1980s. In 1987, she was abducted by the Stasi—East Germany's state security service—which claimed that she had been caught on their side of the Berlin Wall with a fake passport and architectural drawings of GDR headquarters. She was interrogated and held for nearly a month before the Stasi released her. Stasi's records, made public after the fall of the wall and the reunification of Germany, showed that she was brutally tortured but gave up no information.

Her days as a clandestine officer over, she moved up the ranks and became one of our nation's foremost experts on Russia, advising the Joint Chiefs and heading the CIA's Central Eur-

asia Division, which oversaw intelligence operations in the former Soviet satellites and Warsaw
Pact countries, and finally serving on the Senior
Intelligence Service. She was my campaign's top
adviser on Russia. She rarely speaks unless spoken to, but when you wind her up, she can tell
you more about President Dmitry Chernokev
than Chernokev himself probably could.

"What do you think, Erica?" I ask.

"Montejo's playing right into Chernokev's
hands," she says. "Chernokev has wanted an in-
road into Central America since he took office.
This is his best chance to date. Montejo's turning
fascist, giving the Patriotas credibility, making
them look like freedom fighters and not Russian
puppets. He is playing precisely the role that
Chernokev scripted for him. Montejo is a coward
and a moron."

"But he's *our* cowardly moron," Kathy says.

Kathy's right. We can't let the Russian-backed
Patriotas, Chernokev's puppets, into that region.
We could declare any overthrow of President
Montejo a coup d'état and cut off all American
aid, but how would that help our interests? That
would just turn the Honduran government even
more strongly against us, and Russia would be
happy to gain a foothold in Central America.

"Do I have any good options here?" I ask.

Nobody can think of one.

"Let's do Saudi Arabia next," I say. "What the hell happened?"

Erica Beatty handles this one. "The Saudis have arrested several dozen people in what they say was a plot to assassinate King Saad ibn Saud. They apparently recovered weapons and explosives. It never got as far as an attempt on his life, but the Saudis are saying they were in the 'final stages' of putting it together when the Mabahith executed its raids and mass arrests."

Saad ibn Saud is only thirty-five years old, the youngest son of the former king. Only a year ago, his father reshuffled his leadership and surprised a lot of people by naming Saad the crown prince—next in line to the throne. It made a lot of people in the royal family unhappy. And within three months of his elevation, his father died, and Saad ibn Saud became Saudi Arabia's youngest king.

It's been a rocky road for him so far. He's overcompensated by using his internal state police, the Mabahith, to crack down on dissidents, and one night several months ago he executed more than a dozen of them. I didn't like it, but there wasn't much I could do. I need him in that region. His country is our closest ally. And without a stable Saudi Arabia, our influence is compromised.

"Who's behind it, Erica? Iran? Yemen? Was it in-house?"

"They don't know, sir. We don't know. The human rights NGOs are claiming there was no assassination plot, that it's just an excuse to round up more of the king's political rivals. We do know that some of the wealthy but less influential members of the royal family have been swept up, too. It's going to be a rough few days there."

"We're assisting?"

"We've offered. So far, they haven't taken us up on it. It's a...tense situation."

Unrest in the most stable part of the Middle East. While I'm dealing with this problem at home. It's the absolute last thing I need right now.

At 2:30, back in the Oval Office, I say into the phone, "Mrs. Kopecky, your son was a hero. We honor his service to this country. I'm praying for you and your family."

"He loved...he loved his country, President Duncan," she says, her voice trembling. *"He believed in his mission."*

"I'm sure he—"

"I did not," she says. *"I don't know why we still have to be in that country. Can't they figure out how to run their own stupid country?"*

Overhead, the lights flicker, a quick blink-blink. What's with the lights?

"I understand, Mrs. Kopecky," I say.

"Call me Margaret—everyone else does," she says. *"Can I call you Jon?"*

"Margaret," I say to a woman who's just lost her nineteen-year-old son, "you can call me anything you want."

"I know you're trying to get out of Iraq, Jon," she says. *"But do more than try. Get the hell out."*

Ten after three in the Oval Office, with Danny Akers and Jenny Brickman, my political adviser.

Carolyn walks in and makes eye contact with me and gives a curt, preemptive shake of her head—still no news, no change.

It's hard to concentrate on anything else. But I have no choice. The world isn't going to stop for this threat.

Carolyn joins us, taking a seat.

"This is from HHS," says Danny. I wasn't in the mood for the Heath and Human Services secretary's presentation today, wanting to minimize time spent on nonessential matters, so I had Danny get into the issue and break it down for me.

"It's a Medicaid issue," says Danny, "involving Alabama. You recall that Alabama was one of the states that refused to accept the Medicaid expansion under the Affordable Care Act?"

"Sure."

Carolyn pops up from her seat and rushes to the door, which opens just as she reaches it. My secretary, JoAnn, hands her a note.

Danny stops talking, probably seeing the expression on my face.

Carolyn reads the note and looks at me. "You're needed in the Situation Room, sir," she says.

If it's what we're afraid it is—if this is it—we're hearing about it together for the first time.

CHAPTER
11

❖

S even minutes later, Carolyn and I enter the Situation Room.

We know immediately: it isn't what we feared. The attack hasn't commenced. My pulse slows. We're not here for fun and games, but it's not the nightmare. Not yet.

In the room as we enter: Vice President Kathy Brandt. My national security adviser, Brendan Mohan. The chairman of the Joint Chiefs, Admiral Rodrigo Sanchez. The defense secretary, Dominick Dayton. Sam Haber, the secretary of homeland security. And the CIA director, Erica Beatty.

"They're in a town called al-Bayda," says Admiral Sanchez. "Central Yemen. Not a center of military activity. The Saudi-led coalition is within a hundred kilometers."

"Why are these two meeting?" I ask.

Erica Beatty, CIA, answers. "We don't know, Mr. President. But Abu-Dheeq is al-Shabaab's head of military operations, and al-Fadhli is the military commander of AQAP." She raises her eyebrows.

The top generals for the Somali terrorists and Al Qaeda in the Arabian Peninsula, coming together for a meeting.

"Who else is there?"

"Looks like Abu-Dheeq came with just a small entourage," she says. "But al-Fadhli brought his family. He always does."

Right. He brings his family along to make himself a harder target. "How many?"

"Seven children," she says. "Five boys, two girls. Ages two to sixteen. And his wife."

"Tell me where they are, exactly. Not geographically but in terms of civilians."

"They're meeting in an elementary school," she says. Then she quickly adds, "But there aren't any kids there right now. Remember, they're eight hours ahead of us. It's nighttime."

"You mean there aren't any kids," I say, "besides al-Fadhli's five boys and two girls."

"Of course, sir."

That bastard, using his children as a shield, daring us to kill his entire family to get to him. What kind of coward does that?

"There's no chance that al-Fadhli will be separated from his children?"

"He appears to be in a different part of the school, for what that's worth," says Sanchez. "The meeting is taking place in some interior office. The children are sleeping in a large space that is probably a gymnasium or assembly room."

"But the missile will demolish the entire school," I say.

"We have to assume it will, yes, sir."

"General Burke?" I say into the speakerphone. "Any comment?"

Burke is a four-star general and head of US Central Command, on the phone from Qatar. *"Mr. President, you don't need me to tell you that these are two high-value targets. They are the best military minds in their respective organizations. Abu-Dheeq is al-Shabaab's Douglas MacArthur. Al-Fadhli is not only the top military commander but also the top strategist for AQAP. This would be significant, sir. We may never have an opportunity like this again."*

Significant being a relative term. These men will be replaced. And depending how many innocents we kill, we may create more future terrorists in their wake than we kill right now. But this will be a setback to their organizations, no question. And we can't let terrorists think that

106

they're safe as long as they hide behind their families, either.

"Mr. President," says Erica Beatty, "we don't know how long this meeting will last. It could be breaking up right now. There is obviously something important that these two military commanders want to say to each other, or share with each other, and they're afraid to do it through intermediaries or electronically. But for all we know, in five minutes they'll be gone."

It's now or never, in other words.

"Rod?" I say to the Joint Chiefs chairman, Admiral Sanchez.

"I recommend we strike," he says.

"Dom?" I say to the defense secretary.

"I agree."

"Brendan?"

"I agree."

"Kathy?" I say to the vice president.

The vice president takes a quick moment, lets out air. Tucks a strand of her gray hair behind her ear. "He made the choice, not us, to use his family as a human shield," she says. "I agree that we should strike."

I look at the CIA director. "Erica, do you have the children's names?"

She knows me well enough by now. She hands me a piece of paper with seven names written on it.

I read them, from the sixteen-year-old boy, Yasin, to the two-year-old girl, Salma.

"Salma," I say aloud. "That means 'peace,' doesn't it?"

She clears her throat. "I believe it does, sir."

I picture a small child, nestled in her mother's arms, sleeping quietly, knowing nothing of a world filled with hate. Maybe Salma will grow up to become the woman who changes it all. Maybe she'll be the one to lead us away from our divisions and toward understanding. We have to believe that can happen someday, don't we?

"We could wait for the meeting to break up," I say. "When they go their separate ways, we follow Abu-Dheeq's convoy and take it out. That's one dead terrorist leader. It's not two, but it's better than zero."

"And al-Fadhli?" asks Chairman Sanchez.

"We follow his convoy, too, and hope that he separates himself from his family. Then we strike."

"He won't, sir. Separate himself from his family, I mean. He'll return to a populated area and disappear, like he always does. We'll lose him."

"Al-Fadhli rarely comes up for air," says Erica Beatty. "That's why this is such a tremendous opportunity."

"Tremendous." I flip a hand. "Yes. Killing seven children feels…tremendous."

I stand up and move away from my chair, pace along the wall. My back turned to the team, I hear Kathy Brandt's voice.

"Mr. President," she says, "al-Fadhli is no dummy. If we take out Abu-Dheeq within a kilometer or two of where the meeting took place, he'll know you tracked both of them to that elementary school. He'll know why you spared him. He'll spread the word to his brothers in arms. Keep your children close to you, and the Americans won't strike."

"They don't worry about *our* children," says Erica Beatty.

"So we're no different?" I ask. "We're no better? They don't care about our children, so we don't care about theirs?"

Kathy raises a hand. "No, sir, that's not what I'm saying. They *deliberately* target civilians. We're not doing it deliberately. We're doing it as a last resort. We are conducting a precision military strike against a terrorist leader, not randomly choosing civilians and children as targets."

That's the argument, sure. But the terrorists we're fighting don't see the difference between a military strike conducted by the United States and what they do. They can't drop missiles on us from drones. They can't take on our army, our air force. What they do, blowing up or attacking civilian targets, is their version of a precision military strike.

Aren't we different? Don't we draw the line at conducting a military strike that we *know* will kill innocent children? Unintended consequences are one thing. This time we know the result before we start.

Rod Sanchez checks his watch. "This debate could become moot any minute. I doubt they will stay together for very long be—"

"Yes, that point was made already," I say. "I heard it the first time."

I lower my head and close my eyes, shutting out the rest of the room. I have a team of highly competent, well-trained professionals advising me. But I am making this decision alone. There is a reason that the founders of our country put a civilian in charge of the military. Because it is not only about military effectiveness. It's also about policy, about values, about what we stand for as a nation.

How can I kill seven children?

You're not. You're killing two terrorists who are plotting their next slaughter of innocent civilians. Al-Fadhli's killing his children by hiding behind them.

110

True, but that's semantics. It's my choice. They live or they die based on my choice. How do I meet my Maker one day and justify their deaths?

It's not semantics. If you pass on this, you're rewarding them for their cowardly tactics.

But that doesn't matter. Seven innocent children are what matters. Is that what the United States stands for?

But why are those high-value terrorists meeting in person? That's never happened before. They must be planning something big. Something that will result in the deaths of more than seven children. Stop this now, you might stop an attack. A net saving of lives.

I open my eyes. I take a deep breath, waiting for the drumming of my heart to slow. It doesn't. It speeds up.

I know the answer. I always knew the answer. I haven't been searching for the answer. I've been searching for a justification.

I take one more moment and whisper a prayer. I pray for those children. I pray that one day no president will have to make a decision like this.

"God help us," I say. "You have my authorization to strike."

CHAPTER
12

❖

I return to the Oval Office with Carolyn as the clock slowly, agonizingly approaches five. We are silent. A lot of working men and women look forward to five o'clock on Friday because it signals the end of the work week, some much-needed relaxation and time with family.

But for the last four days, Carolyn and I have been waiting and planning for this particular hour of this particular day not knowing whether it's the beginning of something, the end of something, or both.

It was last Monday, just after noon, when I received the phone call on my personal cell. Carolyn and I were grabbing turkey sandwiches in the kitchen. We already knew we were facing an imminent threat. We didn't understand the scope or magnitude of it. We had no idea how to stop it. Our mission in Algeria had already failed in spectacular fashion for all the world to see. Suliman Cindoruk remained on the loose. My entire national security team had been subpoenaed to testify the following day, Tuesday, before the House Select Committee.

But when I put down my sandwich and answered that call in the kitchen, everything changed. The dynamic was completely upended. For the first time, I had the tiniest sliver of hope. But I was also more scared than ever.

"Five p.m. Eastern time, Friday, May the eleventh," I was told.

So as the time approaches five o'clock on Friday, May 11, I am no longer thinking about the seven innocent children in the Republic of Yemen who are dead under a pile of ash and rubble based on a decision I made.

Now I'm wondering what in the hell is about to happen to our country and how I can best deal with it.

"Where is she?" I mumble.

"It's not quite five, sir. She'll be here."

"You don't know that," I say as I pace. "You can't know that. Call down."

Before she can, her phone buzzes. She answers. "Yes, Alex...she—all right...she's alone?...yes...

that's fine, do what you need to do...yes, but be quick about it."

She puts away her phone and looks at me.

"She's here," I say.

"Yes, sir, she's here. They're searching her."

I look out the window, up at the bruised sky, threatening rain. "What is she going to say, Carrie?"

"I wish I knew, sir. I will be monitoring."

The instruction delivered to me was a one-on-one meeting, no exceptions. So I will be alone, physically, in the Oval Office with my guest. But Carolyn will be watching from a monitor in the Roosevelt Room.

I bounce on my toes, not knowing what to do with my hands. My stomach is in full-scale revolt. "God, I haven't been this nervous since..." I can't finish the sentence. "I don't think I've ever been this nervous."

"You don't show it, sir."

I nod. "Neither do you." Carolyn never shows weakness. It's not her way. And it's a comfort right now, because she's the only one I can count on.

She's the only person in the US government, besides me, who knows about this meeting.

Carolyn leaves. I stand by my desk and wait for JoAnn to open the door for my visitor.

After what feels like an endless slog of time, the clock moving in slow motion, JoAnn opens the door. "Mr. President," she says.

I nod. This is it.

"Show her in," I say.

CHAPTER
13

❖

The girl enters the room wearing work boots, torn jeans, and a gray long-sleeved T-shirt bearing the word PRINCETON. She is waif-thin, with a long neck, prominent cheekbones, and narrow eyes spread apart in a way that suggests eastern Europe. Her hair is in one of those styles I've never understood, the right side of her head shaved in a military buzz cut with longer hair hanging over it, down to her bony shoulders.

A cross between a Calvin Klein model and a Eurotrash punk rocker.

She scans the room, but not the way most people who enter the Oval Office do. First-time visitors soak it all in, eagerly devour all the portraits and knickknacks, marvel at the presidential seal, the *Resolute* desk.

Not her. What I see in her eyes, behind the impenetrable wall of her face, is pure loathing. Hatred of me, this office, everything it stands for.

But she's tense, too, on alert—wondering if someone will jump her, handcuff her, throw a hood over her head.

She fits the physical description I received. She gave the name at the gate that we expected. It's her. But I have to confirm, regardless.

"Say the words," I tell her.

She raises her eyebrows. She can't be surprised.

"Say it."

She rolls her eyes.

"'Dark Ages,'" she says, curling her *r*'s, as if the words were poison on her tongue. Her accent is heavily eastern European.

"How do you know those words?"

She shakes her head, clucks her tongue. There will be no answer to my question.

"Your…Secret Service…does not like me," she says. *Doze not like me.*

"You were setting off the metal detectors."

"I do that…always. The…what is your word? The bomb frag—the—"

"Shrapnel," I say. "Parts of a bomb. From an explosion."

"This, yes," she says, tapping her forehead. "They

told me that two…centimeters to the right…and I would not have woken up."

She curls a thumb into the belt loop of her jeans. There is defiance in her eyes, a challenge.

"Would you like to know…what I did to deserve it?"

I'm going to guess it had something to do with some military strike ordered by an American president—maybe me—in some faraway land. But I know next to nothing about this woman. I don't know her real name or where she's from. I don't know her motivation or her plan. After first making contact with me—indirectly—four days ago, on Monday, she fell off the map, and despite my considerable efforts to learn more about her, I failed. I don't know anything about her for certain.

But I am reasonably sure that this young woman holds the fate of the free world in her hands.

"I was walking my…cousin…to mass when the missile hit," she says.

I shove my hands in my pockets. "You're safe here," I say.

Her eyes drift up and away, enlarging them, a beautiful copper color. It makes her look even younger. Less of the hardened image she's trying to project and more the scared kid she must be, underneath it all.

She should be scared. I hope she's scared. I sure as hell am, but I'm not going to show it any more than she will.

"No," she says. "I do not think." *I donut zink.*

"I promise."

She blinks her eyes heavily, looks away with disdain. "The American president promises." She reaches into the back pocket of her jeans and produces an envelope, tattered and folded in half. She straightens it and places it on the table next to the couch.

"My partner does not know what I know," she says. "Only I do. I did not write it down." She taps the right side of her head. "It is in here only."

Her secret, she means. She didn't put it on a computer we could hack or in an e-mail we could intercept. She is storing it in one place only, a place that not even our sophisticated technology can penetrate—her mind.

"And I do not know what my partner knows," she says.

Right. She has separated herself from her partner. Each of them, she is telling me, holds part of the puzzle. Each of them is indispensable.

"I need both of you," I say. "I understand. Your message on Monday was clear about that."

"And you will be alone tonight," she says.

"Yes. Your message was clear on that, too."

She nods, as if we have settled something.

"How do you know 'Dark Ages'?" I ask again.

Her eyes turn down. From the table by the couch, she picks up a photograph of my daughter and me walking from Marine One toward the White House.

"I remember the first time I saw a helicopter," she says. "I was a young girl. It was on the television. There was a hotel in Dubai that was opening. The Mari-Poseidon, it was called. This... majestic hotel on the waters of the Persian Gulf. It had a heli—a heli...pad?"

"A helipad, yes," I say. "A rooftop landing for helicopters."

"This, yes. The helicopter landed on the roof of this hotel. I remember thinking that if people could fly, they could do...anything."

I'm not sure why she's telling me about Dubai hotels or helicopters. Maybe it's nothing more than nervous chatter.

I approach her. She turns, puts down the photo, and steels herself.

"If I do not leave here," she says, "you will never see my partner. You will have no way to stop this."

I lift the envelope from the table. It is nearly weightless, flimsy. I can see a trace of color through the paper. The Secret Service would have inspected it, checked it for any suspicious residue and the like.

She steps back, still wary, still waiting for government agents to burst through the door and whisk her away to some Guantánamo Bay–style interrogation room. If I thought that would work, I'd do it in a heartbeat. But she has set this up so that it wouldn't. This young woman has managed to do something that very few people could pull off.

She has forced me to play this game on her terms.

"What do you want?" I ask. "Why are you doing this?"

For the first time, her stoic expression breaks, her lips curve, but it's not an expression of mirth. "Only the president of this country would ask such a question." She shakes her head, then her face once again becomes a poker-face wall.

"You will find out why," she says, nodding toward the envelope in my hand. "Tonight."

"So I have to trust you," I say.

This draws a look from her, a raised eyebrow, her eyes glistening. "I have not convinced you?"

"You've gotten this far," I say. "But no, you haven't entirely convinced me."

She eyeballs me, a confident, daring look, like

I'd be a fool to call her bluff. "Then you must decide," she says.

"Wait," I say as she heads for the door, reaches for the knob.

She bristles, freezes in place. Still looking at the door, not me, she says, "If I am not allowed to leave, you will never see my partner. If I am followed, you will never see my part—"

"No one's going to stop you," I say. "No one's going to follow you."

She holds still, her hand poised over the knob. Thinking. Debating. About what, I don't know. I could fill a room with what I don't know.

"If anything happens to my partner," she says, "your country will burn."

She turns the knob and leaves. Just like that, she's gone.

And then I'm alone with the envelope. I have to let her go. I have no choice. I can't risk alienating the one chance I have.

Assuming I believe her. Assuming that everything she's saying is true. I'm nearly 100 percent there, but in my line of work, it's hard to get closer than that.

I open the envelope, which tells me where the next meeting will take place, tonight. I replay everything that just happened. So very little did. She had almost nothing of substance to say.

She accomplished two things, I realize. One, she needed to hand me this envelope. And two, she wanted to know if she could trust me, if I would let her leave.

I walk over and sit on my couch, staring at the envelope, trying to glean any hints from what she said. Trying to think ahead on the chessboard.

A knock on the door, and Carolyn enters.

"I passed her test," I say.

"That's all this was," she agrees. "And that," she adds, nodding at the envelope in my hand.

"But did she pass mine?" I ask. "How do I know this is real?"

"I think it is, sir."

"Why?"

Overhead, the lights flicker again, a momentary strobe effect. Carolyn looks up and curses under her breath. Another thing she'll have to address sometime down the road.

"Why do you believe her?" I ask.

"The reason it took me a few minutes to come in, sir." She points at her phone. "We just got word out of Dubai. There was an incident."

An incident in Dubai. "With a helicopter?"

She nods. "A helicopter exploded while landing on the helipad of the Mari-Poseidon Hotel."

I bring a hand to my face.

"I checked the timing, sir. It happened after

123

she'd walked into the Oval Office. There's no other way she could have known about it."

I fall back against the couch. So she accomplished a third goal. She showed me she was the real deal.

"All right," I whisper. "I'm convinced."

CHAPTER
14

❖

Up in the private residence, I open one of the dresser drawers, which contains only a single item: a picture of Rachel. I have plenty of those around here, photos of her vibrant and happy, mugging for the camera or hugging or laughing. This one is for me only. It was taken less than a week before she died. Her face is blotchy from treatments; she has only wisps of hair on her head. Her face is almost skeletal. To most people, this would be hard to look at— Rachel Carson Duncan at her absolute worst, finally succumbing to a ravaging disease. But to me, it's Rachel at her best, her strongest, her most beautiful—the smile in her eyes, her peace and resolve.

The fight was over at that point. It was just a

matter of time, they told us—could be months, but more likely weeks. It turned out to be six days. It was six days I wouldn't trade for any others in my life. All that mattered was us, our love. We talked about our fears. We talked about Lilly. We talked about God. We read from the Bible and prayed and laughed and cried until our wells of tears had run dry. I'd never known intimacy so raw and cathartic. I'd never felt so inseparable from another human being.

"Let me take a picture of you," I whispered to her.

She started to object, but she understood: I wanted to remember this time because, at that moment, I'd never loved her more.

"Sir," says Carolyn Brock, lightly rapping her knuckles on the door.

"Yeah, I know."

I put my fingers to my lips, then touch Rachel's photo. I close the drawer and look up.

"Let's go," I say, dressed in my civvies and holding a small bag over my shoulder.

Alex Trimble's head drops, his jaw clenched with disapproval. When the head of a Secret Service detail dreams his worst nightmare, it is this. He can always console himself with the fact that I gave him an order, that he had no choice but to let me go.

"Just a loose perimeter?" he says. "You'll never see us."

I give him a smile that says no.

Alex has been with me since I was first assigned security protection during the primaries, when I was a governor viewed as a long shot for the nomination. It wasn't until the first major debate that my poll numbers surged, placing me in the top tier of candidates behind the front-runner, Kathy Brandt. I didn't know how the Secret Service doled out its assignments, but I had assumed, as a dark-horse candidate, that I did not receive their best and brightest. But Alex always said to me, "Governor, as far as I'm concerned, you *are* the president," and he was disciplined and organized. His team feared him the same way cadets fear their drill sergeants. And as I told him when I made him the head of the White House detail, nobody killed me, so he must have done something right.

You don't get too close to your security, and they don't get too close to you. Each side of the arrangement understands the need for emotional separation. But I've always seen the goodness in Alex. He married his college sweetheart, Gwen; he reads the Bible every day and sends money to his mother back home every month. He's the first to tell you he wasn't book smart, but he was a hell of a left tackle and got a football scholarship to Iowa State, where he studied criminal justice and dreamed of joining the Secret Service so he could do in life what he did on the gridiron— protect the blind side of his client.

When I asked him to head up my detail at the White House, he kept his standard stoic expression and ramrod posture, but I caught a brief sheen of emotion across his eyes. "It would be the greatest honor of my life, sir," he whispered.

"We'll use GPS," he says to me now. "Just so we'll know where you are."

"Sorry," I say.

"Checkpoints," he tries, a Hail Mary. "Just tell us where you're going—"

"No, Alex," I say.

He doesn't understand why. He is convinced that he could surveil me invisibly. I'm sure he could. So why won't I let him?

He doesn't know, and I can't tell him.

"At least wear a bulletproof vest," he says.

"No," I answer. "Too noticeable." Even the new ones are too bulky.

Alex wants to argue more. He wants to tell me that I'm being a horse's ass, but he'd never speak to me like that. He runs through an entire plea in his head, probably no different from the arguments he's already raised with me, before dropping his shoulders and relenting.

"Be safe," he says, a line that people throw out every day as an innocuous sign-off but that in this case is charged with emotion and dread.

"Will do."

I look at Danny and Carolyn, the only other people in the room. It's time for me to go, alone and off the record. For years I've been constantly going, but never alone and never off the record. The Secret Service takes every step with me, and at least one aide is almost always there, even when I'm on vacation. A record is kept of where I am every hour.

I know this is the only option that will spare the country untold misery and allow me to do my duty to preserve, protect, and defend it. I know my fellow Americans go alone and off the record all the time, though surveillance cameras, cell phones, social media mining, and hacking are shrinking their zones of privacy, too. Still, this is a big change, and I feel a little disoriented and disarmed.

Danny and Carolyn are by my side for the last leg of my dislocation from the trappings of office. We are quiet. They each tried hard to talk me out of this. Now they're resigned to helping me make it work.

It's harder than you might think to get out of the White House unnoticed. We take the stairs from the residence all the way down. We walk slowly, each footfall another movement toward what is about to happen. With every step, I am surrendering more control to an uncertain fate tonight.

"You remember when we first took this route?" I ask, recalling our postelection tour before I took the oath of office.

"Like it was yesterday," says Carolyn.

"I'll never forget it," Danny says.

"We were so full of…hope, I guess. We were so sure we'd make the world a better place."

Carolyn says, "Maybe you were. I was scared to death."

I was, too. We knew the world we were inheriting. We had no illusions that we would leave everything perfect. When I hit the pillow every night during those heady preinauguration days, my mind would veer wildly from dreams of massive strides forward in national security, foreign relations, shared prosperity, and health care and criminal justice reform to nightmares of completely botching the whole thing and plunging the nation into crisis.

"Safer, stronger, fairer, kinder," Danny says, reminding me of the four words I ticked off every morning as we began to put fine points on our policies and build our team for the upcoming four-year term.

Finally we reach the subbasement, where there's a one-lane bowling alley, a bunkerlike but well-furnished operations center that Dick Cheney occupied after 9/11, and a couple of other rooms designed for meeting around simple tables or sleeping on cots.

We pass the doors and head toward a narrow tunnel that connects the building to the Treasury Department, just to the east, on 15th and Pennsylvania. What exactly is beneath the White House has been the subject of myth and rumor going back to the Civil War, when the Union Army feared an attack on the White House and plans were put together to evacuate President Lincoln to a vault in the Treasury Building as a last resort. The real work on the tunnel didn't begin until FDR and World War II, when an air assault on the White House became a real possibility. It was designed in a zigzag pattern precisely to mitigate the impact of a bomb strike.

The entrance to the tunnel has a door alarm, but Carolyn's taken care of that. The tunnel itself is only ten feet wide and seven feet high—not a lot of headroom for someone like me, who's over six feet tall. It could have a claustrophobic effect, but I don't feel it. For someone no longer accustomed to going anywhere without the Secret Service or aides, the empty, open space of the tunnel is liberating.

The three of us walk almost the length of the tunnel before coming to another path, which turns right into a small underground parking garage reserved for high-ranking Treasury officials and important guests. Tonight it also holds my getaway car.

Carolyn hands me car keys, then a cell phone, which I put in my left pocket, next to the envelope that the girl gave me half an hour ago.

"The numbers are preprogrammed," she says, referring to the cell phone. "Everyone we talked about. Including Lilly."

Lilly. Something breaks inside of me.

"You remember the code?" she asks.

"I remember. Don't worry."

From behind my back, I produce an envelope of my own, this one bearing the presidential seal and containing a single piece of paper. When Danny sees it, he almost loses his composure.

"No," he says. "I'm not opening that."

Carolyn puts out her hand and takes it from me.

"Open it," I tell her, "if you need to open it."

Danny puts a hand on his forehead, pushing his hair back. "Jesus, Jon," he whispers, the first time since I took office that he's used my name. "Are you really going to do this?"

"Danny," I whisper, "if anything happens to me—"

"Hey—hey now." He puts his hands on my shoulders. He is faltering, holding back emotion. "She's like flesh and blood to me. You know that. I love that kid more than anything."

Danny's divorced now, with one son in grad school. But he was in the waiting room when Lilly was born; he stood on the altar at her baptism; he teared up at every one of her graduations; he held Lilly's other hand at Rachel's funeral. Early on, he was "Uncle Danny" to Lilly. Somewhere along the line, the "uncle" part got dropped. He will be the closest thing she'll have to a parent.

"You got your Ranger coin?" he asks.

"What, you're popping me with a coin check right now?" I pat my pocket. "Never go anywhere without it," I say. "What about you?"

"Can't say I have mine with me. Guess I owe you a drink. So now you…" His throat catches with emotion. "Now you *have* to come back."

I hold my stare on Danny, my family not in blood but in every way that matters. "Roger that, brother."

Then I turn to Carolyn. We don't have a hugging kind of relationship; other than the nights I won the nomination and then the general election, we've never embraced.

But we do now. She whispers into my ear. "My money's on you, sir. They don't know what they're up against."

"If that's true," I say back, "it's because I have you on my side."

I watch them leave, shaken but resolved. The next twenty-four or forty-eight hours will not be easy for Carolyn, who will have to serve as my point person at the White House. These are unprecedented times. We are, in a real sense, making this up as we go along.

When they are gone, when I am alone in the tunnel, I bend over and put my hands on my knees. I take a few deep breaths to combat the butterflies.

"I hope you know what the hell you're doing," I say to myself. Then I turn and head farther into the tunnel.

CHAPTER
15

❖

I walk into Treasury's underground parking garage with my head angled downward, hands in the pockets of my blue jeans, my leather shoes moving softly along the asphalt. I am not the only person down here at this hour, so my presence is not conspicuous by any means, though I'm dressed more casually than the departing employees of the Treasury Department, with their suits and briefcases and ID badges. It's easy to hide among the sounds of heels clicking on pavement, car remotes beeping, automatic locks on cars releasing, and engines turning over, especially when the departing employees are more concerned with their weekend plans than with the guy in the cotton button-down and blue jeans.

I may be in hiding, and this is no joyride, but I can't deny the small thrill of release I feel while moving about in public without being noticed. It has been more than a decade since I've set foot in a public place without being on display, without feeling like someone might snap a photo of me at any moment, without seeing dozens of people wanting to approach me for a handshake or a quick hello, a selfie, a favor, or even a substantive policy discussion.

As promised, the car is the fourth from the end on the left, a nondescript sedan, an older model, silver, with Virginia plates. I hold out the remote and push the Unlock button for too long, causing every door to unlock and then a series of beeps to sound. I'm out of practice. I haven't opened my own car door for a decade.

Behind the wheel, I feel like someone fresh out of a time machine, transported into the future by this mysterious contraption. I adjust the seat, turn the ignition, gun the gas once, throw it into Reverse, and turn my head to look back, my arm over the passenger seat. As I slowly back out of the space, the car emits a beep that grows more urgent. I hit the brakes and see a woman walking behind the car, on the way to hers. Once she has passed by, the beeping stops.

Some kind of radar, an anticollision device. I

look back at the dashboard and notice a backup camera. So I can drive in Reverse while facing forward, watching the screen? They didn't have that ten years ago, or if they did, *my* car sure as hell didn't have it.

I navigate the sedan through the garage, the lanes surprisingly narrow, the angles sharp. It takes me a few minutes to get the hang of it again, jumping forward too abruptly, braking too harshly, but then it feels like yesterday that I was sixteen, driving that beater Chevy off the lot of Crazy Sam Kelsey's New and Used Autos for twelve hundred dollars.

I watch the cars in front of me in the line to leave the garage. The gate lifts automatically as each car reaches the front. No need for the driver to reach out the window to press a card against some reader or anything like that. It occurs to me that I didn't even think to ask about that.

When it's my turn at the front, the gate rises, letting me leave. I pull slowly up the ramp, approaching daylight, wary of passing pedestrians, before I pull into the street.

Traffic is thick, so my urge to gun the car, to feel the freedom of this temporary independence, is stymied by the congestion at every intersection. I look up through the windshield at the bruised sky, hoping it won't rain.

The radio. I click a knob to turn it on, and nothing happens. I push a button, and nothing happens. I push another button, and the sound blares out, sending a shock wave through me as two people are arguing, talking over each other about whether President Jonathan Duncan has committed an impeachable offense. I push the same button, kill the sound, and focus on driving.

I think about where I'm going, the person I'm about to see, and invariably my mind wanders back…

CHAPTER
16

❖

*P*rofessor Waite strolled across the well of the lecture hall, hands clasped behind his back. "And
what was the point of Justice Stevens's dissent?" He returned to the lectern, looked over his name chart.
"Mr.... Duncan?" He looked up at me.

Shit. I'd thrown a lump of Copenhagen in my cheek
so I could stay awake after a night of getting my paper
done. I'd only skimmed the case for today. I was one of a
hundred in this class, after all, so the odds of my being
called on were slim. But this was my unlucky day. I was
on the spot and unprepared.

"Justice Stevens...disagreed with the majority
in...with..." I flipped through the pages, feeling the heat
rise to my face.

"Well, yes, Mr. Duncan, dissents do typically disagree
with the majority. I do believe that's why they're called

dissents." Nervous laughter rippled through the lecture hall.

"Yes, sir, he...he disagreed with the majority's interpretation of the Fourth Amendment—"

"You must be confusing Justice Stevens's dissent with Justice Brennan's dissent, Mr. Duncan. Justice Stevens's dissent did not so much as mention *the Fourth Amendment."*

"Well, yes, I am confused—I mean confusing..."

"I think you had it right the first time, Mr. Duncan. Ms. Carson, would you be so kind as to rescue us from Mr. Duncan's confusion?"

"Justice Stevens's point was that the Supreme Court should not intervene in state court decisions that, at worst, would have the effect of raising the floor of the federal constitution..."

Burned for the first time by the notorious Professor Waite, this being only the fourth week of my first year at UNC Law, I looked across the room at the woman in the third row who was speaking as I thought to myself, This is the last time you come to class unprepared, you maggot.

And then I fixed my gaze on her, seated in the third row, confidently, almost casually giving her answer. "...It is a floor, not a ceiling, and so long as an adequate and independent state ground exists for the decision..."

I felt like the wind had been knocked out of me.

"Who...is that?" I whispered to Danny, seated next to

me. Danny was two years ahead of me in school—he was a third-year—and he knew pretty much everyone.

"That's Rachel," he whispered back. "Rachel Carson. A 3L. The one who beat me out for editor in chief of the law review."

"What's her story?"

"You mean is she single? No idea. You've made a great first impression, though."

My heart was still pounding as the class ended. I jumped out of my seat and hit the door, hoping to catch her in the hallway amid a sea of students.

Cropped chestnut hair, jean jacket...

...Rachel Carson...Rachel Carson...

There. I spotted her. I navigated the crowd and caught up to her just as she was breaking away from the forward movement of the masses and angling toward one of the doors.

"Hey," I said, my voice shaky. My voice was shaking?

She turned and looked at me, liquid green eyes, eyebrows raised. The most delicate, sculpted face I'd ever seen. "Hi..." she said tentatively, trying to place me.

"Um. Hi." I hiked my backpack over my shoulder. "I, uh, just wanted to say thanks for, y'know, bailing me out in there."

"Oh. No problem. You're a 1L?"

"Guilty as charged."

"Happens to all of us," she said.

I took a breath. "So, uh, what are you…I mean…what are you, y'know, doing right now?"

What the hell was wrong with me? I'd taken every smoke session Sergeant Melton could dish out. I'd been waterboarded, beaten, strung up, and mock-executed by the Iraqi Republican Guard. Suddenly I was tongue-tied?

"Right now? Well, I…" She nodded to one side. For the first time, I focused on the door she'd been about to enter—the ladies' bathroom.

"Oh, you were gonna…"

"Yeah…"

"You should, then."

"Should I?" she said, amused.

"Yeah, I mean, it's not good to—to hold it in, or—I mean—if you gotta go, you gotta go, right?"

What in holy hell was wrong with me?

"Right," she said. "So…it was nice meeting you."

I could hear her laughter inside the bathroom.

A week after I first laid eyes on her, I hadn't been able to get her out of my mind. I scolded myself: the first year of law school is the year to buckle down, the year when you establish yourself. But no matter how hard I tried to focus on the minimum-contacts doctrine of personal jurisdiction or the elements of a negligence claim or the mirror-image rule of contract law, that girl in the third row of my federal jurisdiction elective kept popping into my head.

Danny gave me intel: Rachel Carson was from a small town in western Minnesota, went to Harvard undergrad, and was at UNC Law on a public-interest grant. She was editor in chief of the law review, first in her class, and had a job waiting for her at a nonprofit organization that provides legal assistance to the poor. She was sweet but quiet. She kept a low profile socially, tended to hang out with the older people in school who didn't come straight from undergrad.

Well, shit, *I thought to myself.* I didn't come straight from undergrad, either.

I eventually mustered my courage and found her in the library, sitting at a long table with several of her friends. I told myself again that this was a bad idea. My legs had a different notion, though, and suddenly I was standing by her table.

When she saw me coming, she put down the pen in her hand and stared.

I wanted to do this in private, but I was afraid that if I didn't do it now, I'd never do it.

So go on, you dumb ass, before someone calls security.

I removed the piece of paper from my pocket, unfolded it, and cleared my throat. By now I had the entire table's attention. I started reading:

The first two times you heard me speak, I
   sounded like a fool.

I made about as much sense as a top hat on a mule.
I wasn't sure a third attempt would do me any
    better,
So I decided that I'd put my thoughts down in a
    letter.

*I peeked at her, an amused smile flirting with her face.
"She hasn't walked away yet," I said, getting a chuckle
from one of her friends, a good start.*

My name is Jon. I come from here, a town near
    Boomer.
I have good manners, listen well, a decent sense
    of humor.
I have no money, have no car, no talent as a
    poet,
But I do possess a working brain, though I often
    fail to show it.

*That line got me another chuckle from her friends.
"It's true," I said to Rachel. "I can read and write and
all that junk."
    "I'm sure, I'm sure."
    "May I keep going?"
    "By all means." She swept her hand.*

You're here to study, says my buddy. Remember
    Professor Waite?

But for some reason I just can't concentrate.
I'm reading the section on equal protection, the
 law and racial quotas,
But instead I'm thinking of a green-eyed girl
 from Minnesota.

She couldn't suppress her smile, her face coloring. The rest of the women at the table applauded.

I bowed at the waist. "Thank you very much," I said, doing my best Elvis imitation. "I'll be here all week."

Rachel didn't look at me.

"I mean, if nothing else, the fact that I rhymed Minnesota…"

"No, that was impressive," she agreed, her eyes closed.

"All right, then. Ladies, if you'll excuse me, I'm going to pretend that this whole thing went well, and I'm going to leave while I'm ahead on points."

I walked slowly enough for her to have caught up with me if she wanted.

CHAPTER
17

❖

I snap out of my reverie and slide into the parking space, just where I was told it would be, not three miles from the White House. I park the car and kill the ignition. No one else is in sight.

I grab my bag and get out. The back entrance looks like a loading dock of some sort, with steps up to a large door that has no outside knob.

A voice through an intercom squawks at me. *"Who is it, please?"*

"Charles Kane," I say.

A moment later, the thick door pops ajar. I reach in and pull it open.

Inside is a freight area, empty of people, cluttered with UPS and FedEx boxes, large crates and wheeled dollies. A large elevator is to the right, the doors open, the walls covered with thick padding.

I press the top button, and the doors close. I draw a sharp breath as the elevator reacts clumsily, dropping for a moment before lifting me, the grinding of the gears audible.

Another moment of light-headedness. I put my hand against the padded wall and wait it out while Dr. Lane's words echo in my head.

When I reach the top and the doors open, I step out carefully into a well-appointed hallway, the walls painted a light yellow, Monet prints guiding me toward the only door on the top floor, the penthouse.

When I reach the door, it opens without my doing anything.

"Charles Kane, at your service," I say.

Amanda Braidwood stands inside the penthouse, her arm fully extended as she holds the door open and appraises me. A thin sweater hangs loose over a fitted shirt. She's wearing black stretch pants and nothing on her feet. Her hair is long these days, courtesy of the movie she wrapped a month ago, but tonight it's pulled back into a ponytail, with a few strands hanging down to frame the contours of her face.

"Well, hello there, 'Mr. Kane,'" she says. "Sorry

about the subterfuge, but the doorman at the front entrance is a little busybodyish."

Last year, an entertainment magazine named Mandy one of the twenty most beautiful women on the planet. Another dubbed her one of the top twenty highest-paid actors in Hollywood, less than a year after she took home her second Oscar.

She and Rachel lived together all four years at Harvard and stayed in touch over the years—as closely as a North Carolina lawyer and an international movie star can manage. The code name Charles Kane was Mandy's idea: about eight years ago, over a bottle of wine in the backyard of the governor's mansion, Rachel, Mandy, and I agreed that Orson Welles's masterpiece was the finest movie ever made.

She shakes her head as a smile slowly blooms on her face.

"My, my," she says. "Whiskers, scruff," she adds as she kisses my cheek. "How rugged. Well, don't just stand there looking all outdoorsy—come in."

Her scent, the smell of a woman, lingers with me. Rachel wasn't much for perfume, but her bath gel and body lotion—whatever you call all those creams and lotions and soaps—were both vanilla. I will never smell that scent again, as long as I live, without seeing the image of Rachel's bare shoulder and imagining the softness of her neck.

They say there's no manual for overcoming the death of a spouse. That's truer still when the survivor is the president and all hell is breaking loose, because you have no time to grieve. There are too many decisions to make that won't wait, constant security threats that, with even a momentary lapse in your attention, can have catastrophic consequences. As Rachel hit the end stages of her illness, we watched North Korea and Russia and China more closely than ever, knowing that the leaders of those countries were looking for any hint of vulnerability or inattention from the White House. I considered temporarily stepping down as president—I even had Danny draw up the papers—but Rachel would have none of it. She was determined that her illness would not cause any interruption in my presidency. It mattered to her, in an intense way that she never fully explained and I never fully understood.

Three days before Rachel passed—by that point, we'd returned to Raleigh so she could die at home—North Korea tested an intercontinental ballistic missile off its coast, and I ordered an aircraft carrier into the Yellow Sea. The day we buried her, as I stood at her grave, holding hands with my daughter, our embassy in Venezuela was attacked by a suicide bomber, and I soon found myself in our kitchen with generals and our national security team considering options for a proportional response.

In the short term, it's probably easier to deal with personal loss when the world around you constantly demands your attention. You're too busy to be sad and lonely at first. Then the reality drops in—you've lost the love of your life, your daughter has lost her mother, and a wonderful woman was denied the chance to live a long, rich life. Now you're grateful for the demands of your job. But there are moments of intense loneliness, even when you're the president. I'd never felt it before. I'd had plenty of tough decisions to make in my first two years, plenty of times I could do nothing more than pray that I'd made the right call, times when it didn't matter how many aides I had because the buck stopped with me and me alone. But I never *felt* alone. I always had Rachel there with me, giving me her honest opinion about how I was making the decisions, telling me to do the best I could, then wrapping her arms around my neck when it was over.

I still miss Rachel all the time, in every way a

man can miss his wife. Tonight I miss her un-
canny sense of when to dress me down and when
to back me up, make me believe that no matter
what, everything will turn out all right.

There will never be another Rachel. I know
that. But I do wish I weren't alone all the time.
Rachel demanded that we talk about what would
happen after she died. She used to joke that I'd be
the most eligible bachelor on the planet. Maybe.
Right now I feel like a clueless nerd about to let
everybody down.

"Drink?" Mandy asks over her shoulder.

"No time," I say. "I don't have very long."

"Honestly, I don't even understand why you
want to do this," she says. "But I'm ready. Let's
get to it."

I follow her into the apartment.

CHAPTER
18

❖

T his feels weird," I say.

"You're doing fine," Mandy whispers. "Nobody's ever done this to you?"

"No, and I hope nobody ever does again."

"It will be more enjoyable for both of us," she says, "if you'd stop complaining. For God's sake, Jon, you were tortured in a Baghdad prison and you can't handle this?"

"You do this every day?"

"Most days. Now hold…still. It's easier that way."

Easier for her, maybe. I try to stay as still as possible, seated in a pink chair in the dressing room inside Mandy's bedroom suite as she uses a makeup pencil on my eyebrows. To my right, Mandy's vanity is covered with makeup supplies, bottles and brushes and powders and creams and clays of all different sizes and colors. It looks like something on the set of a B movie about vampires or zombies.

"Don't make me look like Groucho Marx," I say.

"No, no," she says. "But speaking of..." She reaches down and pulls something out of a bag and shows it to me—Groucho Marx glasses, the bushy eyebrows and mustache.

I take them from her. "Rachel's," I say.

When Rachel started getting really sick, it bothered her how sorry for her everyone felt. So when friends would come to visit, she had a little routine to lighten things up. I'd warn people that "Rachel isn't really herself today." And when they'd walk into the room, they'd see Rachel in bed, wearing the Groucho glasses. Sometimes it was a clown nose. She had a mask of Richard Nixon, too, which really got a laugh.

That was Rachel, right there. Always worrying about everyone but herself.

"Anyway," says Mandy, before things get too misty, "don't worry about your eyebrows. I'm just thickening them a little. You'd be amazed how they can change one's appearance. Eyes and eyebrows."

She scoots back in her chair and looks at me.

"Honestly, kiddo, that beard you showed up with was half the battle right there. And it's so red! It almost doesn't look real. You want me to color your hair to match?"

"Definitely not."

She shakes her head, still studying my face like it's a lab specimen. "Your hair isn't long enough to do much with," she mumbles, talking to herself more than to me. "Changing the part from the right to the left wouldn't help. We could forget the part and comb it all forward." She puts her hands in my hair, gripping it, finger-combing it, mussing it. "At least you'd have a hairstyle that matches this decade."

"How about I wear a baseball cap?" I say.

"Oh." She draws back. "Sure, that would be easier. Does that work? Did you bring one?"

"Yeah." I reach down into my bag and pull out a Nationals baseball cap, put it on.

"Reliving your glory days, eh? Okay, well, between the beard and the red baseball cap, the eyebrows, and…hmm." Her head bobs back and forth. "The key is in the eyes," she says, gesturing to her own face. She lets out a sigh. "Your eyes haven't looked the same, honey."

"What do you mean?"

"Since Rachel," she says. "Your eyes haven't looked the same since she died." She snaps out of it. "Sorry. Let's get you in some eyeglasses. You don't wear glasses, do you?"

"Reading glasses when I'm tired," I say.

"Hang on." She goes into her closet and comes out with a rectangular velvet box. She pops it open and reveals about fifty pairs of eyeglasses, each perched in a small divot.

"Jeez, Mandy."

"I borrowed these from Jamie," she says. "When we did the sequel to *London* last year. It's coming out this Christmas."

"Heard about that. Congrats."

"Yeah, well, I told Steven that was the last one I'm doing. Rodney couldn't keep his paws off me the whole time. But I handled it."

She hands me a pair of eyeglasses with thick brown frames. I put them on.

"Hmph," she says. "No. Try these."

I try another pair.

"No, these."

"I'm not trying to win a fashion award," I say.

She gives me a deadpan look. "You're in absolutely no danger of that, my sweet, believe me. Here." She removes another pair. "These. These, yes."

She hands me a pair with thick frames again, but this time the color is more of a reddish-brown. I put them on, and she lights up.

"It blends in with your beard," she says.

I make a face.

"No, I mean it throws off your color completely, Jon. You're fair. Dirty blond and fair-complected. The glasses and beard highlight a deep brown-red."

I stand up and go to the mirror over her vanity.

"You've lost weight," she says. "You were never overweight a day in your life, but you're looking skinny."

"I'm not hearing a compliment in there."

I check myself out in the mirror. I'm still myself, but I see her point about the change in my coloring. The cap, the glasses, and the beard. And I never realized how much slightly thicker eyebrows could change the look of a person. All that and no Secret Service entourage. Nobody will recognize me.

"Y'know, Jon, it's okay to move on with your life. You're only fifty. She wanted you to. In fact, she made me prom—"

She stops on that, some color coming to her face, a sheen over her eyes.

"You and Rachel talked about that?"

She nods, placing a hand on her chest, taking a moment to let the emotion dissipate. "She said to me, and I quote, 'Don't let Jon spend the rest of his life alone out of some misplaced sense of loyalty.'"

I take a sharp breath. Those words—*some misplaced sense of loyalty*—were exactly what she said to me more than once. They bring Rachel right back into this room, as if her breath is on my face, her head angled as it always was when she had something important to say. Her vanilla scent, the dimple in her right cheek, the smile lines by her eyes—

Her hand clutching mine, that last day, her voice groggy from the pain meds, so weak, but strong enough to squeeze my hand tight one last time.

Promise me you'll meet someone else, Jonathan. Promise me.

"My only point," Mandy says, her voice gravelly with emotion, "is that everyone understands that there's a time when you have to get back in the ring. You shouldn't have to disguise your appearance just to go on a date."

I take a moment of my own to recover and to remember something I never should have forgotten—that Mandy has no idea what's happening. Sure, now that I think about it, it makes sense that she'd think I was meeting a woman for a date—dinner or a drink or a movie—and I might not want our first get-together observed by the international press.

"You *are* going on a date, aren't you?" Her perfectly shaped eyebrows come together as she starts thinking things through. If I'm not going on a date, then what am I doing? Why else would a president sneak away from his security detail and travel incognito?

Before I let that imaginative mind of hers go any further down that path, I say, "I'm meeting someone, yes."

She waits for more and is hurt when it isn't forthcoming. But she's handled me with kid gloves since Rachel's death, and she won't push if I don't want to be pushed.

I clear my throat as I check my watch. I'm on a strict schedule. I'm not used to that. I always have a busy schedule, but the president is never late. Everybody waits for him. Not this time.

"I have to go now," I tell her.

CHAPTER
19

❖

I take the freight elevator back down and come out into the alley. My car is still parked in its spot. I drive to the Capitol Hill neighborhood and find a parking lot near 7th Street and North Carolina, leaving my keys with an attendant who hardly glances at my face.

I blend in with the pedestrians and the sounds of people enjoying a spring Friday evening in a vibrant residential neighborhood, restaurants and bars with their windows flung open, people laughing and mingling, pop music blasting from speakers.

I come upon a shabbily dressed man sitting against the wall of a corner coffee shop. A German shepherd, lying next to him, pants in the heat next to an empty bowl. The man, like many of the homeless, is wearing more layers than he needs. He also wears dark, scratched-up sunglasses. The sign he's been holding says HOMELESS VETERAN, but it now leans against the wall of the building. It must be break time. On his other side, a small cardboard box holds a few dollar bills. Music is playing quietly on a boom box.

I remove myself from the wave of pedestrian traffic and bend down next to him. I recognize the song playing, Van Morrison's "Into the Mystic." My mind whirls back to a slow dance in Savannah during basic training, closing time at one of the bars on River Street, my brain foggy from booze, my limbs aching from smoke sessions and training exercises.

"Are you a Gulf War vet, sir?" I ask. By his appearance, I'd almost guessed Vietnam before factoring in the lean years, which likely aged him faster than they should have.

"Sure am," he says, "but I wasn't no 'sir.' I earned my pay, friend. Platoon sergeant in the Big Red One. I was there when they breached Saddam's wire."

I sense the pride well up in him. It feels good to give him that moment. I want to throw another log onto that fire, get this guy a sandwich, listen just a little more. But I also feel the press of time and check my watch.

"First Infantry Division, huh? You guys led the charge into Iraq, right?"

"Tip of the spear, man. We rolled over those Republican Guard pansies like they were caught sleeping."

"Not bad for a leg," I say.

"A leg?" He sounds surprised. "You served? What were you, Airborne?"

"I'm a hooah just like you," I say. "Yeah, spent a couple of years in the Seventy-Fifth."

He sits up a little and raises his ungroomed unibrow. "Airborne Ranger, huh? I bet you saw some shit, boy. Raids and recon missions, right?"

"Not as much as you guys in the bigger units," I say, deflecting the narrative back to him. "What did it take you guys—a week to get halfway up the country?"

"And then we stopped short," he says with a crimped mouth. "Always thought that was a mistake."

"Hey," I say. "I could use a sandwich. How about you?"

"That would be much appreciated," he says. As I move toward the door he adds, "This place makes a killer turkey sandwich, by the way."

"Turkey it is."

When I return, I'm committed to a quick exit,

but not without finding out a few more things. "What's your name, hooah?" I ask.

"Sergeant First Class Christopher Knight," he says.

"Here you go, Sergeant." I hand him the paper sack of food. I put down the dish full of water for the dog, who laps it up until it's gone.

"It's been an honor to meet you, Sergeant. Where do you put your head down at night?"

"Shelter's a couple streets over. I come here most mornings. People are a little nicer."

"I have to move along, but here, Chris, take this."

I pull the change from the meal out of my pocket and give it to him.

"God bless you," he says, squeezing my hand with the still-firm grip of a warrior.

For some reason, that starts a catch in my throat. I've visited clinics and hospitals and done my best to reform the Department of Veterans Affairs, but this is what I don't see, the homeless PTSD vet who can't find or hold down a job.

I move back along the sidewalk, taking out my cell phone to store his name and the coffee-shop location so I can make sure this guy gets some help before it's too late for him.

But there are tens of thousands like him. The familiar feeling passes through me, the sense that my ability to help people is both vast and limited at the same time. You learn to live with the paradox. If you don't, obsessing over the limits will keep you from making the most of what you can do. Meanwhile, you keep looking for chances to push the limits back, to do as much as you can for as many as you can, every day. Even on the bad days, there's always something good you can do.

Two blocks beyond Sergeant Knight, as I walk among the shadows created by the setting sun, the crowd ahead of me has stopped moving. I walk through some people and step into the street to get a better look.

Two police officers from DC Metro are trying to force a man to the ground, an African American kid in a white T-shirt and jeans. He is resisting, trying to swing his arms free while one of the two officers tries to cuff him. They have weapons and Tasers but aren't using them, at least not yet. Two or three people along the sidewalk are holding up their phones and filming the incident.

"Get on the ground! On the ground!" the officers are shouting.

The man they're trying to take into custody stumbles to his right, the officers along with them, spilling over into the street, where traffic has stopped, blocked by the police car.

I take a step forward, instinctively, then step

back. What am I going to do, announce that I'm the president and I'll handle this? There's nothing for me to do but either gawk or leave.

I have no idea what led up to this moment. It could be that this man has committed a violent felony or even a purse snatching, or maybe he just pissed these guys off. I hope the officers are simply responding to a call and acting properly. I know that most cops, most of the time, do the best they can. I know that there are bad cops, just as there are bad actors in every profession. And I know that there are cops who think of themselves as good cops but, even if unconsciously, see a black man in a T-shirt and jeans as more threatening than a white man dressed the same way.

I look around at the watching crowd, people of all races and colors. Ten different people could watch the same thing and come away with ten unique takes on it. Some will see good cops doing their job. Some will see a black person being treated differently because of the color of his skin. Sometimes it's the one. Sometimes it's the other. Sometimes it's a bit of both. Regardless, in the back of every onlooker's mind is the same question: Will this unarmed man leave the scene unshot?

A second squad car rolls down the street as the officers get the man to the ground, cuff him, and lift him to his feet.

I cross the street and head to my next destination. There are no easy solutions to problems like these, so I try to follow my own advice—understand my limitations and keep doing whatever I can to make things better. An executive order, a bill that reaches my desk, speeches, words from my bully pulpit—these things can set the right tone, move us in the right direction.

But it's a battle as old as humanity—us versus them. In every age and time, individuals, families, clans, and nations have struggled with how to treat the "other." In America, racism is our oldest curse. But there are other divides—over religion, immigration, sexual identity. Sometimes the "them" strategy is just a narcotic to feed the beast in all of us. All too often, those who rail against "them" prevail over earnest pleas to remember what "we" can be and do together. Our brains have worked this way for a long time. Maybe they always will. But we have to keep trying. That's the permanent mission our Founding Fathers left us—moving toward the "more perfect union."

The wind whips up as I turn a corner. I look up at a troubled sky, ash-colored clouds.

As I walk to the end of the street, toward the bar on the corner, I fear I'm facing the hardest part of a very tough night.

CHAPTER
20

❖

I take a deep breath and enter the bar.

Inside: banners for the Georgetown Hoyas and Skins and Nationals, televisions perched in the corners of the exposed-brick walls, loud music competing with the animated chatter of the happy-hour crowd. Many are dressed casually, college and grad students, but some are young after-work professionals in their suits with ties pulled loose or in blouses and pants. The outdoor patio is filled to the brim. The floors are sticky, and the odor is one of stale beer. I'm taken back again to Savannah during basic training, when we used to tear up River Street on the weekends.

I nod to the two Secret Service agents, dressed in suits, standing sentry. They've been told that

I was coming and how I'd be dressed. They've been told not to formally acknowledge me, and they follow that directive, only brief nods, a slight stiffening of their posture.

In the back corner, my daughter is seated at a table, surrounded by people—some friends, some who just want to be in the presence of the First Daughter—drinking something colorful and fruity from a glass as another woman whispers something into her ear over the loud music. She reacts to the comment, bringing her hand to her mouth, as if trying to laugh and swallow at the same time. But it looks forced. She's just being polite.

Her eyes scan the room. They pass over me at first but then return to me. Lilly's lips part, her eyes narrow. Finally, her expression softens. It took her a moment, so my disguise must be pretty good.

I keep walking, past the bathrooms into the stockroom at the back of the bar, the door unlocked by design. Inside, it smells like a frat house, with shelves upon shelves of assorted liquors, kegs lined up along the walls, open boxes of napkins and bar glasses on the concrete floor.

My heart swells when she walks in, the infant with the round face and enormous eyes reaching out to touch my face, the little girl lifting herself on her tippy-toes to kiss me with a PBJ-smudged face, the teenager slicing the air with her hand as she argued the merits of alternative-energy in-centives at the state debate finals.

When she draws back and looks me in the eyes, her smile has vanished. "So this is real."

"It's real."

"Did she come to the White House?"

"She did, yeah. I can't say more than that."

"Where are you going?" she asks. "What are you doing? Why don't you have Secret Service? Why are you dressed in some disguise—"

"Hey. Hey." I hold her at the shoulders. "It's okay, Lil. I'm going to meet with them."

"With Nina and her partner?"

I highly doubt that the girl in the Princeton T-shirt gave my daughter her real name. But the less said, the better. "Yes," I say.

"I haven't seen her since she talked to me," says Lilly. "Not once. She completely disappeared from the program."

"I don't think she was ever enrolled in the Sorbonne program," I say. "I think she went to Paris to see you. To deliver the message."

"But why talk to *me,* of all people?"

I don't answer. I don't want to give any more specifics than necessary. But Lilly has her mother's smarts. It doesn't take her long.

"She knew I'd deliver the message to you directly," she says. "No intermediaries. No filter."

That's exactly why.

"So what did she mean?" Lilly asks. "What's 'Dark Ages'?"

"Lil…" I draw her in close but don't say anything.

"You won't tell me. You can't," she adds, giving me the out, forgiving me. "It must be important. So important that you asked me to fly home from Paris, and now you're…doing whatever it is you're doing." She glances over her shoulder. "Where's Alex? Where's your protection? Other than Frick and Frack, the men you sent to guard me?"

Since she graduated from college, Lilly has opted to decline protection, as is her right. But the moment I got the call from her last Monday, I rushed the Service to her side. It took a couple of days to get her home, because she had a final exam, and I was assured she was secure in Paris.

"My protection is around," I say. She doesn't need to know that I'm going it alone. She has enough anxiety as it is. Getting over the loss of her mother, barely a year ago, is still a work in progress. She doesn't need to add the possibility of losing a second parent. She's no child, and mature beyond her years, but she's only twenty-three, for God's sake, still a babe in the woods when it comes to what life will throw at her.

My chest tightens at the thought of what all this could mean to Lilly. But I have no choice. I made a vow to defend this country, and I'm the only person who can do this.

"Listen," I say, taking her hand. "I want you to spend the next few days at the White House. Your room's all ready. If you need anything from your condo, the agents will get it for you."

"I...don't understand." She turns and looks at me, her lips trembling slightly. "Are you in *danger,* Daddy?"

It's all I can do to rein in my emotions. She stopped calling me Daddy during adolescence, though she pulled it out once or twice when Rachel was dying. She reserves it for the times when she's feeling most vulnerable, most terrified. I have stood down sadistic drill sergeants, cruel Iraqi interrogators, partisan lawmakers, and the Washington press corps, but my daughter can punch my buttons like no one else.

I lean over and touch my head against hers. "Me? C'mon. I'm just being cautious. I just want to know that you're safe."

It's not enough for her. She wraps her arms around my neck and squeezes tight. I draw her close, too. I can hear her sobs, feel her body shake.

"I'm so proud of you, Lilly," I whisper, trying to avoid the catch in my throat. "I ever tell you that?"

"You tell me that all the time," she says into my ear.

I stroke the hair of my brilliant, strong, independent girl. She is a woman now, with her mother's beauty and brains and spirit, but she will always be the little girl who lit up when she saw me, who squealed when I'd bombard her with kisses, who couldn't fall back asleep after a nightmare unless Daddy held her hand.

"Go with the agents now," I whisper. "Will you?"

She pulls back from me, wipes the tears off her cheeks, takes a breath, looks at me with hopeful eyes, and nods.

Then she lunges toward me, throwing her arms around me again.

I squeeze my eyes shut, hold her trembling body. Suddenly my grown daughter is fifteen years younger, a grade-schooler who needs her daddy, a father who is supposed to be her rock, who will never let her down.

I wish I could hold her, wipe away her tears, allay her every concern. I had to teach myself, long ago, that I couldn't follow my baby girl around and make sure the world was kind to her. And now I have to pry myself loose and get on with the business at hand when I'd like nothing more than to hold her and never let go.

I cup my hands around her face, my daughter's swollen, hopeful eyes looking up at me.

"I love you more than anything in the world," I say. "And I promise I will come back to you."

CHAPTER
21

❖

After Lilly leaves the bar with the Secret Service agents, I ask the bartender for a glass of water. I reach into my pocket and take out my pills, the steroids that will boost my platelet count. I hate these pills. They mess up my head. But I either operate with a fuzzy brain or I'm out of commission altogether. There's no in-between. And the latter is not an option.

I walk back to my car. The clouds are as bruised as the backs of my legs. No rain has fallen, but the smell of it is in the air.

I pull my phone out of my pocket and call Dr. Lane as I walk. She won't recognize this phone number, but she answers anyway.

"Dr. Lane, it's Jon Duncan."

"Mr. President? I've been trying to reach you all afternoon."

"I know. I've been busy."

"Your count is continuing to drop. You're under six-teen thousand."

"Okay, I'm doubling up on the steroids, like I promised."

"It's not enough. You need immediate treatment."

I almost walk into oncoming traffic, not paying attention as I step into a crosswalk. An SUV driver lays on the horn, in case I hadn't noticed my mistake.

"I'm not at ten thousand yet," I say to Dr. Lane.

"That's a guideline. Everyone is different. You could be suffering internal bleeding as we speak."

"But that's unlikely," I say. "The MRI was negative yesterday."

"Yesterday, yes. Today? Who knows?"

I reach the lot where my car is parked. I hand over my ticket and cash, and the attendant hands me the keys.

"Mr. President, you're surrounded by talented and capable people. I'm sure they could keep on top of things for a few hours while you take a treatment. I thought presidents delegated."

They do. Most of the time. But this I can't delegate. And I can't tell her, or anyone else, why.

"I hear everything you're saying, Deborah. I have to go now. Keep your phone handy."

I punch out the phone, start up the car, and

drive through thick traffic. Thinking about the girl in the Princeton T-shirt—Nina to my daughter.

Thinking about "Dark Ages."

Thinking about my next meeting tonight, threats I can issue, offers I can make.

A man holding a white sign that says PARKING waves me into a lot. I pay money and follow another man's directions to a spot. I keep my keys and walk for two blocks until I stop in front of a medium-rise apartment building bearing the name CAMDEN SOUTH CAPITOL over the entrance. Across the street, there is a roar from the crowd.

I cross the boulevard, no easy task with the traffic. A man passes me saying, "Who needs two? Who needs two?"

I remove the envelope Nina gave me and pull out the single colorful ticket to tonight's game, the Nationals versus the Mets.

At the left-field gate of Nationals Park, attendants are processing people through a metal detector, wanding people who don't pass the test, checking bags for weapons. I wait my place in line, but it's a short wait. The game has already started.

My seat is in section 104, nosebleed seats. I'm accustomed to the best seats in the house, a skybox or behind home plate or right off the dugout on the third-base line. But I like this better, here in the left-field stands. My view isn't the greatest, but it feels more real.

I look around, but there's no point. It will happen when it happens. My job is to sit here and wait.

Ordinarily I'd be like a kid in a candy store here. I'd grab a Budweiser and a hot dog. You can shelve all those microbrews: at a ball game, there is no finer beverage than an ice-cold Bud. And no food ever tasted so good as a dog with mustard at a ball game, not even my mama's rib tips with vinegar sauce.

I'd kick back and remember those days hurling fastballs at UNC, dreams of a pro career when the Royals drafted me in the fourth round, my year in Double A with the Memphis Chicks, sweating on buses, icing my elbow at night in dive motels, playing before crowds numbering only in the hundreds, eating Big Macs and dipping Copenhagen.

But no beer for me tonight. My stomach is already in turmoil as I wait for my visitor, the Princeton girl's partner.

My phone vibrates in the pocket of my jeans. The caller ID on the screen reads C Brock. Carolyn texts a single number: 3. I type back Wellman and hit Send.

This is our code for a status update: so far so good. But I'm not sure everything is so good so far. I'm late to the ball game. Did he already come and go? Did I miss him?

That couldn't be. But there's nothing I can do but sit here and wait and watch the game. The Mets pitcher has a live arm but overthrows his split-fingered fastball, which is why it won't drop. The Nationals leadoff hitter, a lefty, is in an obvious bunt situation with men on first and second and the third baseman staying back. The pitcher should throw high and inside, but he doesn't. He gets lucky when the batter can't get the bunt down either time he tries. Ultimately, with two strikes, the kid lofts a long fly ball to deep left field, toward me. Instinctively the crowd rises, but he got under it too much, and the Mets left fielder hauls it in short of the warning track.

When we all sit back down, someone in my peripheral vision is still standing, angling down the row toward me. He is wearing a Nationals cap that looks brand-new, but otherwise he looks completely out of place at a baseball game. I know instantly that the seat he's going to take is the open one next to mine.

This man is Nina's partner. It's time.

CHAPTER
22

❖

T he assassin known as Bach closes the door, locking herself in the small bathroom. She draws a shaky breath, drops to her knees, and vomits into the toilet.

When she's done, her eyes stinging, her stomach knotted up, she takes a breath and falls back on her haunches. This is no good. Unacceptable.

When she's able to, she stands up, flushes the toilet, and uses Clorox wipes to thoroughly scrub the toilet, then flushes the wipes, too. No trace evidence, no DNA.

That is the last time she will vomit tonight. Period.

She checks herself in the dingy mirror above the sink. Her wig is blond, a bun. Her uniform is sky blue. Not optimal, but she didn't get to pick the outfits worn by the cleaning crew at the Camden South Capitol apartments.

When she emerges from the bathroom into the maintenance room, the three men are still standing there, likewise dressed in light-blue shirts and dark trousers. One of the men is so muscular that his biceps and chest nearly bulge out of his shirt. She took an instant dislike to him when she met him earlier today. First because he stands out. Nobody in their profession should stand out. And second because he has probably relied too often on his brute strength and not enough on wits and skill and a nasty temperament.

The other two are acceptable. Wiry and solid but not physically impressive. Homely, forgettable faces.

"Feeling better?" the muscle-bound guy says. The other two react with a smile until they see the look on Bach's face.

"Better than you're going to feel," she says, "if you ask me that again."

Don't mess with a woman in her first trimester of pregnancy, with morning sickness that isn't limited, apparently, to the morning. Especially one who specializes in high-risk assassinations.

She turns to the leader of the trio, a bald man with a glass eye.

He raises his hands in apology. "No disrespect,

no disrespect," he says. His English is good, though heavily accented—the Czech Republic, if she's guessing.

She puts out her hand. The leader hands her an earbud. She fits it in her ear, and the man does the same.

"Status?" she asks.

Through her earbud comes the answer. *"He has arrived. Our team is ready."*

"Then we will all take our positions," she says.

With her weapon case and duffel bag in tow, Bach takes the freight elevator. While inside, she removes a black coat from her bag and puts it on. She removes her wig for the time being and puts on a black ski cap. She is now dressed from head to toe in black.

She gets off the elevator at the top and climbs the stairs to the door to the roof. As promised, it is unlocked. The wind on the roof is swirling, but it's nothing for which she can't adjust. She feels certain it will rain at some point. But at least it has held off until now. Had this silly sporting event been canceled altogether, her operation would have been aborted.

So now she must be prepared for the rain interrupting this sports contest, forcing thousands of people out at once, hidden amid a sea of umbrellas. She once killed a Turkish ambassador by firing a bullet through an umbrella into his brain, but he was with only one other person on a quiet street. Her problem tonight will be acquiring her target in the first scenario—should a mass of people move simultaneously through the exits.

That's what the ground teams are for.

She opens her weapon case using the thumb recognition and assembles Anna Magdalena, her semiautomatic rifle, mounting the tactical scope, loading the magazine.

She moves into place, crouching down under the cover of near darkness. The sun will set in less than twenty minutes, which will obscure her position on the roof all the more.

She gets herself into position and focuses the scope. She finds the entrance she's looking for, the left-field gate.

She will wait. It could be five minutes. It could be three hours. And then she will be called upon to act almost immediately with deadly precision. But this is what she does, and she has never failed.

Oh, how she longs to put on her headphones and listen to a piano concerto! But every job is different, and for this one, she needs an advance team giving her prompts in her ear. They could come at any time, so instead of listening to Andrea Bacchetti playing Keyboard Concerto no. 4

at the Teatro Olimpico di Vicenza, she listens to automobile traffic, the cheers of a crowded stadium, blasts of organ music revving up the crowd, and occasional updates from the advance team.

She breathes in, breathes out. Lets her pulse slow. Keeps her finger close to but free of the trigger. There is no point in impatience. The target will come to her, as always.

And as always, she will not miss.

CHAPTER
23

❖

The man takes the seat next to me without a word, his head down as he moves past me and sits to my immediate left, settling in as if we are strangers who happened to get tickets for adjacent seats.

We are, in fact, strangers. I know nothing about him. The unexpected is so common in my job as to be expected, but whenever something comes up, I have a team of advisers to help me analyze it, to collect everything we know and break it down, to impose some order amid the chaos. This time, I'm alone and clueless.

He could be nothing but a courier, delivering information that he may not even understand, impervious to interrogation because he has nothing of value to spill. If that's true, he was misrepresented to me, but it's not as if I can trust the source, the woman known as Nina.

He may be an assassin. This whole thing could be a ruse to get me alone and vulnerable. If so, my daughter will be without a living parent. And I will have tainted the office of the president by allowing myself to be suckered into a secret meeting by a simplistic ploy.

But I had to take the chance, all because of those two words, *Dark Ages*.

He turns and gets his first look at me up close, at the man he understands to be President Duncan but who, with the red beard and glasses and baseball cap, doesn't look much like the clean-shaven, suit-wearing commander in chief he sees in the media. He gives a slight nod of his head in approval, which I take to be approval not at my disguise per se but at the fact that I'm wearing a disguise at all. It means I'm playing along—so far, at least. I've agreed to a secret meeting. I've already acknowledged his importance.

It's the last thing I wanted to concede, but I had to. As far as I'm concerned, this man could be the most dangerous person in the world right now.

I glance around us. No one sitting on either side of us, nobody directly behind us, either. "Say the words," I tell the man.

He is young, like his partner, Nina, maybe in

his early twenties at most. Slim, like her. Bone structure suggesting eastern European, like hers. He is Caucasian, but with a darker complexion than his partner. Possibly a Mediterranean influence in his heritage, possibly Middle Eastern or African. His face is largely obscured by a long, ratty beard and thick, ropy hair that juts out from the baseball cap. His eyes are set deeply, as if bruised. His nose is long and crooked—possibly genetic, possibly the result of having been broken.

He is wearing a solid black T-shirt, dark cargo pants, and running shoes. He brought nothing with him in terms of a bag or backpack.

He doesn't have a gun. He wouldn't have made it past security. But there are plenty of things that can be weaponized. You can kill someone with a house key, a piece of wood, even a ball-point pen if you insert it with surgical precision into your target's body. In Ranger training before I shipped out to Iraq, they showed us things— self-defense tactics, opportunistic weapons— that never would have occurred to me. One quick movement with a sharp edge into my carotid artery, and I'd bleed out before medical help could arrive.

I grab his arm, my hand wrapping completely around his bony limb. "Say the words. *Now.*"

He is startled by the move. He looks down at my hand clutching his biceps, then back up at me. Startled, but—I take careful note—not particularly shaken.

"Son," I say, reminding myself to keep my facial expression and voice volume in check, "this is not a game. You have no idea who you're messing with. You have no idea how far in over your head you are."

I wish my position was as strong as I'm making it out to be.

His eyes narrow before he decides to speak. "What words would you like me to say?" he asks. "Armageddon? Nuclear holocaust?"

The same accent as his partner. But his command of English appears stronger.

"Last chance," I say. "You're not going to like what happens next."

He breaks eye contact. "You say these things as if I want something from you. Yet it is you who wants something from me."

That last point is undeniable. My presence here confirms it. But the converse is also true. I don't know what it is he has to tell me. If it's nothing more than information, he has a price. If it's to communicate a threat, he wants a ransom. He didn't go through all this for nothing. I have something he wants, too. I just don't know what it is.

I release the grip on his arm. "You won't make it out of the stadium," I say, rising from my seat.

"'Dark Ages,'" he hisses, as if he's uttered a curse word.

On the field, Rendon bounces a high chopper that the shortstop has to catch and throw on the run for the out at first.

I sit back down in my seat. Take a breath. "What do I call you?" I ask.

"You may call me…Augie."

The defiance, the sarcasm, is gone. A minor victory for me. His cards are probably better than mine, but he's a kid, and I play poker for a living.

"And what…should I call you?" he says, scarcely above a whisper.

"You call me Mr. President."

I put my arm over his chair, as if we are old friends or family.

"Here's how this is going to work," I say. "You're going to tell me how you know those words. And you're going to tell me whatever else you came here to say. And then *I'm* going to decide what to do. If you and I can work together—if I'm satisfied with our conversation—then this could turn out very well for you, Augie."

I give that a moment to sink in, the light at the

end of the tunnel for him. There has to be one in any negotiation.

"But if I'm *not* satisfied," I continue, "I'll do whatever is necessary to you, to your girlfriend, to anyone else you care about in this world, to protect my country. There's nothing I can't do. There's nothing I *won't* do."

His mouth curls into a snarl. There is hatred in that expression, no doubt, hatred of me and everything I represent. But he's scared, too. He's dealt with me thus far from a distance, using his partner to contact my daughter overseas, using his technology remotely, but now he's here, in person, with the president of the United States. He's passed the point of no return.

He leans forward, elbows on knees, an attempt to move away from me. Good. He's rattled.

"You would like to know how I have come upon 'Dark Ages,'" he says, his voice less certain, shaky. "You would also like to know why the electricity in the White House continues to...falter?"

I don't respond to that outwardly. He's saying he's responsible for the flickering of the lights in the White House. A bluff? I try to remember if Nina saw them flicker while she was there.

"Is annoying, one would think," he says. "Engaging in important matters of national security and economic policy and political...machinations in your Oval Office while the lights blink on and off as if you live in a shack in a third-world country."

He draws a deep breath. "Your technicians have no idea why, do they? Of course they do not." The confidence in his voice is restored.

"You have two minutes, kid. Starting now. If you don't talk to me, you will talk to people who work for me who will not be as friendly."

He shakes his head, though it's hard to tell whom he's trying to convince, me or himself. "No, you came alone," he says, hope in his voice, not conviction.

"Did I?"

The crowd roars at the sound of a bat hitting a ball, the people around us getting to their feet and cheering, then fading out as the long fly ball veers foul. Augie does not move, still leaning forward, a hard look on his face as he stares into the back of the seat in front of him.

"One minute, thirty seconds," I say.

In the game, the batter takes a called third strike, a slider that paints the corner, and the crowd hoots and hollers its reaction.

I check my watch. "One minute," I say. "And then your life is over."

Augie leans back to face me again. I keep my

eyes on the field, don't accord him the respect of looking in his direction.

But eventually I turn to him, as if I'm now ready to hear what he has to say. His face is wearing a different expression now, intense and cold.

He's holding a handgun in his lap, trained on me.

"*My* life is over?" he asks.

CHAPTER
24

❖

I focus on Augie, not the gun.
He has it low in his lap, safe from detection by other ticket holders. I understand now why the seats on either side of us are empty, as are the four seats behind and in front of us. Augie bought them all to give us a semblance of privacy.

From its boxy shape I can see it's a Glock, a gun I've never fired but a 9mm all the same, capable of firing a bullet into me at close range.

Once upon a time, I might have stood a chance of disarming him without suffering a fatal shot. But the Rangers was a long time ago. I'm fifty years old and rusty.

It's not, by any means, the first time I've had a gun pointed at me. When I was a prisoner of war, an Iraqi prison guard put a pistol to my head every day and pulled the trigger.

But this is the first time in a long time, and it's my first time as president.

Through the pounding of my pulse, I think it through: he could already have pulled the trigger if his plan was to kill me. He didn't have to wait until I turned to look at him. He wanted me to see the gun. He wanted to alter the dynamic.

I hope I'm right about that. He doesn't look like someone with a lot of experience in handling a firearm. I'm a nervous twitch away from a bullet in the ribs.

"You came here for a reason," I say. "So put that gun away and tell me what it is."

His lips purse. "Perhaps I feel safer this way."

I lean forward, lowering my voice. "That gun makes you *less* safe. It makes my people nervous. It makes them want to put a bullet through your head right now, while you're sitting there in your seat."

He blinks hard in response, his eyes moving about, trying to remain in control. The notion that someone is training a high-powered rifle on you can be unsettling on the nerves.

"You can't see them, Augie. But believe me, they can see you."

There is risk in what I'm doing. It might not

be the wisest move to scare the hell out of a man with his finger on the trigger of a gun pointed at you. But I need him to put that gun away. And I will continue to make him believe that he is not dealing with one man but with a country—one with overwhelming force, shock-and-awe capabilities, and resources beyond his comprehension.

"Nobody wants to hurt you, Augie," I say. "But if you pull that trigger, you'll be dead in two seconds."

"No," he says. "You came…" His voice fades out.

"What, I came alone? You don't really believe that. You're too smart to believe that. So put the gun away and tell me why I'm here. Otherwise I walk."

The gun moves in his lap. His eyes narrow again. "If you walk away," he says, "you will not be able to stop what is going to happen."

"And you'll never get what you want from me, whatever that is."

He thinks about that. It's the smart thing for him to do, all things considered, but he wants it to be his idea, not mine. Finally he nods and hikes up his pants leg, holstering the gun.

I release the breath I've been holding.

"How the hell did you get that gun past the metal detectors?"

He slides down his pants leg. He looks as relieved as I am.

"A rudimentary machine," he says, "knows only what it is told to know. It has no independent thought. If it is told it sees nothing, then it sees nothing. If it is told to close its eyes, it closes its eyes. Machines do not ask why."

I think back to the metal detector as I went through it. There was no X-ray, as there is at an airport. It was just a doorway, and it either beeped or didn't beep as you passed through it, as the security guard stood by, waiting for an audible signal.

He jammed it somehow. He disabled it while he passed through.

He hacked into the electrical system at 1600 Pennsylvania Avenue.

He downed a helicopter in Dubai.

And he knew "Dark Ages."

"Here I am, Augie," I say. "You got your meeting. Tell me how you know 'Dark Ages.'"

His eyebrows rise. He almost smiles. Obtaining that code word is quite an achievement, and he knows it.

"Did you hack in somehow?" I ask. "Or…"

Now he does smile. "It is the 'or' that concerns you. It concerns you so much that you cannot bring yourself to say the words."

I don't argue the point. He's right.

"Because if I was not able to obtain this re-motely," he says, "there is only one other way I could have obtained it. And you know what this means."

If Augie didn't learn "Dark Ages" through a hack—and it's hard to see how he could have—then he got it from a human being, and the list of human beings with access to "Dark Ages" is very, very small.

"It is the reason you agreed to meet me," he says. "You clearly understand the…significance."

I nod. "It means there's a traitor in the White House," I say.

CHAPTER
25

❖

The crowd around us breaks into a cheer. An organ plays. The Nationals are running off the field. Someone inches down the row past us toward the aisle. I envy that person, whose greatest concern at this moment is taking a leak or heading to the concession stand to grab some nachos.

My phone buzzes. I reach for it in my pocket, then realize a sudden movement could cause alarm. "My phone," I explain. "It's just my phone. A well-being check."

Augie's brow furrows. "What is this?"

"My chief of staff. She's checking that I'm okay. Nothing more."

Augie draws back, suspicious. But I don't wait for his approval. If I don't respond to Carolyn, she will assume the worst. And there will be consequences. She will open that letter I gave her.

The text message, again, is from C Brock. Again, just one number, this time, 4.

I type back Stewart and send it.

I put my phone away and say, "So tell me. How do you know 'Dark Ages'?"

He shakes his head. It won't be that easy. His partner wouldn't hand over that information, and neither will he. Not yet. It's part of his leverage. It might be his *only* leverage.

"I need to know," I say.

"No, you do not. You *want* to know. What you *need* to know is more important."

It's hard to imagine anything more important than whether someone in my inner circle has betrayed our country.

"Then tell me what I need to know."

He says, "Your country will not survive."

"What does that mean?" I ask. "How?"

He shrugs. "Truly, when one considers it, it is a simple inevitability. Do you think you can prevent forever a nuclear detonation in the United States? Have you read *A Canticle for Leibowitz?*"

I shake my head, searching my memory bank. Sounds familiar, high school English.

"Or *The Fourth Turning?*" he says. "A fascinating discussion of the...cyclical nature of history.

Mankind is predictable. Governments mistreat people—their own people and others. They always have, and they always will. So the people react. There is action and reaction. This is how history has progressed and how it always will."

He wags his finger. "Ah, but now—now technology allows even one man to inflict utter destruction. It alters the construct, does it not? Mutually assured destruction is no longer a deterrent. Recruiting thousands or millions to your cause is no longer necessary. No need for an army, for a movement. It takes only one man, willing to destroy it all, willing to die if necessary, who is not susceptible to coercion or negotiation."

Overhead, the first sounds from a turbulent sky. Thunder but no lightning. No rain yet. The lights in the ballpark are already on, so the darkening of the sky has little effect.

I lean into him, peering into his eyes. "Is this a history lesson? Or are you telling me something is imminent?"

He blinks. Swallows hard, his Adam's apple bobbing. "Something is imminent," he says, his voice changing.

"How imminent?"

"A matter of hours," he says.

My blood goes cold.

"What are we talking about, exactly?" I ask.

"You know this already."

Of course I do. But I want to hear him say it. I'm not giving anything away for free.

"Tell me," I say.

"The virus," he says. "The one you saw for a moment"—he snaps his fingers—"before it disappeared. The reason for your phone call to Suliman Cindoruk. The virus you have not been able to locate. The virus that has baffled your team of experts. The virus that terrifies you to the core. The virus you will never stop without us."

I glance around, look for anyone paying close attention to us. Nobody.

"The Sons of Jihad is behind this?" I whisper. "Suliman Cindoruk?"

"Yes. You were correct about that."

I swallow over the lump forming in my throat. "What does he want?"

Augie blinks hard, his expression changing, confusion. "What does *he* want?"

"Yes," I say. "Suliman Cindoruk. What does he want?"

"This I do not know."

"You don't..." I sit back in my seat. What is the point of a ransom demand if you don't know what you're demanding? Money, a prisoner release, a pardon, a change in foreign policy—something. He came here to threaten me, to get something, but he doesn't know what he wants?

Maybe his job is to demonstrate the threat. Someone else, later, will make the demand. Possible, but it doesn't feel right to me.

And then it comes to me. It was always a possibility, but as I contemplated the potential scenarios for tonight, it was never very high on my list.

"You're not here representing Suliman Cindoruk," I say.

He raises his shoulders. "My interests are no longer…aligned with Suli, that is true."

"They once were. You were part of the Sons of Jihad."

A snarl curls his upper lip, color rising to his face, fire in his eyes. "I was," he says. "But no longer."

His anger, that emotional response—resentment toward the SOJ or its leader, a power struggle, perhaps—is something I tuck away for later, something I might be able to use.

The crack of a bat on a ball. The crowd rises, cheers. Music plays from the speakers. Someone hit a home run. It feels like we are light-years removed from a baseball game right now.

I open my hands. "So tell me what *you* want."

He shakes his head. "Not yet," he says. *No chet.*

The first sprinkle of rain hits my hand. Light, sporadic, nothing heavy, bringing groans from the crowd but no movement, no rush for shelter.

"We go now," says Augie.

"We?"

"Yes, we."

A shudder passes through me. But I assumed this encounter would eventually move to a different location. It's not safe, but neither was this meeting. Nothing about this is safe.

"Okay," I say and push myself out of the seat.

"Your phone," he says. "Hold it in your hand."

I look at him with a question.

He stands up, too, and nods. "You will understand why in a moment," he says.

CHAPTER
26

❖

B *reathe. Relax. Aim. Squeeze.*
Bach lies on the rooftop, her breathing
even, her nerves still, her eye looking through
the scope of the rifle down at the baseball stadium, the left-field gate. Remembering the words
of Ranko, her first teacher, the toothpick jutting
out from the side of his mouth, his fiery red,
stalklike hair—*a scarecrow whose hair caught fire*, as
he once described himself.

*Align your body with the weapon. Think of the rifle as
part of your body. Aim your body, not the weapon.*

You must remain steady.

Choose your aiming point, not your target.

*Pull straight back on the trigger. Your index finger is
separate from the rest of your hand.*

*No, no—you jerked the weapon. Keep the rest of the
hand still. You're not breathing. Breathe normally.*

Breathe. Relax. Aim. Squeeze.

The first drop of rain hits her neck. The rain could accelerate events rapidly.

She moves her head away from the sniper scope and raises her binoculars to check on her teams.

Team 1 to the north of the exit, three men huddled together, speaking and laughing, by all appearances nothing more than three friends meeting one another on the street and conversing.

Team 2 to the south of the exit, doing the same thing.

Immediately below her perch, across the street from the stadium, out of her sight, should be team 3, similarly huddled together, ready to stop any escape headed in their direction.

The exit will be surrounded, the teams prepared to close in like a boa constrictor.

"He is leaving his seat."

Her heart does a flip, adrenaline pumping through her, as the words spill from her earbud.

Breathe.

Relax.

Everything slows to a crawl. Slow. Easy.

It will not go perfectly as planned. It never does. A small part of her, the competitor in her, prefers it when it doesn't, when she has to make an on-the-spot adjustment.

"Headed for the exit," she hears through the earbud.

"Teams 1 and 2, go," she says. "Team 3, hold ready."

"Team 1, that's a go," comes the response.

"Team 2, that's a go."

"Team 3 holding ready."

She moves her eye up to the scope of her rifle.

She breathes.

She relaxes.

She aims.

She curls her finger around the trigger, ready to squeeze.

CHAPTER
27

❖

Augie and I move toward the exit, the left-field gate through which I entered, my smartphone in hand as instructed. A handful of people have already given up on the game with the first sprinkles of rain, but most of the thirty-some thousand are keeping the faith for the time being, so we are not leaving with a crowd. I would have preferred that. But it's not my decision.

The composure and confidence Augie has shown are gone. As we get closer to the exit, closer to whatever is coming next, he has grown more nervous, his eyes darting about, his fingers wiggling with no purpose. He checks his phone, maybe to see the time, maybe to look for a message, but I can't tell because his hands are cupped around it.

We pass through the stadium gate. He stops while we are still inside the alcove, outside now, looking out at Capitol Street but still protected within the stadium walls. Leaving the stadium is meaningful to him. He must feel safe in a crowd.

I look at the sky, now an endless black, a drop of rain on my cheek.

Augie takes a breath and nods. "Now," he says.

He inches forward, passing beyond the alcove's walls onto the sidewalk. Some people are moving about, but the number is small. To our right, the north, a large utility truck is parked by the curb. Next to it, a couple of sweaty sanitation workers are taking a cigarette break under a streetlamp.

To the south, our left, a DC Metro squad car is parked by the curb, nobody inside.

Pulling up directly behind the squad car is a van, parking by the curb about ten yards away from us.

Augie seems to be peering at it, trying to see the driver. I look, too. Hard to make out details, but the features are unmistakable—the skeletal outline of her shoulders, the sharp angles of her face. Augie's partner, the Princeton woman, Nina.

Seemingly in response, the van blinks its high beams twice. And then turns off its lights completely.

Augie's head drops down to his phone, lighting up in response to his fingers tapping. Then he stops, looks up, and waits.

For a moment, he is still. Everything is still.

Some kind of signal, I think to myself. *Something is about to happen.*

My last thought before everything goes black.

CHAPTER
28

❖

I, Katherine Emerson Brandt...do solemnly swear...that I will faithfully execute the office of president of the United States...and will, to the best of my ability...preserve, protect, and defend...the Constitution of the United States."

Kathy Brandt adjusts her jacket and nods at herself in the bathroom mirror inside the vice president's private quarters.

It hasn't been easy being vice president, though she is well aware that any number of people would trade places with her. But how many of those people came within a breath of winning the nomination only to see their dreams upended by a war hero with rugged good looks and a sharp sense of humor?

She vowed to herself, on the night of Super

THE PRESIDENT IS MISSING

Tuesday, when Texas and Georgia came in late for Duncan, that she wouldn't concede, that she wouldn't endorse him, that—God help her— she wouldn't join his *ticket*.

And then she did all those things.

And now she's a parasite, living off her host. If he makes a mistake, *she* made the mistake. As if that's not bad enough, she has to defend the mistake as if it were her own.

And if she doesn't, if she separates herself and criticizes the president, she's disloyal. The critics will lump her in with Duncan anyway, and her supporters will desert her for her failure to stand by her president.

It's been a delicate dance.

"I, Katherine Emerson Brandt...do solemnly—"

Her phone rings. Instinctively she reaches for the phone on the vanity, her work phone, even as she recognizes that the ringtone belongs to her other phone.

Her personal phone.

She walks into the bedroom and picks up the phone by the bedside. She sees the caller ID. A flutter passes through her.

Here we go, she thinks to herself as she answers the call.

CHAPTER
29

❖

B lack, nothing but black.

Thirty thousand people roar in unison in the stadium behind me as everything plunges into darkness, streetlamps and buildings and traffic signals, all electricity dead for blocks. Headlights from car traffic on Capitol Street are halos of light as they pass, spotlights sweeping a stage, while smartphones are fireflies dancing about in the dark.

"Use your phone," says Augie, his voice frantic, hitting my arm. "Come, hurry!"

We race in darkness toward Nina's van, our phones in front of us for faint illumination.

A light goes on inside the van as the hydraulic side-panel door slides open for us. Now offset against the darkness around us, the Princeton woman's features come into full relief, the sculpted waif-model face, her eyebrows knit tightly together in worry as she grips the steering wheel. She seems to be saying something, probably telling us to hurry—

—just as the glass of the driver's-side window shatters and the left side of her face explodes, blood and tissue and brain matter spattering the windshield.

Her head lolls to her right, the seat belt restraining her, her lips still pursed in midspeech, her doe eyes staring blankly beside a bloody crater on the left side of her skull. A scared, innocent child, abruptly, violently, suddenly no longer scared, now at peace—

If you are obliged to receive the enemy's fire, fall or squat down 'til it's over.

"N—no—no!" Augie shouts—

Augie.

I snap into focus, grab him by the shoulders, and pull him downward, falling against the DC Metro squad car parked north of the van, landing on top of him on the sidewalk. Around us, the pavement erupts with tiny explosions as the air hisses with projectiles. The windows on the squad car shatter, raining glass down on us. The stadium wall spits stone and powder at us.

The chaos of screams and cries, tires squealing,

horns honking, all muffled by the percussion inside my head, the pounding of my pulse. The squad car slumps under the relentless barrage of bullets.

I push Augie flat on the sidewalk and scramble to find his pants leg, the gun holstered at his ankle. Through the rush of adrenaline comes the dull pounding between my ears, ever present during combat. It never leaves a veteran.

The Glock is lighter by a good measure than the Beretta I was trained on, with a better grip, and I've heard it's accurate, but weapons are like cars—you know they have standard stuff like lights and an ignition and windshield wipers, but it still takes a few seconds to figure them out when they're unfamiliar. So I burn precious moments getting a feel for it before I'm ready to point and shoot—

To the south, the light from the van's side door shines out onto the sidewalk. From the shadows, three men come into focus, running toward us. One of them, large and muscular, has the lead on the other two men, running toward me into the van's light, a gun held down with both hands.

I fire the gun twice, aiming for center mass. He staggers and falls forward. The other two I don't see receding into the darkness...where are they...how many rounds do I have...are there others from the other side…is this a ten-round mag…where are the other two guys from the south?

I turn to my left as the top of the squad car takes two bullets, *thunk-thunk,* and drape my body over Augie's. I swivel my head to the left, to the right, to the left, searching through the darkness, more explosions from the sidewalk around us. The sniper is trying every angle to reach us but can't. As long as we hold our ground crouched behind the car, the sniper, wherever he is, can't hit us.

But as long as we hold our ground, we're sitting ducks.

Augie pushes up. "We have to run, we have to run—"

"Don't move!" I shout, pressing down on him, keeping him flat. "We run, we die."

Augie holds still. So do I, in our cocoon of darkness. There is noise from the stadium, general chaos from the blackout, tires screeching, horns honking—but no bullets pelting the squad car.

Or the sidewalk around us.

Or the stadium wall opposite us.

The sniper stopped firing. He stopped firing because—

I spin back to my four o'clock and see a man coming around the driver's side of the van, illuminated by the interior dome light, a weapon up at shoulder level. I pull the trigger once, twice, three times as light explodes from his weapon, too, bullets ricocheting off the hood of the squad car in an exchange of gunfire, but I have the advantage, crouched low in the dark while he's standing by light.

I risk another glance over the hood, my pulse like a shock wave through my body. No sign of the shooter or of the third member of the south team.

The sharp squealing of brakes, men shouting, voices I recognize, words I recognize—

"Secret Service! Secret Service!"

I lower my gun and they are on me, surrounding me with automatic weapons trained in all directions while someone grabs me under the arms and lifts me, and I'm trying to say "sniper" to them but I'm not sure if it comes out, I'm thinking it but I can't speak, and shouts of "Go! Go! Go!" as I'm carried into a waiting vehicle, blanketed on all sides by people trained to sacrifice their lives for mine—

And then blinding light, a loud hum, everything lit up again, as bright as a spotlight in my face, electricity restored all around us.

I hear myself say "Augie" and "bring him" and then the door is shut and I'm lying in the car and

"Go! Go! Go!" and we are speeding away, driving on uneven ground, the grassy median in the middle of Capitol Street.

"Are you hit? Are you hit?" Alex Trimble frantically runs his hands over me, looking for any signs of wounds.

"No," I answer, but he's not taking my word for it, touching my chest and torso, forcibly turning me on my side to check my back, my neck, my head, then my legs.

"He's not hit," Alex calls out.

"Augie," I say. "The...kid."

"We have him, Mr. President. He's in the car behind us."

"The girl who was shot...get her, too."

He lets out a breath, looking out the window behind him, adrenaline decelerating. "DC Metro can handle—"

"No, Alex, no," I say. "The girl...she's dead... get custody of her...whatever...whatever you have to tell DC Metro..."

"Yes, sir."

Alex calls out to the driver. I try to process what's just happened. The dots are there, strewn about like stars in a galaxy, but I can't connect them, not right now.

My phone buzzes. I find it in the footwell of the backseat. Carolyn. Can only be Carolyn.

"I need…the phone," I tell Alex.

He reaches for it and puts it in my still-trembling hand. The number Carolyn texts me is 1. My thoughts are too scattered right now to remember the name of my first-grade teacher. I can picture her. She was tall, a big hook for a nose…

I need to remember it. I need to respond to her. If I don't—

Richards. No, Richardson, Mrs. Richardson.

The phone pops out of my hand. I'm shaking so hard I can't hold it, can't text on it. I tell Alex what to type into the phone, and he does it for me.

"I want to ride…with Augie," I say. "The… man I was with."

"We'll rendezvous at the White House, Mr. President, and we can—"

"No," I say. "No."

"No what, sir?"

"We're not going back…to the White House," I say.

CHAPTER
30

❖

We don't stop until we make it to the highway, then I order Alex to take an exit. The skies have finally opened, a heavy rainfall punishing the windshield, the wipers flying back and forth, an urgent cadence in sync with the pounding of my pulse.

Alex Trimble is barking at someone on the phone but keeping one eye on me, making sure I'm not in shock. *Shock* is the wrong word. Adrenaline crashes through my body as I replay the events, then recedes with the knowledge that I'm safe inside this armored SUV, then returns with still greater vengeance, as if my body is at high tide.

Until I'm dead, I'm alive. It was my constant refrain when I was a POW, when days blurred into nights in my windowless cell, when they'd wrap the towel around my face and dump the water on, when they'd use the dogs, when they'd blindfold me and chant a prayer and press the gun against my temple.

I'm not barely alive. I'm just alive, period, and more than ever, a euphoria that fills my body with electricity, every sense heightened, the smell of the leather seats, the taste of bile in my mouth, the feel of sweat slithering down my face.

"I can't tell you any more than that," Alex says into his phone to someone from the police department, pulling rank—or trying to. It won't be easy. We have a lot of explaining to do. Capitol Street must look like a small war zone. A pockmarked sidewalk, one wall of Nationals Park battered, a DC Metro squad car riddled with bullets, shattered glass everywhere. And bodies, three of them at least—the big guy who ran toward me, the other member of his team who tried to sneak around the van to get at us, and Nina.

I grab Alex's tree limb of an arm. He turns to me, says into the phone, "I have to call you back," and punches out his phone.

"How many dead?" I ask, fearing the worst, that innocent people were caught in the sniper's hail of bullets or the ground team's follow-up.

"Just the girl in the van, sir."

"What about the men? There were two of them."

He shakes his head. "They're gone, sir. Whoever was with them must have taken them away. That was a well-coordinated attack."

No question. A sniper and at least one ground team.

Yet I'm still alive.

"We just removed the girl from the scene, sir. We told them it was a Secret Service counterfeiting investigation."

That was smart. It's not an easy sell—a counterfeiting investigation ending in a bloody shootout outside a baseball stadium—but Alex didn't have any other cards to play.

"I guess that's better than saying the president was sneaking out to a baseball game when someone tried to assassinate him."

"I had the same thought, sir," says Alex, deadpan.

I meet his eyes. He is scolding me. He is saying, without saying it, that this is the kind of complication that results when a president sheds his security.

"The blackout helped," he says, letting me off the hook. "And the stadium noise, too. It was pandemonium. And now it's raining like hell, so thirty, forty thousand people are rushing out of the stadium while the police are trying to figure out what the hell just happened and while the rainfall washes away most of the forensic evidence."

He's right. Chaos, in this case, is good. There will be media all over this, but most of it happened in the pitch-dark, and Treasury will sweep the rest under the rug as an official investigation. Will it work? It better.

"You followed me," I say to him.

He shrugs. "Not exactly, sir. When the woman came to the White House, we had to search her."

"You scanned the envelope."

"As a matter of course," he says.

Right. And it showed a ticket to tonight's game at Nationals Park. My thoughts have been so scattered, I didn't even think of it.

Alex looks at me, giving me the chance to reprimand him. But it's hard to chew out the guy who just saved your life. "Thank you, Alex," I say. "Now, don't ever disobey me again."

We are off the highway now, slowing into an open space, some massive parking lot empty at this time of night. I can barely see our second car through the sheets of rainfall. I can barely see anything.

"Get Augie in here with me," I say.

"He's a threat, sir."

"No, he's not." Not in the way Alex means, at least.

"You don't know that, sir. His job could've been to get you out of the stadium—"

"If I was the target, Alex, I'd be dead. Augie himself could have killed me. And the sniper shot Nina first. I imagine that the second target was Augie, not me."

"Mr. President, my job is to assume that you were the target."

"Fine. Cuff him if you want to," I say. "Put him in a goddamn straitjacket. But he's riding with me."

"He's already cuffed, sir. He's very…upset." Alex thinks for a moment. "Sir, it might be best if I follow in the other car. I need to stay close to what's going on at the stadium. DC Metro wants answers."

And only he can massage that situation. Only he would know what to say and what not to say.

"Jacobson will ride with you, sir."

"Fine," I say. "Just get Augie in here."

He speaks into the radio clipped to his jacket. A moment later, he opens the side door of the SUV with some effort as the violent wind hisses into the car, blowing in the rain that spares no one.

The agents rearrange themselves. Jacobson,

Alex's second in command, bounds into the car a moment later. Jacobson is smaller than Alex, hard and lean with an unrelenting intensity. He is soaked, droplets of rain flinging off his windbreaker as he takes the seat next to me.

"Mr. President," he says in his just-the-facts way, but with a sense of urgency, as he looks out the door, ready to pounce.

A moment later, he does just that, coming forward to take the handoff from another agent. Augie's head comes through the door, then the rest of him, as Jacobson pushes him violently into one of the seats across from me in the rear compartment. Augie's hands are cuffed in front. His ropy hair hangs wet over his face.

"You sit there and don't move, understand?" Jacobson barks at him. "Understand?"

Augie thrashes about, pushing against the seat belt Jacobson has clipped over him.

"He understands," I say. Jacobson sits next to me, leaning forward on the balls of his feet.

Augie's eyes, as best I can see them through the hair hanging down to his cheeks, finally make contact with mine. He has probably been crying, though it's impossible to see on his rain-slicked face. His eyes widen with fury.

"You killed her!" he spits. "You killed her!"

"Augie," I say matter-of-factly, trying to calm

222

him with my tone, "that doesn't make any sense. This was your plan, not mine."

His face contorts into a snarl, tears streaming, blubbering and sobbing. He could be an actor portraying an inmate in an asylum, thrashing about while restrained, moaning and cursing and crying out, except that his pain is real, not the product of a broken mind.

There's no point in my saying anything to him yet. He needs to get this out first.

The car starts moving again, back toward the highway, to our destination. It will be a long trip before we get there.

We ride in silence for some time, as Augie, shackled, mumbles in words that alternate between English and his native tongue, as he hiccups loud bellows of pain, as he struggles for breath through his sobs.

I use the next few minutes to think things over, to sort out what just happened. Asking myself questions. Why am I alive? Why was the girl killed first? And who sent these people?

Lost in these thoughts, I suddenly become aware of the silence in the car. Augie is watching me, waiting for me to notice.

"You expect me..." he says, his voice breaking, "you expect me to help you after this?"

CHAPTER
31

❖

B ach quietly leaves through the rear exit of
the building, her trench coat buttoned to
her chin, a bag over her shoulder, an umbrella
concealing her face, taking on the *rat-a-tat-tat* of
the pelting rain. She moves onto the street as police sirens blare, as law-enforcement vehicles
race down the next street over, Capitol Street,
toward the stadium.

Ranko, her first mentor, the red-haired scarecrow—the Serbian soldier who took pity on her
after what his men did to her father, who took
her under his wing (and under his body)—may
have taught her how to shoot, but he never
taught her extractions. A Serbian sniper had no
need for one, never had to leave Trebevic Mountain, where he fired at will upon citizens and

opposition military targets alike during the war as his army strangled Sarajevo like a python.

No, she taught herself about extractions, planned escape routes and stealth movements when foraging for food in back alleys or in garbage cans at the market, dodging land mines, scanning for snipers and ambushes, listening for the ever-present threat of mortar fire or, at night, the drunken chatter of off-duty soldiers who respected no rules regarding young civilian Bosnian girls they found on the street.

Sometimes, as she hunted for bread or rice or firewood, Bach was fast enough to get away from the soldiers. Sometimes she wasn't.

"We have two extra tickets," comes a man's voice through her earbud.

Two tickets—two men wounded.

"Can you bring them home?" she asks.

"We do not have time," he says. Their medical conditions are urgent, he means.

"It will be fine at home," she says. "Meet you at home."

They should already know that the only option is the extraction point. They are panicking, losing focus. It was probably the arrival of the Secret Service that did it. Or maybe the blackout, which she must admit was an impressive tactical maneuver. She was ready, of course, to switch her scope to night-vision mode, but it clearly affected the ground teams.

She removes her earbud and stuffs it into the right-hand pocket of her trench coat.

She reaches into the left-hand pocket and places a different earbud into her ear.

"The game is not over," she says. "They went north."

CHAPTER
32

❖

It was…your people," Augie says, his chest heaving, his eyes so puffy and red from crying that he looks like a different person. He looks like a boy, which is exactly what he is.

"My people didn't shoot your friend, Augie," I say, trying to convey compassion but also, more than anything, calm and reason. "Whoever shot her was shooting at *us*, too. My people are the reason we're safe and sound in this SUV."

It does nothing to stop his tears. I don't know his specific relationship with Nina, but it's clear that his distress is more than just fear. Whoever she was, he cared deeply for her.

I'm sorry for his loss, but I don't have time to be sorry. I have to keep my eye on the prize. I have three hundred million people to protect. So my only question is how I can use his emotions to my advantage.

Because this could go south on me quickly. If I believe what Nina told me in the Oval Office, she and Augie held different pieces of information, different parts of the puzzle. And now she is dead. If I lose Augie now, too—if he clams up on me—I have nothing.

The driver, Agent Davis, is quiet as he focuses on the road in the treacherous weather. The front-seat passenger, Agent Ontiveros, pulls the radio from the dashboard and speaks softly into it. Jacobson, next to me in the rear compartment, has a finger up to his earpiece, listening intently as he receives updates from Alex Trimble in the other car.

"Mr. President," says Jacobson. "We've impounded the van she was driving. So she and the van are both cleared of the scene. All that's left is a chopped-up sidewalk and a DC Metro squad car shot to hell. And a bunch of pissed-off cops," he adds.

I lean over to Jacobson, so only he can hear me. "Keep the woman's body and the van under guard. Do we know how to hold a corpse?"

He nods briskly. "We'll figure it out, sir."

"This stays with Secret Service."

"Understood, sir."

"Now give me the key to Augie's handcuffs."

Jacobson draws back. "Sir?"

I don't repeat myself. A president doesn't have to. I just meet his eyes.

Jacobson was Special Forces, just as I was a long time ago, but that's where our similarities end. His intensity is not born of discipline or devotion to duty so much as it is a way of life. He doesn't seem to know another way. He's the type who falls out of bed in the morning and bangs out a hundred push-ups and stomach crunches. He is a soldier looking for a war, a hero in search of a moment of heroism.

He hands me the key. "Mr. President, I suggest you let me do it."

"No."

I show Augie the key, as I might extend a cautionary hand to a wounded animal to signal my approach. We have now shared a traumatic experience, but Augie is still a mystery to me. All I know is that he once was part of the Sons of Jihad and now is not. I don't know why. I don't know what he wants out of this. I just know that he isn't here for nothing. Nobody does anything for nothing.

I move across the rear chamber of the SUV to his side, the smell of wet clothes and sweat and body odor. I lean around and fit the key into the handcuffs.

"Augie," I say into his ear, "I know you cared about her."

"I loved her."

"Okay. I know what it's like to lose someone you love. When I lost my wife, I had to go on without missing a beat. That's what we have to do right now, you and me. There will be lots of time to grieve, but not now. You came to me for a reason. I don't know what that reason is, but it must have been important if you went to all this trouble and took this much risk. You trusted me before. Trust me now."

"I trusted you, and now she is dead," he whispers.

"And if you don't help me now, who *are* you helping? The people who just killed her," I say.

The sound of his accelerated breathing is audible as I pull back from him, returning to my seat, the handcuffs dangling from my finger.

Jacobson pulls out my shoulder restraint for me. I take it the rest of the way and fasten the seat belt. These guys really are full-service.

Augie rubs his wrists and looks at me with something other than hatred. Curiosity. Wonder. He knows what I'm saying makes sense. He knows how close he and I came to dying, that

I could have him locked up, interrogated, even killed—but instead I've done his bidding from the start.

"Where are we going?" he asks, his voice without affect.

"Somewhere private," I say as we take the highway onto the bridge over the Potomac, crossing into Virginia. "Somewhere we can be safe."

"Safe," Augie repeats, looking away.

"What's *that?*" snaps Davis, the driver. "Bike path, two o'clock—"

"What the—"

Before Agent Ontiveros can finish his sentence, something hits the center of the windshield with a thunderous splat, blanketing it in darkness. The SUV fishtails as bursts of fire erupt from our right, bullets pelting the right side of our armored vehicle, *thunk-thunk-thunk.*

"Get us out of here!" Jacobson shouts as I crash into him, as he fumbles for his weapon, as our vehicle spins out of control on the rain-slick 14th Street Bridge under hostile fire.

CHAPTER
33

❖

B ach angles the umbrella to hold off the
rain, blown sideways by the relentless
wind, forcing her to walk in a more plodding
fashion than she would prefer.

It rained like this the first time the soldiers came.
She remembers the pelting of the rain on the
roof. The darkness of her house, after electricity
had been cut for weeks in the neighborhood. The
warmth of the fire in the family room. The burst
of cold air as the front door to their house flew
open, her initial thought being that it was caused
by the gusty wind. Then the shouts of the soldiers, the gunfire, dishes crashing in the kitchen,
her father's angry protests as they dragged him
from the house. It was the last time she ever
heard his voice.

Finally she reaches the warehouse and enters through the rear door, fitting her umbrella behind her through the door and placing it open, upside down, on the concrete floor. She hears the men near the front of the open-air space, where they are tending to the wounded, shouting at one another, blaming one another in a language she doesn't understand.

But she understands panic in any tongue.

She lets her heels click loudly enough for them to hear her coming. She didn't want to preannounce her arrival lest there be an ambush awaiting her—old habits die hard—but likewise she finds no advantage in startling a group of heavily armed, violent men.

The men turn to the sound of her heels echoing off the high ceiling of the warehouse, two of the nine instinctively reaching for their weapons before relaxing.

"He got away," says the team leader, the bald man, still in his powder-blue shirt and dark trousers, as she approaches.

The men part, clearing a path for her as she finds two men leaning up against crates. One is the bodybuilder, the one she never liked, eyes squeezed shut, grimacing and moaning, his shirt removed and a makeshift gauze-and-tape bandage near his right shoulder. Probably a clean through-and-through, she imagines, plenty of muscle and tissue but no bone.

The second one is also shirtless, breathing with difficulty, his eyes listless, his color waning, as another man presses a bloody rag against the left side of his chest.

"Where's the medical help?" asks another man.

She did not select this team. She was assured it contained some of the best operatives in the world. Given that they hired her, and given what they paid her, she assumed they were sparing no expense in obtaining the best nine operatives available for this part of the mission.

From the pocket of her trench coat she removes her handgun, the suppressor already attached, and fires a bullet through the temple of the bodybuilder, then another through the skull of the second one.

Now *seven* of the best operatives available.

The other men step back, stunned into silence by the rapid *thwip-thwip* that ended the lives of two of their partners. None of them, she notes, reaches for a weapon.

She makes eye contact with each of them, settling the *are-we-going-to-have-a-problem* question with each one to her satisfaction. They can't be surprised. The one with the chest wound was going to die anyway. The bodybuilder, absent an infection, could have made it, but he'd turned from an asset into a liability. These are zero-sum games they play. And the game isn't over.

The final man she seeks out is the bald man, the team leader. "You will dispose of these bodies," she says.

He nods.

"You know where to relocate?"

He nods again.

She walks over to him. "Do you have any further questions of me?"

He shakes his head, an emphatic no.

CHAPTER
34

❖

W e are under attack, repeat, we are under
       attack..."
Our SUV veering wildly, rapid bursts of fire
coming from one side of the bridge, the sick-
ening, helpless feeling of hydroplaning as Agent
Davis furiously struggles to regain control.

The three of us in the backseat are jerked like
human pinballs, straining against our seat belts,
Jacobson and I crashing into each other as we
lurch from one side to the other.

A car slams into us from behind, spinning our
SUV across traffic, then another collision from
the right, the headlights only inches from Jacobson's face, the impact felt in my teeth, my neck,
as I hurl to my left.

Everything in a spin, everyone shouting, bullets pummeling the armor of our vehicle, left and right, north and south indistinguishable—

The rear of our SUV crashes against the concrete barrier, and we are suddenly at rest, spun around in the wrong direction on the 14th Street Bridge, facing north in southbound traffic. The explosion of fire from automatic weapons comes from our left now, relentless, some of the bullets bouncing off, some of them embedding in the armor and bulletproof glass.

"Get us an exit!" Jacobson shouts. The first order of business—find a route of escape for the president and extract him.

"Augie," I whisper. He is slung against his seat belt, conscious and unharmed but dazed, trying to gather his bearings, trying to catch his breath.

The thought flickers through my head: you could almost see the White House from this bridge, facing this direction. A score of agents, a SWAT team, only six blocks away yet as useless as if they were on the other side of the planet.

Agent Davis cursing as he struggles to change gears, as the windshield clears enough to see in front of us, southbound. Gunfire erupting not only from the pedestrian path but also from our backup car, Alex Trimble and his team firing at our attackers.

How do we get out? We're trapped. We have to make a run for it—

"Go! Go! Go!" Jacobson yells in that practiced cadence, as he remains restrained by his seat belt but holds his automatic weapon at the ready.

Davis finally gets the car in reverse using the dashboard radar, and after the tires grip the slick pavement we hurtle backward, the firefight in front of us shrinking from view and then disappearing altogether as another vehicle comes into our lane, bigger than our Suburbans.

A truck, bearing down on us at twice our speed.

We race and slide backward, Davis trying to pick up speed as best he can but no match for the truck closing the distance quickly from the front. I steel myself for the impact as the grille of the truck is the only thing visible through the windshield.

Davis, his hands at nine and three on the wheel, whips his right hand over to nine, his left to three, and spins the car into an evasive J-turn. I plow into Jacobson as the rear fishtails to the right again, the car now profiled in the path of the oncoming truck, turned sideways in the lane at the moment of impact.

The concussive *whump* of the impact knocks the breath from me, sends stars dancing before my eyes and a shock wave through my body. The grille of the truck caves in the front passenger side, flinging Ontiveros into the driver, Davis, like a floppy doll, the back end of the SUV twisting right at a sixty-degree angle while the front end stays locked to the grille of the truck in a crunch of whining armor. Hot wet air invades the rear compartment as the SUV desperately tries to hold itself together in one piece.

Jacobson somehow manages to roll the window down, firing his MP5 submachine gun up at the cab of the truck as hot wind and rain pummel us. The vehicles, joined together, come to a halt. Jacobson fires relentlessly as the backup car approaches, Alex and his team already shooting at the truck from their SUV's side windows.

Get Augie out.

"Augie," I say, releasing my seat belt.

"Don't move, Mr. President!" Jacobson yells as the hood of our SUV bursts into a ball of orange flame.

Augie, his face white with terror, unhooks his seat belt. I open the left passenger door, pulling Augie by the wrist. "Stay low!" I shout as we run along the back of the SUV, shielding us from the cab of the truck, then run toward Alex's car in the thrashing rain, removing any angle the shooters in the truck's cab would have on us—if they survive Jacobson's merciless assault.

"Mr. President, get in the car!" Alex shouts from the middle of the bridge as we approach. By now, he and the two other agents have left the second SUV and are pounding the truck with machine-gun fire.

Augie and I race to the second vehicle. Behind that SUV, a pileup of cars on the bridge, turned in all directions.

"Get in the back!" I shout at him, rain smacking my face. I take the driver's seat. I put the car in gear and floor the accelerator.

The rear of the vehicle is damaged, but the car's still operable, still enough to get us out of here. I don't like leaving my men behind. It goes against everything I learned in the service. But I have no weapon, so I'm no help. And I am protecting the most important asset—Augie.

The inevitable second explosion comes as we cross the bridge into Virginia, with more questions than ever before and not a single answer.

But until we're dead, we're alive.

CHAPTER
35

❖

My hands tremble as I grip the steering wheel, my heart races as I peer through a windshield pockmarked with bullets, splattered by rain, wipers flailing furiously back and forth.

Sweat dripping down my face, a fire blazing in my chest, wishing I could adjust the temperature but afraid to take my eyes off the road, afraid to stop the SUV or even slow down, checking the rearview mirror only for signs of another vehicle following me. There is damage to the rear of this SUV, the sound of metal scraping on a tire, a slight hitch as we drive. I can't drive it much longer.

"Augie," I say. "Augie!" Surprised at the rage, the frustration in my voice.

My mysterious companion sits up in the backseat but doesn't speak. He looks utterly shell-shocked, overwhelmed, staring off into the distance, his mouth open slightly in a small O, wincing at every bolt of lightning or bump on the road.

"People are dying, Augie. Whatever you know, you better damn well tell me, and tell me now!"

But I don't even know if I can trust him yet. Since I met him, with his cryptic references to Armageddon at the ballpark, we've spent every moment just trying to stay alive. I don't know if he's friend or foe, hero or operative.

Only one thing is for sure—he's important. He's a threat to someone. None of this would be happening otherwise. The more they try to stop us, the more his significance grows.

"Augie!" I shout. "Damn it, kid, snap out of it! Don't go into shock on me. We don't have time for shock right—"

My phone buzzes in my pocket. I reach for it with my right hand, struggling to free it from my pocket before it goes to voice mail.

"*Mr. President, you're okay*," says Carolyn Brock, the relief evident in her voice. "*Was that you on the 14th Street Bridge?*"

Not surprising she'd already know. It wouldn't take but a minute for something like that to reach the White House, less than a mile away. There would be immediate concerns about terrorism, a strike on the capital.

"Lock down the White House, Carrie," I say as I follow the road, the overhead lights a blur of color against the wet windshield. "Just as a—"

"It's already locked down, sir."

"And secure—"

"The vice president is already secured in the operations center, sir."

I take a breath. God, do I need a port in the storm like Carolyn right now, anticipating my moves and even improving on them.

I explain to her, in as few words as possible, trying not to ramble, struggling to remain calm, that yes, what happened on the bridge, what happened at Nationals Park, involved me.

"Are you with Secret Service right now, sir?"

"No. Just me and Augie."

"His name is Augie? And the girl—"

"The girl is dead."

"Dead? What happened?"

"At the baseball stadium. Someone shot her. Augie and I got away. Listen, I have to get off the road, Carrie. I'm headed to the Blue House. I'm sorry, but I don't have a choice."

"Of course, sir, of course."

"And I need Greenfield on the phone right now."

"You have her on your phone, sir, unless you want me to patch you through."

Right, that's right. Carolyn put Liz Greenfield's number into this phone.

"Got it. Talk soon," I say.

"Mr. President! Are you there?" The words, Alex's voice, squawk through the dashboard. I drop my phone on the passenger seat and pull the radio from the dash, press the button with my right thumb to speak.

"Alex, I'm fine. I'm just driving on the highway. Talk to me." I release my thumb.

"They're neutralized, sir. Four dead on the pedestrian path. The truck blew. No idea how many casualties inside the truck, but definitely no survivors."

"A truck bomb?"

"No, sir. They weren't suicide bombers. If they were, none of us would still be alive. We penetrated the gas tank and caused a gasoline fire. No other explosives on board. No civilian casualties."

That tells us something, at least. They weren't true believers, not radicals. This wasn't ISIS or Al Qaeda or any of their cancerous branches. They were mercenaries for hire.

I take a breath and ask the question I've dreaded. "What about our people, Alex?" A silent prayer as I wait for the answer.

"We lost Davis and Ontiveros, sir."

I slam my fist against the wheel. The vehicle swerves, and I quickly adjust, instantly reminding me that I can't let go of my obligations for even one second.

If I do, then my men just gave their lives in vain.

"I'm sorry, Alex," I say into the radio. "I'm so sorry."

"Yes sir," he says, all business. *"Mr. President, it's a shitstorm here right now. Fire trucks. DC Metro and Arlington PD. Everyone's trying to figure out what the hell happened and who's in charge."*

Right. Of course. An explosion on a bridge between Washington and Virginia, a jurisdictional nightmare. Mass confusion.

"Make it clear that *you're* in charge," I tell him. "Just say 'federal investigation' for now. Help is on the way."

"Yes, sir. Sir, stay on the highway. We'll track you on GPS and have vehicles surrounding you soon. Stay in that vehicle, sir. It's the safest place you can be until we can get you back to the White House."

"I'm not going back to the White House, Alex. And I don't want a convoy. One vehicle. One."

"Sir, whatever this is, or was, the circumstances have changed. They have intelligence and technology and manpower and weapons. They knew where you'd be."

"We don't know that," I say. "They could've set

up multiple ambush points. They were probably ready for us if we went to the White House, too, or if we headed south from the stadium. Hell, they were probably *hoping* we'd cross the bridge over the Potomac."

"We don't know, Mr. President, that's the point—"

"One vehicle, Alex. That's a direct order."

I click off and find my phone on the passenger seat. I find the number on my phone for FBI Liz and dial it.

"Hello, Mr. President," says the acting FBI director, Elizabeth Greenfield. *"You're aware of the bridge explosion?"*

"Liz, how long have you been acting director?"

"Ten days, sir."

"Well, Madam Director," I say, "it's time to take off the training wheels."

CHAPTER
36

❖

*N*ext *house down, sir."* Jacobson's voice squawks through my dashboard, as if I didn't already recognize the house.

I pull the Suburban up to the curb, relieved that I made it this far. These Secret Service vehicles are battleships, but I wasn't sure how long I could drive with the rear-end damage.

Jacobson's vehicle pulls up behind me. He caught up to me on the highway and used GPS to guide me here. I've been to the house many times but never paid much attention to the various roads that got me here.

I put the car in Park and kill the ignition. When I do so, I feel the tidal-wave rush, as I knew I would—the shakes, the post-adrenaline, post-traumatic physical reaction. Until this moment, I had to keep control to get Augie and myself out of harm's way. My work is far from over—more complicated than ever, in fact—but I allow myself this brief respite, taking a few deep breaths, trying to get past the life-or-death crises, trying to empty out all the panic and anger bottled up inside me.

"You have to keep it together," I whisper to myself, trembling. "If you don't, nobody else will, either." I treat it like any other decision, like it's something I can completely control, willing myself to stop shaking.

Jacobson jogs over and opens my car door. I don't need help getting out of the vehicle, but he helps me anyway. Some cuts and dirt on his face aside, he looks generally intact.

Standing, I feel momentary wooziness, unsure of my legs. Dr. Lane would not be happy with me right now.

"You okay?" I ask Jacobson.

"Am *I* okay? I'm fine. How are you, sir?"

"Fine. You saved my life," I say to him.

"Davis saved your life, sir."

That's also true. The evasive-driving maneuver, the J-turn that spun our vehicle perpendicular to the oncoming truck, was Davis's way of taking the brunt of the impact so I wouldn't, in the rear. It was a brilliant bit of driving by a well-trained agent. And Jacobson was no slouch, either, firing on the cab of the truck before the two intertwined vehicles had even stopped. Augie and I couldn't have escaped without that cover.

Secret Service agents never get the credit they deserve for what they do every day to keep me safe, to trade their own lives for mine, to do what no sane person would ever willingly do—step in front of a bullet, not away from it. Every now and then, an agent does something stupid on the taxpayer's dime, and that's all anybody remembers. The ninety-nine times out of a hundred they perform their jobs perfectly never get mentioned.

"Davis had a wife and little boy, didn't he?" I ask. Had I known the Secret Service was going to track me tonight, I would have done what I always do when I visit one of the hot spots around the world, one of the places where the Service is most insecure about my safety—Pakistan or Bangladesh or Afghanistan: I would have insisted that nobody with young children accompany me.

"Comes with the job," says Jacobson.

Tell that to his wife and son. "And Ontiveros?"

"Sir," he says, shaking his head curtly.

He's right. It will matter down the road. I will make sure that we don't forget Davis's family and whatever family Ontiveros left behind. That is my personal vow. But I can't deal with it right now, not tonight.

Mourn your losses later, after the fight's over, Sergeant Melton used to say. *When you're in the fight, fight.*

Augie gets out of the Suburban on shaky legs, too, planting his foot in a puddle on the road. It's stopped raining, leaving an earthy, fresh smell in its wake on this sleepy, dark residential street, as if Mother Nature is telling us, *You made it to the other side, a fresh start.* I hope that's true, but it doesn't feel that way.

Augie looks at me like a lost puppy, in a foreign place with no partner anymore, nothing to call his own except his smartphone.

The house before us is a stucco-and-brick Victorian with a manicured lawn, a driveway leading up to a two-car garage, and a lamp that lights the walkway to the front porch—the only light that appears to be on past ten o'clock in the evening. The stucco is painted a soft blue, the origin of the nickname the Blue House.

Augie and Jacobson follow me up the driveway.

The door opens before we reach it. Carolyn Brock's husband was expecting us.

CHAPTER
37

❖

G reg Morton, Carolyn Brock's husband, is wearing an oxford-cloth shirt and blue jeans with sandals on his feet, waving us in.

"Sorry to come here, Morty," I say.

"Not at all, not at all."

Morty and Carolyn celebrated fifteen years of marriage this year—though given her role as chief of staff to the president, the celebration, as I recall, was just a long weekend on Martha's Vineyard. Morty, age fifty-two, retired after a lucrative career as a trial lawyer that ended with a heart attack in a Cuyahoga County courtroom as he stood before a jury. His second child, James, was less than a year old at the time. He wanted to see his children grow up, and he couldn't spend all the money he'd already made, so he hung up the boxing gloves. These days, he makes documentary short films and stays home with the two kids.

He looks us over, me and my ragtag crew. I had forgotten that I'd gone to such lengths to disguise my appearance—the beard nobody's ever seen, my casual, rain-soaked clothes, my hair still dripping rainwater into my face. Then there's Augie, already shaggy before the rain did its work on him. At least Jacobson looks the part of the Secret Service agent.

"It sounds like you have quite a story to tell," says Morty in the baritone voice that swayed many a juror over the years. "But I'll never hear a word of it."

We step inside. Halfway down the winding staircase that ends in the foyer, the two kids sit and stare at us through the balusters—six-year-old James, in Batman pajamas, hair standing on end, and ten-year-old Jennifer, her mother's face staring back at me. I'm nothing new to them at this point, but I don't usually look like something the cat dragged in from the garbage.

"If I had any ability to control the minions," says Morty, "they'd be in bed right now."

"You have a red beard," says Jennifer, wrinkling her nose. "You don't look like a president."

"Grant had a beard. Coolidge had red hair."

"Who?" asks James.

"They were presidents, genius," his sister tells him with a swat in his direction. "Like, a really long time ago. Like, when Mom and Dad were little."

"Whoa—how old do you think I am?" says Morty.

"You're fifty-two," says Jennifer. "But we're aging you prematurely."

"You got *that* right." Morty turns to me. "Carrie said the basement office, Mr. President. Is that what you want?"

"That's great."

"You know the way. I'll get you some towels. And my kids are going to bed, aren't you, children?"

"Awwww…"

"Enough with the sound effects. Bed!"

Carolyn had the basement finished as an elaborate office, complete with secure lines of telecommunication, allowing her to work in the late evenings from home.

Jacobson goes first, taking the stairs down and clearing the area before giving me a thumbs-up.

Augie and I head down. The basement is neat and well-appointed, as one would expect in Carolyn's home. There is a large open playroom furnished with beanbag chairs as well as a desk and chair and couch; there is also a TV mounted on the wall, a wine cellar, a movie room with a projection screen and deep, lush seats, a full bathroom in the hallway, a bedroom, and Carolyn's office in the back. Her office contains a horseshoe-shaped desk topped with multiple computers, a large corkboard on the wall, several file cabinets, and a large flat-screen TV.

"Here you guys go." Morty hands each of us a towel. "Are you ready for Carrie, Mr. President? Just tap this button right here." He points at a mouse by the computer.

"One second. Is there someplace my friend could go?" I ask, meaning Augie. I haven't introduced him to Morty, and Morty hasn't asked for an introduction. He knows better.

"The rec room," says Morty. "The large open space by the stairs."

"Great. Go with him," I say to Jacobson.

The two of them leave the room. Morty nods to me. "Carrie said you'd want a change of clothes."

"That would be great." The bag I'd carried with me, including clothes for Saturday, was left behind in the car I'd parked in the baseball stadium lot.

"Will do. Well, I'll leave you to it. I'll be praying for you, Mr. President."

I look at him questioningly. Those are strong words. This has been unorthodox, no doubt, my showing up incognito this way. He's a bright guy, but I know Carolyn doesn't share classified information with him.

He leans into me. "I've known Carrie for eighteen years," he says. "I've seen her lose a congressional election. I've seen her when she miscarried, when I nearly died from a myocardial infarction, and when we lost Jenny in a shopping mall in Alexandria for two hours. I've seen her with her back against the wall; I've seen her concerned; I've seen her worried. But before tonight, I've never seen her terrified."

I don't say anything to that. I can't. He knows that.

He extends his hand. "Whatever it is, I'm betting on the two of you."

I shake his hand. "All the same," I say, "go ahead and say those prayers."

CHAPTER
38

❖

I close the door to Carolyn's basement office, enclosing myself in soundproofed walls, and sit at the desk. I pick up the computer mouse. When I do, the computer changes from a black screen to fuzz, then a somewhat clear screen split in two.

"Hello, Mr. President," says Carolyn Brock, speaking from the White House.

"Hello, Mr. President," says Elizabeth Greenfield, acting FBI director, on the second half of the split screen. Liz became the acting director after her predecessor died in office ten days ago from an aneurysm. I've nominated her for the permanent position, too. By every measure, she's the best person for the job—former agent, federal prosecutor, head of the criminal division at Jus-

tice, respected by everyone as nonpartisan and a straight arrow.

The strike against her, which I don't consider a strike at all, is that more than a decade ago, she joined protests against the invasion of Iraq, so some of the hawks in the Senate have suggested she lacks patriotism, presumably forgetting that peaceful protest is one of the most admirable forms of patriotism.

They also said I just wanted to be the first president to appoint an African American woman to run the FBI.

"Tell me about the bridge," I say, "and Nationals Park."

"We have very, very little from the ballpark. It's early, of course, but the blackout erased any visuals, and the rain has washed away most of the forensics. If men were killed outside the stadium, we have no trace of it. If they left behind any forensic evidence of their existence, it might be days before we find it. And the likelihood is low."

"And the sniper?"

"The sniper. The vehicle was removed by Secret Service, but we have the bullets fired into the sidewalk and the stadium wall, so we can make out a decent angle. From what we can gather, it looks like the sniper was shooting from the roof of an apartment building across the street from the stadium, a building called the

Camden South Capitol. *We didn't find anyone up there, of course, but the problem is we didn't find anything, period. So the sniper did a good job of cleaning up. And of course there's the rain."*

"Right."

"Mr. President, if they set up in that building, we will figure out who they are. It would have required advance planning. Access. Stolen uniforms, probably. Internal cameras. Facial recognition. We have ways. But you're telling me there's no time."

"Not much, no."

"We're working as quickly as we can, sir. I just can't promise you we'll have answers within hours."

"Try. And the woman?" I ask, referring to Augie's partner.

"Nina, yes. The Secret Service just turned over the vehicle and the body. We'll have her fingerprints and DNA within minutes, and we'll run them. We'll trace the car, everything."

"Good."

"What about the bridge?" asks Carolyn.

"The bridge is still a work in progress," says Liz. *"The fire is out. We've removed the four dead subjects from the pedestrian path and are running their vitals through the database. The ones inside the truck will be harder, but we're working on it. But Mr. President, even if we can learn their identities, whoever hired these people wouldn't leave a trail behind. There will be cutouts.*

Intermediaries. We can probably trace it back eventually, but not, I don't think —"

"Not within a matter of hours. I understand. It's still worth the effort. And do it discreetly."

"You want me to keep Secretary Haber in the dark about this?"

Liz is still new to the job, so she doesn't consider herself on a first-name basis with the other members of my national security team, including Sam Haber, from Homeland Security.

"Sam can know that you're tracking these people. He'd expect that, at any rate. But don't report your findings to anybody but me or Carolyn. If he asks — if anyone else asks — your answer is, 'We don't have anything yet.' Okay?"

"Mr. President, may I speak freely?"

"Always, Liz. I'd be upset with you if you didn't." There is nothing I value more in subordinates than their willingness to tell me I'm wrong, to challenge me, to sharpen my decision making. Surrounding yourself with sycophants and bootlickers is the surest route to failure.

"Why, sir? Why wouldn't we coordinate this as openly as possible? We're more effective if one hand talks to the other. If 9/11 taught us anything, it's that."

I look at Carolyn's face on the split screen. She shrugs in response, agreeing with me that it's worth telling the acting director.

"The code word 'Dark Ages,' Liz. Only eight people in the world know that code word besides me. It's never been written down, on my order. It's never been repeated, outside our circle, on my order. Right?"

"Yes, of course, sir."

"Even the task force of technicians trying to locate and neutralize the virus, the Imminent Threat Response Team—not even they know 'Dark Ages,' right?"

"Correct, sir. Only the eight of us and you."

"One of those eight people leaked it to the Sons of Jihad," I say.

A pause as the acting director takes that in.

"Which means," I say, "that the person did more than leak."

"Yes, sir."

"Four days ago," I say, "Monday, a woman whispered those words into my daughter's ear in Paris, to relay to me. That woman is Nina—the one shot at the stadium by the sniper."

"My God."

"She approached my daughter and told her to say 'Dark Ages' to me and to tell me that I was running out of time and that she'd meet me Friday night."

The acting director's chin rises slightly as she processes the information.

"Mr. President…I'm one of those eight," she says. *"How do you rule me out?"*

Good for her. "Before I tapped you as acting director, ten days ago, you weren't in the loop. Whatever outside actor is doing this to us, whoever among our eight is helping them—this would have taken time to develop. It wouldn't happen overnight."

"So I'm not the traitor," she says, *"because I wouldn't have had time."*

"The timing rules you out, yes. So besides you, Carolyn, and me, that leaves six people, Liz. Six people who could be our Benedict Arnold."

"Have you considered that one of those six might have told a spouse or friend who sold the information? They'd be violating your directive of confidentiality, but still…"

"I have considered that, yes. But whoever's betraying us did more than leak a code word. They're a part of this. Nobody's spouse or friend would have the kind of access and resources to do that. They'd need the government official."

"So it's one of our six."

"It's one of our six," I say in agreement. "So you understand, Liz, that you're the only one we can fully trust."

CHAPTER
39

❖

When I finish with Acting Director Greenfield, Carolyn tells me my next call is
ready.

A moment later, after some fuzz and screen
garble, the image of a man, thick-necked and
deadly serious, with a manicured beard and bald
head, comes onto the screen. The bags underneath his eyes are a testament not to his age but
to the week he's had.

"Mr....President," he says. His English is perfect,
his foreign accent almost imperceptible.

"David, good to see you."

*"It's good to see you as well, Mr. President. Given the
events of the last few hours, that statement is more than
a mere pleasantry."*

True enough. "The woman is dead, David. Did
you know that?"

"It is what we assumed."

"But the man is with me," I say. "He calls himself Augie."

"He told you his name is Augie?"

"He did. Is that the truth? Did you get a shot of his face?"

After I received the ticket to the Nationals game from Nina, I called David and told him where I'd be sitting in the left-field stands. He had to scramble, but his team got tickets to the game and positioned themselves so they could get an image of Augie's face that they could run through facial-recognition software.

"We were able to get a reliable image, yes, in spite of the baseball cap he wore. We believe that the person sitting next to you at the baseball game is Augustas Koslenko. Born in 1996 in Sloviansk, in the Donetsk province, in eastern Ukraine."

"Donetsk? That's interesting."

"We thought so as well. His mother is Lithuanian. His father is Ukrainian, a laborer in a machine factory. No political affiliation or activism that we know of."

"What about Augie himself?"

"He left Ukraine in middle school. He was a mathematics prodigy, a genius. He attended boarding school in eastern Turkey on a scholarship. We believe—we assume that this is where he met Suliman Cindoruk.

263

Before then, we know of nothing he did or said in the way of activism of any kind."

"But he's the real article, you're saying. He was part of the Sons of Jihad."

"Yes, Mr. President. But I am not confident I would use the past tense."

I'm not, either. I'm not confident of anything when it comes to Augie. I don't know what he wants or why he's doing this. Now, at least, I know he gave me his real name, but if he's as smart as we think he is, he probably figured I'd learn his identity anyway. And if his whole basis for legitimacy is that he was affiliated with the Sons of Jihad, he'd *want* me to know his name, he'd want me to confirm that fact. So I'm no further than I was before with Augie.

"He said he had a falling-out with the SOJ."

"He said. You've obviously considered the possibility that he is still in their employ? That he is doing their bidding?"

I shrug. "Sure, of course, but—to what end? He could have killed me at the stadium."

"True."

"And somebody wants him dead."

"Apparently so. Or they want you to believe that, Mr. President."

"Well, David—if that's a fake, it's a pretty damn good fake. I don't know how much your people saw outside the stadium, and I assume you didn't see anything on the bridge. They weren't pretending. We could have easily died either time."

"I do not doubt what you are saying, Mr. President. I only offer the thought that you should remain open to other possibilities. In my experience, these individuals are brilliant tacticians. We must constantly reassess our position and thinking."

It's a good reminder.

"Tell me what you're hearing out there," I say.

David is quiet for a moment, measuring his words. *"We are hearing talk of America being brought to its knees. We are hearing doomsday prophecies. The end of days. We often hear such things in generic chatter from the jihadists, of course—that the Great Satan's day will come, the time is near—but..."*

"But what?"

"But we have never heard a firm date placed on such things. And what we are hearing now is that it will happen tomorrow. Saturday, they are saying."

I take a breath. Saturday is less than two hours away.

"Who's behind this, David?" I ask.

"We cannot know for sure, Mr. President. Suliman Cindoruk answers to no official state actor, as you know. We are hearing a multitude of suspects. The usual suspects, I suppose you would say. ISIS. North Korea.

China. My country. Even your country—they say the event will be propaganda, a self-created crisis to justify military retaliation, typical conspiracy-theory nonsense."

"Your best guess?" I say. But I'm relatively sure I know the answer. The tactical spread of chatter, the communication of clandestine information that in fact was intended all along to be overheard by intelligence intercepts. Counterespionage at its most devious, tradecraft at its finest. It bears the mark of one country over all others.

David Guralnick, the director of Israel's Institute for Intelligence and Special Operations—Mossad—takes a deep breath. For dramatic measure, the screen cuts in and out before his face becomes clear again.

"Our best guess is Russia," he says.

CHAPTER
40

❖

I click off the transmission with the director of
Mossad and gather my thoughts before I talk
to Augie. There are many ways to play this, but I
have no time for subtlety.

Saturday, David said. Ninety minutes away.

I push myself out of the chair and turn for
the door when a wave of vertigo strikes me, like
someone is playing spin the bottle with my internal compass. I grab hold of the desk for balance
and measure my breaths. I reach into my pocket
for my pills. I need my pills.

But my pills are gone. There are no more in my
pocket, and the rest were left behind in the bag,
in the sedan in the stadium parking lot.

"Damn it." I dial Carolyn on my phone. "Carrie, I need more steroids. I don't have any more

at the White House, and I lost the bottle I had. Call Dr. Lane. Maybe she has some ex—"

"I'll make it happen, Mr. President."

"Great." I click off and leave the soundproofed office, walking carefully down the hall toward the rec room, near the staircase. Augie is sitting on the couch, looking to all appearances like an ordinary scraggly teenager lounging in front of the television.

But he's neither a teenager nor ordinary.

The mounted television he's watching is set to cable news, coverage of the assassination attempt on King Saad ibn Saud of Saudi Arabia and the growing unrest in Honduras.

"Augie," I say. "Stand up."

He does what I ask, facing me.

"Who attacked us?" I ask.

He pushes his hair out of his face, shrugs. "I do not know."

"Do better than that. Let's start with who sent you. You said you no longer see eye to eye with Suliman Cindoruk and the Sons of Jihad."

"Yes, that is true. I do not."

"So who sent you?"

"Nobody sent us. We came of our own will."

"Why?"

"Is it not obvious?"

I grab a fistful of his shirt. "Augie, a lot of people died tonight. Including someone you cared about and two Secret Service agents *I* cared about, men who left young families behind. So start answering my—"

"We came to stop it," he says, breaking free of my grip.

"To stop Dark Ages? But—why?"

He shakes his head, hiccups a bitter chuckle. "Do you mean, what do I stand to gain? What is…in it for me?"

"That's what I mean," I say. "You didn't want to tell me before. Tell me now. What does a kid from Donetsk want from the United States?"

Augie draws back, surprised for only a moment. Not that surprised at all, really. "That did not take long."

"Are you part of the pro-Russian camp or the pro-Ukraine camp? They have lots of both in Donetsk, last I checked."

"Yes? And when was the last time you checked, Mr. President?" His face changing color, fuming. "When it suited your purposes, that's when. This," he says, shaking his finger at me, "this is the difference between you and me. I want nothing from you, that's what I want. I want…to not destroy a nation full of millions of people. Is that not enough?"

Is it that simple? That Augie and his partner

were simply trying to do the right thing? These days, it's never your first instinct to believe that.

I'm not sure I do now, either. I don't know what to believe.

"But you created Dark Ages," I say.

He shakes his head. "Suli, Nina, and I created it. But Nina was the real inspiration, the driving force. Without her, we never could have created it. I helped with the coding and particularly with the implementation."

"Nina? That's her real name?"

"Yes."

"They created it, and you infiltrated our systems."

"More or less, yes."

"And you can stop it?"

He shrugs. "This I do not know."

"What?" I grab him by the shoulder, as if shaking him will produce a different answer. "You said you could, Augie. You said that before."

"I did, yes." He nods, looks at me with shiny eyes. "Nina was alive before."

I release him, walk over to the wall, and pound my fist against it. It's always one step forward, two steps back.

I take a deep breath. What Augie's saying makes sense. Nina was the superstar. That's why she was the sniper's first target. From a practical standpoint, it would have made more sense to shoot Augie first, because he was mobile, and then go for Nina, who was seated in a parked car. Nina was clearly the highest priority.

"I will do my best to help," he says.

"Okay, well, who attacked us?" I ask for the second time. "Can you at least help me with that?"

"Mr. President," he says, "the Sons of Jihad is not a…democracy. This kind of information Suli would not have shared with me. I can only tell you two things. One, obviously, is that Suli knows that Nina and I broke away from him, and he clearly tracked us somehow to the United States."

"Obviously," I say.

"And the second thing," he says, "is that as far as I am aware, Suli's capabilities are limited to computers. He is formidable. He can do considerable damage, as you well know. But he does not have at his disposal trained mercenaries."

I put my hand against the wall. "Meaning…"

"Meaning he is working with someone else," says Augie. "A nation-state, some country that wishes to bring the United States to its knees."

"And one that compromised someone in my inner circle," I add.

CHAPTER
41

❖

O kay, Augie, next question," I say. "What does Suliman want? He must want something. Or they—whoever's working with him. What do they want?"

Augie cocks his head. "Why do you say this?"

"Why do I say that? Well, why else would they have shown us the virus in advance?" I put out my hand. "Augie, two weeks ago, a virus suddenly popped up on our systems inside the Pentagon. It appeared, then it disappeared. You know this. You said it to me yourself at the baseball stadium. It suddenly appeared and then just as suddenly disappeared"—I snap my fingers—"like that."

"A peekaboo."

"A peekaboo, yes, that's what my experts called it. A peekaboo. Without any warning, without triggering any of our state-of-the-art security alerts, suddenly this virus flashed all over our internal Defense Department systems then disappeared just as quickly, without a trace. That's how this whole thing started. We called it Dark Ages and formed a task force. Our best cyberspecialists have been working around the clock trying to find it, trying to stop it, but they can't."

Augie nods. "And it terrifies you."

"Of course it does."

"Because it infiltrated your system without any warning and evaporated into thin air just as quickly. You realize that it might come back again, or it might never have left. And you have no idea what it's capable of doing to your systems."

"All those things, yes," I say. "But there was a reason for this sneak preview, this peekaboo. If whoever did this simply wanted to take down our systems, they would've just done it. They wouldn't have *warned* us first. You only warn someone first if you want something, if you're going to make a ransom demand."

"Ransomware," he says. "Yes, I understand your reasoning. When you saw the warning, you expected it to be followed by a demand of some kind."

"Right."

"Ah, so this—this is why you made that phone call to Suli." Augie nods. "To ask him what his demand was."

"Yes. He was trying to get my attention. So I let him know he did. I wanted to hear his demand without directly asking him for it, without intimating that the United States would give in to blackmail."

"But he did not give you a demand."

"No, he didn't," I say. "He played coy. He seemed…at a loss for words. Like he hadn't expected my call. Oh, he made disparaging comments about my country, the usual type of stuff—but no demand. No acknowledgment of the peekaboo. So all I could do was threaten him. I told him that if his virus hurt our country, I'd come after him with every resource I could muster."

"It must have seemed like…an odd conversation."

"It was," I said in agreement. "My tech people were certain this was the work of the SOJ. And they said the peekaboo was no glitch; it was intentional. So where was the ransom demand? Why would he go to the trouble of the peekaboo without demanding anything?"

Augie nods. "And then Nina came along. You thought she was going to deliver the ransom demand."

"I did. You or Nina. So?" I throw up my hands, exasperation getting the better of me. "Where the hell is the goddamn ransom demand?"

Augie draws a deep breath. "There is not going to be a ransom demand," he says.

"There's—why not? Then why'd they send the warning?"

"Mr. President, the Sons of Jihad did not send that peekaboo," he says. "And whoever may be sponsoring the Sons of Jihad did not send it, either."

I stare at him. It takes me a moment. Eventually I get there.

"You sent it," I say.

"Nina and I, yes. To warn you," he says. "So you could start preparing mitigation protocols. And so that when Nina and I contacted you, you would take us seriously. Suliman knew nothing of this. The last thing he would ever do is give you an early warning of this virus."

I work this over. Augie and Nina sent the early warning to us two weeks ago. And then, more than a week later, Nina found Lilly in Paris and whispered the magic words to her.

They came to warn me. To help me.

That's the good news.

The bad news? That means that Suliman Cindoruk and the foreign agent who is behind him never wanted the United States to know about it in advance.

They aren't going to ask for something. They aren't seeking a change in our foreign policy. They don't want prisoners released. They don't want money.

They aren't going to demand a ransom at all.

They're just going to detonate the virus.

They want to destroy us.

CHAPTER
42

❖

H ow long do we have?" I ask Augie. "When does the virus detonate?"

"Saturday in America," he says. "This is all I know."

The same thing the director of Mossad said.

"Then we have to go right now," I say, rushing past Augie, grabbing his arm.

"Go where?"

"I'll tell you in the—"

I turn too quickly, feeling like I overspun the room, a loss of balance, a sharp pain in my ribs, wood stabbing me—the edge of the couch—the ceiling flashing before my eyes and spinning—

I take a step forward, but something doesn't work, my leg buckling, the ground not where it's supposed to be—everything sideways—

"Mr. President!" Jacobson, his arms under me, catching me, my face only inches from the carpet.

"Dr. Lane," I whisper, reaching into my pocket. The room dancing around me.

"Call…Carolyn," I manage. I hold up my phone, weaving back and forth, before Jacobson takes it from my hand. "She knows…what to do…"

"Ms. Brock!" Jacobson shouts into the phone. Instructions given, orders received, all in a faint echo, not Jacobson's normal voice, in combat mode.

Not now. It can't be now.

"He's gonna be okay, right?"

"How soon?"

Saturday in America. Saturday in America will be very soon.

Mushroom cloud. Searing red heat sweeping the countryside. Where is our leader? Where is the president?

"Not…now…"

"Tell her to hurry!"

We have no ability to respond, Mr. President.

They disabled our systems, Mr. President.

What are we going to do, Mr. President?

What are you going to do, Mr. President?

"Stay down, sir. Help is on the way."

I'm not ready. Not yet.

No, Rachel, I'm not ready to join you, not yet.

Saturday in America.

Silence, the soft ring of dead, endless, shapeless space.

"Where the hell is the doctor?"

And bright light.

SATURDAY IN
AMERICA

CHAPTER
43

❖

V ice President Katherine Brandt opens her eyes, snatched from the fog of a dream. She hears the sound again, knuckles rapping on her bedroom door.

The door parts slightly, and the knock is louder. The face of Peter Evian, her chief of staff, peering through her door. "Sorry to wake you, Madam Vice President," he says.

She recognizes nothing around her for a moment, takes a second to get her bearings. She is in the subbasement, sleeping alone, though *alone* is a relative term, considering that agents are standing outside the door of this small bedroom.

She reaches for her phone on the nightstand and checks the time: 1:03 a.m.

"Yes, Peter, come in." She speaks calmly. Always

be ready. She says it to herself every day. Because it could happen any time, day or night, without notice. A bullet. An aneurysm. A heart attack. Such is the life of a vice president.

She sits up in bed. Peter, dressed in a shirt and tie as always, walks in and hands her his phone, open to a website, a newspaper article.

The headline: THE PRESIDENT IS MISSING.

Sources at the White House, says the article, confirm that the president is not at the White House. And more to the point, they don't know *where* he is.

The speculation is all over the place, ranging from plausible to implausible to downright ridiculous: a return of his blood disease, and he's gravely ill. He left town to prepare for the select committee hearings. He's huddling with close aides to prepare a resignation speech. He's running off with ill-gotten money from Suliman Cindoruk, fleeing the country to avoid prosecution.

The president and vice president are secure, the official statement said last night, after the explosion on the bridge, the shoot-out at Nationals Park. That was it. That was probably the right way to go. Tell everyone their leaders are safe and sound, but don't specify their precise location. Nobody would expect or demand otherwise.

But this article is saying that his own people don't know where he is.

She doesn't, either.

"I need Carolyn Brock," she says.

CHAPTER
44

❖

C arolyn Brock, notes the vice president, is wearing the same suit as she was wearing yesterday. As if that weren't enough, her blood-shot eyes confirm her lack of sleep.

It seems the indefatigable chief of staff never went home last night.

They sit inside a conference room in the operations center below the White House, at opposite ends of a long table. The vice president would have preferred to hold the meeting in her private office in the West Wing, but she was sent underground last night as part of the continuity-of-government protocol, and she sees no reason to rock that boat right now.

"Where's Alex Trimble?" she asks.

"He's not available, Madam Vice President."

Her eyes narrow. That squint, her aides used to tell her, was what everyone feared the most, her steely but silent way of communicating her unhappiness with an answer.

"That's it? He's 'not available'?"

"Yes, ma'am."

Her blood boils. Technically, Katherine Brandt is the second-most-powerful person in the country. Everyone treats her as such, at least officially. She must admit that, however much she resented Jon Duncan for leapfrogging her and snatching away the nomination that was rightfully hers, and however hard she had to bite her tongue and accept her place as second fiddle, the president has given her the role he promised, seeking her input, giving her a seat at the table for all major decisions. Duncan has kept up his end of the bargain.

Still, they both know that Carolyn is the one with the real power in this room.

"Where's the president, Carolyn?"

Carolyn opens her hands, ever the diplomat. Brandt can't resist a grudging respect for the chief of staff, who has twisted arms in Congress, kept the trains running on time, and held the West Wing staff in line, all in service of the president's agenda. Back when Carolyn was in Congress herself, before that unfortunate stumble she had on a live mike, a lot of people had her pegged as a future Speaker, maybe even a presidential candidate. Well spoken, well prepared, quick on her feet, a solid campaigner, attractive but not beauty-queen gorgeous—the perpetual tightrope women in politics must walk—Carolyn could have been one of the best.

"I asked you where the president is, Carolyn."

"I can't answer that, Madam Vice President."

"Can't or won't?" The vice president flips her hand. "Do *you* know where he is? Can you tell me *that* much?"

"I know where he is, ma'am."

"Is he…" She shakes her head. "Is he okay? Is he secure?"

Carolyn's head leans to one side. "He's with the Secret Service, if that's what—"

"Oh, Jesus *Christ*, Carolyn, can't you give me a straight answer?"

They lock eyes for a moment. Carolyn Brock is no pushover. And her loyalty to the president transcends all else. If she has to take a few bullets for the man, she'll do it.

"I am not authorized to tell you where he is," she says.

"The president said that. He said you can't tell me."

"The order wasn't specific to you, of course, ma'am."

"But it includes me."

"I can't give you the information you want, Madam Vice President."

The vice president slams her hands down on the table, pushes herself out of her chair. "Since when," she says after a moment, "does the president go into hiding from *us?*"

Carolyn stands, too, and they stare at each other again. She doesn't expect Carolyn to respond, and Carolyn doesn't disappoint her. Most people would wilt under the gaze, under the discomfort of silence, but Brandt is pretty sure that Carolyn will stare back at her all night if that's what it takes.

"Is there anything else, Madam Vice President?" That same cool efficiency in her voice, which only unnerves the vice president all the more.

"Why are we on lockdown?" she asks.

"The violence last night," says Carolyn. "Just a precau—"

"No," she says. "The violence last night was an FBI and Secret Service investigation, right? A counterfeiting investigation? That's what was announced publicly, at least."

The chief of staff doesn't speak, doesn't move. That story always sounded bogus to Brandt.

"That violence—it might require a brief lockdown initially," she continues. "A few minutes, an hour, while we sort it all out. But I've been down here all night. Am I supposed to remain down here?"

"For the time being, yes, ma'am."

She walks toward Carolyn and stops just short. "Then don't tell me it's because of the violence in the capital last night. Tell me why we're *really* on lockdown. Tell me why we're in a continuity-of-government protocol. Tell me why the president fears for his life right now."

Carolyn blinks hard a few times but otherwise remains stoic. "Ma'am, I was given a direct order by the president for a lockdown, for COG protocol. It's not my place to question that order. It's not my place to ask why. And it's not—" She looks away, curls her lips inside her mouth.

"And it's not *my* place, either—is that what you were going to say, Carolyn?"

Carolyn turns and looks her in the eye. "Yes, ma'am. That's what I was going to say."

The vice president slowly nods, doing a slow burn.

"Is this about impeachment?" she asks, though she couldn't imagine how.

"No, ma'am."

"Is this a matter of national security?"

Carolyn doesn't answer, makes a point of remaining still.

"Is this about Dark Ages?"

Carolyn flinches but doesn't, won't, answer that question.

"Well, Ms. Brock," she says, "I may not be president—"

Yet.

"—but I *am* the vice president. I don't take orders from you. And I haven't heard a lockdown order from the president. He knows how to reach me. I'm in the phone book. Anytime he wants to ring me and tell me what the *hell* is going on."

She turns and heads for the door.

"Where are you going?" Carolyn asks, her voice different, stronger, less deferential.

"Where do you *think* I'm going? I have a full day. Including an interview with *Meet the Press,* whose first question I'm sure will be 'Where's the president?'"

And more important, and before that: the meeting she scheduled last night, after receiving the phone call in her personal residence. It could be one of the most interesting meetings of her life.

"You aren't leaving the operations center."

The vice president stops at the doorway. She turns to face the White House chief of staff, who just spoke to her in a way that nobody ever has since the election—since long before that, actually. "Ex*cuse* me?"

"You heard what I said." The chief of staff is done, apparently, with any semblance of deference. "The president wants you in the operations center."

"And *you* hear *me*, you unelected flunky. I only take orders from the president. Until I hear from him, I'll be in my office in the West Wing."

She walks out of the room into the hallway, where her chief of staff, Peter Evian, looks up from his phone.

"What's happening?" he asks, keeping pace with her.

"I'll tell you what's *not* happening," she says. "I'm not going down with this ship."

CHAPTER
45

❖

The calm before the storm.

The calm, that is, not for him but for them, for his people, his small crew of computer geniuses, who've spent the last twelve hours living the good life. Fondling women who normally would never bother to glance in their direction, who screwed them ten different ways, showed them delights they'd never experienced in their young lives. Drinking Champagne from bottles that typically reach the lips of only the world's elite. Feasting on a smorgasbord of caviar and paté and lobster and filet mignon.

They are sleeping now, all of them, the last of them retiring only an hour ago. None of them will be up before noon. None of them will be of any use today.

That's okay. They've done their part.

Suliman Cindoruk sits on the penthouse terrace, cigarette burning between his fingers, smartphones and laptops and coffee on the table next to him, pulling apart a croissant as he lifts his face into the morning sunlight.

Enjoy this tranquil morning, he reminds himself. *Because when the sun rises over the river Spree this time tomorrow, there will be no peace.*

He puts his breakfast to the side. He can't find peace himself. Can't bring himself to eat, the acid swimming in his stomach.

He pulls over his laptop, refreshes the screen, scrolls through the top news online.

The lead story: the aborted plot to assassinate King Saad ibn Saud of Saudi Arabia and the dozens of arrests and detentions of suspects in its wake. The possible motives, according to the newswires and the supposedly "informed" pundits who fill the cable channels: The new king's pro-democracy reforms. His liberalization of women's rights. His hard-line stance against Iran. Saudi involvement in the civil war in Yemen.

Story number two: the events in Washington last night, the firefight and explosion on the bridge, the shoot-out at the stadium, the temporary lockdown of the White House. Not terrorism, the federal authorities said. No, it was all part of a counterfeiting investigation conducted jointly by the FBI and the Treasury Department. So far, the media seems to be buying it, only a few hours into the story.

And the blackout at the stadium immediately preceding the shoot-out—a coincidence? Yes, say the federal authorities. Just mere happenstance that a stadium full of people, and everyone within a quarter-mile radius, happened to experience a massive power outage just a heartbeat or two before federal agents and counterfeiters lit up Capitol Street as if they were reenacting the famous gunfight at the O.K. Corral.

President Duncan must know that this ludicrous story will not hold forever. But he probably doesn't care. The president is just buying time.

But he doesn't know how much time he has.

One of Suli's phones buzzes. The burner. The text message traveled around the globe before reaching him, through anonymous proxies, pinging remote servers in a dozen different countries. Someone trying to trace the text message would land anywhere from Sydney, Australia, to Nairobi, Kenya, to Montevideo, Uruguay.

Confirm we are on schedule, the message reads.

He smirks. As if they even know what the schedule is.

He writes back: Confirm Alpha is dead.

"Alpha," meaning Nina.

In all the stories online about the violence last night at the baseball stadium, the shoot-out and explosion on the bridge between the capital and Virginia, there was no mention of a dead woman.

He hits Send, waits while the text message travels its circuitous route.

A flutter runs through him. The sting of betrayal, Nina's betrayal. And loss, too. Perhaps even he didn't fully appreciate his feelings for her. Her revolutionary mind. Her hard, agile body. Her voracious appetite for exploration, in the world of cyberwarfare and in the bedroom. The hours and days and weeks they spent collaborating, challenging each other, feeding each other ideas, offering up and shooting down hypotheses, trials and errors, huddling before a laptop, theorizing over a glass of wine or naked in bed.

Before she lost interest in him romantically. That he could live with. He had no intention of remaining with one woman. But he could never understand how she could take up with Augie, of all people, the homely troll.

Stop. He touches his eyes. There's no point.

The reply comes through:

We are told Alpha is confirmed dead.

That's not quite the same thing as confirmation. But they've assured him of the professionalism and competence of the team they dispatched to America, and he has no choice but to believe them.

Suli sends back: If Alpha is dead, we are on schedule.

The response comes so quickly that Suli assumes it crossed paths with his message:

Beta is confirmed alive and in custody.

"Beta," meaning Augie. So he made it. He's with the Americans.

Suli can't help but smile.

Another message, so soon after the last one. They are nervous.

Confirm we are on schedule in light of this development.

He answers quickly: Confirmed. On schedule.

They think they know the schedule for the detonation of the virus. They don't.

Neither does Suli at this point. It's now entirely in Augie's hands.

Whether he realizes it or not.

CHAPTER
46

❖

"...need to wake him."

"He'll wake up when he wakes up."

"My wife says to wake him up."

Far above me, the surface of the water. Sunlight shimmering on the rippling waves.

Swimming toward it, my arms flailing, my legs kicking.

A rush of air into my lungs, and the light so bright, searing my eyes—

I blink, several times, and squint into the light on my face, my eyes slowly coming into focus.

Focus on Augie, sitting on the couch, wearing shackles on his wrists and ankles, his eyes dark and heavy.

Floating, time meaning nothing, as I watch his eyes narrowed in concentration, his lips moving slightly.

Who are you, Augustas Koslenko? Can I trust you?
I have no choice. It's you or nothing.

His wrist turning slightly, almost imperceptibly. Not looking at the iron shackle. Looking at his watch.

His watch.

"What time...what day..." I start forward, stopped by pain in my neck and back, an IV protruding from my arm, the tube strung along behind me.

"He's awake, he's awake!" The voice of Carolyn's husband, Morty.

"Mr. President, it's Dr. Lane." Her hand on my shoulder. Her face coming between me and the light. "We performed a platelet transfusion. You're doing well. It's 3:45 in the morning, Saturday morning. You've been out for a little over four hours."

"We have to..." I start up again, leaning forward, feeling something under me, some kind of a cushion.

Dr. Lane presses down gently on my shoulder. "Easy now. Do you know where you are?"

I try to shake out the cobwebs. I'm off balance, but I definitely know where I am and what I'm facing.

"I have to go, Doctor. There's no time. Take out this IV."

"Whoa. Hold on."

"Take out the IV or I will. Morty," I say, seeing him with his phone to his ear. "Is that Carrie?"

"Stop!" Dr. Lane says to me, the smile gone. "Forget Morty for one minute. Give me sixty seconds and listen to me for once."

I take a breath. "Sixty seconds," I say. "Go."

"Your chief of staff has explained that you can't stay here, that you have somewhere to be. I can't stop you. But I *can* go with you."

"No," I say. "Not an option."

She works her jaw. "Same thing your chief of staff said. This IV," she says. "Take it with you in the car. Finish the bag. Your agent, Agent..."

"Jacobson," he calls out.

"Yes. He says he has some wound-control training from his time with the Navy SEALs. He can remove the IV when it's done."

"Fine," I say, leaning forward, feeling like I've been kicked in the head six or eight times.

She pushes me back. "My sixty seconds isn't up yet." She leans in closer. "You should be on your back for the next twenty-four hours. I know you won't do that. But you must limit your physical exertion as much as possible. Sit, don't stand. Walk, don't jog or run."

"I understand." I hold out my right hand, wiggle my fingers. "Morty, give me Carolyn."

"Yes, sir."

Morty places the phone in my hand. I put it to my ear. "Carrie, it's going to be today. Get word to our entire team. This is my formal acknowledgment that we are to move to stage 2."

It's all I need to say to get us ready for what we are about to face. Under "normal" disaster scenarios, at least those occurring after 1959, I would reference the DEFCON levels, either for all military systems worldwide or for selected commands. This is different—we are facing a crisis never conceived of in the fifties, and pieces must be set in motion in ways far different from what we would do during a conventional nuclear attack. Carrie knows exactly what stage 2 means, partly because we've been at stage 1 for two weeks.

Nothing from the other end but the sound of Carrie's breath.

"Mr. President," she says, *"it may have already started."*

I listen, for two of the quickest—and longest—minutes of my life.

"Alex," I call out. "Forget driving. Get us on Marine One."

CHAPTER
47

❖

J acobson drives. Alex sits next to me in the backseat of the SUV, the IV bag perched between us. Augie sits across from me.

On my lap is a computer, open to a video. The video is satellite footage, looking down on a city block, an industrial area in Los Angeles. Most of the block is consumed by one large structure, complete with smokestacks, some kind of large factory.

Everything is dark. The time stamp in the corner of the screen shows 02:07—just past two in the morning, about two hours ago.

And then fireballs of orange flame explode through the roof and the side windows, rocking and ultimately caving in the side of the industrial plant. The entire city block disappears in a cloud of black-and-orange smoke.

I pause the video and click on the box in the corner of the screen.

The box opens onto the full screen, which itself is split three ways. In the center screen is Carolyn, from the White House. To her left is acting FBI director Elizabeth Greenfield. To Carolyn's right is Sam Haber, secretary of homeland security.

I'm wearing headphones plugged into the laptop, so the conversation from their end will reach only my ears. I want to hear this first, in full, without Augie overhearing.

"Okay, I saw it," I say. "Start at the start." My voice is scratchy as I shake off the hangover from the treatment and try to focus.

"Mr. President," says Sam Haber. *"The explosion was about two hours ago. The blaze has been enormous, as you can imagine. They're still trying to get it under control."*

"Tell me about the company," I say.

"Sir, it's a defense contractor. They're one of the Defense Department's largest contractors. They have a number of sites around Los Angeles County."

"What's special about this one?"

"Sir, this plant builds reconnaissance aircraft."

I'm not making the connection. A defense contractor? Recon planes?

"Casualties?" I ask.

"We believe in the tens, not the hundreds. It was the

middle of the night, so basically just security personnel. Too soon to know for sure."

"Cause?" I ask, careful to limit my side of the conversation.

"Sir, all we can say with certainty is a gas explosion. Which doesn't automatically suggest a hostile actor. Gas explosions happen, obviously."

I look up at Augie, who is watching me. He blinks and looks away.

"There's a reason I'm hearing about this," I say.

"Sir, that's correct. The company reached out to Defense. Their technicians insist that something, somehow, reset the pump speeds and valve settings. Sabotage, in other words, that produced pressures that overwhelmed the joints and welds. But it wasn't done manually, there in person. Those places have tighter security than government offices."

"Remotely," I say.

"Sir, that's correct. They think it was done remotely. But we can't yet say for certain."

But I bet I know who could. I peek over at Augie, who glances at his watch, unaware that I'm watching him.

"Suspects?" I ask.

"Nothing obvious to us yet," Sam says. *"We have ICS-CERT looking into it."*

He's referring to DHS's cyber-emergency response team for industrial control systems.

"*But we know this much, sir. The Chinese tried to hack into our gas pipeline systems back in 2011, 2012,*" he says. "*Maybe this means they succeeded. If they ex-filtrated credentials from a system user, they could do whatever they wanted inside the system.*"

The Chinese. Maybe.

"I guess the number one question is, do we think…"

I glance at Augie, who is looking out the window.

Carolyn says, "*Could this be Dark Ages?*" She understands my reluctance to say too much in front of Augie. Once again, she's right there with me, reading my thoughts, finishing my sentence so Augie won't hear it.

I'm asking the question because I want to know.

But I'm also asking because I want to hear the secretary of homeland security's response. Sam is one of the circle of eight who know about Dark Ages. Carolyn didn't leak it. Liz Greenfield didn't leak it. I've ruled out two of the eight.

Sam Haber is one of the six I haven't ruled out.

Sam lets out air, shakes his head, like it feels wrong to him. "*Well, Mr. President, Ms. Brock just informed me that we have reason to believe that today is the day.*"

"Correct," I say.

"*She didn't tell me our source for that information.*"

"Correct," I repeat. My way of saying, *And we're not going to tell you the source, Sam.*

He waits a beat and realizes that more will not be forthcoming. Cocks his head, but otherwise doesn't respond. *"All right, well, sir, if that's the case, then I acknowledge that the timing is suspect. But still, I must tell you that this feels different. Dark Ages is malware, a virus we discovered."*

Well, we didn't exactly discover it. They— Augie and Nina—showed it to us. But Sam doesn't know that. He doesn't know that Augie even exists.

Or does he?

"But this—this seems to be a more conventional method, like spear-phishing," he continues. *"Trying to compromise a company executive, lulling him into opening an attachment on an e-mail or clicking on a link, which installs a malicious code that lets the hacker gain access to credentials and all kinds of sensitive information. Once you exfiltrate credentials and have that kind of access, you could do all sorts of things—like what happened here."*

"But how do we know that's different from Dark Ages?" Carolyn presses. *"We can't say that Dark Ages didn't come from spear-phishing. We have no idea how the virus got on the system."*

"You're correct. I can't rule it out yet. It's only been a couple of hours. We'll get right to work on it. We'll get an answer ASAP."

ASAP has a new meaning today.

"*Mr. President,*" says Sam, "*we've reached out to all the gas companies about pipeline security. ICS-CERT is working with them on emergency mitigation protocols. We're hopeful we can stop this from happening again.*"

"Mr. President." Alex nudges me. Our SUV has reached the helipad in eastern Virginia, the majestic green-and-white Marine helicopter illuminated only by the lights around the pad.

"Sam, I'm going to let you get back to it for now," I say. "Keep Carolyn and Liz in the loop at all times. And only them. Is that clear?"

"*Yes, sir. I'm signing off.*"

Sam's third of the screen disappears. The screen adjusts, and Carolyn and Liz appear in larger images.

I turn to Alex. "Get Augie onto Marine One. I'll be right there."

I wait for Alex and Augie to leave the SUV. Then I turn to Carolyn and Liz.

I say, "Why would they want to blow up a defense contractor's airplane plant?"

CHAPTER
48

❖

"I have no idea," says Augie when I ask him the same question.

We are sitting inside Marine One, seated across from each other in lush, cream-colored leather seats, as the helicopter lifts silently into the air.

"I am not aware of any such action," he says. "I played no part in such a thing."

"Hacking into a pipeline system. Or a defense contractor's system. You never did things like that?"

"Mr. President, if we are speaking generally, then yes, we have done such things. You are talking about spear-phishing, you said?"

"Yes."

"Then yes, we have done these things. The

Chinese perfected the art initially. They attempted to hack into your gas pipeline systems, did they not?"

The same point Sam Haber made.

"This is a matter of public knowledge, what the Chinese did," says Augie. "But we did not do that here. Or I should say, *I* did not do that."

"Is Suliman Cindoruk capable of hacking into our pipelines without you?"

"Of course he is. He has a team of such people. I would say that I was probably the most advanced, but we are not speaking of something that is difficult. Anyone can load a virus onto an e-mail and then hope that the target clicks on it."

The Wild, Wild West, this cyberterrorism. This new, scary frontier. Anyone sitting on a couch in his underwear could undermine the security of a nation.

"You never heard anything about Los Angeles."

"No."

I sit back in my chair. "So you don't know anything about this."

"I do not," he says. "And I cannot understand what would be to gain from blowing up a company that builds airplanes for you."

I can't disagree. What purpose would it serve to destroy a manufacturing plant?

There has to be something more to this.

"Okay. Okay, Augie." I rub my eyes, fighting off exhaustion from the platelet transfusion, fighting off exasperation at constantly not knowing what is coming next. "So tell me. Tell me how you infiltrated our systems, and tell me what damage it will cause."

Finally we have the chance. Since we first met at the stadium, what with dodging bullets and escaping from car ambushes and my collapsing near midnight, we haven't had the chance to lock this down.

"I can assure you that our efforts were not so rudimentary as sneaking viruses into e-mails and hoping someone would open them," he says. "And I can assure you that your code word 'Dark Ages' is an appropriate one."

CHAPTER
49

❖

I force down some coffee on Marine One, hoping to snap out of the medication-induced fog. I have to be on my game, 100 percent. This next step could be the most critical of all.

Dawn is just breaking, the clouds a magnificent fiery orange. Ordinarily I'd be deeply moved by the sight, a reminder of the omnipotence of nature, of how small we are in this world we inherited. But the clouds are instead a reminder of the fireball I just watched in Los Angeles via satellite images, and the rising sun tells me that the clock is ticking in deep, echoing gongs.

"They're ready for us," Alex Trimble tells me, looking up at me from conversations he's having through his headset. "The communications room

311

is secure. The war room is secure. The grounds are swept and secure. Barricades and cameras are in place."

We land effortlessly in a spot designed for helicopter landing, a square of open land among the vast woodlands of southwestern Virginia. We're in the middle of an estate owned by a friend of mine, a venture capitalist who, by his own admission, doesn't know a damn thing about what he calls "computer-technical stuff" but recognized a winner when he smelled it, investing millions in a start-up software company and turning those millions into billions. This is his getaway, his place to fish on the lake or hunt deer when he's not in Manhattan or Silicon Valley. More than a thousand acres of Virginia pines and wildflowers, hunting and boating, long hikes and campfires. Lilly and I came here a few weekends after Rachel's death, sitting on the pontoon, taking long walks, trying to find the secret to coping with loss.

"We're the first ones here, right?" I ask Alex.

"Yes, sir."

Good. I want at least a few minutes first, to put some pieces in place and clean myself up a bit. There is no room for error now.

In the next few hours, we could be altering world history for generations.

South of our landing spot there are paths lead-ing to the boat dock, but otherwise all you can see is dense woodlands. North of us is a cabin built more than a decade ago out of white pine logs, the color of the wood having turned over the years from yellow-brown to a darker orange that almost matches the sky at dawn.

One of the best things about this place, partic-ularly from Alex's perspective, is its lack of ac-cessibility. There is no way to enter this property from the south or west, because it is protected by a thirty-foot-high electric fence fitted with sen-sors and cameras. The east side of the property abuts a massive lake, which is guarded by Se-cret Service agents standing on the dock. And to access the property by car, you have to find an unmarked gravel road off the county highway, then turn down a dirt road barricaded by Secret Service vehicles.

I insisted on light protection, because this loca-tion must remain secret. What is about to happen has to remain completely confidential. And the Secret Service tends to stand out when it's in full force—it's intended to stand out. We've struck a good balance between secure and inconspicuous.

I walk on unsteady legs up the slight incline, carrying the IV stand in my hand because the wheels do not comfortably roll across the thick grass. The air out here is so different, so fresh and clean and sweet with the scent of wildflowers, that I am tempted to forget for the moment that the world may be on the brink of catastrophe.

On one side of the open lawn, a tent has been set up, all black. If not for the color, and the fact that a drape covers all sides, it would look like any other tent set up for an outdoor party. Instead it is a tent set up to allow private conversations, either in person or electronic, to occur in utter seclusion, jamming out all other signals, any attempts at eavesdropping.

There are going to be a lot of critical and confidential conversations today.

The agents have the cabin open. Inside, the rustic theme has been retained to a large extent—some wildlife trophies mounted on the walls, pictures hung in pine frames, a carved-out canoe serving as a bookcase.

A man and woman stand at attention as I enter, taking note of the IV in my arm but saying nothing. The man is Devin Wittmer, age forty-three, looking like a college professor—a sport jacket and trousers, dress shirt open at the collar, his long hair brushed back, some gray peppering the beard covering his thin face—otherwise youthful in appearance but with bags under his eyes that reflect the stress he's endured over the last two weeks.

The woman is Casey Alvarez, age thirty-seven, slightly taller than Devin and with a bit more of a corporate-America look—her ink-black hair pulled back, red eyeglasses, a blouse and black pants.

Devin and Casey are the cochairs of the Imminent Threat Response Team, part of a task force I assembled after the virus we dubbed Dark Ages made its cameo peekaboo appearance on Pentagon servers two weeks ago. I told my people that I wanted only the best, whatever it took, wherever they came from, whatever it cost.

We assembled thirty people, the brightest cybersecurity minds we have. A few are on loan, pursuant to strict confidentiality agreements, from the private sector—software companies, telecommunications giants, cybersecurity firms, military contractors. Two are former hackers themselves, one of them currently serving a thirteen-year sentence in a federal penitentiary. Most are from various agencies of the federal government—Homeland Security, CIA, FBI, NSA.

Half our team is devoted to threat mitigation—how to limit the damage to our systems and infrastructure after the virus hits.

But right now, I'm concerned with the other half, the threat-response team that Devin and Casey are running. They're devoted to stopping the virus, something they've been unable to do for the last two weeks.

"Good morning, Mr. President," says Devin Wittmer. He comes from NSA. After graduating from Berkeley, he started designing cyberdefense software for clients like Apple before the NSA recruited him away. He has developed federal cybersecurity assessment tools to help industries and governments understand their preparedness against cyberattacks. When the major health-care systems in France were hit with a ransomware virus three years ago, we lent them Devin, who was able to locate and disable it. Nobody in America, I've been assured, is better at finding holes in cyberdefense systems or at plugging them.

"Mr. President," says Casey Alvarez. Casey is the daughter of Mexican immigrants who settled in Arizona to start a family and built up a fleet of grocery stores in the Southwest along the way. Casey showed no interest in the business, taking quickly to computers and wanting to join law enforcement. When she was a grad student at Penn, she got turned down for a position at the Department of Justice. So Casey got on her computer and managed to do what state and federal authorities had been unable to do for years—she hacked into an underground child-pornography website and disclosed the identities of all the website's patrons, basically gift-wrapping a federal prosecution for Justice and shutting down an operation that was believed to be the largest purveyor of kiddie porn in the country. DOJ hired her on the spot, and she stayed there until she went to work for the CIA. She's been most recently deployed in the Middle East with US Central Command, where she intercepts, decodes, and disrupts cybercommunications among terrorist groups.

I've been assured that these two are, by far, the best we have. And they are about to meet the person who, so far, has been better.

There is a hint of reverence in their expressions as I introduce them to Augie. The Sons of Jihad is the all-star team of cyberterrorists, mythical figures in that world. But I sense some competitive fire, too, which will be a good thing.

"Devin and Casey can show you to their war room," I say. "And they're in touch with the rest of the threat-response team back at the Pentagon."

"Follow me," says Casey to Augie.

I feel a small measure of relief. At least I've

got them together. After everything we went through, that itself is a small victory.

Now I can focus on what comes next.

"Jacobson," I say once they've left. "Remove this IV."

"Before it's finished, sir?"

I stare back at him. "You know what's about to happen, don't you?"

"Yes, sir, of course."

"Right. And I'm not going to have a damn tube in my arm. Take it out."

"Sir, yes, sir." He gets to work, snapping on rubber gloves from his bag and gathering the other supplies. He starts talking to himself, like a kid trying to memorize the steps in an instruction manual—*close the clamp, stabilize catheter, pull dressing and tape toward the injection site, and…*

"Ouch."

"Sorry, sir…no sign of infection…here." He places a gauze pad over the site. "Hold this down."

A moment later, I'm taped up and ready to go. I go straight to my bedroom, into the small bathroom inside it. I pull out an electric razor and shave off most of the red beard, then use a razor and shaving cream to finish the job. Then I shower, taking the moment to enjoy the pressure of the steaming water on my face, awkward as it may be with my left arm hanging outside the shower, protecting the gauze pad and tape, doing everything with one hand. Still. I needed a shower. I needed a shave. I feel better, and appearances still matter, at least for one more day.

I put on the clean clothes that Carolyn's husband gave me. I'm still wearing my jeans and shoes, but he gave me a button-down shirt that fits okay, plus clean boxers and socks. I've just finished combing my hair when I get a text message from FBI Liz telling me that we need to talk.

"Alex!" I call out. He pops into the bedroom. "Where the hell are they?"

"I understand they're close, sir."

"But everything's okay? I mean, after what we went through last night..."

"My understanding, sir, is that they are secure and on their way."

"Double-check that, Alex."

I dial my FBI director's number.

"Yes, Liz. What is it?"

"Mr. President, news on Los Angeles," she says. *"They weren't targeting the defense contractor."*

CHAPTER
50

❖

I head to the basement, to a room on the east end, where the owner of this cabin, with the help of the CIA, was good enough to install a soundproof door and set up secure communications lines for my use when I visit. This communications room is several doors down from the war room, on the west side of the basement, where Augie, Devin, and Casey are set up.

I close the door and plug the secure line into my laptop and pull up the triumvirate of Carolyn Brock, Liz Greenfield, and Sam Haber of Homeland Security on a three-way split screen.

"Talk to me," I say. "Hurry."

"Sir, on the same block as the defense contractor's plant was a private health laboratory that was in a partnership with the state of California and our CDC."

THE PRESIDENT IS MISSING

"The Centers for Disease Control," I say.

"*Correct, sir. Within the CDC, we have a Laboratory Response Network. It—essentially, we have about two hundred laboratories around the country designed as first responders to biological and chemical terrorism.*"

A cold wave passes through my chest.

"*The largest member of the Laboratory Response Network in the greater Los Angeles area was next door to the defense contractor's plant. It was decimated in the fire, sir.*"

I close my eyes. "Are you telling me that the primary lab charged with responding to a bioterrorism attack in LA was just burned to the ground?"

"*Yes, sir.*"

"Holy shit." I rub my temples.

"*Yes, sir. That about sums it up.*"

"And what, exactly, does that lab do? Or *did* it do?"

"*It was the first to diagnose,*" he says. "*The first to treat. Diagnosis being the most critical aspect. Understanding what, exactly, our citizens have been exposed to is the first order of business for first responders. You can't treat the patient if you don't know what you're treating.*"

Nobody speaks for a moment.

"Are we looking at a biological attack on Los Angeles?" I ask.

"Well, sir, we're making that assumption right now. We're in touch with the local authorities."

"Okay, Sam—do we have protocols in place to divert CDC operations around the country?"

"We're doing it right now, sir. We're mobilizing resources from other cities on the West Coast."

A predictable response. What the terrorists would expect. Is this a head fake? Are they feinting toward LA so we'll move everything on the West Coast there, then hit another spot like Seattle or San Francisco while our guard is down?

I throw up my hands. "Why do I feel like we're chasing our goddamn tails here, people?"

"Because it always feels that way, sir," says Sam. *"It's what we do. We play defense against invisible opponents. We try to smoke them out. We try to predict what they might do. We hope it never happens but try to be as ready as possible if it does."*

"Is that supposed to make me feel better? Because it doesn't."

"Sir, we're on this. We'll do everything we can."

I run my fingers through my hair. "Get to it, Sam. Keep me updated."

"Yes, sir."

The screen adjusts to show just Carolyn and Liz as Sam signs off.

"Any more good news?" I ask. "A hurricane on

322

the East Coast? Tornadoes? An oil spill? Is a god-damn volcano erupting somewhere?"

"One thing, sir," says Liz. *"About the gas explosion."*

"Something new?"

She cocks her head. *"More like something old,"* she says.

Liz fills me in. And I didn't think I could feel any worse.

Ten minutes later, I open the thick door and leave the communications room as Alex approaches me. He nods to me.

"They just reached the security perimeter up the road," says Alex. "The Israeli prime minister has arrived."

CHAPTER
51

❖

The delegation for the Israeli prime minister, Noya Baram, arrives as planned: one advance car that arrived earlier and now two armored SUVs, one carrying a security detail that will leave once she has safely arrived and the other carrying the prime minister herself.

Noya emerges from the SUV wearing sunglasses, a jacket, and slacks. She looks up at the sky for a moment, as if to confirm that it's still there. It's one of those days.

Noya is sixty-four, with gray dominating her shoulder-length hair and dark eyes that can be both fierce and engaging. She is one of the most fearless people I've ever known.

She called me the night I was elected president. She asked if she could call me Jonny, which nobody in my life had ever done. Surprised, off balance, giddy from the win, I said, "Sure you can!" She's called me that ever since.

"Jonny," she says to me now, removing her sunglasses and kissing both my cheeks. With her hands clasped over mine, a tight smile on her face, she says, "You look like someone who could use a friend right now."

"I certainly could."

"You know that Israel will never leave your side."

"I do know that," I say. "And my gratitude knows no bounds, Noya."

"David has been helpful?"

"Very."

I reached out to Noya when I discovered the leak in my national security team. I didn't know whom I could trust and whom I couldn't, so I was forced to outsource some of my reconnaissance work to the Mossad, dealing directly with David Guralnick, its director.

Noya and I have had disagreements over the two-state solution and settlements on the West Bank, but when it comes to the things that bring us together today, there is no daylight between our positions. A safe and stable United States means a safe and stable Israel. They have every reason to help us and no reason not to.

And they have the finest cybersecurity experts in the world. They play defense better than anybody. Two of them have arrived with Noya and will join Augie and my people.

"I am the first to arrive?"

"You are, Noya, you are. And I wouldn't mind a word with you before the others get here. If I had time to give you a tour—"

"What—a tour?" She waves her hand. "It's a cabin. I've seen cabins before."

We walk past the cabin into the yard. She acknowledges the black tent.

We walk toward the woods, the trees thirty feet high, the wildflowers yellow and violet, following the stone path to the lake. Alex Trimble follows from behind, speaking into his radio.

I tell her everything she doesn't already know, which isn't very much.

"What we have heard about so far," she says, "did not sound like plans for a biological attack in a major city."

"I agree. But maybe the idea is to destroy our ability to respond, then introduce some biological pathogen. That would include destroying physical buildings and our technological infrastructure."

"True, true," she says.

"The gas pipeline explosion could be telling," I say.

"How so?"

"Some computer virus—some malware—caused a disruption," I say. "We just confirmed it a few minutes ago. The virus prompted a forced increase in pressure that caused the explosion."

"Yes? And?"

I let out air and stop, turn to her. "Noya, in 1982, we did the same thing to the Soviets."

"Ah. You sabotaged one of their pipelines?"

"My FBI director just told me. Reagan learned that the Soviets were trying to steal some industrial software," I say. "So he decided to let them steal it. But we tampered with it first. We booby-trapped it. So when the Soviets stole it and used it, it caused a tremendous explosion in the Siberian pipeline. Our people said that the satellite imagery showed one of the biggest explosions they'd ever seen."

She laughs, in spite of the circumstances. "Reagan," she says, shaking her head. "I had not heard this story. But it sounds just like him." She angles her head, looks up at me. "This is ancient history, though."

"Yes and no," I say. "We learned that a number of people were disciplined for the mistake. It was a huge embarrassment for the Kremlin. A lot of people were punished. Some went to prison for life. We never knew all the details. But one of the KGB agents who was never heard from again was named Viktor Chernokev."

Her smile disappears. "The Russian president's father."

"The Russian president's father."

She nods knowingly. "I knew his father was KGB. I didn't know how he died. Or why."

She chews on her lip, something she always does when she concentrates.

"So…what are you going to do with this information, Jonny?"

"Mr. President—excuse me, sir. Excuse me, Madam Prime Minister."

I turn to Alex. "What is it, Alex?"

"Sir," he says, "the German chancellor is arriving."

CHAPTER
52

❖

Juergen Richter, the German chancellor, steps out of his SUV looking like something out of British royalty in his pin-striped three-piece suit. He has a slight paunch, but he has the height—six feet four—and the perfect posture to carry it off.

His long, regal face lights up when he sees Noya Baram. He bows at the waist in exaggerated fashion, which she waves off with a laugh. Then they embrace. She's more than a foot shorter than he is, so she rises up and he leans down so they can exchange kisses.

I offer my hand, and he accepts it, clasping my shoulder with the other hand, the large hand of a former basketball player for West Germany in the 1988 Olympics. "Mr. President," he says. "Always these difficult situations, we meet."

The last time I saw Juergen was at Rachel's funeral.

"How is your wife, Mr. Chancellor?" I ask. His wife now has cancer, too, and is getting treatment in the United States.

"Ah, she is a strong woman, Mr. President, thank you for your concern. She has never lost a battle. Certainly none with me." He looks over at Noya for a laugh, which she gives him. Juergen is one of those larger-than-life personalities, always trying for humor. His need to shine has bought him trouble more than once in interviews and press conferences, where he's been known to make an occasional off-color remark, but his voters seem to appreciate his freewheeling style.

"I appreciate your coming," I say.

"When one friend has a problem, another friend helps," he says.

True. But the principal reason I invited him is to convince him that the problem is not only my country's but his—and all of NATO's—too.

I show him around the grounds briefly, but my phone is buzzing before long. I excuse myself from the group and answer the phone. Three minutes later, I'm back downstairs, communicating by laptop on the secure line.

Again, it's the same three people involved. Carolyn and Liz, whom I trust, and Sam Haber, who has to be involved in homeland security issues, and whom I would really like to believe I can trust, too.

Sam Haber was a case officer in the CIA thirty years ago who returned to Minnesota and was elected to Congress. He ran for governor, lost, and managed to get an appointment as one of the CIA's deputy directors. My predecessor appointed him secretary of DHS, and he was given high marks. He lobbied me to be CIA director, but I chose Erica Beatty for that post and asked him to stay on at DHS. I was pleasantly surprised when he agreed. Most of us thought he'd serve in a sort of interim capacity, bridging administrations before moving on to something else. But he's lasted more than two years in the job, and if he's unhappy, he hasn't made that known to anyone.

Sam's eyes are in a nearly permanent squint, his forehead always etched in wrinkles below the ever-present crew cut. Everything about him is intense. It's not a bad trait in a secretary of homeland security.

"Where exactly did it happen?" I ask.

"It's in a small town outside Los Angeles proper," says Sam. *"It's the largest water treatment plant in California. It pumps more than half a billion gallons of water a day, mostly into LA County and Orange County."*

"So what happened?"

"Sir, after the explosion at the private biological lab, we were in touch with state and local officials, focusing on critical public infrastructure—gas, electricity, commuter rail—but most urgently on water lines."

Makes sense. The most obvious target among public utilities for a biological attack. You introduce a biological pathogen into the water, it spreads faster than wildfire.

"The Metropolitan Water District of Southern California and members of DHS and EPA conducted an emergency inspection and discovered the breach."

"Explain the breach," I say. "In English."

"They hacked into the computer software, sir. They managed to alter the settings on the chemical applicators. But they also disabled the alert functions that would normally detect anomalies in the purification process."

"So dirty water that was supposed to be passing through a chemical application wasn't receiving that chemical application, and the alert functions in the system, designed to detect that very problem…"

"Weren't detecting. Sir, that's correct. The good news is that we caught it quickly. We caught it within an hour of the cyberintrusion. The untreated water was still in the finished-water reservoirs."

"No tainted water left the plant?"

"Sir, that's correct. Nothing had passed into the water mains yet."

"Did the water contain any biological pathogens? Anything like that?"

"Sir, we don't know at this point. Our rapid-response team in that area—"

"The lab you'd normally use burned down four hours ago."

"Sir, that's correct."

"Sam, I need your full attention here." I lean forward toward the screen. "You can tell me with 100 percent confidence—no tainted water was sent to the citizens of LA or Orange Counties."

"Sir, that's correct. This was the only plant they breached. And we can pinpoint precisely when the cyber event occurred, when the chemical-applicator software and detection systems were compromised. There is no physical way that any untreated water left the plant."

I release a breath. "Okay. Well, that's something, at least. Well done, Sam."

"Yes, sir, a good team effort. But the news isn't all good, sir."

"Of course it isn't. Why in the hell would we expect only good news?" I wave off my tantrum. "Tell me the bad news, Sam."

"The bad news is that none of our technicians has ever seen a cyberattack like this. They've been unable so far to reengage the chemical applicators."

"They can't fix it?"

"Exactly, sir. For all practical purposes, the primary

water treatment plant serving Los Angeles County and Orange County is closed for business."

"Okay, well—surely there are other plants."

"Yes, sir, most certainly, but there is no practical way to compensate for the loss for very long. And sir, I'm concerned that the hacking isn't over yet. What if they hit another plant around LA, too? We're watching closely now, of course. We'll shut down any affected system and prevent untreated water from reaching the water mains."

"But you'd have to shut the plant down, too," I say.

"Yes, sir. We could have multiple water treatment plants shut down at once."

"What are you telling me, Sam? We could have a massive water shortage in Los Angeles?"

"That's what I'm telling you, sir."

"How many people are we talking about? Los Angeles and Orange Counties?"

"Fourteen million, sir."

"Oh, Jesus." I put my hand over my mouth.

"We're not just talking about hot showers and lawn sprinklers," he says. *"We're talking about potable water. We're talking about hospitals and surgery wards and first responders."*

"So, what—this will be Flint, Michigan, all over again?"

"It will be Flint, Michigan," says Sam, *"multiplied by a factor of one hundred forty."*

CHAPTER
53

❖

*B*ut not immediately," says Carolyn. *"Not today."*
"Not today, but soon. LA County alone is bigger than many states in population, and this is its biggest supplier of clean water. We'll have a crisis starting today. Not Flint, Michigan, not yet—but a real true-blue crisis."

"Mobilize FEMA," I say.

"Already done, sir."

"We can have a federal disaster declaration."

"Already have it written for you, sir."

"But you have something else in mind."

"Yes, sir. Fixing the problem, sir."

That's what I thought he was going to say.

"Sir, you know as well as I do that there are many very good, highly competent individuals under our umbrella when it comes to cyberdefense. But it looks like

very good and highly competent isn't going to cut it today in Los Angeles. Our people there are telling us they've never seen a virus like this. They don't know what to do."

"You need the best."

"Yes, sir. We need the threat-response team you assembled."

"Devin Wittmer and Casey Alvarez are with me, Sam."

Sam doesn't immediately reply. I'm keeping him in the dark. We both know that. I have a source telling me today is the day for the attack, but I haven't identified the source to him. That's unusual. And on top of that, now I'm telling him what he probably already figured out for himself—that our country's two most elite cybersecurity experts are with me in an undisclosed location. None of this makes any sense to him. He's the secretary of homeland security—of all people in the world, why wouldn't I tell him?

"Sir, if we can't have Wittmer and Alvarez, at least send part of the team."

I rub my face, think it over.

"This is Dark Ages, sir. There's no chance this is a coincidence. This is the beginning. Where it ends, I don't know. The rest of the water plants? The electrical grid? Are they going to open the dams? We need them in Los

Angeles. We got lucky once today. I don't want to count on luck again."

I get out of my chair, feeling claustrophobic down here. Pacing helps me. Gets the juices flowing. I need them all flowing in the direction of the best possible decision.

The gas explosion…the decimated biological lab…the tampering at the water lab.

Wait a minute. Wait just a—

"*Was* it luck?" I ask.

"Finding the malfunction in the water purification plant? I don't know what else I'd call it. It could have been days before they caught this. This was a highly sophisticated hacking."

"And it's only because of the destruction of the bioterrorism-response laboratory that we thought to manually check the control functions at that water plant."

"Correct, sir. It was an obvious first-step precaution to take."

"I know," I say. "That's my point."

"I'm not following, sir."

"Sam, if you were the terrorists, what order would you do things in? Would you contaminate the water supply first or blow up the lab first?"

"I…well, if I—"

"I'll tell you what *I'd* do if I were the terrorists," I go on. "I'd contaminate the water supply first.

It wouldn't be immediately noticeable. Maybe within hours, maybe within days. And *then* I'd blow up the lab. Because if you blow up the lab first...if you blow up a lab dedicated to emergency biological-terror response first..."

"You show your hand," says Carolyn. *"You know the first thing the federal government will do is check things like the water supply."*

"Which is exactly what we did," I say.

"They showed their hand," Sam mumbles, as much to himself as to us, thinking it over.

"They *deliberately* showed their hand," I say. "They tipped us off. They wanted us to go inspect all the water plants. They wanted us to find the cyberintrusion."

Sam says, *"I don't see how that helps—"*

"Maybe they don't want to poison the water in Los Angeles. Maybe they just want us to *think* they do. They want us to send the best, the most elite cybersecurity experts in the nation to LA, to the other side of the country, so that our pants are at our ankles when the virus strikes."

I put my hands on top of my head, work it over again.

"We're taking an awfully big risk in making that assumption, sir."

I start pacing again. "Liz, you have any thoughts here?"

She looks surprised that I'm asking. *"You want to know what I'd do?"*

"Yes, Liz. You went to one of those Ivy League schools, didn't you? What would you do?"

"I—Los Angeles is a major metropolitan area. I wouldn't risk it. I'd send the team to LA to fix that system."

I nod. "Carolyn?"

"Sir, I understand your logic, but I have to agree with Sam and Liz. Imagine if it ever came out that you decided not to send—"

"No!" I shout, pointing at the computer screen. "No politics today. No worrying about what might come out later. This is the whole freakin' show, people. Every decision I make today is a risk. We are on the high wire without a net. I make the wrong decision, either way, and we're screwed. There's no safe play here. There's only a right play and a wrong play."

"Send some of the team, then," Carolyn says. *"Not Devin and Casey, but some of the threat-response team at the Pentagon."*

"That team was put together as a cohesive unit," I say. "You can't cut a bicycle in half and still expect it to work. No—it's all or nothing. Do we send them to LA or don't we?"

The room is silent.

Sam says, *"Send them to LA."*

"Send them," says Carolyn.

"I agree," Liz chimes in.

Three highly intelligent people, all voting the same way. How much of their decision is based on reason and how much on fear?

They're right. The smart money says send 'em. My gut says otherwise.

So what's it going to be, Mr. President?

"The team stays put for now," I say. "Los Angeles is a decoy."

CHAPTER
54

❖

S aturday morning, 6:52 a.m. The limousine is
parked on 13th Street Northwest by the curb.
Vice President Katherine Brandt sits in the
back of the limo, her stomach churning, but not
from hunger.

Her cover is airtight: every Saturday morning
at 7:00 a.m., she and her husband have a standing
reservation for omelets just around the corner
on G Street Northwest at Blake's Café. They
have a table ready for her, and by now her order
is assumed—egg whites with feta cheese and
tomatoes, extra-crispy hash browns.

So she has every reason to be here right now.
Nobody would say otherwise if she were ever
confronted.

Her husband, thank goodness, is out of town,
another golfing trip. Or maybe it's fishing. She

loses track. It was easier when they lived in Massachusetts and she was gone during the week when she was in the Senate. Living together in Washington has been hard on them. She loves him, and they still have good times together, but he has no interest in politics, hates Washington, and has nothing to do since he sold his business. It's put a strain on their relationship and makes it harder for her to put in her standard twelve-hour days. In this case, well-timed absences do make the heart grow fonder.

How is he going to like being First Husband?

We may find out sooner rather than later. Let's see how the next half hour goes.

Next to her, filling in for her husband as a breakfast partner: her chief of staff, Peter Evian. He holds out his phone, showing her the time: 6:56.

She gives him a quick nod.

"Madam Vice President," he says, loud enough for the agents in front to hear, "since we have a few minutes before our reservation, would you mind if I made a personal call?"

"Not at all, Pete. Go right ahead."

"I'll just step out."

"Take your time."

And she knows, for appearance's sake, that Peter will do just that—he will call his mother and have a nice long documented phone call with her.

Peter leaves the car and walks up 13th Street with his phone to his ear just as a group of three joggers turns the corner from G Street Northwest and moves past him toward the vice president's limo.

The joggers slow as they near the vice-presidential motorcade. The man in the front of the pack, far older and less fit than his two partners, looks at the limo and seems to mention something to the others. They slow to a walk and engage with the Secret Service agents standing at their posts by her vehicle.

"Madam Vice President," says her driver, tapping his ear, "the Speaker of the House is right out there. One of those joggers."

"Lester Rhodes? You're kidding," she says, trying not to overdo her show of surprise.

"He wants to say a quick hello."

"I'd sooner set my hair on fire," she says.

The agent doesn't laugh. He turns his head, waiting for more. "Shall I tell him—"

"Well, I can't very well refuse him, can I? Tell him to come in."

"Yes, ma'am." He speaks into his earpiece.

"Give us privacy, Jay. I wouldn't want you and Eric to get burned by any fireworks."

This time the agent chuckles appropriately. "Yes, ma'am."

Never hurts to be careful. Secret Service agents are subject to subpoena just like anyone else. So are the Capitol Police guarding the Speaker. Everyone would tell the same story under oath now, if it ever came to that. It was all a coincidence. The Speaker just happened to jog by while the vice president was waiting for the café to open.

The two agents in the front seat leave the limousine. The smell of sweat and body odor sweeps into the car as Lester Rhodes pops into the back, next to Katherine. "Madam Vice President, just wanted to say hello!"

The door closes behind him. Just the two of them inside the car.

Lester doesn't look great in running gear. He needs to lose three or four inches in the midsection, and someone should have told him to wear longer running shorts. At least he's wearing a hat—slate blue, with US CAPITOL POLICE in red stenciling—so she doesn't have to look at that dopey perfectly sharp part he makes in his silver hair.

He lifts his hat and wipes his forehead with a sweatband. This idiot is wearing a sweatband.

Correction. He's no idiot. He's a ruthless tactician who orchestrated the takeover of the House, who knows his members better than they know themselves, who plays a long political game, who never forgets anyone who crosses him, however slight the insult or disrespect, who moves the pieces of the chessboard only after careful deliberation.

He turns to her, his lethal blue eyes reduced to a squint. "Kathy."

"Lester. Be brief."

"I have the votes in the House," he says. "The House is wrapped up like a bow. Is that brief enough?"

One of the things she has learned over the years is the art of not responding too quickly. It buys you time and makes you seem more deliberative.

"Don't act so uninterested, Kathy. If you weren't interested, we wouldn't be here right now."

She allows his point. "What about the Senate?" she asks.

His shoulders rise. "You're the president of the Senate, not me."

She smirks. "But your party controls it."

"You get twelve on your side, I guarantee my fifty-five will vote to convict."

The vice president adjusts in her seat to face him squarely. "And why are you telling me this, Mr. Speaker?"

"Because I don't have to pull this trigger." He sits back in the seat, settles in. "I don't have to impeach him. I could just let him twist in the wind, wounded and ineffective. He's dead in the water, Kathy. He won't be reelected. I'll own him for the next two years. So why would I impeach him and watch the Senate remove him from office and give the voters a fresh face like you to run against?"

That possibility had occurred to her—that the president was of more use to Lester Rhodes wounded than gone. "Because you'll be immortalized in your party for removing a president, that's why," she says.

"Maybe so." He seems to relish that thought. "But there are more important things."

"There's something more important to you than being Speaker for life?"

Lester helps himself to a bottle of water in the side compartment, screws off the top, takes a big swallow, then smacks his lips with satisfaction. "One thing is more important, yes," he says.

She opens her hands. "Do tell."

A wide smile crosses his face, then disappears.

"It's something President Duncan would never do," he says. "But President Brandt, in her infinite wisdom, might."

CHAPTER
55

❖

T here's going to be a vacancy on the Court,"
says Lester.

"Oh?" She hadn't heard that. You never know
with these justices, most of whom stay in their
seats until they're well into their eighties.
"Who?"

He turns and looks at her, his eyes narrowing,
a poker face. *Deciding,* she thinks. *Deciding whether
to tell me.*

"Whitman got some very bad news from his
doctor a week ago," he says.

"Justice Whitman is…"

"It was bad news," he says. "Voluntarily or otherwise, he won't make it through this presidential
term. He's being urged to step down right now."

"I'm sorry to hear that," she says.

"Are you?" A wry smile creeps across his face. "Anyway, do you know what hasn't happened in a long time? There's been no midwesterner on the Supreme Court since John Paul Stevens. Nobody from a federal court like...oh, like the Seventh Circuit. The heartland."

The United States Court of Appeals for the Seventh Circuit. If memory serves her, that court covers federal cases from Illinois, Wisconsin...

...and Indiana, Lester's home state.

Of course.

"Who, Lester?"

"The former attorney general of Indiana," he says. "Female. Moderate. Well respected. Got nearly unanimous approval from the Senate four years ago for the appeals court, including your vote. Good and young—forty-three years old— so that's good legacy building. She could sit on the court for thirty years. She's from my side of the aisle, but she'll vote your way on the issues your people seem to care about."

The vice president's mouth drops open. She leans into him.

"Jesus, Lester," she says. "You want me to put your daughter on the Supreme Court?"

She tries to remember what she knows about Lester's daughter. Married with a few kids. Harvard undergrad, Harvard law. She worked in

Washington, moved back home to Indiana, and ran for attorney general as a moderate counterweight to her father's fire-and-brimstone politics. Everyone assumed the next step was the governorship, but then she went wonky and took an appointment to the federal appeals court.

And yes, then Senator Katherine Brandt voted yes on her nomination to the appeals court. The report on her was that she was nothing like her father—if anything she veered in the other direction, party affiliation notwithstanding. Smart and sensible.

Lester frames a newspaper headline with his hands. "Bipartisan, bipartisan, bipartisan," he says. "A new day after the gridlock of the Duncan administration. She'll be confirmed easily. I can guarantee the senators on my side, and your side will be happy. She's pro-choice, Kathy, which seems to be all your people care about."

It…might not be so crazy.

"You'll start your presidency with a big win. Hell, you play this right, Kathy, you could serve nearly ten years in office."

The vice president looks out the window. She remembers that rush when she first announced, when she was the favorite, when she could see it, feel it, taste it.

"Otherwise," says Lester, "you won't serve one

day. I'll keep Duncan in office, he'll get crushed in the reelection, and you'll be at a dead end."

He's probably right about the next election. She wouldn't be at a dead end, as he's saying, but it would be an uphill battle to run four years later as a former vice president who lost a reelection bid.

"And you're okay," she says, "with my serving two and a half terms as president?"

The Speaker of the House slides toward the door, reaches for the handle. "What the hell do *I* care who the president is?"

She shakes her head, bemused but not particularly surprised.

"You gotta get those twelve votes in the Senate, though," he says, wagging a finger.

"And I suppose you have an idea how I would do that."

Speaker Rhodes moves his hand off the door handle. "As a matter of fact, Madam Vice President, I do."

CHAPTER
56

❖

The assembled dignitaries eat a light breakfast of bagels and fruit and coffee in the
eat-in kitchen overlooking the backyard and
woods as I update them on where we are so far.
I've just received an update on Los Angeles,
where Homeland Security and FEMA, under
DHS's umbrella, are working with the city and
the state of California on the delivery of clean
water. There have always been contingency plans
for the suspension or failure of water-
purification plants, so in the short term, while
there will be a sense of urgency to get the plant
up and running again, with any luck it will never
bloom into a full-scale crisis. I won't send my Imminent Threat Response Team out there, but
we're sending everyone else we have.

I may be wrong about LA. It may not be a decoy. It might be ground zero for whatever is coming. If that's true, I've made an enormous mistake. But without more to go on, I am not letting go of my team. They're currently in the basement with Augie and the cybersecurity experts from Israel and Germany, working in concert with the rest of our team, stationed at the Pentagon.

Chancellor Juergen Richter sits with his one aide, a fair-haired young man named Dieter Kohl, the head of Germany's BND, its international intelligence service. Prime Minister Noya Baram brought her chief of staff, a stout, formal, older man who once served as a general in the Israeli army.

We're trying to keep this meeting a secret, which means we had to keep it small. One leader and one aide each, plus their technical gurus. This isn't 1942, when FDR and Churchill met secretly at a spot just off the Intracoastal Waterway, in southern Florida, for a series of war conferences. They ate at a great restaurant called Cap's Place and sent the owner letters of appreciation, which are now the treasures of an eatery otherwise known for its seafood, Key lime pie, and 1940s atmosphere.

Nowadays, with an emboldened and ravenous

press, the Internet and social media, all eyes on world leaders day and night, it is exceptionally difficult for any of us to move about incognito. The only thing in our favor is security: given terrorism threats these days, we are able to keep the specifics of our travel plans under wraps.

Noya Baram is attending a conference tomorrow in Manhattan and said she was using Saturday to visit family in the United States. Considering she has a daughter who lives in Boston, a brother outside Chicago, and a grandchild completing her freshman year at Columbia, her alibi is plausible. Whether it will hold up is another story.

Chancellor Richter used his wife's cancer as a cover, moving up a scheduled trip to Sloan Kettering to yesterday, Friday. Their stated plan is to spend the weekend in New York City with friends.

"Excuse me," I say to the group gathered in the cabin's living room as my phone buzzes. "I have to take this call. It's—it's one of those days."

I wish I had an aide with me, too, but I need Carolyn at the White House, and there isn't anybody else I can trust.

I move onto the deck overlooking the woods. The Secret Service is taking the lead, but there is a small contingent of German and Israeli agents in the yard and spread out around the property.

"Mr. President," says Liz Greenfield. *"The girl, Nina. Her fingerprints came back. Her name is Nina Shinkuba. We don't have much of a dossier on her, but we think she was born almost twenty-six years ago in the Abkhazia region of the republic of Georgia."*

"The separatist territory," I say. "The disputed territory." The Russians backed Abkhazia's claim of autonomy from Georgia. The 2008 war between Russia and Georgia was fought over it, at least ostensibly.

"Yes, sir. Nina Shinkuba was suspected by the Georgian government of bombing a train station on the Georgian side of the disputed border in 2008. There was a series of attacks on both sides of the border before the war broke out between Abkhazia and Georgia."

Which became the war between Russia and Georgia.

"She was a separatist?"

"Apparently. The republic of Georgia calls her a terrorist."

"So that would put her in the category of anti-Western," I say. "Would it also make her pro-Russian?"

"The Russians were with them. The Russians and Abkhazians fought on the same side of that war. It's a logical inference."

But not an automatic one.

"Should we reach out to the Georgians to see what else we can learn about her?"

"Hold that thought," I say. "I want to ask someone else first."

CHAPTER
57

❖

I only knew her as Nina," says Augie, haggard from his work in the basement, rubbing his eyes as we stand together in the cabin's living room.

"No last name. That didn't strike you as odd? You fell in love with a woman and you didn't know her last name?"

He lets out a sigh. "I knew she had a past she was escaping. I did not know the details. I did not care."

I watch him, but he doesn't say more, doesn't seem to be struggling to explain himself any more than that.

"She was an Abkhazian separatist," I say. "They worked with the Russians."

"So you have said. If she was…sympathetic to

Russia, it was never something she shared with me. You have always known, Mr. President, that the Sons of Jihad attacked Western institutions. We oppose the influence of the West in southeastern Europe. Of course, this is consistent with the Russian agenda. But this does not mean that we work for the Russians. My understanding is that, yes, Suliman has accepted money from the Russians in the past, but he no longer needs their money."

"He sells his services to the highest bidder," I say.

"He does whatever he wants. Not always for money. He answers to no man but himself."

That's how our intelligence has understood it, too.

"That's how Nina was injured," I say. "That shrapnel in her head. She said a missile struck close to a church. It was the Georgians. It must have been."

Augie's eyes trail away, looking off into the distance, filling with tears. "Does it really matter?" he whispers.

"It matters if she was working with the Russians, Augie. If I can figure out who's behind this, I have more options at my disposal."

Augie nods, still looking off in the distance. "Threats. Deterrence. Mr. President," he says, "if we cannot stop this virus, your threats will be empty. Your attempts at deterrence will mean nothing."

But the virus hasn't hit yet. We are still the most powerful country in the world.

Maybe it's time I reminded Russia of that fact.

Augie returns to the basement. I pull out my phone and dial Carolyn.

"Carrie," I say, "are the Joint Chiefs in the Situation Room?"

"Yes, sir."

"I'll be on in two minutes," I say.

CHAPTER
58

❖

"Mr. President," says Chancellor Richter with his usual regal formality, as he shoots the French cuffs on his shirt. "I require no convincing of the Russians' involvement in this attack. As you know, Germany has experienced several such incidents in our recent past. The Bundestag affair, the CDU headquarters. We are still experiencing the effects today."

He's referring to the 2015 hacking into the servers of the German Bundestag, the lower house of the federal legislature. The hackers scooped up e-mails and loads of sensitive information before the Germans finally detected it and patched it up. Leaks of that information continue to spill out on the Internet, strategic drip by strategic drip, to this day.

And the headquarters of Germany's Christian Democratic Union party—Chancellor Richter's party—was hacked as well, involving the theft of many documents containing sensitive and sometimes blunt exchanges on topics of political strategy, campaign coordination, and key issues.

Both these attacks have been attributed to a group of cyberterrorist hackers known as APT28, or Fancy Bear, affiliated with the GRU, Russia's military intelligence service.

"We are aware of approximately seventy-five attempted cyberterrorist incidents since Bundestag and the CDU," says Richter's aide, Dieter Kohl, Germany's top foreign intelligence officer. "I speak of phishing expeditions into the servers belonging to federal and local governments and various political parties, all of them hostile to the Kremlin. I speak of incidents involving government institutions, industry, labor unions, think tanks. All of them," he says, "attributed to Fancy Bear."

"Much of the information they have…" Chancellor Richter turns to his colleague, searching for the right word. "Exfiltrated, yes. Much of the information they have exfiltrated has not yet been leaked. We are expecting, as the election season approaches, to be seeing it. So, Mr. President, I can say to you that Germany requires no convincing on the question of whether the Russians are involved."

"But this is different," says Prime Minister Noya Baram. "If I am right about the virus you detected on the Pentagon server, there were no...bread crumbs, I believe you'd say."

"Correct," I say. "This time the hackers didn't leave behind any trace. No fingerprints. No bread crumbs. It just showed up out of nowhere and disappeared without a trace."

"And that is not the only difference," she continues. "Your concern, Jonny, is not the theft of information. Your concern is the stability of your infrastructure."

"It's both," I say, "but you're correct, Noya. I'm worried that they're attacking our systems. The place where the virus showed up, when it winked at us before disappearing—it's part of our operational infrastructure. They aren't stealing e-mails. They're compromising our systems."

"And I am told," says Chancellor Richter, "that if anyone can do it, it is the Sons of Jihad. Our people"—he looks at his foreign intelligence chief, who nods—"they tell us the SOJ is the best in the world. One would think that we could find people just as competent. But what we are learning is no, in fact there are very few elite cyberterrorists and just as few, if not fewer, elite cyberdefense experts. In our country, we have formed a new cybercommand, but we are having trouble filling the positions. We have maybe a dozen, more or less, who would qualify as good enough to defend against the most able cyberterrorists."

"It's like anything else," I say. "Sports, the arts, academia. There are some people at the very top of the pyramid who are simply more skilled than everyone else. Israel has many of them on the defense side. Israel has the best cyberdefense systems in the world." I nod to Noya, who accepts the compliment without objection; it is a source of pride for the Israelis.

"And if Israel plays the best defense," says Richter, "Russia plays the best offense."

"But now we have Augie."

Richter nods, his eyes narrowing. Noya looks at Richter, then at me. "And you are confident you can trust this man, this Augustas Koslenko?"

"Noya." I open my hands. "I'm confident that I have no other choice *but* to trust him. Our people can't unlock this thing. They can't even find it." I sit back in my chair. "He tipped us off to it. If it weren't for him, we wouldn't even know about it."

"So he says."

"So he says," I concede. "True. Look, whoever

is ultimately behind this, the SOJ or Russia or someone else—yes, they may have sent Augie to me. He may have some ulterior motive. I've been waiting to hear it. I've been waiting for some demand, some ransom. I'm not hearing it. And remember, they tried to kill him. Twice. So for my money, he's a threat to them. Which means he's an asset to us. I have my best people, and *your* best people, and Juergen's best people, watching every move he makes downstairs, listening and learning and probing. We even have a camera on the room, just to keep an eye on him." I throw up my hands. "If anyone has a better idea, I'm open to it. Otherwise, this is the best thing I can do to try to avoid…" My words trail off. I can't bring myself to say them.

"To avoid…what?" asks Richter. "Do we have a sense of the possible harm? We can all speculate. We can all conjure up nightmare scenarios. What does the boy say?"

It's a good segue, one of the principal reasons I've asked the German chancellor here today.

I turn to Alex, standing in the far corner of the living room. "Alex, bring Augie up here," I say. "You all should hear this for yourselves."

CHAPTER
59

❖

Augie stands before the world leaders present in the living room, fatigued and frazzled, wearing ill-fitting clothes we found for him after a shower, overwhelmed in every way by the events of the last twelve hours. Yet this young man seems not even slightly fazed by the company he is keeping. They are men and women of tremendous accomplishments, with incredible power at their fingertips, but in this arena, he is the teacher, and we are the pupils.

"One of the great ironies of the modern age," he begins, "is that the advancements of mankind can make us more powerful and yet more vulnerable at the same time. The greater the power, the greater the vulnerability. You think, rightly so, that you are at the apex of your power, that you can do more things than ever before. But I see you at the peak of your vulnerability.

"The reason is reliance. Our society has become completely reliant on technology. The Internet of Things—you are familiar with the concept?"

"More or less," I say. "The connection of devices to the Internet."

"Yes, essentially. And not just laptop computers and smartphones. Anything with a power switch. Washing machines, coffeemakers, DVRs, digital cameras, thermostats, machine components, jet engines—the list of things, large and small, is almost endless. Two years ago, there were fifteen billion devices connected to the Internet. Two years from now? I have read estimates that the number will be fifty billion. I have heard one hundred billion. The layperson can hardly turn on a television anymore without seeing a commercial about the latest smart device and how it will do something you never would have thought possible twenty years ago. It will order flowers for you. It will let you see someone standing outside the front door of your home while you are at work. It will tell you if there is road construction up ahead and a faster route to your destination."

"And all that connectivity makes us more vulnerable to malware and spyware," I say. "We understand that. But I'm not so concerned, right at the moment, about whether Siri will tell me the weather in Buenos Aires or whether some foreign nation is spying on me through my toaster."

Augie moves about the room, as if lecturing on a large stage to an audience of thousands. "No, no—but I have digressed. More to the point, nearly every sophisticated form of automation, nearly every transaction in the modern world, relies on the Internet. Let me say it like this: we depend on the power grid for electricity, do we not?"

"Of course."

"And without electricity? It would be chaos. Why?" He looks at each of us, awaiting an answer.

"Because there's no substitute for electricity," I say. "Not really."

He points at me. "Correct. Because we are so reliant on something that has no substitute."

"And the same is now true of the Internet," says Noya, as much to herself as to anyone else.

Augie bows slightly. "Most assuredly, Madam Prime Minister. A whole host of functions that were once performed without the Internet now can *only* be performed *with* the Internet. There is no fallback. Not anymore. And you are correct—the world will not collapse if we cannot ask our smartphones what the capital of Indonesia is. The world will not collapse if our microwave ovens stop heating up our breakfast burritos or if our DVRs stop working."

Augie paces a bit, looking down, hands in his pockets, every bit the professor in midlecture.

"But what if *everything* stopped working?" he says.

The room goes silent. Chancellor Richter, raising a cup of coffee to his lips, freezes midstream. Noya looks like she's holding her breath.

Dark Ages, I think to myself.

"But the Internet is not as vulnerable as you are saying," says Dieter Kohl, who may not be Augie's equal on these matters but is far more knowledgeable than any of the elected officials in the room. "A server may become compromised, slowing or even blocking traffic, but then another one is used. The traffic routes are dynamic."

"But what if every route were compromised?" Augie asks.

Kohl works that over, his mouth pursed as if about to speak, suspended in that position. He closes his eyes and shakes his head. "How would...that be possible?"

"It would be possible with time, patience, and skill," says Augie. "If the virus was not detected when it infiltrated the server. And if it stayed dormant after infiltration."

"How did you infiltrate the servers? Phishing attacks?"

Augie makes a face, as if insulted. "On occasion. But primarily, no. Primarily we used misdirection. DDoS attacks, corruption of the BGP tables."

"Augie," I say.

"Oh, yes, I apologize. Speak English, you said. Very well. A DDoS attack is a distributed denial-of-service attack. A flood attack, essentially, on the network of servers that convert the URL addresses we type into our browsers into IP numbers that Internet routers use."

"Augie," I say again.

He smiles in apology. "Here: you type in www.cnn.com, but the network converts it to a routing number to direct traffic. A flood attack sends bogus traffic to the network and overwhelms it, so the network stalls or crashes. In October of 2016, a DDoS attack shut down many servers, and thus many prominent websites in America, for nearly an entire day. Twitter, PlayStation, CNN, Spotify, Verizon, Comcast, not to mention thousands of online retail operations, were all disrupted.

"And then the corruption of the BGP tables—

the border gateway protocol tables. The service providers, such as, for example, AT&T—they will essentially advertise on those tables who their clients are. If Company ABC uses AT&T for Internet service, then AT&T will advertise on those tables, 'If you want to access Company ABC's website, go through us.' Let's say you're in China, for example, using VelaTel, and you want to access Company ABC's website. You will have to hop from VelaTel to NTT in Japan, and then hop to AT&T in America. The BGP tables tell you the path. We, of course, just type in a website or click on a link, but often what is happening almost instantaneously is a series of hops across Internet service providers, using the BGP tables as a map.

"The problem is that these BGP tables are set up on trust. You may recall that several years ago, VelaTel, called ChinaTel at the time, claimed one day that it was the final hop for traffic to the Pentagon, and thus for some period of time, a good portion of Internet traffic intended for the Pentagon was routed through China."

I know about it now, but I wasn't aware of it then. I was just the governor of North Carolina back then. Simpler times. The understatement of the century.

"A sophisticated hacker," says Augie, "could

invade the BGP tables at the top twenty Internet service providers around the world, scramble the tables, and thus misdirect traffic. It would be the same effect as a DDoS attack. It would temporarily shut down Internet service to anyone served by that provider."

"But how does that relate to the installation of the virus?" asks Noya. "The object of a DDoS attack, as I understand it, is to shut down Internet service to a provider."

"Yes."

"And it sounds as if this—this scrambling of the BGP tables has the same effect."

"Yes. And as you can imagine, it is very serious. A service provider cannot afford to lose service to its customers. That is its whole reason for existence. It must act immediately to fix the problem or it will lose its customers and go out of business."

"Of course," says Noya.

"As I said before, misdirection." Augie waves a hand. "We used the BGP tables and the DDoS attacks as platforms to invade the servers."

Noya raises her chin, getting it now. Augie had to explain all this to me more than once. "So while they were focusing on that emergency, you snuck in and planted the virus."

"An accurate enough summary, yes." Augie

cannot help but beam with pride. "And because the virus was dormant—because it was hidden and performed no malicious function—they never noticed."

"Dormant for how long?" asks Dieter Kohl.

"Years. I believe we started..." He looks upward, squints. "Three years ago?"

"The virus has been lying dormant for three years?"

"In some cases, yes."

"And you've infected how many servers?"

Augie takes a breath, a child prepared to deliver bad news to his parents. "The virus is programmed to infect every node—every device that receives Internet service from the provider."

"And..." Kohl pauses, as if afraid to probe further, afraid to open the door to the dark closet to find out what's hidden inside. "Approximately how many Internet service providers did you infect?"

"Approximately?" Augie shrugs his shoulders. "All of them," he says.

Everyone wilts under the news. Richter, unable to sit still, rises from his chair and leans against the wall, folding his arms. Noya whispers something to her aide. People of great power, feeling powerless.

"If you have infected every Internet service provider in the country, and those providers have, in turn, passed on the virus to every client, every node, every device, that means…" Dieter Kohl falls back in his chair.

"We have infected virtually every device that uses the Internet in the United States."

The prime minister and chancellor both look at me, each turning pale. The attack we are discussing is on America, but they know full well that their countries could be next.

Which is part of the reason I wanted Augie to explain this to them.

"Just the United States?" Chancellor Richter asks. "The Internet connects the entire world."

"A fair point," says Augie. "We targeted only the ISPs in the United States. No doubt there will be some transfer to other countries as data from American devices is sent abroad. There is no way to know for certain, but we wouldn't expect the spread to be significant. We were focusing on the United States. The goal was to cripple the United States."

This is far broader than our worst fears. When the virus peeked at us, it was on a Pentagon server. We all thought military. Or government, at least. But Augie is telling us it goes far, far beyond government usage. It will affect every industry, countless aspects of daily life, every household, all facets of our lives.

"What you're telling us," says Chancellor Richter, his voice shaky, "is that you're going to steal the Internet from America."

Augie looks at Richter, then at me.

"Yes, but that's just the beginning," I say. "Augie, tell them what the virus will do."

CHAPTER
60

❖

The virus is essentially what you call a wiper virus," says Augie. "As the name suggests, a wiper attack erases—wipes out—all software on a device. Your laptop computers will be useful only as doorstops, your routers as paperweights. The servers will be erased. You will have no Internet service, that is surely true, but your devices will not work, either."

Dark Ages.

Augie picks an apple out of the fruit bowl and tosses it in his hand. "Most viruses and attack codes are designed to infiltrate surreptitiously and steal data," he explains. "Think of a burglar who sneaks in through a window and tiptoes quietly through a house. He wants to get in and out without detection. And if the theft is ever detected, it's too late.

"Wiper attacks, on the other hand, are noisy. They *want* you to know what they're doing. There's no reason to hide. Because they want something from you. They are, essentially— well, not essentially—they are *actually* holding the contents of your device hostage. Pay the ransom or say good-bye to all your files. Of course, they have no particular desire to delete all your data. They just want your money."

He opens his hand. "Well, our virus is a silent wiper attack. We have entered quietly and infiltrated to the maximum extent possible. But we do not want ransom. We *want* to delete all your files."

"And backup files are no help," says Dieter Kohl, shaking his head. "Because you have infected them as well."

"Of course. The virus has been uploaded onto the backup files by the very act of backing up the systems on a routine basis."

"They're time bombs," I say. "They've been hiding inside devices waiting for the moment they're called into action."

"Yes."

"And that day is today."

We look around the room at one another. I've had a couple of hours to digest this, having had all this explained to me by Augie on Marine One.

I was probably wearing the same holy-shit expression on that helicopter that all of them are wearing right now.

"So you appreciate the consequences," says Augie. "Fifty years ago, you had typewriters and carbon paper. Now you only have computers. Fifty years ago—in most cases, *ten or fifteen* years ago—you didn't rely on connectivity to run so many of your operations. But now you do. It is the only way you operate. Take it away, and there is no fallback."

The room is quiet. Augie looks down at his shoes, maybe out of respect for the grieving, or maybe out of apology. What he is describing is something that he had a big hand in creating.

"Give us an idea of..." Noya Baram rubs her temples.

"Oh, well." Augie begins to stroll around again. "The examples are limitless. Small examples: elevators stop working. Grocery-store scanners. Train and bus passes. Televisions. Phones. Radios. Traffic lights. Credit-card scanners. Home alarm systems. Laptop computers will lose all their software, all files, everything erased. Your computer will be nothing but a keyboard and a blank screen.

"Electricity would be severely compromised. Which means refrigerators. In some cases, heat.

Water—well, we have already seen the effect on water-purification plants. Clean water in America will quickly become a scarcity.

"That means health problems on a massive scale. Who will care for the sick? Hospitals? Will they have the necessary resources to treat you? Surgical operations these days are highly computerized. And they will not have access to any of your prior medical records online.

"For that matter, will they treat you at all? Do you have health insurance? Says who? A card in your pocket? They won't be able to look you up and confirm it. Nor will they be able to seek reimbursement from the insurer. And even if they could get in contact with the insurance company, the insurance company won't know whether you're its customer. Does it have handwritten lists of its policyholders? No. It's all on computers. Computers that have been erased. Will the hospitals work for free?

"No websites, of course. No e-commerce. Conveyor belts. Sophisticated machinery inside manufacturing plants. Payroll records.

"Planes will be grounded. Even trains may not operate in most places. Cars, at least any built since, oh, 2010 or so, will be affected.

"Legal records. Welfare records. Law enforcement databases. The ability of local police to identify criminals, to coordinate with other states and the federal government through databases—no more.

"Bank records. You think you have ten thousand dollars in your savings account? Fifty thousand dollars in a retirement account? You think you have a pension that allows you to receive a fixed payment every month?" He shakes his head. "Not if computer files and their backups are erased. Do banks have a large wad of cash, wrapped in a rubber band with your name on it, sitting in a vault somewhere? Of course not. It's all data."

"Mother of God," says Chancellor Richter, wiping his face with a handkerchief.

"Surely," Augie continues, "banks were some of the first companies to realize their vulnerability and to segregate some of their records onto separate systems. But we had already infected them. That was the first industry we targeted. So their segregated networks are just as compromised.

"The financial markets. There are no longer trading floors. It is all electronic. All trading through American exchanges will stop.

"Government functions, of course. The government depends on the collection of revenue. The tax rolls for income tax. The collection of sales taxes, excise taxes, and the like. All of it, gone. Where will the government get the money to function, to the extent it *can* function?

"The flow of currency will be suddenly reduced to hand-to-hand transactions in cash. And cash from where? You will not be able to go to your local bank, or to your nearest ATM, and withdraw cash, because the bank has no record of you.

"The economy in this country will screech to a halt. Entire industrial sectors dependent exclusively on the Internet will have no means of surviving. The others will be severely compromised. The impact will inevitably lead to massive unemployment, an enormous reduction in the availability of credit, a recession the likes of which would make your Depression in the 1930s look like a momentary hiccup.

"Panic," he says. "Widespread panic. A run on the banks. Looting of grocery stores. Rioting. Massive crime. The outbreak of diseases. All semblance of civil order gone.

"And I have not even mentioned military and national security capabilities. Your ability to track terrorists. Your surveillance capabilities. Your highly sophisticated air force will be grounded. Your missile-launching capability? No more. Radar and sonar? The high-tech telecommunications capabilities in your military? Gone.

"The United States will be vulnerable to attack in ways it has never been before," he says. "Your military defenses will be at nineteenth-century levels against enemies with twenty-first-century capabilities."

Like Russia. And China. And North Korea.

Dieter Kohl raises a hand. "If the Internet were *permanently* taken down, then it would be a…a catastrophe of epic proportions. But these problems would be fixed. It is not as if America would *forever* lose the Internet."

Augie nods, bows slightly. "You are correct, sir, that Internet capability would eventually be restored. It would probably take months to rebuild the entire network, from the Internet service providers all the way down to the end-use devices, all of whose systems, at every step of the chain, will have been destroyed completely. During that time, the United States will be vulnerable to a military attack or a terrorist strike as never before. During that time, entire sectors of the economy, heavily if not exclusively reliant on the Internet, will be destroyed. During that time, desperately sick people will not receive their treatments or their medical procedures. Every company, every bank, every hospital, every government office, every individual, will have to buy new devices because their old ones were destroyed.

"How long can the entire country go without clean drinking water? Without electricity? Without refrigeration? Without the ability to perform vital medical procedures and surgeries? Surely the United States would focus first on such critical needs and services, but how quickly could it restore even those things to a country of three hundred million people? Certainly not within a week, not to the entire country. Two weeks? Several months, more likely. The death toll, I should think, would be staggering.

"And even when Internet service is eventually restored, consider the damage that would be irreparable. Everyone in America will have lost all their savings, all their investments, all those records permanently erased. They will be utterly penniless except for the cash they happened to have on them when the virus struck. The same is true of their pensions, their health insurance, their welfare and Social Security benefits, their medical records. That data will never be recovered. Or if it were somehow recovered, without electronic data it would be an imperfect, unverifiable process—and it would take years. *Years.* How long can a person go without money?

"And if people do not have money, how can *any* sector of the economy remain viable? Not a single store on any street in this country, from your

Fifth Avenues and your Magnificent Miles and your Rodeo Drives down to the smallest stores in the smallest towns—how can any of them exist without customers? To say nothing of the Internet-based sectors of the industry. There will be nothing, absolutely nothing, left of the American economy."

"Great God," Chancellor Richter mumbles. "It's much worse than I had imagined."

"It's worse than anyone could imagine," says Augie. "The United States of America will become the largest third-world country on earth."

CHAPTER
61

❖

Augie leaves my two guests, Prime Minister
Noya Baram and Chancellor Juergen
Richter, dazed and silenced. Richter removes his
suit jacket, revealing his vest, and again wipes his
forehead with a handkerchief. Noya serves herself a large glass of water.

"Why..." Richter brings a hand to his chin,
rubbing it. "Why would Russia do this?"

If it's Russia, I think to myself.

"Is it not obvious?" asks Noya Baram after a
long drink of water, dabbing her lips with a
napkin.

"To me it is not. Is there a military component
here? If America's military capabilities are compromised, if her infrastructure is in tatters—
does that make the United States vulnerable to

a military attack? It cannot be. Can it? Russia would attack the United States? Surely…" He waves a hand. "Surely the United States—perhaps she would be momentarily vulnerable, yes, but surely America would rebuild her might. And then, of course, there is Article 5."

Under Article 5 of the North Atlantic Treaty, an attack on one NATO nation is an attack on all. An attack on the United States could trigger a world war.

Theoretically, at least. That doctrine has never been put to the ultimate test. If Russia disabled our military infrastructure and followed it up by hitting us with nuclear weapons, would our nuclear NATO members—Germany, for example, or the UK or France—respond in kind against Russia? It would test our alliance as never before. Each one of those countries, should it do so, would be guaranteed a retaliatory nuclear strike.

That's why it's so important for Richter to realize that Germany could be next, that he can't let Russia—or whoever is responsible—get away with this.

"But who is Russia's greatest impediment?" Noya asks. "Whom does Russia fear the most?"

"NATO," says Richter.

Noya's shoulders rise. "Well, yes—yes, Juergen. Yes, NATO's expansion to the borders of

Russia is of great concern to them. But in Russia's eyes, and of course I mean no disrespect, Juergen—but in Russia's eyes, when it sees NATO, it sees America. America, first and foremost, and then its allies."

"So what does Russia gain?" I get out of my chair, unable to sit still. "I can understand Russia wanting to disable us. To set us back. To leave us wounded. But destroy us?"

"Jonny," says Noya, setting down her water. "During the Cold War, the United States—you always believed that the Soviets wanted to destroy you. And they assumed the same of you. A lot has changed over the last twenty-five, thirty years. The Soviet empire collapsed. Russia's military degraded. NATO expanded to Russia's borders. But has anything *really* changed? Russia feels as threatened by you as ever. Ultimately, given the chance, do you not think it would be a viable option once more? Are you willing to risk being wrong?" Her head tilting to the side, a heavy sigh released, she says, "You have no choice but to prepare for the possibility of a direct strike on America."

It's almost unfathomable. Almost. But my job is to prepare for the worst, even as I work for the best. And anyone who thinks he fully understands President Chernokev is mistaken. The man plays a long game. But that doesn't mean he wouldn't take a shortcut if he could.

Chancellor Richter checks his watch. "We are still one delegation short," he says. "I would have thought they'd be here by now."

"They have a few things on their minds," I say.

Alex Trimble walks into the room. I turn to him.

"They've arrived, Mr. President," he says. "The Russians are here."

CHAPTER
62

❖

The convoy of black SUVs pulls into the driveway. Russian security agents emerge from the first SUV, conferring with Jacobson and others from Secret Service.

I stand ready to receive them, one thought dominating all others:

This is how wars begin.

I asked President Chernokev to attend our summit at the same time I reached out to Israel and Germany. I didn't know of Russia's involvement at the time—I still don't, not for certain—but that country has the best cyberterrorists in the world, and if they aren't behind this, then they can help, and they have just as much to fear as we do. If the United States is vulnerable, so is everybody else. Including Russia.

And if Russia *is* behind this, it still makes sense to have the country represented here. When Sun Tzu said, "Keep your friends close and your enemies closer," he had a point.

But it was also a test. If Russia was behind Dark Ages, I didn't think President Chernokev would be willing to come and sit with me while this virus detonated and spread mass destruction in its wake. He would send someone in his stead, for appearance's sake.

The Russian agents open the rear door of the second SUV.

One official steps out: Prime Minister Ivan Volkov.

Chernokev's handpicked second in command, a former colonel in the Red Army. To some, the Butcher of Crimea.

The military leader behind suspected war crimes in Chechnya, Crimea, and, later, Ukraine, from the rape and murder of innocent civilians to the merciless torture of POWs and the suspected use of chemical weapons.

He is built like a stack of bricks, short and solid, his hair cut so tight that only a small strip of dark hair on top of his head is visible, almost like a Mohawk. He is near sixty but physically fit, a former boxer who spends time every day in the gym, as far as we understand, with sharp wrinkles on his prominent forehead and a flat nose that has been broken more than once in the ring.

"Mr. Prime Minister," I say, standing alone on the driveway, my hand extended.

"Mr. President." His expression implacable, his dark eyes peering into mine, he shakes my hand with an iron grip. He is dressed in a black suit and a tie that is a solid blue on the top half, red on the bottom, two-thirds of the Russian flag.

"I was disappointed that President Chernokev could not come personally."

I was more than disappointed.

"As is he, Mr. President. He has been ill for several days. Nothing serious, but he was not available to travel. I can assure you that I speak with his full authority. And the president wanted me to convey his disappointment as well. In fact more than disappointment. Concern. Deep concern over recent provocative actions by your country."

I gesture down to the backyard. He nods, and we start to walk into the backyard. "The tent, yes," he says. "Appropriate for this conversation."

The black tent has no door, no zipper, only heavy overlapping flaps on the front. I put my hands together and slide them through, divide the flaps and enter, as Prime Minister Volkov follows.

Inside, all outside light is blocked out, the only illumination provided by artificial kerosene lamps in the corners. A small wooden table and chairs have been set up, as if a picnic were planned, but I make no move for them. For this conversation, just the two of us—just me and a man reported to be responsible for the savage butchering of innocent civilians, a man representing a country that may well be behind this terrifying attack on my country—I prefer to stand.

"President Chernokev has been quite alarmed at your provocative military actions of the last thirty-six hours," he says. With his thick accent, the words drip from his tongue, particularly *provocative*.

"Just training missions," I say.

A sour smile passes and fades from his lips. "Training missions," he says, the words bitter on his tongue. "Just as in 2014."

In 2014, after Russia invaded Ukraine, the United States sent two B-2 stealth bombers to Europe for "training missions." The message was clear enough.

"Just like that, yes," I say.

"But far more extensive," he says. "The movement of aircraft carriers and nuclear-armed submarines into the North Sea. Your stealth aircraft exercises over Germany. And of course the joint military exercises in Latvia and Poland."

Two current members of NATO. One of them, Latvia, sharing a border with Russia, and the other, Poland, not far away, on Belarus's southwestern flank.

"Including a simulated nuclear strike," he adds.

"Russia has done the same thing recently," I note.

"Not within *fifty miles of your borders.*" His jaw muscles clench, squaring off his face. There is a challenge in his words, but there is fear, too.

The fear is real. Neither of us wants war. Neither of us will win. The question is always, how far are we willing to be pushed? That's why we must be so careful about drawing lines in the sand. If those lines are crossed and we do nothing, we lose credibility. If they are crossed and we respond—well, that response is the war that neither of us wants.

"Mr. Prime Minister," I say, "you know the reason I invited you. The virus."

He blinks, his thick eyebrows bend, as if surprised at the segue. But that's a feint. He knows one thing follows the other.

"We discovered the presence of the virus about two weeks ago," I say. "And when we did, the first thing that occurred to us was our vulnerability to a military attack. If the virus were to disable our military effectiveness, we would be open to an attack. So, Mr. Prime Minister, we immediately did two things.

"The first thing we did was re-create our continental systems, here at home. We basically started over. Call it reinventing the wheel, reverse engineering, whatever you like. We've rebuilt our operational systems, disconnected from any device that could possibly be infected by the virus. New servers, new computers—everything new.

"We started with the things that matter the most—our strategic-defense systems, our nuclear fleet—and made sure that they were re-created free of any virus. And then we went from there. I'm happy to report, Mr. Prime Minister, that we have successfully completed that operation. It took us every second of these two weeks, but we did it. We have rebuilt our entire military operational infrastructure in the continental United States. We built those systems the first time around, after all, so it wasn't as hard as you might think to re-create them."

Volkov is stoic, taking this in. He doesn't trust me any more than I trust him. We didn't publicize any of this work. Our re-creation of our military infrastructure was done, for obvious reasons, in utter secrecy. From his perspective, I might be bluffing. He can't confirm anything I've just told him.

So now we're going to talk about something he *can* confirm.

"The second thing we did, simultaneously," I say, "was make sure we disconnected our *overseas* military infrastructure from anything stateside. The same kind of reverse engineering. The long and short of it is, any computerized systems in our European arsenal that depended on our continental infrastructure—well, we replaced them with new systems. We made them independent. We wanted to make sure that, if all our systems in the United States crashed, if all our computers went kaput…"

Something seems to dim in Volkov's eyes. He blinks and looks away, but then quickly returns his eyes to mine.

"We wanted to make sure, Mr. Prime Minister," I say, "that even if someone utterly and completely destroyed our stateside military operational systems, we were armed and ready with our European resources—that we were prepared to respond militarily against any nation responsible for the virus. Or any nation that had the ridiculous idea that it could take advantage of the United States during that difficult time by, say, attacking us.

"So clearly, these European training exercises were necessary," I say. "And the good news is, they have all been successful. You probably already know that."

The color in his face changes. He does know that. The Russians, obviously, closely followed our training exercises. But he's not going to give me the satisfaction of acknowledging that fact.

The truth? There was only so much we could accomplish in two weeks. Only our generals know how thin and provisional these new systems are, how rudimentary compared to our existing systems. But they assure me they are effective and secure. Commands will go through. Missiles will fire. Targets will be hit.

"We now have full confidence," I continue, "that even if somehow the virus still managed to infect our stateside operational network, we have the full capacity to engage in warfare of any kind—nuclear, air, conventional, what have you—from our NATO bases in Europe. Anyone responsible for this virus, Mr. Prime Minister, or any nation that tries to take advantage of this difficult time to attack the United States or its allies—we reserve the right, and we will have the full capacity, to respond with overwhelming force.

"So it's nothing specific to Russia. It just so happens that many of our NATO allies happen to be in your backyard. Right," I say, drawing it out, "in your backyard."

Volkov's eyebrows flare a bit with that reminder. The expansion of NATO to the Russian borders, as Noya pointed out, has been the cause of great consternation in the Kremlin.

"But if Russia had nothing to do with this virus, as President Chernokev has assured us, and as long as Russia makes no attempt to take advantage of us, Russia has nothing to worry about." I wave a hand. "Nothing at all."

He nods slowly, some of the vinegar in his expression lost now.

"I'll say it to anyone," I say, "whoever is responsible for this virus. We *will* find out who did this. And if that virus detonates, we will consider it an act of war."

Volkov is still nodding, his Adam's apple bobbing as he swallows that down.

"We will not strike first, Mr. Prime Minister. That is my solemn vow. But if we are struck, we will strike back."

I put my hand on the prime minister's shoulder. "So please relay that to President Chernokev. And please convey to him that I hope he's feeling better."

I lean in to him. "And then let's see if you can help us stop that virus," I say.

CHAPTER
63

❖

N oya Baram and I stand on the dock looking at the lake, the midday sun gaining
ground in the sky, its beams reflecting off the
shimmering water, the serenity and beauty of the
scene grotesquely contrasted with the feeling of
impending doom taking up residence in my gut.
Not since Kennedy stared down Khrushchev
over the missiles in Cuba has our nation been
this close to world war.

I've done it now. I've drawn the line in the sand.
Now they know our military structure is operational, the virus notwithstanding. And now they
know that if they planted this virus and it detonates, the United States will consider it a first
strike and respond accordingly.

One of my Secret Service agents stands near

the dock with one member each of the security details from Germany and Israel. About fifty yards from the shore, three men sit in a gray twenty-five-foot motorboat, two of them lazily holding fishing rods for show, though they are not there to catch largemouth bass or catfish. All three are Secret Service—men without young children, at my insistence. Their boat is a Defender-class "Charlie" boat used by Homeland Security and the Coast Guard, this one recently taken out of rotation at Guantánamo Bay and snatched up by Secret Service. Now it looks pretty much like an ordinary motorboat, but that's because it's impossible to tell that its updated hull is armored and bulletproof. The agents have thrown tarps over the machine guns mounted on the port and starboard sides by the cabin as well as the .50-caliber machine gun on the bow.

They are on a small bay of water that feeds into the larger man-made reservoir, staying close to the narrow opening that protects this private bay from the rest of the lake.

I look back up the trail toward the cabin, toward the black tent on the lawn. "Volkov has been in and out of that tent so many times you'd think he was going for a merit badge."

For the last three hours, Volkov has been repeatedly summoned by Moscow for more phone calls, sending him back into the tent.

"It means he believed you," Noya says.

"Oh, they believe we're capable of a counter-strike," I say. "Those training exercises left no doubt. Do they believe I'll actually do it? That's another question."

Instinctively I brush my hand against the wallet in my pocket, which holds the nuclear codes.

Noya turns and looks at me. "Do *you* believe you'll do it?"

That's the million-dollar question. "What would you do, Noya?"

She moans. "Imagine if the virus detonates," she says. "Economic collapse, panic, mass hysteria. In the midst of that, do you send troops to Russia? Do you launch nuclear missiles at Moscow?"

"They'd respond in kind," I say.

"Yes. So not only are you facing unprecedented domestic problems, but millions of Americans are also exposed to nuclear radiation. Could your nation survive all that at once?"

I put my hands on my knees. An old habit, when I'm nervous, from my days on the baseball mound.

"But the flip side of the coin," she says, "is how do you *not* respond? What will become of the

United States if there is no retaliation? You *must* retaliate in some way, yes?"

I find a stone in the grass, pick it up, and hurl it into the lake. I had a live fastball. It occurs to me that if I hadn't trashed my shoulder falling out of a Black Hawk helicopter in Iraq, I wouldn't be here right now.

"The United States will retaliate," I say. "There's no scenario in which we don't retaliate."

She says, "Your Joint Chiefs prefer a conventional war, I assume."

Of course they do. A nuclear war is a lose-lose proposition. You only launch if you have no choice, because the other side launched first. That's why nobody has triggered that option. Mutually assured destruction has worked for a reason.

"But a ground invasion of Russia?" she says. "Even if your NATO allies join in, it will be long and bloody."

"We'd win," I say. "Eventually. But then what would Chernokev do? He'd use nuclear weapons, that's what he'd do. If his back was against the wall? If he was going to be ousted? He'd have nothing to lose. He cares more about his own ass than his people."

"So you're right back at a nuclear holocaust."

"Right. We lose thousands of men and women

on the Russian battlefield, and then he launches nukes anyway."

Noya is quiet. What can she say?

"Okay, well." I throw up my hands. "None of that is an option. The only option is stopping that goddamn virus and not having to make that decision."

"And you've done what you can, Jonny. You've given Russia every reason to want to help you."

I rub my face with my hands, as if I can cleanse away the stress. "Well, that was the point of my threat." I gesture up the path, toward the cabin. "Volkov's still in the black tent, communicating back home. I hope they're taking the message seriously."

"Assuming it's Russia," she reminds me. "We don't know this for certain. How is China responding to the Japanese exercises?"

We just did essentially the same thing in Japan that we did in Europe, the air exercises and the nuclear simulation.

"Beijing wasn't happy," I say. "My defense secretary basically read from the same script. He told them we were testing new technology, independent of our continental systems. He didn't mention the virus, but if China's behind it, they got the message."

"They're probably concerned about what Pyongyang is thinking."

Yes, we can expect more fire-and-brimstone language from the North Korean dictator.

Noya grips my arm. "If it's any consolation, I would not do anything differently from what you've done. You've fortified your military capabilities, you've demonstrated those fortified capabilities for all the world to see, you've issued an ultimatum to Volkov, and you've assembled the best minds you can possibly gather together to stop this virus."

"You have no idea how consoling that is," I say as we turn and begin the walk up the path toward the cabin.

"Then believe in the plan," she says.

We approach the black tent in the backyard, where the Russian security detail remains, standing at attention. Then the men step back, and Prime Minister Volkov emerges from the tent, fixing his tie, nodding at his men.

"If he leaves now," I whisper to Noya, "we'll have the answer to our question."

"He'll make an excuse. He'll say he's leaving to protest your military exercises off their border."

Right. But the stated reason won't matter. If the Russians leave now, after the threat I've issued, there will be no doubt that they're behind this.

Volkov turns and sees us approach.

"Mr. President, Madam Prime Minister." Seeing

Noya for the first time, he greets her with a handshake, all formality.

Then he looks at me. I don't say anything. It's his move.

"President Chernokev assures you, Mr. President, that Russia remains committed to helping you prevent this horrific virus from detonating." He gestures to the cabin. "Shall we head inside?" he says.

CHAPTER
64

❖

P lan B.
　　This is it. Her last job. Her last kill. And
then she will be done, wealthy and free to raise
her unborn daughter somewhere far away from
all this. Her daughter will know love. She will
know happiness. War and violence will be something she reads about in books or hears about on
the news.

She checks her watch. It's almost time.

She squints up at the afternoon sun. The morning sickness is there as always, aggravated by the
gentle rocking of the boat on the lake, but her
adrenaline overwhelms it. She has no time for
nausea right now.

She glances over at the other team members on
the boat, ridiculous as they look with their hats

and fishing poles. They've kept their distance after she killed two of their comrades. That's fine with her. In all likelihood, their role in the mission is over now anyway, other than giving her a ride.

She may need to reconsider her opinion of men now. Studies say that children with two parents are happier, healthier, more well adjusted. So maybe she'll marry. It's hard to imagine. She's simply never felt the need for a man.

Sex? Sex to her was a price to be paid. A price to be paid by her mother to the Serbian soldiers for allowing her and her two children to remain in their home after they killed her father, officially because she was Christian, not Muslim, like her husband, but in reality because of her beauty and willingness, for her children's sake, to satisfy the soldiers' needs on demand on a nightly basis. Sex was the price Bach paid for the bread and rice she would steal in the marketplace on those evenings when she couldn't escape the soldiers' ambush. Sex was the price to be paid to get close to Ranko, the Serbian soldier who agreed to teach her how to fire a rifle from long range.

And of course it was the price to be paid for having a child of her own. The man who impregnated her, Geoffrey, was a good man, a man she chose deliberately for that purpose after careful research. Brains: a radiologist who studied here in the States, at Yale. Musical ability: played the cello. Athletic: played rugby in college. Handsome, with good bone structure. No history of cancer or mental illness in his immediate family. His parents were still alive, in their eighties. She slept with him no more than three times a week to maximize his potency. She stuck around until she got a positive test result, then left Melbourne without another word. He never knew her real name.

"Is time," says one of the men, tapping his watch.

Bach hikes the oxygen tank onto her back. Piles on her other bag. Slings her rifle, Anna Magdalena, protected in its case, over her shoulder.

She puts on the mask, adjusts it, and nods at the rest of her team, giving each of them one last look. When this is over, she wonders, will they in fact transport her back to the extraction point? Or will they try to kill her once she's performed the mission, once she is no longer useful to them?

The latter, probably. Something she will deal with when the time comes.

She falls backward off the boat, into the lake water.

CHAPTER
65

❖

I nside the communications room, I am talking to my CIA director, Erica Beatty. Danny always calls her spooky, not as a pun on her career-long allegiance to the agency but because of her poker-face demeanor and the dark circles under her hooded eyes. *I know she's seen and done a lot,* he has said, *and who knows what the East Germans really did to her in captivity, but damn, I can't shake the image of her brewing potions in a boiling cauldron inside her gingerbread house.*

Spooky, yes. But she's my spook. And she knows more about Russia than anyone with a pulse.

She's also one of the six people who could have leaked "Dark Ages."

"So what does he do, Erica?"

She nods her head, digesting everything I've told her. *"Mr. President, this is not Chernokev's style,"* she says. *"He is ruthless, yes, but not reckless. Of course he would be interested in causing great damage to our country, but the risk is too high. If Russia is implicated in this, he knows we will retaliate with great force. I don't see him taking this chance."*

"But answer my question," I say. "If he is behind this virus, and now he sees that we have restored our military capabilities, what does he do?"

"He abandons his plan," she says. *"The risk is far greater to him now, because no matter how paralyzed we might be at home, we could still strike him. But Mr. President, I do not see Russian fingerprints on this."*

My phone buzzes: C. Brock.

"I have to run, Erica."

"Are you near the computer?" Carolyn asks when I answer the phone.

Moments later, my computer screen is split between Carolyn Brock, at the White House, and a video, currently frozen on an image of Tony Winters, the host of *Meet the Press,* his hair expertly coiffed, his tie knotted perfectly, his hands raised and mouth pursed in midspeech.

"They completed it a half hour ago," says Carolyn. *"They're going to start running excerpts this morning. Full interview runs tomorrow morning."*

"They're going to start running excerpts this morning. Full interview runs tomorrow morning."

I nod. The video starts to play.

Winters, caught in midsentence: *"—vernight reports that the president is missing, that not even his aides know where he is. Madam Vice President, is the president missing?"*

Kathy nods, as if expecting the question, her expression somber. I'd have expected mirth, as in, *What a ridiculous question.* She raises a hand and brings it down like a hatchet. *"Tony, the president is working day and night for the people of this country, to bring back jobs, to keep America safe, to provide tax relief to the middle class."*

"But has he gone missing?"

"Tony—"

"Do you know where he is?"

She smiles politely. Finally. *"Tony, I don't keep tabs on the president of the United States. But I can only assume that he is surrounded by aides and Secret Service at all times."*

"The reports say even his aides don't know where he is."

She opens her hands. *"I'm not going to respond to speculation."*

"Reports suggest that the president is getting away from Washington and preparing for his testimony this week before the House Select Committee. Others suggest

that his blood disease has flared up again and he's in treatment."

The vice president shakes her head.

"Here," says Carolyn. *"Right here."*

"Tony," says Kathy, *"I'm sure his critics would love to paint the picture of a president having a nervous breakdown, hiding under his covers, or fleeing the capital in a panic. But that's not the case. Whether I know his precise whereabouts at this moment or not, I know that he is in full control of the government. And that's all I'm going to say on the topic."*

The clip ends. I sit back in my chair.

Carolyn explodes. *"His* critics *would love to paint the picture of a nervous breakdown and hiding under his covers? Fleeing in panic?* She *just painted that picture! A nervous breakdown? Are you kidding me?"*

"This is why you called me?" I ask.

"That sound bite will run all day. Everyone's going to pick it up. The Sunday papers will lead with it."

"I don't care."

"None of those overnight reports said anything about a nervous breakdown or fleeing in—"

"Carrie."

"Mr. President, this was calculated. She's no rookie. She knew she was going to be asked the question. She had that response—"

"Carrie! I get it, okay? She did it on purpose. She stabbed me in the back. She's distancing herself from me. I don't care! Do you hear me? I. Don't. Care!"

"We have to respond. It's a problem."

"There's only one problem right now, Carrie. Have you heard? It's the one that might bring our country to its knees any minute now. We have"— I look at my watch; it's just past 2:00 p.m.—"about ten hours before 'Saturday in America' comes to an end, and any time between now and then, our country could go up in flames. So as much as I appreciate your loyalty, keep your eye on the prize. Got it?"

Carolyn bows her head, chastened. *"Yes, sir, I apologize. And I'm sorry I let her leave the operations center. She refused to listen. I couldn't very well order Secret Service to detain her."*

I breathe out, try to calm down. "That's on her, not you."

Politics aside, is Kathy's disloyalty significant? Kathy is, after all, one of the six people I haven't ruled out of suspicion.

If I'd died last night, she'd be president right now.

"Carrie, get hold of her," I say. "Tell her I want her back in the operations center in the subbasement. Tell her that when she gets there, I'll call her."

CHAPTER
66

❖

Bach positions herself on the seacraft, gripping the arms, much as a child would hold a kickboard when learning to swim. Except those kickboards aren't propelled by twin jet thrusters.

She pushes the green button on the left arm and aims the vehicle downward, plunging below the surface of the lake until she evens out at thirty feet below the surface. She pushes the button to accelerate the thrusters until she's moving at ten kilometers per hour through the murky water. She has a fair distance to travel. She is at the eastern end of this huge body of water.

"Boat to your north," says the voice in her earbud. *"Veer south. Left. Veer left."*

She sees the boat on the surface of the water,

but not before her team did, with their GPS and radar capabilities on the boat.

She veers left, thrusting through the foggy green water, the weeds and fish. The GPS on her console shows her the destination with a blinking green dot, and the number below ticks off her distance.

1800 m . . .

1500 m . . .

"Water skier from the right. Hold. Hold."

She sees the boat above her, to her right, its engine chopping at the water, followed by the skimming of the water by the skier.

She doesn't stop. She's well below them. She guns the watercraft and speeds past them, beneath them.

She'll have to get herself one of these toys.

1100 m . . .

She slows the watercraft. The lake bottoms out at fifty meters at its deepest, but as she gets close to shore, the land rises up sharply to the water, and the last thing she needs is to slam into the earth.

"Hold. Hold. Stay down. Stay down. Sentry. Sentry."

She comes to an abrupt halt nine hundred meters from the shore and doesn't move in the water, nearly losing her grip on the watercraft, allowing herself to drift lower in the lake. A member of the security detail—US Secret Service or the Germans or Israelis—must be in the woods near the shore, looking around.

There can't be very many of them patrolling the woods. It would require hundreds of people to secure more than a thousand acres of heavy woods, and their security details are light.

Last night—of course the agents walked the entire acreage, swept it thoroughly, before the president arrived.

But now they can't afford to patrol the woods. Most of the security will be around or inside the cabin, with a few at the dock and a few in the backyard, where the woods end.

"All clear," the voice finally says.

She gives it another minute for good measure, then proceeds onward. When she's three hundred meters from shore, she kills the engine entirely. She rides the momentum of this fun little toy upward until she's coasting on top of the water, much like someone riding a surfboard to shore. She stays low—as low as she can with an air tank, her rifle, and a bag tied to her back—until she beaches on the small clip of sand.

She removes the scuba mask and breathes fresh air. She glances around and sees nobody. This part of the lake bends around, so that she is entirely out of the sight line of anyone by the dock. The Secret Service cannot possibly see her.

She climbs up onto the land and finds the spot where she is to hide the watercraft and scuba gear. She does so quickly, stripping off the gear and throwing on clean, dry fatigues from her bag. She towel-dries her hair and makes sure her face and neck are free of any moisture before she applies the camouflage paint.

She uncases her rifle and slings it over her shoulder. Checks her sidearm.

She is ready to do this now. Alone, as she prefers it, as she's always been.

CHAPTER
67

❖

T he woods provide Bach excellent cover.
The tall, lush canopy trees block most of
the sunlight, which renders visibility difficult for
two reasons—the darkness itself and the inter-
mittent strips of sunlight penetrating the canopy,
which play tricks on the eyes. It's hard to see
much of anything in here.

She finds herself back in the Trebevic mountainside, on the run, in hiding, after it was over,
after she turned the tables on the sniper, Ranko,
the redheaded Serbian soldier who, for pity or
sex or both, had taught her how to fire a rifle.

"Here, again, you're using your arms too much!"
Ranko said as they sat up in the bombed-out nightclub
that served as a sniper's hideaway in the mountains.
"I do not understand you, girl. One day you can shoot

a bottle of beer off a tree stump from a hundred meters away, and today your mechanics are those of a beginner? Let me show you once more." Taking the gun from her, settling into the perch. "Hold steady, like this," he said, his last words before she stuck the kitchen knife into his neck.

Taking his rifle, on which she was now well trained, to the open window of the nightclub overlooking Sarajevo, aiming down at Ranko's comrades, the patrolling Serbian soldiers who had beaten her father to death and carved a cross in his chest, all for the crime of being Muslim. Pop-pop-pop-pop-pop, firing the rifle in rapid succession, picking them off one after the other after the other, having to lead the last one as he dropped his weapon and sprinted toward the trees.

She hid in the mountains for more than a week afterward, hungry and thirsty and cold, moving about constantly, afraid to stay in the same spot, as they hunted for the young girl who killed six Serbian soldiers, one of them up close and the others from a hundred meters away.

With the pack and rifle on her back, she moves forward gingerly; with each step, she plants her foot before shifting weight onto it. To her right, something jumps, and her heart skips a beat as she reaches for her sidearm. Some little animal, a rabbit or squirrel, gone before she can make it out. She waits for the adrenaline to drain.

"Two kilometers due north," they tell her in her earbud.

She continues her gentle, quiet movements forward. Her instinct is to move quickly to her spot, but discipline is essential. She doesn't know these woods. She never scouted the location, as she'd normally prefer. The ground is dark and uneven, obscured by the brush and lack of light, full of tree roots and branches and who knows what else.

Foot forward, weight forward, stop and listen. Foot forward, weight forward, stop and listen. Foot forward, weight for—

Movement.

Up ahead, appearing from around a tree.

The animal is no bigger than a large dog, with thick salt-and-pepper fur, tall ears perked at attention, a long snout, and beady black eyes that focus on her.

There aren't supposed to be any wolves around here. A coyote? Must be.

A coyote that is standing between her and her destination.

Another one now, a second one, popping its head up, farther down, about the same size.

A third one, a bit smaller and darker in color, separating itself from the others, moving to Bach's left, eyes on her, something fleshy dripping from its mouth.

A fourth one, to her right. A semicircle of four, in what she can only assume is some kind of formation.

A defensive formation. Or an attack formation. The latter, she decides.

Eight beady eyes on her.

She takes a step forward and hears a low growl, sees the sides of the first animal's long snout tremble, revealing teeth—presumably jagged fangs—that she's too far away to make out. The others, spurred on by their leader, join in, snarling and growling.

Are they coyotes? They're supposed to be afraid of humans.

Food, she thinks. They must be close to food or already feasting, maybe something big and tasty, like a deer carcass. They must see her as a threat to their lunch.

Unless they see *her* as the lunch.

She doesn't have time for this. It would be too risky and time-consuming to alter her path. One side is going to have to move, and it isn't going to be hers.

Her body otherwise still, she removes her sidearm, her SIG Sauer with the long suppressor.

The lead animal lowers its head, the growling louder, snapping at her.

She aims her weapon at the small space between its eyes. Then she adjusts her aim for its ear and fires once, a single suppressed *thwip*.

The animal yelps and spins around, bounding away in a flash, nothing worse than a small flesh wound on the tip of its ear. The others disappear just like that, too.

It might have been a problem if they'd all attacked at once, coming from different directions. She would have taken them all out, but it would have required more ammunition and probably made more noise.

It's always easier just to take out the leader.

If there is nothing else to learn from history, it's that from humans to animals, from the most primitive to the most civilized, most individuals want to be led.

Take out the leader, and the rest of the pack panics.

CHAPTER
68

❖

I t would be better if it came from you," I say
to Chancellor Richter as we confer in the
room I would call the cabin's family room. "The
other leaders in the European Union look to you,
Mr. Chancellor. That's no secret."

"Yes, well." Richter places his coffee cup on its
saucer, searches for a place to set it down, buying himself a moment to think. It never hurts to
stroke the boundless ego of the chancellor, the
longest-serving leader in the EU and, my flattery
aside, increasingly the most influential.

Never mind the fact that if the virus activates
and decisions of war must be made, I will be
making the same phone calls, with more or less
the same pleas, to the leaders of France, the UK,
Spain, Italy, and the other NATO countries.

If we have to invoke Article 5 of the NATO treaty and go to war with Russia or whatever country is behind this, I'd rather the motion to invoke came from someone other than the United States. Better yet, as was the case after 9/11, a motion joined by all NATO members. It would be better if it looked like an unsolicited decision rather than a plea from a wounded superpower.

He doesn't answer right away. I didn't expect him to. Still, it is the first time I've seen Juergen Richter at a loss for words.

In the background, from the corner, the television plays a continuous string of bad news: the water-supply difficulties in Los Angeles, possibly caused by terrorism; North Korea vowing another ballistic-missile test after our military exercises in Japan; the civil unrest in Honduras, where half the president's cabinet has resigned; further developments in the assassination plot against the Saudi king. But the lead story, of course, is the upcoming testimony of the president of the United States before the House Select Committee and, courtesy of my vice president, the question of whether the president is suffering from a "nervous breakdown" or has "fled the capital in a panic."

My phone buzzes—FBI Liz—saving the chancellor from the awkward silence. "Excuse me," I say.

I tap my earbud as I stand in the kitchen looking out over the backyard, the black tent, and the wall of endless trees beyond. "Go ahead, Liz," I say.

"The team members that the Secret Service killed on the bridge," says the acting FBI director, Elizabeth Greenfield. *"We've identified them."*

"And?"

"They are a part of a group called Ratnici. It means "warriors," basically. They're mercenaries. They come from all over the world, and they've fought all over the world. The narcos used them in Colombia. They fought for the rebels in Sudan until the government hired them to switch sides. They fought for the Tunisian government against the ISIS insurgency there."

"It's what we figured. Cutouts. Untraceable."

"But Ratnici doesn't work for free. They're soldiers, not ideologues. Somebody paid them. And for something like this, Mr. President, you can only imagine how much money they'd demand."

"That's right," I say. "Good. You're going to follow the money."

"We're trying, sir. It's our best lead."

"Keep at it, as fast as you can," I say as the door leading to the basement opens behind me.

Up walk the Americans on our tech team,

Devin Wittmer and Casey Alvarez, a wave of cigarette smoke wafting off them. I don't know them
to be smokers, but I assume some of the Europeans are.

Devin is no longer wearing his sport jacket. His
shirt has come partially untucked, and his sleeves
are rolled up. The wear on his face is evident.

But he has a smile on his face.

Some of Casey's ponytail is undone. She removes her glasses and rubs her eyes, but the up-
turn of her mouth is promising.

I feel something flutter through my chest.

"We located it, Mr. President," says Devin. "We
found the virus."

CHAPTER
69

❖

*F*oot forward, weight forward, stop and listen.
  Foot forward, weight forward, stop and listen.
It worked for her when foraging for food in the
markets of Sarajevo. It worked for her when hiding from the Serbian army in the mountainside
as they searched for the half-Muslim Bosnian
girl who killed six of their men.

It worked for her a week later, when she finally
summoned the courage to sneak down from the
mountains to her home.

A home that had burned to the ground. A two-
story house, now little more than a heap of gray
ash and rubble.

Next to it, her mother's naked body, tied to a
tree, her throat slashed open.

Two kilometers. Bach could run the distance

in twelve minutes, even with this pack on her back. She could walk it in twenty. But it takes her almost forty minutes in this cautious, plodding fashion.

Along the way, little animals bounce out of her path, even a few deer, freezing in place on her approach, then bounding away. But no more coyotes, or whatever they were. Maybe word got out not to mess with the girl with the gun.

She hasn't strayed far from the east side of the acreage, heading due north during her jaunt and sticking close to the lake's shoreline. The patrols aren't likely to come from that side but rather from the north, south, or west.

She reaches the tree, the thickest one she's seen in these woods. Sixty feet high and two feet in diameter, she was told, which to her means about eighteen meters high and sixty centimeters wide. Tall and skinny.

This is where it will happen. This is where she will kill him.

Above her, the tree is thick with leaves and strong branches, easy to climb. But from the ground, there is nothing to latch onto. Full climbing gear—a lanyard, foot spikes—would be too cumbersome, too heavy to transport.

From her bag, she removes the cord of rope with a noose on one end. She throws it up over the lowest-hanging branch, a good four meters above ground—about thirteen feet high. It takes her three tries to get the noose end over the branch. Then she raises up the other side of the rope as the noose side lowers down to her.

Once she has it in her hand, she slides the straight end of the rope through the noose. Then she pulls down on the straight end slowly, careful to avoid any snags, as the noose end slowly rises again. On the branch, the two sides come together in a knot.

She puts on the backpack again, and the rifle, and grips the rope. She'll need to do this fast. It's a lot of weight to put on the branch, so the less time it takes, the better.

She takes a breath. Her nausea has subsided, but she is bone-tired, weary and shaky. She fantasizes about sleep, about stretching out her legs and closing her eyes.

Her team may have had a point about her going it alone. They wanted to deploy a force of ten or twelve in the woods. That would have been fine with her, but the risk was too great. She couldn't know how heavy the patrols of the woods would be. It was hard enough for her to make it to her spot alone without incident. Multiply one person by twelve, and that's a dozen different opportunities for detection. It would only take one mistake, one person who was too loud or clumsy, and the entire operation would be blown.

She looks around one more time, seeing nothing, hearing nothing.

She climbs the rope, inching upward, her arms straining, one hand over the other, legs scissored over the rope.

She's just reaching for the branch when she hears it.

A noise, in the distance. Not the sound of small animals scurrying away. Not the low growl or angry bark of a predator.

Human voices, coming her way.

It's a burst of laughter she first hears, then animated chatter, muted by distance.

Does she drop down and remove her sidearm? The rope would still be visible, dangling from a branch.

The voices get closer. More laughter.

She removes her feet from the rope and puts them taut against the tree to steady herself, feeling the strain of the branch. If she holds completely still, they may never see her. Movement draws the eye more than anything else, more than color or sound.

Still, if the tree branch snaps, the noise will be unmistakable.

She holds still, no small chore when suspended in the air, her arms straining, sweat dripping into her eyes.

She sees them now, two of them, through the trees to the west, semiautomatic weapons in their hands, their voices growing louder.

Her right hand lets go of the rope, moving to the grip of her sidearm.

She can't dangle here forever. The branch won't hold. And sooner or later, the one arm holding her up will give out, too.

She manages to pull her sidearm free.

They draw closer, not specifically walking in her direction—more of a southeasterly direction—but getting near. If she can see them, they can see her.

Trying to obscure the movement of the weapon, she holds it close to her side. She'll have to take out both of them before they can rattle off a single round, before they can reach their radios.

And then she'll have to figure out what happens next.

CHAPTER
70

❖

I check my watch: nearly 3:00 p.m. The virus could go off any minute, but no later than nine hours from now.

And my people found the virus.

"So—that's great, right?" I say to Devin and Casey. "You found it!"

"Yes, sir, *great* is the right word." Casey pushes her glasses up against the bridge of her nose. "Thanks to Augie. We never would've located it ourselves. We tried for two weeks. We tried everything. We even did manual searches, we ran customized—"

"But now you found it."

"Yes." She nods. "So that's step 1."

"What's step 2?"

"Neutralizing it. It's not like we can just hit a

Delete button and make it go away. And if we do it wrong, well—it's like a bomb. If you don't disable it properly, it goes off."

"Right, okay," I say. "So…"

Devin says, "So we're trying to re-create the virus on the other computers."

"Can Augie do that?"

"Augie was the hacker, sir, remember. Nina was the code writer. Actually, if anyone's been most helpful, it's the Russians."

I cast a glance around me and lower my voice. "Are they really helping or just appearing to help? They could be taking you down the wrong road."

"We've been on guard for that," says Casey. "But it doesn't seem like they're misleading us. They've told us things we've never known about what they do. It seems like their orders were to do everything possible to help us."

I nod. That's certainly what I was aiming for. I can't know if it's true.

"But they didn't write this code, either," she adds. "This virus Nina created—Augie says she created it three years ago. It's more advanced than anything we've ever seen. It's quite amazing."

"We can give her a posthumous award for best cyberterrorist ever when this is over, okay? Tell me what's going to happen. You're going to re-create the virus and then learn how to neutralize it. Like a simulated war game?"

"Yes, sir."

"And you have all the supplies you need?"

"I think we have enough laptops here, sir. And there are thousands at the Pentagon for the rest of the threat-response team."

I had a hundred computers shipped here for this very purpose. We have another five hundred under Marine guard at the airport, not three miles away.

"And water, coffee, food—all that?" The last thing I need is for these experts to falter physically. They have enough pressure on them mentally. "Cigarettes?" I say, waving my hand at the stench.

"Yeah, we're fine. The Russians and Germans smoke up a storm."

"It's totally polluted down there." Devin makes a face. "At least we got them to agree to smoke in the laundry room. There they can open a window."

"They—there's a window?"

"Yeah, in the laundry—"

"Secret Service locked all the windows," I say, realizing, of course, that it doesn't stop someone from unlocking them from the inside.

I head down the stairs to the basement, Devin and Casey following me.

"Mr. President?" Alex calls out, following me down the stairs as well.

I hit the bottom of the stairs and turn to their war room, moving quickly, feeling a ringing in my ears along with my doctor's words of warning.

The war room is filled with desks and laptops, dozens more off to the side, and a large white-board. Other than the security camera in the corner of the room, it looks like an ordinary classroom. Six people are here—two each from Russia, Germany, and Israel, chatting while they open laptops and bang away on keyboards.

No Augie.

"Check the laundry room, Alex," I say. I hear him move behind me. I hear his words, too, from two rooms away.

"Why is this window open?"

It only takes Alex a minute to sweep the entire basement, including the room I've taken over as the communications room. I already know the answer before he tells me.

"He's gone, Mr. President. Augie is gone."

CHAPTER
71

❖

T he two members of the security patrol are
dark and burly, crew-cut and square-jawed
and wide-bodied. Whatever they're saying to
each other in German, as they march toward her,
must be humorous. They'll stop laughing if either of them, moving southeast, turns his head to
the left.

Her head only inches from the branch above
her, suspended in air by one hand on a rope,
Bach feels her strength failing. She blinks away
the sweat in her eyes as her arm begins to tremble furiously. And she can hear the branch, with
all her weight on one isolated part, start to give
way, a steady creaking.

Her bag and clothes may be camouflaged, her
face and neck may be painted pine green to

match the tree foliage, but if that branch even begins to crack, the game is over.

If she shoots, she must end it right there, two quick shots. And then what? She could steal their radios, but it wouldn't take the rest of the team very long to realize that two of their sentries have gone missing. She'll have no choice but to abort.

Abort. She's never dropped a job or failed one. She could do it now, yes, and probably expect retaliation from the people who hired her. But that's not the problem: she doesn't fear retaliation. Twice in the past, on jobs she carried out successfully, the people who hired her tried to kill her afterward to tie up loose ends, and she's still here; the people they sent are not.

The problem now is Delilah, the name she will give her child—her mother's name. Delilah will not grow up with that burden. She will not know what her mother has done. She will not live in fear. She will not experience terror so great and long-lasting that it seeps into your pores, never leaves you, colors everything that comes afterward.

The men move past her sight line for a moment, disappearing behind the tree from which she is hanging. When they pass by on the other side of the tree, she will be completely exposed, no more than ten meters from them. If either of them looks to his left, due east, they won't miss her.

They come into sight again, on the other side of the tree.

And they stop. The closer one has a mole on his cheek and a deformed ear that looks like it's taken some hits over the years. He drinks from a water bottle, his Adam's apple bobbing on his unshaved throat. The other man, smaller, is standing in the shadows of the woods, a beam of light shooting upward, scanning the trees, scanning the ground.

Don't look to your left.

But they will, of course. And there's no time. She can't hold on much longer.

The branch groans out a larger creak.

The first man lowers the water bottle, looks up, then turns to his left, toward her—

Bach already has her SIG aimed at the first man, a bead on the space between his eyes—

A loud squawk comes from both radios at the same time, something in German, but by any measure indicating that something has gone wrong.

Each man reaches for the radio on his waist. A few words are exchanged, and they turn and run north in headlong flight back toward the cabin.

What just happened? She doesn't know, doesn't care.

With no time and no strength left, Bach puts the sidearm in her mouth, her teeth clamping down on the long suppressor. Her right hand free now, she swings it up and grabs the thickest part of the branch, nearest the tree's body. Then her left hand comes off the rope and grabs the branch, too, just quickly enough to avoid a free fall to the ground. With a groan that is far too loud, but not caring about the consequences now, she summons whatever energy she has left and does a pull-up, her face scraping against the branch. She pushes her feet against the base of the tree and runs them upward until she manages to get her left leg over the branch.

Not the most graceful maneuver she's ever performed, but she is finally in an upright position, straddling the tree branch, almost losing her backpack and rifle in the process. She breathes out, wipes her forehead, slick with sweat, camouflage paint be damned. She gives herself one minute. She counts aloud to sixty, managing to reholster her sidearm, ignoring the burn in her arm, slowing her breathing.

She unties the knot and pulls the loose rope up. She wraps it around her neck, unable at the moment to access the backpack.

She's not going to spend another minute on this branch, even if she's sitting over the thickest part now.

She steadies herself against the tree and gets to her feet, reaches for the next branch, and starts climbing. When she arrives at the top, she'll find a secure perch, and she'll be in perfect position to carry out her job without detection.

CHAPTER
72

❖

Cowboy's gone missing. Repeat, Cowboy's gone missing. We need a full search of the woods. Alpha teams, stay home."

Alex Trimble clicks off the radio and looks at me. "Mr. President, I'm sorry. This is my fault."

It was my idea to keep security light—to keep this meeting secret. We had to. And what security we have has been devoted to watching for anyone trying to come *in* the cabin. We weren't worried about someone trying to *leave*.

"Just find him, Alex."

On our way to the stairs, I pass Devin and Casey, ashen, as if they've done something wrong. Both of them with their mouths open, trying to find words.

"Fix the problem," I say, pointing back to the

war room. "Figure out how to kill that virus. That's all that matters. Go."

Alex and I head up the stairs and stand in the kitchen, looking out the window to the south, the expansive backyard and then the woods that seem to have no end. Alex is giving instructions through his radio, but he will remain at my side. The agents are now scrambling, most of them moving into the woods, searching for Augie, but a small number of agents—the Alpha team— hold back to secure the perimeter.

I don't know how he got to the woods without being seen. But I do know that if Augie's in there, it will be very difficult for our small team of agents to find him.

More important: why run?

"Alex," I say, about to express these thoughts, "we should—"

But my words are interrupted by the noise from the woods, unmistakable even from inside the cabin.

The *rat-tat-tat* of gunfire from an automatic weapon.

CHAPTER
73

❖

"M
    r. President!"
    I ignore Alex, bounding down the stairs and into the woods, over uneven ground, turning sideways to pass between trees.

"Mr. President, *please!*"

I keep going through dark terrain, shrouded by the tree canopy, hearing the shouts of men up ahead.

"At least let me go in front of you," he says, and I allow him to overtake me. Alex has his automatic weapon at the ready and is swiveling his head from side to side.

When we reach the clearing, Augie is sitting on the ground, leaning against a tree, seizing his chest. Above him, the tree has been splintered to near devastation from bullets. Two Russian agents stand with their automatic weapons at their sides, while Jacobson is giving them an ear-ful, stabbing the air with his finger.

When Jacobson sees us, he stops and turns, showing us his palm in a stop gesture. "We're okay. Everyone's okay." He glares one more time at the Russians, then approaches us.

"Our comrades from the Russian Federation saw him first," he says. "They opened fire. They say they were just warning shots."

"Warning shots? Who needed warning shots?"

I walk toward the Russians, pointing back to the cabin. "Go back to the cabin! Get out of my woods!"

Jacobson says something to them, a word or two in Russian. Their expressions implacable, they nod, turn, and leave us.

"Thank God I was close," says Jacobson. "I ordered them to cease fire."

"Thank God you were close...as in, you think the Russians were trying to kill him?" I ask.

Jacobson ponders that, expelling air through his nose. He throws up a hand. "The Russian National Guard, they're supposed to be the best Russia has. If they wanted to kill him, he'd be dead."

President Chernokev recently created a new internal security force, answering directly to him. The word is that his National Guard is the elite of the elite.

"How sure are you of that?" I ask Jacobson.

"Not sure at all, sir."

I pass between the Secret Service agents and walk over to Augie. I squat down next to him. "What the hell were you doing, Augie?"

His lips quiver, his chest still heaves with deep breaths, and his eyes are wide and unfocused.

"They..." His throat chokes up. He swallows hard. "Tried to kill me."

I glance up at the tree above him. A quick glance reveals that the bullets that riddled the tree were about five feet off the ground. Doesn't feel like "warning shots" to me. But I suppose it depends on where he was standing.

"Why'd you run, Augie?"

A faint shake of the head, and his eyes drift off. "I...I can't stop this. I can't be there when it...when it..."

"You're scared? Is that it?"

Augie, almost sheepishly, his body still shaking, nods.

Is that all this is? Fear, remorse, feeling overwhelmed?

Or have I missed something about Augie?

"Get up." I grab his arm and force him to his feet. "This is no time for scared, Augie. Let's you and I have a talk in the cabin."

CHAPTER
74

❖

B ach finally reaches the perch she's seeking high up in the white pines, her arms and back feeling the strain of climbing upward with a sizable bag and rifle on her back. In her earbuds, she listens to Wilhelm Friedemann Herzog performing his playful rendition of the Violin Concerto in E Major three years ago in Budapest.

Through the pines, she has a clear view of the cabin in the distance and the grounds to the south.

The branches next to the trunk of the tree are thick enough to hold her. She straddles a branch and places her case in front of her. She opens it with her thumbprint and removes Anna Magdalena, assembling it in less than two minutes, looking out over the trees as she does so.

She sees sentries patrolling the grounds, men with weapons.

A black tent.

Four men climbing the stairs to the porch, moving quickly—

She adjusts the scope feverishly. She has no time to create a platform and mount the rifle and get into position, instead bringing it to her shoulder and looking through the scope. Not ideal, and she will only have one chance at a shot before blowing her cover, blowing everything up, so she can't make a mistake—

She works forward to back as they approach the door to the cabin.

A large dark-haired man, earpiece.

Shorter, lighter man, earpiece.

The president, passing between the men, disappearing into the cabin.

Followed by a short man, frail, tangled dark hair—

Is that him?

Is it him?

Yes.

One second to decide.

Take the shot?

CHAPTER
75

❖

I take Augie by the arm and pull him into the cabin. Alex and Jacobson, behind us, step in and close the cabin door.

I move Augie into the living room and put him on the couch. "Get him some water," I tell Alex.

Augie sits on the couch, still looking dazed and distraught. "This is not...what she wanted," he whispers. "She would not...want this."

Alex returns with a cup of water. I put out my hand. "Give it to me," I say.

I walk over to Augie and throw the water in his face, dousing his hair and shirt. He gasps in surprise, shakes his head, sits up straight.

I lean down over him. "Are you being straight with me, kid? There's a lot riding on you."

"I...I..." He looks up at me, different from before, scared not just of the circumstances but also of me.

"Alex," I say. "Show me the footage from the war room."

"Yes, sir." From his pocket, Alex removes his phone and clicks on it before handing it to me. It's the real-time feed from the security camera inside the war room, showing Casey on the phone, Devin on a computer, the other tech geniuses working on laptops and drawing on the whiteboard.

"Look at that, Augie. Are any of those people giving up? No. They're terrified, every one of them, but they're not giving up. Hell, you're the one who located the virus. You just did what my best people couldn't do for two weeks."

He closes his eyes and nods. "I'm sorry."

I kick his shoes, jarring him. "Look at me, Augie. Look at me!"

He does.

"Tell me about Nina. You said this isn't what she wanted. What do you mean? She didn't want to destroy America?"

Augie, eyes down, shakes his head. "Nina was tired of running. She said she'd been running for so long."

"From the Georgian government?"

446

"Yes. Georgian intelligence had been chasing her. They almost killed her once in Uzbekistan."

"Okay, well—so she was tired of running. What did she want? To live in America?"

My phone buzzes in my pocket. I pull it out. It's Liz Greenfield. I decline the call and stuff it back in my pocket.

"She wanted to go home," says Augie.

"To the Georgian republic? Where she's wanted for war crimes?"

"She was hoping you would...assist in that re-gard."

"She wanted me to intervene. She wanted me to ask Georgia to grant her amnesty. As a favor to the United States."

Augie nods. "And would you not expect Georgia to do such a thing under the circumstances? If America was in peril, and one of its allies—es-pecially one that could use America as a friend, with the Russians on its border—do you not think Georgia would have granted you that favor?"

They probably would have. If I pressed hard enough, if I explained the situation thoroughly enough—yes, we would have figured some-thing out.

"So I want to be sure I have this straight," I say. "Nina helped Suliman Cindoruk build this virus."

"Yes."

"But she never wanted to destroy America with it?"

He pauses. "You must understand Suli," he says. "The way he operates. Nina built a magnificent virus. A devastating stealth wiper virus. I worked, as you might say, on the other side of the business."

"You were the hacker."

"Yes. My job was to infiltrate American systems and spread the virus as far and wide as possible. But our positions were…segregated, you would say."

I think I'm getting it now. "She built a brilliant virus but didn't know, exactly, to what use it would be put. And you spread the virus through American servers but didn't know, exactly, what it was you were spreading."

"What you are saying, yes." He nods. He seems to be calming down now. "I do not mean to portray either of us as innocents. Nina knew the destructive nature of her virus, obviously. But she had no idea how far and wide it was going to be distributed. She did not know it was going to be spread throughout the United States to destroy the lives of hundreds of millions of people. And I…" He looks away. "Suli told me it was an advanced form of spyware I was disseminating. That he would sell it to the highest bidder to finance our other jobs." He shrugs. "When we realized what we had done, we could not sit idly by."

"So Nina came here to stop the virus," I say. "In exchange for my help getting her amnesty."

He nods again. "We hoped you would agree. But we couldn't predict your response. The Sons of Jihad has been responsible for the deaths of Americans in the past. And the United States is hardly what we would consider an ally. So she insisted on meeting you first, alone."

"To see how I would respond."

"To see if you would let her leave the White House. As opposed to arresting her, torturing her, whatever else you might do."

That sounds right. It felt like a test at the time.

"I objected to her going to the White House alone," he says. "But she would not be deterred. By the time we met in the States, she clearly had a plan in mind."

"Wait." I touch his arm. "By the time you met in the States? What does that mean? You weren't together all along?"

"Oh, no," he says. "No, no. The day we sent the peekaboo to your Pentagon server?"

Saturday, April 28. I'll never forget when I first heard about it. I was in Brussels, on the first leg of my European trip. I got the call in the presidential suite. I'd never heard my defense secretary so rattled.

"That was the day Nina and I left Suliman in Algeria. We split up, though. We thought it was safer that way. She came to the United States through Canada. I came through Mexico. Our plan was to meet on Wednesday in Baltimore, Maryland."

"Wednesday—this past Wednesday? Three days ago?"

"Yes. Wednesday, at noon, by the statue of Edgar Allan Poe at the University of Baltimore. Close enough to Washington but not too close, a logical place for people of our age to fit in and a fixed point we both could find."

"And that's when Nina told you the plan."

"Yes. By then she was certain she had a plan in place. She would visit the White House on Friday night, alone, to test your reaction. Then you would meet me at the baseball stadium—another test, to see if you would even appear. And if you did, I would make my own judgment as to whether we could trust you. When you appeared at the stadium, I knew you had passed Nina's test."

"And then I passed yours."

"Yes," he says. "If nothing else, the fact that

I pulled a gun on the president of the United States and nobody immediately shot me or arrested me—I knew you believed us and would work with us."

I shake my head. "And then you contacted Nina?"

"I texted her. She was waiting for my signal to pull up to the stadium in her van."

How close we came, right there.

Augie lets out a noise that sounds like laughter. "That was supposed to be the moment," he says, looking ruefully off in the distance. "We would have all been together. *I* would have located the virus, *you* would have contacted the Georgian government, and *she* would have stopped the virus."

Instead someone stopped Nina.

"I will get back to work, Mr. President." He pushes himself off the couch. "I am sorry for my momentary—"

I push him back down. "We're not done, Augie," I say. "I want to know about Nina's source. I want to know about the traitor in the White House."

CHAPTER
76

❖

I remain hovering over Augie, all but shining a
bright light in his face. "You said by the time
you met Nina in Baltimore three days ago, she
was committed to a plan."

He nods.

"Why? What happened between the time you
split up in Algeria and the time you met in Baltimore? What did she do? Where did she go?"

"This I do not know."

"That doesn't wash, Augie."

"I'm sorry? Wash?"

I lean in farther still, nearly nose to nose with
him. "That doesn't ring true to me. You two
loved each other. You trusted each other. You
needed each other."

"What we *needed* was to keep our information

separate," he insists. "For our own protection. She could not know how to locate the virus, and I could not know how to disarm it. This way we both remained of value to you."

"What did she tell you about her source?"

"I have answered this question more than once—"

"Answer it again." I grab his shoulder. "And remember that the lives of hundreds of millions of people—"

"She did not tell me!" he spits, full of emotion, a high pitch to his voice. "She told me I would need to know the code word 'Dark Ages,' and I asked her how she could possibly know this, and she said it did not matter how, that it was better I did not know, that we were both safer that way."

I stare at him, saying nothing, searching his face.

"Did I suspect she was in communication with someone of importance in Washington? Of course I did. I am not an imbecile. But that gave me *comfort*, not discomfort. It meant we had a credible chance of success. I trusted her. She was the smartest person I'd ever—"

He chokes up, unable to finish the sentence.

My phone buzzes. FBI Liz again. I can't keep ignoring it.

I put my hand on his shoulder. "You want to

honor her memory, Augie? Then do everything you can to stop that virus. Go. Now."

He takes a deep breath and pushes himself off the couch. "I will," he says.

Once Augie is out of earshot, I bring the phone to my ear. "Yes, Liz."

"Mr. President," she says. *"The cell phones in Nina's van."*

"Yes. Two of them, you said?"

"Yes, sir, one on her person, one found under the floorboard in the rear compartment."

"Okay…"

"Sir, the one we found hidden in the rear of the van—we haven't cracked it yet. But the phone that was in her pocket—we finally broke the code. There is an overseas text message that is particularly interesting. It took us a long time to track it, because it was scrambled over three continents—"

"Liz, Liz," I say. "Cut to the chase."

"We think we've found him, sir," she says. *"We think we've located Suliman Cindoruk."*

I suck in my breath.

A second chance, after Algeria.

"Mr. President?"

"I want him alive," I say.

CHAPTER
77

❖

Vice President Katherine Brandt sits quietly, her eyes downcast, taking it all in. Even over the computer screen, with its occasional fuzz, its sporadic image-jumping, she looks TV-ready, heavily made up from her appearance on *Meet the Press*, dressed in a smart red suit and a white blouse.

"That's almost..." She looks up at me.

"Incomprehensible," I say. "Yes. It's far worse than we imagined. We have been able to secure our military, but other areas of federal government, and the private sector—the damage is going to be incalculable."

"And Los Angeles...is a decoy."

I shake my head. "That's my best guess. It's a smart plan. They want our tech superstars on the other side of the country, trying to solve the problem at the water-filtration plant. Then, when the virus detonates, we are cut off from them in every way—no Internet connectivity, no phones, no airplanes or trains. Our best people, stranded on the West Coast, thousands of miles away from us."

"And I'm just learning all this that's happening to our country, and everything you're doing, even though I'm vice president of the United States. Because you don't trust me. I'm one of the six you don't trust."

Her image is not sufficiently clear to gauge her reaction to all this. It wouldn't be a good thing to learn that your boss, the commander in chief, thinks you might be a traitor.

"Mr. President, do you really think I would do such a thing?"

"Kathy, I wouldn't have imagined, in a million years, that any of you would. Not you, not Sam, not Brendan, not Rod, not Dominick, not Erica. But one of you did."

That's it. Sam Haber of DHS. Brendan Mohan, national security adviser. Rodrigo Sanchez, chairman of the Joint Chiefs. Defense secretary Dominick Dayton. And CIA director Erica Beatty. Plus the vice president. My circle of six, all under suspicion.

Katherine Brandt remains silent, still at attention but lost in concentration.

Alex walks in and slips me a note from Devin. It's not a good note.

When I turn back to Kathy, she looks ready to tell me something. I have a good idea what it will be.

"*Mr. President,*" she says, "*if I don't have your trust, the only thing I can do is offer you my resignation.*"

CHAPTER
78

❖

In the tech war room, Devin looks up when he sees me. He taps Casey on the shoulder, and they leave the others—all wearing headsets or banging on computers—to speak with me. Dead laptop computers are piled up against the wall. On the whiteboard, various words and names and codes are scribbled: PETYA and NYETNA, SHAMOON and SCHNEIER ALG., DOD.

The room itself smells like coffee and tobacco and body odor. I'd offer to open a window if I were in a joking mood.

Casey gestures to a corner where a stack of laptop computers lines the wall, the boxes stacked so high that they almost reach the security camera peering down at us from the ceiling.

"All dead," she says. "We're trying everything. Nothing can kill this virus."

"Seventy computers so far?"

"More or less," she says. "And for every one we're using here, the rest of our team at the Pentagon is using three or four. We've racked up close to three hundred computers."

"The computers are…wiped clean?"

"Everything wiped," says Devin. "As soon as we try to disarm it, the wiper virus goes off. Those laptops are no better than a pile of bricks now." He sighs. "Can you get the other five hundred laptops?"

I turn to Alex and make the request. The Marines will get them over to us in no time. "Is five hundred enough?" I ask.

Casey smirks. "We don't have five hundred ways to stop this thing. We've thought of just about everything we know already."

"Augie's not a help?"

"Oh, he's brilliant," says Devin. "The way he buried this thing inside the computer? I've never seen anything like it. But when it comes to actually disabling it? It's not his specialty."

I look at my watch. "It's four o'clock, people. Start getting creative."

"Yes, sir."

"Anything else you need from me?"

Casey says, "Any chance you can capture Suliman and bring him here?"

I pat her on the arm but don't answer.

We're working on it, I do not say.

CHAPTER
79

❖

I return to my communications room, where I find Vice President Katherine Brandt, her eyes cast down, her posture slumped. Before I interrupted our talk, she had said something meaningful to me.

She perks up when she sees me enter the room, her posture stiffening.

"No luck on the virus yet," I say, sitting down. "Whoever created that thing is playing chess, and we're playing checkers."

"Mr. President," says Kathy, *"I just offered you my resignation."*

"Yes, I remember," I say. "This is not the time for that, Kathy. They've tried to kill Augie and me twice. And I'm not well, as I just explained to you."

"I'm sorry to hear that. I hadn't realized your condition was acting up again."

"I didn't tell anybody. This isn't a good time for our friends or our enemies to think the president is in poor health."

She nods her head.

"Listen, Carolyn has been a few floors above you in the White House the whole time. She knows everything. We have it all written up in a document, too. If something had happened to me, Carolyn would have told you everything within minutes. Including my various plans for what to do, depending on how bad this virus is. Including military strikes on Russia, China, North Korea—whoever is behind this virus. Contingency plans for martial law, the suspension of habeas corpus, price controls, rationing of critical goods—the works."

"But if I am the traitor, Mr. President," she says, barely able to spit out that word, *"why would you trust me to stop these people? If I'm in cahoots with them."*

"Kathy, what choice did I have? I can't just switch you out with somebody new. What was I supposed to do four days ago when I learned about the leak from Nina through my daughter? Demand your resignation? And then what? Think about how long it would take to replace you. A vetting process, the nomination process, approval by both houses. I didn't have that kind of time. And if you left and there was a vacancy, think who is next in line of succession."

She doesn't respond, breaking eye contact. The reference to Speaker Lester Rhodes does not seem to sit well with her.

"More important than that, Kathy—I couldn't be sure it was you. I couldn't be sure it was any of you. Sure, I could have fired all six of you, just to make sure I got rid of the leaker. Just to be safe. But then I'm losing essentially my entire national security team when I need them most."

"You could have polygraphed us," she says.

"I could have. That's what Carolyn wanted. Give all of you lie-detector tests."

"But you didn't."

"No, I didn't."

"Why not, sir?"

"The element of surprise," I say. "The only thing I had going for me was that I knew there was a leaker, but the leaker didn't know I knew. If I put all of you on a box and asked you whether you leaked information about Dark Ages, I'd show my hand. Whoever was behind this would know that I knew. It was better to play dumb, so to speak.

"So I got to work fixing the problem," I continue. "I called in the under secretary of defense and had her check, independently, that the re-vamping of our military systems was being done properly. Just in case Secretary Dayton was the Benedict Arnold. I had General Burke at Central Command verify the same thing overseas, just in case Admiral Sanchez was the traitor."

"And you were assured things were done properly."

"Properly enough. We couldn't completely re-create everything in two weeks by any means, but we're up and running enough to launch mis-siles, to deploy air and ground forces. Our train-ing exercises were successful."

"Does that mean Dayton and Sanchez are crossed off your list? The list is down to four now?"

"What do you think, Kathy? Should they be crossed off?"

She thinks about that a minute. *"If one of them is the traitor, they wouldn't be so obvious as to sab-otage something that was their direct responsibility. They might anonymously leak the code word. They might provide some information to the enemy. But these specific tasks you've assigned them—there's a spotlight directly on them. They can't screw it up. They'd be exposed. Whoever did this gave it a lot of thought."*

"My thinking exactly," I say. "So no, they aren't crossed off the list."

This is a lot for Kathy to take in, and she understands that as I talk about the traitor, in my mind I could be talking about her. It wouldn't be easy for anyone to accept. Then again, she isn't exactly wearing a white hat in all this.

Finally, she says, *"Mr. President, if we get through this—"*

"When," I say. "When we get through this. There's no 'if.' 'If' is not an option."

"When we get through this," she says, *"at the appropriate time, I will tender you my resignation to do with what you will. If you can't trust me, sir, I'm not sure how I can serve you."*

"And then who's next in line?" I say, returning to that theme.

She blinks a few times, but the answer isn't exactly a hard one. *"Well, obviously I wouldn't step down until you secured a replacement—"*

"You don't even want to say his name, do you, Kathy? Your friend Lester Rhodes."

"I...I don't think I'd call him my friend, sir."

"No?"

"I certainly wouldn't. I—I did happen to run into him this morn—"

"Stop right there," I say. "You can lie to yourself all you want, Kathy. But do not lie to me."

Her mouth still works for a moment, searching for something, before she closes it and remains still.

"The first thing I did four days ago, when I learned of the leak," I say. "The first thing I did. You know what it was?"

She shakes her head but can't bring herself to speak.

"I had each of you surveilled," I say.

She brings a hand to her chest. *"You had…me…"*

"All six of you," I say. "FISA warrants. I signed the affidavits myself. Those judges had never seen *that* before. Liz Greenfield at the FBI executed them. Intercepts, eavesdropping, the works."

"You've been…"

"Spare me the indignation. You would have done the same thing. And do *not* sit there and act like you just happened to 'run into' Lester Rhodes this morning on your way to breakfast."

There's not a lot she can say. She doesn't have a leg to stand on, given what she did. She looks as if she wants to crawl under a rock and hide right now.

"Focus on the problem," I say. "Forget politics. Forget the hearing next week. Forget about who might be president a month from now. Our country has a very big problem, and all that matters is solving it."

She nods, unable to speak.

"If something happens to me, you're up to bat,"

I say. "So get your head out of your ass and be ready."

She nods again, first slowly, then more adamantly. Her posture straightens, as if she is setting everything else aside, focusing on a new course of action.

"Carolyn's going to show you the contingency plans. They're for your eyes only. You'll stay in the operations center. You won't be able to communicate with anyone but Carolyn or me. Understood?"

"*Yes,*" she says. "*May I say something, sir?*"

I sigh. "Yes."

"*Give me a polygraph,*" she says.

I draw back.

"*The element of surprise is lost now,*" she says. "*You've told me everything. Give me a lie detector and ask me if I leaked 'Dark Ages.' Ask me about Lester Rhodes if you want. Ask me anything. But make damn sure to ask me if I have ever, in any way, betrayed our country.*"

That one, I must admit, I didn't see coming.

"*Ask me,*" she says, "*and I'll tell the truth.*"

CHAPTER
80

❖

I t is 11:03 p.m. in Berlin, Germany.

Four things happen at the same time.

One: a woman in a long white coat enters the front door of the high-rise condominium building, multiple shopping bags, like bulky appendages, in hand. She walks straight to the clerk at the front desk. She looks around and spots the camera in the corner of the ornate, spacious lobby. She sets down the bags and smiles at the clerk. He asks for her identification, and she opens her flip wallet, revealing a badge.

"Ich bin Polizistin," she says, losing her smile. *"Ich brauche Ihre Hilfe jetzt."*

Identifying herself as a cop. Telling him she needs his help right away.

Two: a large orange waste-disposal truck bear-

ing the company name Berliner Stadtreini-
gungsbetriebe pulls alongside the same building
to the east, as the wind off the river Spree swirls
around it. When the vehicle comes to a stop,
the back door lifts open. Twelve men, members
of the KSK, the Kommando Spezialkräfte, Germany's elite rapid-response special-forces unit,
emerge from the truck dressed in tactical gear—
vests, helmets, heavy boots—and armed with
HK MP5 submachine guns, or riot-control rifles.
The nearby door to the condo building pops
open automatically, courtesy of the front desk,
and they enter the building.

Three: a helicopter, painted white and bearing
the name of a local television station, but in fact
a KSK stealth helicopter with reduced-noise-
operation capability, hovers silently over the top
of that same building. Four KSK commandos,
likewise dressed in tactical gear, fall from the helicopter, lowering themselves thirty feet down
to the rooftop, softly landing and detaching the
cords from their belts.

And four: Suliman Cindoruk laughs to himself
as he watches his team inside the penthouse
suite. His four men—the remaining four members of the Sons of Jihad, besides him. Still recovering from last night's festivities, stumbling
around, half dressed and scraggly, hungover if

not still intoxicated. Since they all awakened, some time midday, they have done a grand total of nothing.

Elmurod, his stomach stretching his bright purple T-shirt, drops onto the couch and uses the remote to turn on the TV. Mahmad, wearing a stained undershirt and boxers, his hair standing on end as he sucks down a bottle of water. Hagan, the last one to awaken, in midafternoon, shirtless, wearing sweatpants, munches on grapes from the spread of food left over from last night. Levi, gangly and awkward and wearing only underwear, who assuredly lost his virginity last night, puts his head against a pillow on the couch, wearing an easy smile.

Suli closes his eyes and feels the breeze on his face. Some people complain about the winds coming off the Spree, especially in the evening, but it's one of the things he enjoys the most. One of the things he will miss the most.

He checks the firearm at his side by force of habit. Something he does almost every hour of the day. Checking the magazine, making sure it is loaded.

Loaded, that is, with a single bullet.

CHAPTER
81

❖

They climb the stairs with the proper tactical approach, securing each staircase with a single soldier—a scout—before the rest of the team proceeds upward. There are blind spots everywhere. Ambush opportunities on each level. Their contact at the front desk has given an all-clear on the stairwells, but he is only as competent as the cameras he monitors.

The team 1 leader is a man named Christoph, eleven years now with the KSK. When the twelve-man team reaches the landing on the penthouse floor, he radios in to the commander. "Team 1 in red position," he says in German.

"Hold in red position, team 1," calls out the commander from his location, in a vehicle down the street.

471

The commander for this mission is the brigadier general himself, KSK's leader. That's a first as far as Christoph's ever heard—KSK's highest-ranking officer personally commanding a mission. But then again, this is the first time the brigadier general received a call from the chancellor himself.

The target is Suliman Cindoruk, Chancellor Richter told the brigadier general. *He must be taken alive. He must be apprehended in a condition that allows him to be immediately interrogated.*

Thus the ARWEN in Christoph's hands, the riot-control weapon containing nonlethal plastic baton rounds, capable of unloading the entire five-round magazine in four seconds. Six of the twelve men have ARWENs to incapacitate their targets. The other six have standard MP5 submachine guns should lethal rounds prove necessary.

"Team 2, status," the commander calls out.

Team 2, the four men on the roof: *"Team 2 in red position."* Two of the KSK soldiers prepared to rappel from the roof onto the balcony below. Two others secure the roof in the event of an escape attempt.

But there won't be an escape, Christoph knows. *This guy's mine.*

This will be his bin Laden.

Through his earpiece, the commander: *"Team 3, confirm number and location of targets."*

Team 3 is the stealth helicopter overhead, using high-powered thermal imaging to detect the number of people on the penthouse level.

"Five targets, Commander," comes the response. *"Four inside the penthouse, congregated in the front room, and one on the balcony."*

"Five targets, confirmed. Team 1, proceed to yellow position."

"Team 1, proceeding to yellow position." Christoph turns back to his men and nods. They raise their weapons.

Christoph slowly turns the latch on the staircase door, then gently but swiftly pulls it open with a rush of adrenaline.

The hallway is empty, quiet.

They proceed slowly, the twelve of them in a crouch, guns raised, measuring each step to minimize footfalls on the carpeted floor, slinking toward the single door on the right. His senses on high alert, Christoph feels the heat and energy of the men behind him, smells the lemon scent off the carpet, hears the heavy breathing behind him and the vague sound of laughter down the hallway.

Eight meters away. Six meters. Performance adrenaline coursing through him. Heartbeat racing. But his balance steady, his confidence high—

Click-click-click.

His head whips to the left. The sound is subtle but distinct. A tiny square box on the wall, a thermostat—

No, not a thermostat.

"Shit," he says.

CHAPTER
82

❖

Suliman lights a cigarette and checks his phone. Nothing new on the international front. They do seem concerned about the water problem in Los Angeles. *Did the Americans fall for it?* he wonders.

Inside the penthouse, Hagan grabs a silver bowl off the table of food and vomits in it. It was probably the expensive Champagne, Suli decides. Hagan may be a brilliant code writer, but he was never much of a drink—

A high-pitched beep comes from Suli's phone, a tone reserved for only one thing.

A breach. The hallway sensor.

Instinctively his hand brushes against the pistol at his side, the one with the single bullet.

He's always vowed to himself that he wouldn't

be taken alive, he wouldn't be caged and interrogated, beaten and waterboarded, made to live like an animal. He prefers to go out on his own terms, cupping the pistol under his chin and pulling the trigger.

But he always knew, for all his promises to himself, there would be a moment of truth. And he always wondered if he'd have the courage to go through with it.

CHAPTER
83

❖

W e're burned!" Christoph says in a harsh whisper. "Team 1 proceeding to green position."

"Proceed to green position, team 1."

All pretense of a sneak attack gone, the men rush to the door, fanning out in dual-entry position, five men on each side, two men standing back with the rammer, poised to charge.

"The target on the balcony has entered the penthouse," says the leader of team 3, on the helicopter with the thermal imaging.

That's him, Christoph knows, steeling himself.

They blow into the door with a staggering jolt. It bursts from its hinges, the top falling forward into the apartment like a drawbridge cut from its chain.

The soldiers closest to the door on each side flip their flashbangs into the apartment and quickly turn away from the threshold. A second later, the stun grenades detonate, producing a concussive blast of 180 decibels and a searing, blinding light.

For five seconds, the occupants will be blind, deaf, and unbalanced.

One, two. Christoph is first through the door as the white light evaporates, the afterbuzz of the blast still audible.

"Don't move! Don't move!" he shouts in German as one of the team members shouts the same in Turkish.

He scans the room, head on a swivel.

Fat guy in purple shirt, half fallen off a couch, eyes squeezed shut. *Not him.*

Man in undershirt and boxers, staggering backward as he clutches a bottle of water, collapsing to the floor. *Negative.*

Shirtless guy, dazed, on the floor, a bowl of fruit spilled over his chest. *No.*

Christoph moves to the other side of the couch, where a man wearing only underwear has fallen over the couch and lies unconscious. *Not—*

And over by the sliding glass door to the balcony, the final target, lying prone on the floor: a young Asian girl wearing a bra and panties and a pained expression.

"Only five targets, team 3?" he cries.

"Affirmative, team leader. Five targets."

Christoph moves past the Asian girl, already subdued by one of the soldiers. He slides the glass door open and bounds onto the balcony in a crouch, swinging his anti-riot weapon from side to side. Empty.

"Rest of the apartment is clear," his second in command tells him as Christoph walks back into the living room, the adrenaline draining, his shoulders slumping.

He looks around, defeated, as the five targets are zip-tied and lifted to their feet, still dazed— if they're conscious at all.

Then his eyes move up to the corner of the room.

At the camera looking down on him.

CHAPTER
84

❖

*G*uten Tag," Suliman says, giving a small salute to the soldier who cannot see him. The soldier looks so disappointed that Suli almost feels sorry for him.

Then he closes up his laptop as he is approached by the waiter at the outdoor tavern on the Spree, twenty kilometers away from the penthouse.

"Will there be anything else tonight, sir?" says the waiter.

"Just the bill," says Suliman. He needs to get going. It's a long boat ride.

CHAPTER
85

❖

I nside the black communications tent, Chancellor Richter ends his phone call. "I'm sorry, Mr. President."

"Gone without a trace?" I ask.

"Yes. The other people captured in the raid say he left approximately two hours ago."

He was one step ahead of us, as usual.

"I…I need to think," I say.

I part the flaps of the tent and walk back up to the cabin. My hopes were up, more than I cared to admit. That was our best chance. The last person who could stop the virus.

I walk into the basement, Alex Trimble trailing me. I hear them even from the hallway, before I enter the war room.

I stop at the door, keeping a distance. The

techies are huddled over a speakerphone, no doubt talking with the rest of our threat-response team at the Pentagon.

"I'm saying if we inverted the sequence!" Devin is saying into the phone. "You do know what *inverted* means, don't you? You have a dictionary there somewhere?"

From the speakerphone: *"But WannaCry didn't—"*

"This isn't WannaCry, Jared! This isn't ransomware. This is nothing like WannaCry. This is nothing like anything I've ever freakin' seen." Devin throws an empty water bottle across the room.

"Devin, listen, all I'm saying is the back door…"

As the speaker continues talking, Devin looks up at Casey. "He's still talking about WannaCry. He's making *me* wanna cry."

Casey paces back and forth. "This is a dead end," she says.

I turn and leave the room. They've already answered my question.

"I'm going to the communications room," I tell Alex. He follows me to the door, but I enter alone.

I close the door behind me. Turn off the light.

I sink to the floor and squeeze my eyes shut, though it is already dark.

I reach into my pocket, take out my Ranger coin, and start reciting.

"I volunteered as a Ranger, fully knowing the hazards of my chosen profession..."

The utter destruction of a nation of three hundred million people. Three hundred *million* people, ruined and desperate and terrified, everything stolen from them—their safety, their security, their savings, their dreams—everything shattered by a few geniuses with a computer.

"...my country expects me to move further, faster and fight harder than any other soldier...

"...I will shoulder more than my share of the task, whatever it may be, 100 percent and then some..."

Hundreds of test computers, used and useless. Our best experts utterly clueless about how to stop the virus. A virus that could hit at any minute, the one man capable of stopping the virus toying with us, watching from a remote location as German special forces invaded his penthouse.

"...I shall defeat them on the field of battle...

"Surrender is not a Ranger word."

Maybe not, but if the virus takes hold, I will have no choice but to impose the most authoritarian of measures just to keep people from

483

killing one another for food, clean water, and shelter.

If that happens, we will be unrecognizable. We will no longer be the United States of America as anyone has ever known it or conceived of it. To say nothing of the fact that with all the troubles on the streets of America, there's a real chance we'll find ourselves in a war with the likelihood of nuclear exchanges greater than at any time since Kennedy and Khrushchev.

I need to talk to somebody besides myself. I grab my phone and dial my go-to guy. After three rings, Danny Akers picks up.

"Mr. President," he says.

Just hearing his voice lifts my spirits.

"I don't know what to do, Danny. I feel like I've walked right into an ambush. I'm out of rabbits and hats to pull them out of. They might beat us this time. I don't have the answer."

"You will, though. You always do, always have."

"But this is different."

"Remember when you deployed with Bravo Company to Desert Storm? What happened? Even though you hadn't even been to Ranger School yet, they made you a corporal so you could be team leader after Donlin got wounded in Basra. Probably the fastest rise to team leader in Bravo Company history."

"That was different, too."

"You didn't get promoted for no reason, Jon. Especially over all the other people who'd been to the academy. Why?"

"I don't know. But that was—"

"Shit, I even heard about it stateside. It got around. The lieutenant said that when Donlin went down and you were under enemy fire, you stepped up. He called you 'a born leader who kept his head and found a way.' He was right. Jonathan Lincoln Duncan—and I'm not saying this because I love you—there is no one I'd rather have in charge right now."

Whether he's right or not, and whether I believe it or not, I am in charge. Time to quit whining and suck it up.

"Thanks, Danny." I push myself to my feet. "You're full of shit, but thanks."

"Keep your head and find a way, Mr. President," he says.

CHAPTER
86

❖

I punch out the phone call and flip on the overhead light. Before I can open the door, I get another call. It's Carolyn.

"Mr. President, I have Liz on the line."

"Mr. President, we conducted the polygraph on the vice president," says Liz. *"The results were inconclusive."*

"Meaning what?" I ask.

"Meaning 'no opinion on deception,' sir."

"So what do we make of that?"

"Well, sir, candidly, it was the most likely outcome. We threw together questions quickly when we would normally draft them with great care. And the stress level she's under, whether innocent or guilty, is tremendous."

I passed a lie-detector test once. The Iraqis gave me one. They asked me all kinds of questions about troop movements and locations of assets. I lied to them six ways to Sunday, but I passed. Because I was taught countermeasures. It was part of my training. There are ways to beat the box.

"Do we give her points for volunteering for a polygraph?" I ask.

"No, we don't," says Carolyn. *"If she fails the test, she blames it on stress and she asks that very question—why would I volunteer for a polygraph if I knew I'd fail it?"*

"And besides," Liz Greenfield adds, *"she had to know that sooner or later we'd come around to polygraphing her and everyone else. So she was volunteering for something she knew she'd have to do eventually anyway."*

They're right. Kathy would be tactical enough to have thought this through.

Jesus, we can't catch a break.

"Carolyn," I say, "it's time to make the phone calls."

CHAPTER
87

❖

M r. Chief Justice, I wish I could tell you more," I say into the phone. "All I can say right now is that it's important that the members of the Court are secure, and it's critical that I keep an open communications channel with you."

"I understand, Mr. President," says the chief justice of the United States. *"We are all secure. And we are all praying for you and our country."*

The phone call with the Senate majority leader goes much the same way as he and his leadership team are moved to underground bunkers.

Lester Rhodes, instinctively suspicious of me after I lay out as much as I can for him, says, *"Mr. President, what kind of a threat are we looking at?"*

"I can't give you that right now, Lester. I just

need you and your leadership team secured. As soon as I can tell you, I will."

I hang up before he can ask me what this means for next week's select committee hearing, which assuredly was on his mind. He probably thinks I'm trying to throw up some diversion to distract the country from what he's trying to do to me. A guy like Lester, it's the first place his mind would travel. Here we are, treating this like a DEFCON 1 scenario, including taking action to secure the continuity of our government, and he's still treating it like cheap politics.

Inside the communications room, I click on the laptop and summon Carolyn Brock.

"Mr. President," she says, *"they're all secure in the operations center."*

"Brendan Mohan?" I say, referring to my national security adviser.

"He's secure, yes."

"Rod Sanchez?" Chairman of the Joint Chiefs.

"He's secure," Carolyn says.

"Dom Dayton?" The secretary of defense.

"Secure."

"Erica Beatty?"

"Secure, sir."

"Sam Haber?"

"Yes, sir."

"And the vice president."

My circle of six.

Carolyn says, *"They're all secure in the operations center."*

Keep your head and find a way.

"Have them ready to speak with me in a few minutes," I say.

CHAPTER
88

❖

I return to the war room, where the computer techs are still giving it every effort they can muster. With their relatively young faces, their tired, bloodshot eyes, and the urgency of their actions, they look as much like students cramming for finals as they do cybersecurity experts trying to save the world.

"Stop," I say. "Everyone stop."

The room goes quiet. All eyes on me.

"Is it possible," I say, "that you people are too damn smart?"

"Too smart, sir?"

"Yes. Is it possible that you have so much knowledge, and you're up against something so sophisticated, that you haven't considered a simple solution? That you can't see the forest for the trees?"

Casey looks around the room, throws up a hand. "At this point, I'm open to—"

"Show me," I say. "I want to see this thing."

"The virus?"

"Yes, Casey, the virus. The one that's going to destroy our country, if you weren't sure which virus I meant."

Everyone's on edge, frazzled, an air of desperation in the room.

"Sorry, sir." She drops her head and goes to work on a laptop. "I'll use the smartscreen," she says, and for the first time I notice that the whiteboard is really some kind of computer smartboard.

I look over at the smartscreen. A long menu of files suddenly appears. Casey scrolls down until she clicks on one.

"Here it is," she says. "Your virus."

I look at it, doing a double take:

Suliman.exe

"How humble of him," I say. He named the virus after himself. "This is the file we couldn't find for two weeks?"

"Sir, it avoided detection," says Casey. "Nina programmed it so it bypassed logging and— well, so it basically disappeared whenever we looked for it."

I shake my head. "So can you open this thing? Does it open?"

"Yes, sir. It took us a while to do even that." She types on her laptop, and the contents of the virus pop up on the smartscreen.

I don't know what I expected. Maybe a little green gargoyle, ready to gobble up data and files like some demented Pac-Man.

It's just a bunch of scrambled jumble. Six lines of symbols and letters—ampersands and pound signs, capital and lowercase letters, numbers and punctuation marks—that bear no resemblance to a written word in any language.

"Is this some kind of encrypted code we're supposed to unravel?"

"No," says Augie. "It is obfuscated. Nina obfuscated the malicious code so it cannot be read, it cannot be reverse-engineered. The whole point is to make it unreadable."

"But you re-created it, didn't you?"

"We did, to a large extent," says Augie. "You've got great people in this room, but we can't be sure we re-created everything. And we know we did not re-create the timing mechanism."

I exhale, putting my hands on my hips, dropping my head.

"Okay, so you can't disable it. Kill it. Whatever."

Casey says, "That's correct. When we try to disable or remove the virus, it activates."

"Explain 'activates' to me. You mean it deletes all the data?"

"It overwrites all active files," she says. "They can't be reconstructed."

"So it's like deleting a file and then deleting it again from the trash, like when I had my Macintosh in the nineties?"

She wrinkles her nose. "No. Deleting is different. When something is deleted, it's marked as deleted. It's inactive, and it becomes unallocated space that could eventually be replaced when storage hits capacity—"

"Casey, for Christ's sake. Would you speak English?"

She pushes her thick glasses up on the bridge of her nose. "It doesn't really matter, sir. All I was saying was, when the user deletes a file, it doesn't disappear immediately and forever. The computer marks it as deleted, so that space opens up in the memory, and it disappears from your active files. But an expert could reconstruct it. That's not what this virus is doing. The wiper virus overwrites the data. And *that* is permanent."

"Show me," I say again. "Show me the virus overwriting the data."

"Okay. We made a simulation in case you ever

wanted to see it." Casey runs through a couple things on the computer so fast that I don't even know what she's done. "Here is a random active file on this laptop. See it here? All the rows, the various properties of the file?"

On the smartscreen, a box has opened up showing a single file's properties. A series of horizontal rows, each occupied by a number or word.

"Now I'll show you that same file after the overwrite."

Suddenly a different image appears on the smartscreen.

Again, I'd envisioned something dramatic, but the actual visual experience is decidedly anticlimactic.

"It's identical," I say, "except the last three rows have been replaced with a zero."

"That's the overwrite. The zero. We can never reconstruct it once it's gone."

A bunch of zeros. America will be transformed into a third-world country by a bunch of zeros.

"Show me the virus again," I say.

She pops it back on the screen, the amalgamation of numbers and symbols and letters.

"So this thing goes kaboom, and everything vanishes like that?" I snap my fingers.

"Not quite," says Casey. "Some wiper viruses

act that way. This one goes file by file. It's fairly quick, but it's slower than the snap of a finger. It's like the difference between dying suddenly from a massive coronary versus dying slowly from cancer."

"How slow is slowly?"

"Maybe, I don't know, about twenty minutes."

Find a way.

"That thing has a timing mechanism inside it?"

"It might. We can't tell."

"Well, what's the other possibility?"

"That it's waiting for a command to execute. That the viruses in each affected device are communicating with one another. One of them will issue a command to execute, and they all will, simultaneously."

I look at Augie. "Which is it?"

He shrugs. "I do not know. I'm sorry. Nina did not share that with me."

"Well, can't we play with the time?" I ask. "Can't we change the time on the computer so it's a different year? If it's set to go off today, can't we change the clock and calendar back a century? So it thinks it has to wait a hundred years to go off? I mean, how the hell does this virus know what date and what year it is if we tell it something different?"

Augie shakes his head. "Nina would not have

tied it to a computer's clock," he says. "It's too imprecise and too easy to manipulate. Either it's master-controlled or she gave it a specific amount of time. She would start back from the desired date and time, calculate it in terms of seconds, and tell it to detonate in that many seconds."

"Three years ago she did that?"

"Yes, Mr. President. It would be simple multiplication. It would be trillions of seconds, but so be it. It's still just mathematics."

I deflate.

"If you can't change the timer," I ask, "how did you guys make this virus go off?"

"We tried to remove the virus or disable it," says Devin. "And it detonated. It has a trigger function, like a booby trap, that recognizes hostile activity."

"Nina did not expect anyone to ever detect it," says Augie. "And she was correct. No one did. But she installed this trigger in case someone did."

"Okay," I say, pacing the room. "Work with me. Think big picture. Big picture but simple."

Everyone nods, concentrating, as if readjusting their thinking. These people are accustomed to sophistication, to brainteasers, to matching wits with other experts.

"Can we—can we somehow quarantine the virus? Put it inside a box that it can't see out of?"

Augie is shaking his head before I've finished my sentence. "It will overwrite all active files, Mr. President. No 'box' would change that."

"We tried that, believe me," says Casey. "Many different versions of that idea. We can't isolate the virus from the rest of the files."

"Can we…couldn't we just unplug every device from the Internet?"

Her head inclines. "Possibly. It's possible that this is a distributive system, meaning the viruses are communicating from device to device, like we just said, and one of them will send an 'execute' command to the other viruses. It's possible that she set it up that way. So if she did, then yes, if we disconnected everything from the Internet, that 'execute' command wouldn't be received and the wiper virus wouldn't activate."

"Okay. So…" I lean forward.

"Sir, if we disconnect everything from the Internet…we disconnect everything from the Internet. If we order every Internet service provider in the country to shut off…"

"Then everything reliant on the Internet would shut down."

"We'd be doing their work for them, sir."

"And we'd be doing that not even knowing if it

would be successful, sir," says Devin. "For all we know, each virus has its own internal timer, independent of the Internet. The individual viruses might not be communicating with one another. We just don't know."

"Okay." I spin my hands around each other. "Keep going. Keep thinking. What about…what happens to the wiper virus after it's done wiping?"

Devin opens his hands. "After it's done, the computer's crashed. Once the core operating files are overwritten, the computer crashes forever."

"But what happens to the virus?"

Casey shrugs. "What happens to a cancer cell after the host body dies?"

"So you're saying the virus dies when the computer dies?"

"I…" Casey looks at Devin, then Augie. "*Everything* dies."

"Well, what if the computer crashed but you reinstalled the operating software and booted the computer back up? Would the virus be right there waiting for us again? Or would it be dead? Or asleep forever, at least?"

Devin thinks about that for a second. "It wouldn't matter, sir. The files you care about are already overwritten, gone forever."

"Could we—I don't suppose we could just turn off all our computers and wait for the time to pass?"

"No, sir."

I step back and look at all three of them, Casey, Devin, and Augie. "Back to work. Be creative. Turn everything upside down. Find. A. Way."

I storm out of the room, nearly running into Alex in the process, and head to the communications room.

It will be my last chance. My Hail Mary.

CHAPTER
89

❖

My circle of six, all appearing before me on the computer screen. One of these six individuals—Brendan Mohan, NSA head; Rodrigo Sanchez, chairman of the Joint Chiefs; Dominick Dayton, secretary of defense; Erica Beatty, CIA director; Sam Haber, secretary of homeland security; and Vice President Katherine Brandt—one of them...

"A traitor?" says Sam Haber, breaking the silence.

"It had to be one of you," I say.

I can't deny a certain relief, having finally spilled it. For the last four days I've known that there was someone on the inside working with our enemy. It's colored my every interaction with this group. It feels good to finally reveal the truth to them.

"So here's where we are," I say. "Whoever you are, I don't know why you did it. Money, I suppose, because I can't bring myself to believe that any of you, who have devoted your lives to public service, would hate this country so much that you'd want to see it go down in flames.

"Maybe you got in over your head. Maybe you thought this was some garden-variety hack. Some theft of sensitive information or something. You didn't realize that you'd be unleashing the hounds of hell on our country. And by the time you *did* realize it, it was too late to turn back. I could believe that. I could believe that you didn't intend for things to get this bad."

What I'm saying must be true. I can't believe that our traitor really wants to destroy our country. He or she may have been compromised somehow with blackmail, or may have succumbed to good old-fashioned bribery, but I just can't believe that one of these six people is secretly an agent of a foreign government who wants to destroy the United States.

But even if I'm wrong, I want the traitor to think I'm seeing things this way. I'm trying to give him or her an out.

"But none of that matters now," I continue. "What matters is stopping this virus before it detonates and wreaks its havoc. So I'm going to do something I never thought I'd do."

I can't believe I'm doing this, but I have no other choice.

"Whoever you are, if you step forward and help me stop the virus, I'll pardon you for all the crimes you've committed."

I search the faces of the six as I say these words, but the screens are too small to note any particular reaction.

"Whoever you are, the other five of you are witnesses to what I've just said. I will pardon you of all your crimes if you cooperate with me, if you help me stop the virus and tell me who is behind this.

"And I will classify the information. You will resign your position and leave the country immediately and never come back. Nobody will know why you left. Nobody will know what you did. If you received money from our enemy, you can keep it. You will leave this country, and you'll never be allowed back in. But you'll have your freedom. Which is one hell of a lot more than you deserve.

"If you don't come forward now, know this: you will not get away with it. I will not rest until we figure out who is responsible. You will be prosecuted and convicted of so many crimes I couldn't list them all. But one of them will be treason against the United States. You will be sentenced to death."

I take a breath. "So that's it," I say. "You can choose freedom, and probably riches, with a complete cover-up of what you've done. Or you can be remembered as the Ethel and Julius Rosenberg or the Robert Hanssen of this generation. This is the easiest decision you'll ever have to make.

"This offer expires in thirty minutes or until the virus goes off, whichever is sooner," I say. "Make a good decision."

I terminate the connection and walk out of the room.

CHAPTER
90

❖

I stand in the kitchen looking out over the backyard, the woods. The light is quickly dimming outside. It's an hour, give or take, until sunset, and the sun has fallen behind the trees. "Saturday in America" has only five hours remaining.

And it's been eleven minutes and thirty seconds since I issued my offer to the circle of six.

Noya Baram walks up beside me. Takes my hand, wraps her bony, delicate fingers in mine.

"I wanted to give my country a new spirit," I say. "I wanted to make us closer. I wanted us to feel like we were all in this together. Or at least get us moving in that direction. I thought I could. I really thought I could do that."

"You still can," she says.

"I'll be lucky if I can keep us alive," I say. "And keep us from killing each other over a loaf of bread or a gallon of gas."

Our nation will survive this. I do believe that. But we will be set so far back. We will suffer so much in the process.

"What haven't I done, Noya?" I ask. "What am I not doing that I should be doing?"

She exhales an elaborate sigh. "Are you preparing to mobilize all active and reserve forces if necessary to preserve order?"

"Yes."

"Have you secured the leadership of the other two branches of government?"

"Yes."

"Are you preparing emergency measures to stabilize the markets?"

"Already drafted," I say. "What I mean, Noya, is what am I not doing to stop this?"

"Ah. What do you do when you know an enemy is coming and you can't stop it?" She turns to me. "There are many world leaders in history who would have liked to know the answer to that question."

"Count me as one of them."

She looks at me. "What did you do in Iraq when your plane was shot down?"

A helicopter, actually—a Black Hawk on a

search-and-rescue mission for a downed F-16 pilot near Basra. The time between the Iraqi SAM obliterating our tail section and the bird spiraling to the ground couldn't have been more than five or ten seconds.

I shrug. "I just prayed for myself and my team and told myself I wouldn't give up any information."

That's my standard line. Only Rachel and Danny know the truth.

I'd somehow been tossed from the rapidly descending aircraft. To this day it's a blur of spinning, stomach-churning motion, the smoke and smell of aircraft fuel gagging me. Then the desert sand rose up to absorb much of my contorted hard landing but knocked the wind from me nonetheless.

Sand in my eyes, sand in my mouth. I couldn't move. I couldn't see. But I could hear. I could hear the animated shouts of the Republican Guard approaching, calling out to one another in their native tongue, their voices growing closer.

My rifle was nowhere in sight. I tried to make my right arm work. I tried to roll over. But I couldn't reach it. My sidearm was pinned underneath my body.

I couldn't move at all. My collarbone was shattered, my shoulder badly dislocated, my arm like an appendage broken off a toy doll under the weight of my body.

So the next best thing I could do—the only thing I could do, helpless as I was—was lie perfectly still and hope that when the Iraqis arrived to claim their prize, they'd think I was already—

Wait.

I grab Noya's arm. She jumps in surprise.

Without another word to her, I rush down the stairs to the war room. Casey almost jumps out of her chair when she sees me, the look on my face.

"What?" she asks.

"We can't kill this thing," I say. "And we can't clean up its damage afterward."

"Right..."

"What if we tricked it?" I ask.

"Tricked it—"

"You said when you delete files, they become inactive, right?"

"Yes."

"And the virus only overwrites active files, right? That's what you said."

"Yes. So..."

"So?" I rush over to Casey, grab her by the shoulders.

"What if we play dead?" I say.

CHAPTER
91

❖

"P lay dead," says Casey, repeating my words. "We destroy the data before the virus can destroy it?"

"Well—I'm going by what you told me," I say. "You said when files are deleted, they aren't really deleted. They're just *marked* as deleted. They don't disappear forever, but they become inactive."

She nods.

"And you told me the virus only overwrites *active* files," I continue. "So it won't overwrite inactive, marked-as-deleted files."

Augie, standing near the smartboard now, wags a finger. "You are suggesting we delete all active files on the computer."

"Yes," I say. "When it's time for the virus to

activate, it opens its eyes and sees no active files to delete. It's like—well, here: it's like the virus is an assassin, an assassin whose job is to walk into a room and shoot everyone inside. But when he gets inside, everyone's already dead. Or so he thinks. So he never pulls out his gun. He just turns around and leaves, because his work was already done for him."

"So we mark every active file as deleted," says Casey. "Then the virus activates. It doesn't do anything, because it sees no active files to overwrite."

She looks at Devin, who seems skeptical. "And then what?" he asks. "At some point we have to recover those files, right? I mean, that's the whole point—to save those files, to save all that data. So when we recover them, when we unmark them and make them active again—the virus just overwrites them then. It happens later instead of sooner, but it still happens. We're just delaying the inevitable."

I look around at everyone in the room, unwilling to let this go. I have the tiniest fraction of their knowledge, but the more I interact with them, the more I think that might be an advantage. They are way too engulfed in the trees to see the forest.

"Are you sure?" I ask. "After the virus does its

job, are we sure it doesn't go back to sleep, or die, or whatever? I asked you that before, and you responded by asking what happens to a cancer cell after the host body dies. Use my analogy instead. The assassin walks into the room, ready to kill everybody, and finds them all dead. Does the assassin leave, thinking his job is already accomplished? Or does he wait around forever, just in case someone wakes up?"

Casey, thinking it over, starts nodding. "He's right," she says to Devin. "We don't know. In every model we've run, the virus overwrote the core operating files and killed the computer. We've never asked ourselves what happens to the virus afterward. We've never run a model where the computer *survives* afterward. We can't say for certain the virus would remain active."

"But why *wouldn't* it remain active?" asks Devin. "I can't imagine Nina would've programmed the Suliman virus to stop at any point. Would she?"

All eyes turn to Augie, his hands stuffed in his pockets, eyes in a focused squint, peering off into some point in the present or the past. I can all but hear the tick of the clock. I want to grab him and shake him. But he's working this through. When his mouth opens, everyone in the room seems to lean toward him.

"I think your plan is possible," he says. "Certainly worth trying on a trial run."

I check my watch. Eighteen minutes have passed since I made my offer of a pardon. No attempts to contact me.

Why not? It's the deal of a lifetime.

"Let's run a test right now," says Casey.

Devin folds his arms, not looking convinced.

"What?" I ask him.

"This isn't going to work," he says. "And we're wasting time we don't have."

CHAPTER
92

❖

A group of scraggly, frumpy, frazzled computer experts stares at the smartboard in the room as Devin completes his preparations for the test run.

"Okay," says Devin, hovering over the keyboard of one of the test computers. "Every single file on this computer has been marked as deleted. Even the core operating files."

"You can delete the core operating files and still run the computer?"

"Normally, no," he says. "But what we did was—"

"Never mind. I don't care," I say. "So…let's do it. Activate the virus."

"I'll delete the virus, which should activate it."

I turn to the smartboard as Devin performs one of the few things that even a dinosaur like me could do—clicking on the Suliman.exe file and hitting Delete.

Nothing happens.

"Okay, it resisted my deletion," says Devin. "It's triggered the activation process."

"Devin—"

"The virus is active, Mr. President," says Casey, translating. "The assassin has entered the room."

A series of files pops up on the screen, just like the random files they showed me before, a series of boxes, the properties in a group of descending rows for each file.

"It's not overwriting them," says Casey.

The assassin hasn't found anyone to kill yet. So far so good.

I turn to Casey. "You said it took about twenty minutes to look for all the files. So we have twenty—"

"No," she says. "I said it took twenty minutes to overwrite them all, one by one. But it *finds* them much quicker. It—"

"Here." Devin works the keyboard, popping up an image of the Suliman virus.

Completing scan...
62%

She's right. It's moving much faster.

70 percent…80 percent…

I close my eyes, open them, look at the smart-board:

Scan completed
Number of files located: 0

"Okay," says Devin. "So it didn't overwrite anything. Not a single file affected."

"Now let's see if the assassin will leave the room, mission accomplished," I say.

Augie, who has remained quiet in the corner, tapping his foot, hand cupping chin, chimes in. "We should delete the virus now—again—now that it has performed its function. It might not resist."

"Or it might reactivate it," says Devin. "Wake it back up," he says to me.

"If that happens," says Augie, "then we will run the model again but not delete it."

I'm suddenly realizing why every move they make has consequences, why every tactic they've employed is subject to multiple iterations—why it was necessary to have so many test computers, so many trials.

Devin says, "We should do it my way first. There's a better chance of the virus coexisting with the—"

An argument erupts in the room, in multiple languages. Everyone has an opinion. I raise my hand and shout above the din. "Hey! Hey! Do it Augie's way," I say. "Delete the virus again, see what happens." I nod at Devin. "Do it."

"Okay," he says.

On the smartscreen, I watch Devin move the cursor over the only active file in the entire computer, the Suliman.exe virus. Then he hits Delete.

The icon disappears.

A collective exhalation of air escapes from the room as the world's foremost cyberops experts gasp in wonder at the empty screen.

"Holy shit!" Casey blurts out. "You know how many times we've tried to erase that stupid thing?"

"About five hundred?"

"That is literally the first time that's happened."

"The wicked witch is dead?" Devin says. He furiously works the computer, the computer screen changing so fast I can't look at it. "The wicked witch is dead!"

I temper my enthusiasm, suppress a wave of relief. We're not there yet.

"Recover all the other files," says Casey. "Let's see if the assassin really has left the room."

"Okay, recovering all marked-as-deleted files," says Devin, his finger strokes like little animal chirps as he feverishly works to recover the files. "Except the virus, of course."

I turn away, unable to look. The room is silent.

I glance at my phone to check the time. Twenty-eight minutes have passed since I made the offer of a pardon. Nobody has called. I don't understand it. I didn't expect anyone to confess on the spot, of course. No doubt it would be a big moment, admitting to something like this, a monumental thing, the biggest moment in a person's life. They'd need a few minutes to consider it.

But consider it they would: the tremendous chance of being caught committing treason against America and the horrific consequences it would bring—prison, disgrace, ruin for the family. And here I'm offering a free pass, as free a pass as I could possibly offer—not just avoiding prison or the death penalty but avoiding infamy, too. I promised to keep this classified. Nobody would ever know what the traitor did. If they got paid off, which presumably they did, they could keep the money, too.

No prison, no disgrace, no forfeiture—why would anyone turn down that offer? Does no one believe me?

"Mr. President," says Devin.

I turn to him. He nods to the screen. A bunch of files are pulled up, their properties listed in those descending rows.

"No zeros," I say.

"No zeros," says Devin. "The files are recovered and active, and the virus isn't touching them!"

"Yes!" Casey punches a fist in the air. "We tricked the freakin' virus!" Everyone is hugging, high-fiving, releasing hours of frustration.

"See? I knew this was a good idea," Devin jokes.

And my phone buzzes.

"Get ready to do this for real!" I shout at Devin, at Casey, at all of them. "Get set up on the Pentagon server."

"Yes, sir!"

"How long, guys? Minutes?"

"A few minutes," says Casey. "Maybe twenty, thirty? It will take us some time—"

"Hurry. If I'm not standing here when you're ready, find me."

Then I leave the room to answer my phone.

It's been twenty-nine minutes since I offered

the pardon. Whoever it is used nearly every second of the thirty minutes.

I remove my phone from my pocket and look at the face, the caller ID.

FBI Liz, it reads.

CHAPTER
93

❖

I n the hallway outside the war room, I answer a call from someone I had already ruled out of suspicion—

"Mr. President?"

"Director Greenfield," I say.

"We just unlocked Nina's second phone," she says. *"The one we found in the back of the van."*

"That's great, right?"

"Let's hope. We're downloading everything right now. We'll have it for you soon."

Why would Nina have two phones? I have no idea.

"There has to be something good on that phone, Liz."

"It's certainly possible, sir."

"There *has* to be," I say, looking at my watch. Thirty-one minutes have now passed. My offer of a pardon has expired, without a word from anyone.

CHAPTER
94

❖

High up in the white pine tree, Bach listens and waits, the scope of the rifle trained on the rear of the house through the branches.

Where is it? she wonders. *Where is the helicopter?*

She missed her chance. That was him, she is certain now—the scrawny, scraggly-haired man who passed into the cabin after the president. Had she even a few more seconds to confirm, that man would be dead now and she would be on a plane.

But Ranko's words during that summer, those three months that he taught her: *a missed shot is far worse than no shot.*

Caution was the better play. He might have come back out sometime over the last several hours, giving her another chance. The fact that he did not, that he has not reemerged from the cabin, does not render her decision at the time unreasonable or even wrong.

Playing gently through her earbuds is the Gavotte in D Major, performed by Wilhelm Friedemann Herzog some twelve years ago, a tutorial for Suzuki students. It is by no means her favorite of Johann Sebastian's work: truth be told, she never particularly cared for the piece and would rather hear it played with a full ensemble than as a violin solo.

But she cannot let go of the piece. She remembers playing it on her mother's violin, at first so choppy and awkward, ripening with time, maturing from a series of notes to something graceful and moving. Her mother hovering over her, gently instructing her, correcting every stroke. *Bow distribution!...Now big!...First one's strong—strong, little, little...do it again...balance your bow,* draga... *slow down your fingers, but not the bow—not the bow! Here,* draga, *let me show you.*

Her mother taking the violin herself, playing the gavotte from memory, her confidence and passion, losing herself in the music, shutting out the bombs and artillery fire outside, the house safe within the gentle spell of the music.

Her brother, so much more talented on the

violin, not only because he is two years older, with two more years' instruction, but also because it came so effortlessly to him, as if it were an extension of him and not a separate musical instrument, as if producing beautiful music was as natural as speaking or breathing.

For him, a violin. For her, a rifle.

Yes, a rifle. One last time.

She checks her watch. It's time. It's past time.

Why has nothing happened?

Where is the helicopter?

CHAPTER
95

❖

I can't thank you enough," I say to Chancellor Juergen Richter.

"Well, I am most disappointed by our failure in Berlin."

"It wasn't your failure. He knew you were coming." Then I add, using his first name, a rare thing with him, a man of such formality, "Juergen, your influence on NATO will be critical, if it comes to that."

"Yes." He gives a grave nod. He knows that this is the principal reason I brought him here, to look him squarely in the eye and make sure that our NATO partners will stand with the United States should a military conflict become necessary. Article 5, the commitment of NATO itself, will be tested as never before if the traditional roles are reversed and the world's greatest super-power is the one that needs assistance in what could easily turn into World War III.

"Noya." I give her a long hug, enjoying the comfort of her warm embrace.

"I could stay, Jonny," she whispers in my ear.

I pull back. "No. It's already past seven. I've already kept you longer than I planned. If this... happens...if the worst...I don't want to be responsible for your safety. And you'll want to be back home anyway."

She doesn't argue. She knows I'm right. If this virus activates and does the worst of what we fear, the reverberations will be felt around the world. These leaders will want to be home when that happens.

"My experts could stay," she offers.

I shake my head. "They've done all they can do. My people are doing their work on the Pentagon server now, and we have to keep that work internal, as you can imagine."

"Of course."

I shrug. "Besides, this is it, Noya. This is our last chance to stop the virus."

She takes my hand in hers, wrapping her delicate, wrinkled hands around mine. "Israel has no greater friend," she says. "And I have no greater friend."

The best decision I made was bringing Noya here today. Without my aides here with me, I felt her presence and guidance to be a comfort beyond description. But in the end, no number of aides or advice can change the fact that this all comes down to me. This is happening on my watch. This is my responsibility.

"Mr. Prime Minister," I say, shaking the hand of Ivan Volkov.

"Mr. President, I trust that our experts have been of assistance."

"They have, yes. Please convey my gratitude to President Chernokev."

As far as my people can tell, the Russian techs were on the up-and-up. At a minimum, Casey and Devin saw no signs that they were trying to sabotage the process. But that doesn't mean they couldn't have withheld something. There's no way to know.

"My experts tell me that your plan to stop this virus could be successful," says Volkov. "We are most hopeful this is so."

I wait for the trace of a smirk, a sense of irony, from the stone-faced, cold-blooded man.

"Everyone should be hopeful," I say. "Because if we're hurt, *everyone's* hurt. But the people responsible for this should be the most worried, Mr. Prime Minister. Because the United States will retaliate against anyone responsible. And I'm assured by our NATO allies that they will stand with us."

He nods, the furrowed brow, the look of deep concern. "In the coming days," he says, "leaders will have to make decisions deliberately and cautiously."

"In the coming days," I say, "we will find out who are America's friends and who are America's enemies. Nobody will want to be an enemy."

With that, Volkov takes his leave.

The three leaders, their aides, and their computer experts walk down the back stairs.

A Marine helicopter lands on the helipad in the backyard, preparing to whisk them away.

CHAPTER
96

❖

Here we go.
From her perch in the white pine, Bach looks through the scope of her rifle at the backyard.

Breathe. Relax. Aim. Squeeze.

The military helicopter, using sound suppression that reduces the roar of the rotating blades to a gentle whisper, sets down on the pad.

The cabin door opens. She steels herself.

The leaders walk out of the cabin, illuminated by the porch lights.

She marks each of them as they exit, sees the opportunity for clean shots to the head.

The Israeli prime minister.

The German chancellor.

The Russian prime minister.

Others walking out, too. She scans their faces.

One second, that's all she will need now that she's ready —

Breathe. Relax. Aim. Squeeze.

A dark-haired man —

—her finger caresses the trigger —

Negative.

Adrenaline surging through her body. This is it, and she's done forever —

Long-haired man —

No. Not her target.

The cabin door remains open.

And then it closes.

"Jebi ga," she curses to herself. He never came out. He's still inside.

The helicopter lifts. She feels the rush of air as it rises and angles away, quickly disappearing in relative silence.

He won't leave the cabin. He won't come to them. So they'll have to go to him.

She sets down her rifle and lifts her binoculars. US Secret Service remaining on the lawn, manning the back porch as well. They have laid down flares around the perimeter of the yard to enhance the lighting in the dark.

What happens next will be much riskier.

"Team 1 in position," she hears in her ear.

"Team 2 in position."

And much bloodier.

CHAPTER
97

❖

H urry," I say to Devin and Casey in the
basement, while Devin, plugged into the
Pentagon systems, works to mark all Pentagon
files as deleted. Realizing, as I say it, that he's going as fast as he can and that my badgering
doesn't help matters.

My phone buzzes. "Liz," I say, answering it.

*"Mr. President, we downloaded the contents of Nina's
second phone. You need to see them right away."*

"Okay. How?"

"I'll send them straight to your phone, right now."

"Everything? What am I looking for?"

*"There was only one thing she ever used the phone
for,"* Liz says. *"Just one thing. She was using a burner
phone and texting with another burner. Nina was communicating with our insider, Mr. President. She was
text-messaging with our…our traitor."*

My blood goes cold. There was always a small part of me that wanted to believe that there was no traitor, that Nina and Augie had learned the code word "Dark Ages" some other way, that none of my people was capable of doing this.

"Tell me who, Liz," I say, a tremble in my voice. "Who did it?"

"No names, sir. I just sent it."

"I'll read it and call you back."

I end the call.

"Devin, Casey!" I call out. "I'm going into the communications room. The moment you're ready, you call out to me."

"Yes, sir."

My phone beeps an instant later, a message from Liz. There is a document attached, which I open as I head into the communications room, Alex behind me.

The document displays as a transcript, the participants in the communication designated as either "Nina" or "U/C," for "unknown caller"— I prefer "traitor" or "Judas" or "Benedict Arnold"—and broken down by date and time.

The first text message comes from the unknown caller on May 4. That was a Friday. That was the day after I returned from my European trip, the day after the news broke that the United States had thwarted an assassination attempt on

Suliman Cindoruk and that the mother of a dead CIA operative was demanding answers.

I look at the first grouping of texts from May 4 and notice the location of the unknown caller:

1600 Pennsylvania Avenue

The text messages came from the White House. Whoever it is communicated from within the walls of the White House. It's…unfathomable. I put that aside and start reading:

Friday, May 4
U/C: 1600 Pennsylvania Avenue
Nina: Location unknown
**** All times Eastern Standard Time ****

U/C (7:52 AM): I read your note, obviously. Who are you, and how do I know this is serious?

Nina (7:58 AM): U know I'm real. How else would I know the precise moment, down 2 the second, that the virus appeared on your Pentagon server?

Nina (8:29 AM): No response? U have nothing to say?

Nina (9:02 AM) U don't believe me? Fine. Then watch your country go down in 🔥 Instead of being hero, u can explain to the POTUS that u could have stopped this but didn't. From hero to 🐐 so sad!!

Nina (9:43 AM): Why would I lie about this? What do u have 2 lose? Why r u ignoring me??

I think back to the timing. We had a meeting of the national security team that morning. My inner circle, all in the White House.

Whoever this is was texting from that meeting. I keep reading. Nina continues to pursue the unknown caller:

Nina (9:54 AM): I guess u don't want to be the hero, then just bury head in sand and pretend like I don't exist ??? 🙈 🙉 🙊

Nina (9:59 AM): 💧💧💧💧💧💧💧

Nina (10:09 AM): Maybe u will believe me after Toronto

Toronto. Right. That Friday was the day the Toronto subway system screeched to a halt, shut down entirely by a computer virus that we assumed was the work of the Sons of Jihad. It happened during the evening rush hour. Nina was texting about it that morning, before it happened. Just as she told me about the helicopter crash in Dubai before it happened.

So that explains how this came about, at least. I've been wondering how this whole thing began, how a cyberterrorist and a member of my national security team ever got acquainted in the first place. *Nina* initiated the conversation. She somehow got word to the Judas in our inner circle.

But whoever that insider is, why didn't he or she just tell me right away? The moment that note was received, why not tell me about it? Why keep it a secret?

How differently this all could have turned out if the insider had just come to me at that point.

I scroll down. That's it for May 4.

The next communication is the following day—Saturday, May 5, in the morning. Again, the unknown caller texting from the White House.

Smart, I realize. The traitor recognized that his or her location might be traced all the way down to the street address, to 1600 Pennsylvania, and made sure to be in the presence of other high-level security officials at that time. Hiding within the inner circle. Cautious. Smart.

I read:

Saturday, May 5
U/C: 1600 Pennsylvania Avenue
Nina: Location unknown
** All times Eastern Standard Time **

U/C (10:40 AM): So you're serious. Is that what you're going to do to our military systems, what you did to the Toronto subway last night?

Nina (10:58 AM): That times a million. I have your attn now!!

U/C (10:59 AM): Yes, I believe you now. You can stop this virus?

Nina (11:01 AM): Yes I can tell u how to stop it

U/C (11:02 AM): Telling me wouldn't help. I don't know enough about computers.

Nina (11:05 AM): U don't need to know anything I will tell u what u need simple simple

U/C (11:24 AM): Then turn yourself in. Go to the nearest US embassy.

Nina (11:25 AM): And go straight to Gitmo? No thanx!!!

U/C (11:28 AM): Then just tell me how to stop the virus.

Nina (11:31 AM): Give up my leverage?? That's the only reason u will give me amnesty. If I go first and tell u how to stop the virus, how do I know u will keep up your end of the deal?? No sorry that's one thing I won't do. Never

U/C (11:34 AM): Then I can't help you. You have to do this yourself.

Nina (11:36 AM): Why can't u help me?????

U/C (11:49 AM): Because I'm in trouble now. You told me about Toronto yesterday, before it happened, and I didn't say anything or tell anyone.

Nina (11:51 AM): Why didn't u tell anyone??

U/C (11:55 AM): I didn't believe you. And have you read the news? The president is getting crucified just for calling Suliman. And here I am, texting with someone who works with him. I made a mistake. But I can't do anything about that now.

But I believe you. Let me figure this out, ok? Just wait to hear from me, ok? Do we have time for that? When does the virus strike?

Nina (11:57 AM): In one week. I will give u til tmrw no longer

That's the end of the Saturday, May 5, exchange. My mind is racing, trying to make sense of this. So this wasn't some long-standing treasonous plan? It wasn't blackmail. It wasn't money. Just a mistake in judgment? One bad decision piled on top of another, and suddenly we're in this mess?

The next text comes from our Benedict Arnold, again from the White House, the following morning, Sunday, May 6:

U/C (7:04 AM): I have an idea of how we can do this while keeping me out of it. Are you close to Paris?

CHAPTER
98

❖

A white van, bearing the logo of Lee's Boats and Docks, turns off the Virginia county highway onto a gravel road. Up ahead, a barrier has been erected with a sign attached to it that reads PRIVATE PROPERTY—NO TRESPASSING. Beyond it, two black SUVs are parked perpendicular to the road.

The driver of the van, who goes by Lojzik, stops the van and looks in the rearview mirror at the eight men in the rear compartment, all dressed in body armor. Four of them armed with AK-47s. The other four manning shoulder-launched assault weapons loaded with armor-penetrating rockets.

"If I take off my hat," he says, reminding them of the signal.

Lojzik gets out of the car, looking the part of a lake guy, wearing a hat with a ripped visor, a flannel shirt, and torn jeans. He approaches the SUVs at the barricade, raising a hand as if posing a question.

"Hello?" he says. "You fellas know how I find County Road 20?"

No answer. The windows of the SUVs are tinted, so he can't see inside.

"Anyone there?" he asks.

He asks again. And again. It's what they thought: nobody's occupying those SUVs. The Secret Service is spread too thin, especially with the other security now flying off in a Marine helicopter.

So Lojzik doesn't remove his cap, and the gunners don't spill out to fire their rockets at the convoy.

Good. They'll need them for the cabin.

Lojzik returns to the car and nods at the men. "Looks all clear to the cabin," he says. "Hold on."

He drops the gear into Reverse and backs up to the end of the gravel road. Then he stops, puts the gear in Drive, and floors the gas pedal, hurtling the van toward the barricade.

*   *   *

Moments later, a speedboat drifts slowly toward the small bay where Secret Service agents sit in a boat, well lit at dusk. Unlike team 1's van, penetrating from the north, the boat only contains four men, the opportunity for concealment being far less.

Two men stand at the bow of the boat. At their feet on the deck: the other two men, lying prone, and four AK-74 assault rifles fitted with under-barrel grenade launchers.

"Stop your boat!" the Secret Service agent calls out through a megaphone. *"This is restricted water!"*

The leader, a man named Hamid, cups his hand and yells toward the agents. "Can you tow us ashore? Our engine's dead!"

"Turn your boat around!"

Hamid opens his arms. "I can't. Engine's dead!"

The man standing next to Hamid, his head turned downward only slightly, says to the men at his feet, "On my command."

"Then drop anchor and we will send for help!"

"You want me to—"

"Do not advance! Drop anchor now!"

The agents on the boat scramble, one heading to each side of the boat, one to the bow, each of them yanking off tarps, exposing mounted machine guns.

"Now!" whispers Hamid, reaching down for one of the weapons.

The hidden men jump to their feet with their AK-74s, their grenade launchers, and open fire on the Secret Service.

CHAPTER

99

❖

I n the communications room, reading the text messages between Nina and our Benedict Arnold from Sunday, May 6, I now see how Lilly became involved. It was our insider's way of getting Nina to access me directly without going through anyone else, keeping the insider's fingerprints off the whole thing. Nina's reply:

Nina (7:23 AM): You want me to tell the president's daughter?

U/C (7:28 AM): Yes. If you give her the information, she will deliver it straight to her father. And the president will deal with you directly.

Nina (7:34 AM): Do you think the president will make this deal with me?

U/C (7:35 AM): Of course he will. Amnesty from your home government in exchange for saving our country? Of course he will! But you'll have to go see him. Can you do that? Can you get to the US?

Nina (7:38 AM): Do I have to see him in person?

U/C (7:41 AM): Yes. He wouldn't take your word for this over the phone.

Nina (7:45 AM): I don't know. How do I know he won't ship me to Gitmo and torture me?

U/C (7:48 AM): He wouldn't. Trust me.

The truth is, I don't know *what* I would have been willing to do to stop this virus. I would have interrogated Nina if I thought it would get me answers.

But it never got that far, because Nina made it clear—through Lilly, and then when she came to see me—that she had a partner who knew the other half of the puzzle. They were a package deal, Nina said, and if I detained her at the White House, I'd never meet the other half of the puzzle, and I'd never be able to stop the virus.

Which is where we find ourselves now.

Nina (7:54 AM): If I do this if I go see his daughter in Paris how do I know the president will take me seriously?

U/C (7:59 AM): He will.

Nina (8:02 AM): Why? U didn't

U/C (8:04 AM): Because I'm going to give you a code word that will give you instant credibility. The moment he hears that code, he will take you seriously. No question.

Nina (8:09 AM): OK what is code

U/C (8:12 AM): I have to trust you. This is codeword-classified information I'm disclosing. I wouldn't just have to resign my position. I'd go to prison. You get that?

Nina (8:15 AM): Yeah Edward Snowden Chelsea Manning?

U/C (8:17 AM): Basically. I'm risking everything to help you. I'm trusting you.

Nina (8:22 AM): We have to trust EACH

OTHER. I won't ever tell anyone who you are or what you told me. Swear to God!!

U/C (9:01 AM): All right. I am taking the risk of my life right now. I hope you understand that. I hope I can trust you.

Nina (9:05 AM): I do. U can

So that's how Nina learned "Dark Ages." And the day after this exchange of text messages— just five days ago, this past Monday—Nina found Lilly in Paris at the Sorbonne and whispered "Dark Ages" in her ear. Lilly called me, and I've spent the last four-plus days trying to figure out who the insider is.

So far I'm no closer to knowing that. I scroll down to the next page—

"Mr. President!" The voice of Casey, calling to me. "We're ready!"

I rush out of the communications room, Alex following me, and find Casey, Devin, and Augie in the war room.

"Ready to activate the virus?" I say. I put down my phone on a desk and stand behind Devin.

Casey turns to me. "Mr. President, before we do this: you understand that we don't know whether the virus is communicating between devices. It's possible that each virus on each device around the country is independently timed to go off. But it's also possible that the virus on one computer will signal to the others, that it will send an 'execute' command to set off the virus simultaneously on all affected devices."

"Yes, you said that before."

"My point being, sir, I hope this works—but if it doesn't, and the virus detonates on the Pentagon server, it might activate on the millions and probably billions of devices around the country. Our worst-case scenario will come true if our plan doesn't work."

"It worked on the trial run," I say.

"Yes, it did. We've done our best to reverse-engineer the virus for our trials. But I cannot tell you with 100 percent certainty that our re-creation was perfect. We've only had hours to do this, working quickly. So I can't tell you this will work on the real virus."

I take a deep breath. "If we do nothing, this virus will go off soon anyway," I say. "Maybe a minute from now, maybe a few hours at most—but it's coming soon. And this scheme we devised—it's the closest thing we've come up with to stop the virus. Right?"

"Yes, sir. It's the only thing that's even remotely succeeded."

"So?" I shrug. "Do you have a better idea?"

"I don't, sir. I just want you to understand. If this doesn't work…"

"Everything could go to shit. I get it. This could be a big win for us, or it could be Armageddon." I look at Augie. "What do you think, Augie?"

"I agree with your reasoning, Mr. President. This is our best bet. Our only bet."

"Casey?"

"I agree. We should try it."

"Devin?"

"Agreed, sir."

I rub my hands together. "Let's do it, then."

Devin's fingers hover over the keyboard. "Here goes—"

"What?" Alex Trimble, standing near me, jumps as he puts his finger against his earbud. "North route has been breached? Viper!" he yells into his radio. "Viper, do you copy, Viper?" In one fluid motion, Alex is on me, gripping my arm and pulling me. "In the communications room, Mr. President! We need to lock down. It's the safest—"

"No. I'm staying here."

Alex tugs on me, not relenting. "No, sir, you have to come with me right now."

"Then they're coming with," I say.

"Fine. But let's go."

Devin unhooks the laptop. Everyone rushes to the communications room.

Just as the sound of heavy gunfire echoes in the distance.

CHAPTER
100

❖

After barreling the white van through the barricade, Lojzik slows it almost to a complete stop as he searches for the unmarked dirt road. There. He missed it. He stops, throws the van in Reverse, backs up past the road, and makes the left turn. If he hadn't been told it was there, he would have missed it altogether.

The path is narrow enough to accommodate only a single vehicle. And it's dark, the falling sun completely shrouded by the tall trees on each side. Lojzik grips the steering wheel and cranes his neck forward, unable to gain too much speed on the uneven terrain but slowly accelerating.

Only a half mile until they reach the cabin.

* * *

On the lake, a firefight.

Team 2 fires smoke grenades and batters the Secret Service boat with rounds from the AK-74s. The boat returns machine-gun fire, forcing the attackers down to the deck, using the hull of their boat as a bunker.

The few remaining Secret Service agents are on foot, covering the backyard. They scramble toward the dock, raising their weapons and opening fire on team 2's boat as well.

Once the agents on foot reach the dock, their attention fully trained on the attack boat, Bach rushes along the perimeter of the yard, covered by the darkness and distraction, and jumps into the window well in front of the basement laundry room.

CHAPTER
101

❖

Alex Trimble shuts and locks the heavy door to the communications room. He removes a phone from his pocket and clicks it on.

Devin sits in the chair, laptop open, ready to go.

"Go, Devin," I say. "Activate the virus."

I look over Alex's shoulder at his phone. The Secret Service installed cameras on the roof, and Alex and I watch the feed from the camera facing north—a white van barreling down the dirt path toward us.

"Where are you, Viper!" Alex cries into his radio.

As if responding to a stage director's cue, a Marine helicopter, part of a new fleet of Viper attack helicopters, appears out of nowhere, swooping down as it closes on the van from behind. A Hellfire air-to-surface missile launches from its wing, spiraling toward the van.

The van explodes, a ball of orange flame, bouncing end over end before coming to rest on its side. Secret Service agents shuffle forward, automatic weapons poised—

The screen changes as Alex clicks a button: we are looking to the southeast, watching a firefight on the lake, agents on a boat and agents on the dock firing at another boat, trying desperately to keep it from reaching shore.

Alex, a finger pressed to the earbud in his ear, calls into his radio, "Navigator, clear a path! Clear a path! All agents stand clear for Viper!"

With that, the Secret Service boat reverses course, backing away from the attack boat, and the agents on the dock scramble back to ground and dive to the earth.

The Viper arrives, firing another Hellfire and completely incinerating the attack boat, a ball of flame along with a fountain of lake water. The Secret Service boat capsizes, too.

"Now drop me a perimeter of Marines!" Alex calls out into his radio, immediately moving to the next phase. The Marines, stationed at the local airport with the Viper, were his idea, letting us keep a low profile at the cabin, as I insisted, but keeping some heavy backup nearby.

"The agents in the water!" I say to Alex, pushing his shoulder.

He lowers his radio. "They have life preservers. They're okay." Back to his radio. "Where are my Marines? And I need a casualty report!"

"Okay, the virus is activated on the Pentagon server," says Devin.

My head on a swivel, I focus on Devin as Alex moves to the door of the communications room and continues to shout instructions.

"Let's see if this works." Devin releases a breath. "Say a prayer."

He types on the computer. We don't have the smartscreen now, huddled as we are in the communications room, so I watch over his shoulder along with Casey and Augie as he pulls up the file properties, to see if the marked-as-deleted files will survive.

"That's a zero," I say, looking at the bottom row of the properties box. "A zero's bad, right?"

"It's…no…no," says Devin. "It's overwriting the files."

"You deleted them?" I ask. "You marked them as del—"

"Yes, yes, yes." Devin grabs the laptop in frustration. "Shit!"

I watch the same file properties, the boxes of

descending rows of words and numbers, but seeing the zero in the bottom rows.

"Why isn't it working?" I ask. "What's—"

"We must not have completely reconstructed the virus in our tests," says Augie. "The parts that we could not decrypt."

"We missed something," Casey says.

My blood goes cold. "The Pentagon server's going to be erased?"

Casey raises a hand to her ear, her earpiece. "Repeat!" she says, closing her eyes in concentration. "Are you sure?"

"What, Casey?"

She turns to me. "Mr. President, our team at the Pentagon—they're saying…the virus we just activated issued an 'execute' command throughout the system. The virus is detonating at Treasury…" She taps her ear. "Homeland Security. Transportation. Ev—everywhere, sir." She looks at her smartphone. "My phone, too."

I reach for my phone. "Where's my phone?"

"Oh, no," says Augie. "Oh no oh no oh no."

"My phone, too," says Devin. "It's happening. Jesus, it's going off everywhere! The virus is attacking everywhere."

Casey falls to a crouch, gripping her hair.

"It's happening," she says. "God help us."

For a moment I am stunned, in disbelief. Deep

down, I always believed that somehow, in some way, it would never happen, that we'd figure something out.

God help us is right.

Dark Ages has arrived.

CHAPTER
102

❖

The private jet lands on a narrow runway outside of Zagreb. Suliman Cindoruk stretches, gets up, and takes the stairs down onto the tarmac.

Two men greet him, each with a rifle slung over his shoulder. Tall, dark men with no expressions other than respectful acknowledgments to Suli. He follows them to a Jeep. They get in the front, and he gets in the back. Soon they are driving on a two-lane road parallel to the magnificent Mount Medvednica, so majestic in its—

He jumps at the sound of the ringtone on his phone. A ringtone he's been expecting. The sound of a bomb exploding. The ringtone he reserved for just one event.

It's early by a few hours. The Americans must have tried to delete it.

He pulls it up on his phone and reads the delicious words: Virus activated.

He closes his eyes and lets the warmth of satisfaction spread through him. There is nothing so sexy as a good, destructive overwrite, the power he can deploy from a keyboard thousands of miles away.

As the Jeep continues onward, the wind blowing his hair back, he savors the rush. *He* did this.

One man, who changed the course of history.

One man, who brought the world's only superpower to its knees.

One man, who will soon be rich enough to enjoy it.

CHAPTER
103

❖

T his can't be right!"
"No, God, no—"
Panic, cursing, wailing all around me. My body trembling, still in a suspended state of disbelief, waiting to awaken from the nightmare, I move to the computer in the communications room, secured by a separate line that Dark Ages can't touch.

We've moved to the threat-mitigation phase. I need to get hold of Carolyn.

First: get word to the congressional leaders— bring the House and Senate in, as soon as possible, to pass legislation authorizing the nationwide use of the military in our streets, the suspension of habeas corpus, wide-ranging executive authority to impose price controls and rationing.

Second: file the executive orders—

"Wait, what?" Devin cries out. "Wait, wait, wait! Casey, look at this."

She rushes to his side. I do, too.

Devin works the computer, some kind of accelerated scrolling, jumping from one set of files to another. "It…I don't get it…it…"

"It *what?*" I shout. "Speak!"

"It…" Devin types on the computer, various screens appearing and disappearing. "It started…it overwrote a few files, like it was trying to show us it could…but now it's stopped."

"It stopped? The virus *stopped?*"

Casey angles past me, peering at the computer screen. "What is *that?*" she asks.

CHAPTER
104

❖

B ach stands in the window well as the gunfight rages on the lake. "Team 1, status,"
she says, awaiting word from Lojzik, the Czech
team leader.

"We are proceeding—what is—what—"

"Team 1, status!" she hisses, trying to keep her
voice down.

"Helikoptéra!" Lojzik cries in his native tongue.
"Odkud pochází helikoptéra?"

A helicopter?

"Team 1—"

She hears the explosion in stereo, coming from
the north and from her earbuds via Lojzik's
transmitter. She looks to the north, the flames
coloring the sky.

An attack helicopter? Something inside her sinks.

She tries the window into the laundry room. Locked.

"*Jebi ga,*" she hisses, feeling a trickle of panic. She holds her sidearm by the suppressor, leans in toward the window—

"*Ularning vertolyotlari bor!*" Hamid, the team 2 leader, shouts into her earbud. She doesn't speak Uzbek, but she has a feeling—

"*They have helicopter! They*—"

The explosion is even louder this time, a massive eruption from the direction of the lake, pummeling her eardrum through the earbud as well, causing her a moment of imbalance.

It is unfamiliar, the fear blossoming inside her, raising her temperature, fluttering through her stomach. Not since Sarajevo has she truly felt afraid of anything or anyone. She hadn't realized she was still capable of it.

She flicks the gun's handle against the window, shattering the glass. She reaches in and unlocks the latch, waits for any reaction to the breaking glass from inside, her standard precaution. Five seconds. Ten seconds. No sound.

She pushes open the window and slides into the laundry room feetfirst.

CHAPTER
105

❖

W hat?" I ask. "Tell me what's happening."
"It's a…" Devin shakes his head.
"Nina put a circuit breaker in."

"A what?"

"A—she put a stopper in and installed a password override."

"What the hell is going on, people?"

Augie touches my arm. "Apparently," he says, his voice panicky, "Nina installed a mechanism that suspended the virus after it began to activate. As Devin said, it began to overwrite a small amount of data, to demonstrate its power to do so, but now it is suspended, giving us the opportunity to provide a password to stop it."

"We didn't replicate that when we reconstructed the virus," says Casey. "We didn't know it was there."

"What about the viruses on the other computers and devices around the country?" I ask. "It's talking to them, you said. Are they stopping, too?"

Casey speaks urgently into her headset. "Jared, we have a circuit breaker suspending the virus—are you getting that? You should be getting that…"

I stare at her, waiting.

Twenty seconds have never passed more slowly.

Her face lights up, her hand out like a stop sign. "Yes," she says. "Yes! The virus on the Pentagon server must have sent out a 'suspend' command throughout the distributive system."

"So…the virus is suspended everywhere?"

"Yes, sir. We have new life."

"Let me see this password-override circuit-breaker thing." I move Augie aside and look at the computer screen.

Enter Keyword: _____ 28:47

"The clock," I note. "It's counting down from, what, thirty minutes."

28:41…28:33…28:28…

"So the virus is in suspension for twenty-eight minutes and change?"

"Yes," says Augie. "We have twenty-eight minutes remaining to enter the keyword. Or the virus activates in full. Across the entire system of devices."

"You've gotta be kidding me," I say, gripping my hair. "No, this is good, this is good, we're still in the game. One last chance. Okay, a keyword." I turn to Casey. "Don't we have software that can decode passwords?"

"Well…yes, but not that we can install and operate in twenty-eight minutes, especially with *this* virus. It would take hours, more likely days or weeks—"

"Okay, then we have to guess. We have to guess."

Simple, Nina had said in her text message, when she said she could explain how to stop the virus. You don't need to be an expert, she said.

Simple. Simple if you know the keyword.

"What the hell is the keyword?" I turn to Augie. "She never mentioned anything?"

"I did not know of this at all," he says. "I can only guess it was her way of protecting me, keeping our knowledge separate—"

"But maybe she said something to you. Like,

in hindsight, she was giving you a clue? Think, Augie, *think*."

"I..." Augie puts his hand on his forehead. "I..."

I try to think of anything Nina might have said to me in the Oval Office. She talked about the country burning, about being a package deal with Augie. She gave me a ticket to the Nationals game. The helicopter in Dubai...

It could be anything.

"Type 'Suliman,'" I tell Devin.

He types in the word and hits Enter. The word disappears.

Enter Keyword: _____ 27:46

"Use all caps," says Casey. "It might be case-sensitive."

Devin does. Nothing.

"All lowercase."

"Nope."

"Type his whole name, Suliman Cindoruk," I say.

Devin types it. No response.

"Jesus, how are we supposed to do this?" I say.

Simple, Nina said in the text message.

I pat my pockets. I look around the room. "Where's my phone? Where the hell's my phone?"

"Try 'Nina,'" says Augie.

"Nope. Not in all caps, either," says Devin after trying both. "Not in all lowercase."

"Try 'Nina Shinkuba,' all the different ways."

"How do you spell Shinkuba?"

Everyone looks at Augie, who shrugs. "I never knew her last name until you told me," he says to me.

I never saw it written. Liz gave me the information. I need to call her. I pat my pockets again, look around the room. "Where's my phone?"

"Probably s-h-i-n-k-u-b-a," says Casey.

Devin tries it a number of ways:

Nina Shinkuba
nina shinkuba
NINA SHINKUBA
NINASHINKUBA
ninashinkuba

No luck. I look at the timer:

26:35

"Where the hell is my phone?" I say again. "Has anyone—"

Then I remember. I left my phone in the war

room. I set it down while Devin was about to activate the virus. When Alex got word of the attack outside and hustled us into the communications room, I forgot it.

"I'll be right back," I say.

Alex, still on his radio, still monitoring things outside, sees my movement and rushes to block the door.

"No, sir! We're in lockdown. We don't have the all clear."

"My phone, Alex. I need it—"

"No, sir, Mr. President."

I grab his shirt, surprising him. "I'm giving you a direct order, Agent. That phone is more important than my life."

"Then I'll get it," he says.

He reaches into his pocket.

"Then go, Alex! Go!"

"One moment, sir," he says, removing something from his pocket.

"Keep trying!" I yell to my team. "Try Augie's name! Augie Koslenko!"

CHAPTER
106

❖

B ach, sitting atop the stackable washer and dryer, pushes herself off and drops quietly to the floor of the dark room. She looks through the doorway. As she'd been told, the basement is not some maze of rooms but rather one long hallway with several rooms on each side and a staircase in the middle of the hallway on her left.

Behind her, from the open window, she hears something outside: the thump of a vessel landing, the commotion of commands being shouted, feet stomping the ground, men fanning out.

The helicopter again. Marines arriving, maybe Special Forces.

Footfalls. They are running. Running toward the open window—

She squats down, raising her weapon.

The men rush past and stop. One of them stops right near the window.

What are they—

Then she hears a voice: "West team, in position!"

West team.

This is the west side of the cabin. The west team. There are presumably north, south, and east teams, too.

They have surrounded the perimeter.

In just that instant, she thinks of her mother, Delilah, and what she endured during those nightly visits from the soldiers, what she did for her children every night, placing her son and daughter in a room far away from the bedroom, inside the closet, cocooning them with the headphones she placed on their ears so they would listen to the Passacaglia or the Concerto for Two Violins, not the sounds emanating from the bedroom. "Listen only to the music," she told Bach and her brother.

Bach steels herself and steps out of the room, into the threshold of the first room on the left. The war room, they call it.

She peeks in. A large white screen displaying the words:

Enter Keyword: _____ 26:54

Then a word typed into the box: Nina Shinkuba

The word disappears. Another word: nina shinkuba

The words keep coming, then disappearing:

NINA SHINKUBA
NINASHINKUBA
ninashinkuba

The number to the side of the box—some kind of timer.

26:42
26:39
26:35

She springs into the room, her weapon out. Sweeps the room, seeing nothing. Quickly checks behind a file cabinet, a stack of boxes. Nobody hiding.

The room is empty. This is where he was supposed to be, but nobody's here.

She looks back at the white screen, new words being typed:

Augie Koslenko
AugieKoslenko
augiekoslenko
Augustas Koslenko

She knows that name, of course, but not why it's being typed on a screen.

She jumps at the buzzing sound, the movement of a phone as it vibrates on a wooden desk. The face of the phone reads FBI Liz.

Then her eyes glance upward.

And for the first time, she notices the security camera looking down at her from the corner, the blinking red light leaving no doubt that it's activated, watching her.

She shuffles to the right. The camera moves along with her.

A shiver runs through her.

She hears a noise from the laundry room, someone kicking at the window, trying to enter from the outside.

And urgent footfalls upstairs, so many men she can't count, running to the door leading to the basement. The door swinging open.

More footfalls pummeling the staircase as the men rush down.

Bach moves to the door of the war room, locks it, and backs away, one step behind another, until she hits the far wall.

She unscrews the suppressor on her firearm.

She breathes in deeply, fights the banging pulse in her throat. Her vision now shrouded with warm tears.

She gently touches her stomach. "You are my beautiful gift, *draga*," she whispers in her native tongue, her voice shaking. "I will always be with you."

She unclasps her phone from her waist, unhooks the earphones that snake under her bodysuit up to her ears. "Here, *draga*," she says to the child inside her. "Listen to this, my beautiful angel."

She chooses the church cantata *Selig ist der Mann*. The tenderness of the strings, led by Wilhelm Friedemann Herzog's violin; the delicate introduction of the vox Christi; the impassioned cries of the soprano.

Ich ende behände
mein irdisches Leben,
mit Freuden zu scheiden
verlang ich itzt eben.

I swiftly end my earthly life, I long at this time to
depart with joy.

She slides against the wall, down to the floor. She places the phone against her belly and turns up the volume.

"Listen only to the music, *draga*," she says.

CHAPTER
107

❖

Alex and I watch the feed from the war room on his handheld monitor as the assassin sinks to the floor, eyes closed, her camouflage-painted face seemingly at peace.

She puts the pistol under her chin. She puts her phone against her stomach.

"She knows she's cornered," I say.

"We're all clear otherwise," Alex says to me. "The rest of the downstairs and the rest of the cabin are clear. Just her. The go team is just outside her door, ready to storm it. Now it's time for *us* to go, Mr. President."

"We can't go, Alex, we have to—"

"She could be wearing explosives, sir."

"She's wearing a skintight bodysuit."

"She could be wearing it underneath. The

phone might be a detonator. She's holding it down low by her stomach. Why would she be doing that?"

I look at the screen again. She detached her headphones before placing the device against her stomach.

A memory of singing to Lilly, when she was inside Rachel's swollen belly.

"We have to go right now, sir." Alex grabs my arm. He's going to drag me if I don't go willingly.

Devin, Casey, and Augie are continuing to try to guess the keyword.

"How much time, Devin?"

"Twenty-two minutes."

"Can you take that laptop onto Marine One? Will it work from there?"

"Yes, of course."

"Then let's go. Everyone."

A team of Marines is standing on the other side of the door when Alex opens it. They escort us up the stairs, through the house, onto the balcony, down the stairs, and to the helipad, where Marine One awaits us. Alex all but mugs me as we go, Devin cradling the laptop as if it were a human infant.

"I need my phone," I tell Alex as we hustle inside the helicopter. "Get us in the air, a safe distance, but keep us close. I need someone to bring me the phone."

We get inside the copter, the familiarity of it a comfort, Devin dropping into a cream leather seat and going back to work on the keyboard.

"Just hit twenty minutes," he says as Marine One lifts off the ground and angles over the trees, over the fire on the lake, the remnants of the boat the Viper wiped out.

As I look over Alex's shoulder at the monitor in his hand, I call out to Devin. "Try 'Sons of Jihad,' 'SOJ,' variations of that. Maybe just 'jihad.'"

"Yes, sir."

On the monitor, the assassin remains motionless. The gun under her chin, the phone pressed against her stomach.

Against her womb.

Alex raises his radio. "Marines, the president is clear. Take the room."

I take the radio from Alex. "This is President Duncan," I say. "I want her alive if you can."

CHAPTER
108

❖

S he closes her eyes and hums to the music, nothing in the world but her developing child, Delilah, and the playful strings, the soulful chanting of the chorus.

Not the sound of the door busting open.

Not the orders of the soldiers to drop her weapon, to surrender.

The SIG still pressed under her chin, she watches the men fan out, assault weapons trained on her. They must have orders to take her alive. She'd already be dead if they did not.

They can't hurt her now. She is at peace with her decision.

"This is the best I can do for you, *draga*," she whispers.

She tosses the gun in front of her and comes forward, palms out, lying facedown on the carpet.

The Marines lift her in an instant, as if she were weightless, and rush her out of the room.

CHAPTER
109

❖

G et us down on the ground!" I say to Alex. "I need that phone!"

"Not yet." Alex raises his radio. "Tell me when she's clear!" When she's confirmed as not having explosives, he means, or when they've moved her far enough away to eliminate the threat to me.

The Marines quickly whisk her out of the room, one soldier holding each of her limbs, and disappear from the camera's view.

"Anything?" I say to Devin, already knowing the answer.

"No on 'SOJ' and 'jihad' and their variations."

"Try 'Abkhazia' or 'Georgia,'" I say.

"How do you spell Abkhazia?"

"A-b-…I need to write. Where's paper? *Where's paper and a pen!*"

Casey shoves a small memo pad in my hand, gives me a pen. I write the word out and read it to him.

He types it in. "No on regular case…no all caps…no on all lowercase…"

"Add an *n*. 'Abkhazian.'"

He does so. "No."

"Are you sure you spelled it right?"

"I…think so."

"You *think so?* Don't just *think so,* Devin!" I'm pacing now, walking over to his computer screen to peek at the timer—

18:01

17:58

—and trying to remember anything that Nina told me, anything I saw in the text messages—

"All clear!" Alex calls out. "Let's get this copter back on the ground!"

The pilot moves more quickly than I've ever experienced on Marine One, almost nose-diving downward and then righting the aircraft, gently touching down on the helipad we just left.

Agent Jacobson pops into the copter and hands me my phone.

I pull up the document, the transcript of the

text messages, which I have yet to finish reading in the chaos of the last hour.

The phone buzzes in my hand. FBI Liz, says the caller ID.

"Liz," I answer. "There's no time, so make this quick."

CHAPTER
110

❖

I dial Carolyn, my chief of staff, with whom I've spoken dozens of times today, but it feels like ages since we last talked, what with everything that's happened in the interim—the "play-dead" test run, the FBI unlocking Nina's other phone, the attack on the cabin, the discovery of the stopper Nina installed along with the keyword.

"Mr. President! Thank God! I've been—"

"Listen, Carrie, listen. I don't have time to explain. We have less than six minutes before the virus goes off."

I hear Carolyn suck in her breath.

"There's a keyword," I continue. "Nina created a keyword to stop the virus. If we can figure out the keyword, we disable it across all systems.

If we don't, it detonates across all systems—it's Dark Ages. I've tried everything with our tech experts. We're down to simply guessing. I need the smartest people I know. I need our national security team. Get everyone together."

"Everyone?" she asks. *"Including the vice president?"*

"Especially the vice president," I say.

"Yes, sir."

"It was her, Carrie. I'll explain later. You should know, too. I just ordered a search of the vice president's office in the West Wing. When the FBI shows up, someone will probably tell you. Just let them do it."

"Yes, sir."

"Get everyone on the conference, and patch me in through Marine One, which is where I am now."

"Yes, sir."

"Do it now, Carrie. We're at…five minutes."

CHAPTER
111

❖

I walk past Devin and Casey, who have all but collapsed in the plush leather chairs in the center cabin of Marine One, their expressions washed out, their hair matted with sweat, their eyes staring upward. They've been through a pressure cooker, and they've done everything they could. I don't need them anymore. Now it's up to me and the national security team.

And Augie, the closest connection we have to Nina.

I walk into the rear cabin and close the door behind me after letting Augie through. My hands are shaking as I lift the remote on the flat-screen TV and push the button, the faces of eight people immediately popping on—Liz, Carolyn, and the "circle of six."

Augie sits in one of the leather chairs, the laptop in his lap, ready to type.

"Carolyn briefed you?" I say to my team on the television. "We have a keyword, and we have…"

I look at my phone, which has a timer of its own that I synced up with the virus's timer.

4:26
4:25

"…four and a half minutes to figure it out. We tried every variation of her name, of Augie's name, of Suliman Cindoruk's name, of 'Abkhazia' and 'Georgia' and 'Sons of Jihad.' I need ideas, people, and I need them now."

"What's her birthday?" asks the CIA director, Erica Beatty.

Liz, holding Nina's dossier, answers: *"We believe it's August 11, 1992."*

I point to Augie. "Try it. 'August 11.' 'August 11, 1992,' or '8-11-92.'"

"No," says Erica. *"Europeans would put the day before the month: '11-8-92.'"*

"Right." I turn to Augie, my heart kicking up. "Try it both ways, I guess."

He types quickly, head down, brow furrowed in concentration. "No," he says on the first try.

"No" on the second one.

"No" on the third one.

"No" on the fourth.

3:57

3:54

My eyes on Vice President Kathy Brandt, who so far has remained silent.

Then Kathy lifts her head. *"What about her family? Family names. Mother, father, siblings."*

"Liz?"

"Mother is Nadya, n-a-d-y-a, maiden name unknown. Father is Mikhail, m-i-k-h-a-i-l."

"Try it, Augie, all variations—all caps, all lowercase, normal, whatever. Try their names together, too," which of course means every combination of spacing and caps. Every guess has multiple permutations. Every permutation takes more time off the clock.

"Keep going while he types, people. Siblings are good. What about—"

I snap my fingers, interrupting myself. "Nina had a niece, right? Nina told me she was killed in a bombing. Nina caught shrapnel in her head. Do we know the niece's name? Liz? Augie?"

"I don't have that information," says Liz.

"The family names didn't work," says Augie. "I tried every combination."

3:14

3:11

"What about the niece, Augie? Did she ever tell you about the niece?"

"I…believe her name started with an *r*…"

"Started with an *r*? I need more than 'started with an *r*.' Come on, people!"

"What moved her?" asks Carolyn. *"What was most important to her?"*

I look at Augie. "Freedom? Try that."

Augie types it in, shakes his head.

"Her passport number," says the defense secretary, Dominick Dayton.

Liz has it. Augie types it in. No.

"Where was she born?" asks Rod Sanchez, chairman of the Joint Chiefs.

"A pet—a dog or cat," says Sam Haber of Homeland Security.

"The name of the train station she blew up," says Brendan Mohan, national security adviser.

"How about 'virus,' 'time bomb,' 'boom.'"

"Armageddon."

"Dark Ages."

"Your name, Mr. President."

"USA. United States."

All of them good ideas. All of them typed into

the computer in their various iterations of all caps and the like.

All of them coming up empty.

2:01
1:58

As best I can see her, the vice president stares forward in steely concentration. What is going through that mind right now?

"She was on the run—isn't that what we know?" Carolyn again.

"Yes."

"So can we work with that? What was most important to her?"

I look at Augie and nod my head.

"She wanted to go home," says Augie.

"That's right," I say. "But we've tried that."

"Maybe...Abkhazia's on the Black Sea, right?" says Carolyn. *"Did she miss the Black Sea? Anything like that?"*

I point to Augie. "That's good. Try 'Black Sea,' all variations."

As Augie types, as everyone joins in with another idea, I watch only my vice president, the person I selected to be my running mate over many other people who gladly would have accepted, who would have loyally served me and this country.

She is stoic, but her eyes are moving around the room she's in, within the operations center below the White House. I wish I could see her face better. I wish I could know if, at the very least, this is weighing on her.

"No on 'Black Sea,'" says Augie.

More suggestions come:

"Amnesty."

"Liberty."

"Family."

"But where is home, specifically?" Carolyn asks. *"If that's all she thought about, if that was her whole goal…what city is she from?"*

"She's right," I say. "We should look at that. Where did she live, Augie? Where specifically? Or Liz. Anyone? Do we know where the hell she lived?"

Liz says, *"Her parents lived in the city of Sokhumi. It's considered the capital of the Abkhazian republic."*

"Good. Spell it, Liz."

"S-o-k-h-u-m-i."

"Go, Augie—'Sokhumi.'"

"Are you sure?" Carolyn asks.

I check my phone, my heartbeat pounding in my throat.

0:55

0:52

Watching the vice president, her lips parting. She says something, but it's drowned out by other suggestions being thrown out—

"Stop, everyone stop," I say. "Kathy, what did you say?"

She seems to steel herself, surprised at my focus on her. *"I said, try 'Lilly.'"*

I deflate. I shouldn't be surprised, but for some reason I am.

I point to Augie. "Do it. Try my daughter's name."

0:32
0:28

Augie types it in. Shakes his head. Tries it a different way, all caps. Shakes his head. Tries it another way—

"Mr. President," says Carolyn. *"Sokhumi can be spelled more than one way. When I was on the intelligence committee, I always saw it with two u's, no o."*

I drop my head and close my eyes. That's how I remember it being spelled, too.

"No on 'Lilly,'" says Augie.

"S-*u*-k-h-u-m-i," I tell him.

He types it in. The room goes silent.

0:10
0:09

Augie's fingers lift off the keypad. He raises his hands as he watches the monitor.

0:04
0:03

"The keyword has been accepted," he says. "The virus is disabled."

CHAPTER
112

❖

C asey, now in the rear chamber with me, holding the laptop in her hands, says, "We've confirmed that the 'stop' command was transmitted throughout the system. The virus is stopped. Everywhere."

"What about the computers and other devices that are offline right now, without Internet access?" I ask. "They didn't get the 'stop' message."

"Then they didn't get the 'execute' message, either," says Devin. "And now they never will. It's on a permanent 'stop' message."

"But all the same," says Casey, "I'm not letting this laptop out of my sight. I'm going to watch that screen like a hawk."

I take one of the deepest breaths I've ever

taken, sweet, delicious oxygen. "So not a single device will be hurt by this virus?"

"Correct, sir."

And just to be sure, just on the off chance that the Suliman virus comes back to life, Homeland Security is blasting out the keyword "Sukhumi" through a rapid-response system created by various executive orders signed either by me or my predecessor as part of an enhanced system to combat industrial cyberterrorism. Basically, we can blast out information to a designated recipient, a point person at each company, at any hour of the day or night. Every Internet service provider, every state and local government, every member of every industrial sector—banks, hospitals, insurance companies, manufacturers, as many small businesses as we have persuaded to sign up: within the next few seconds, all of them will receive this keyword.

The keyword will also be blasted out over our Emergency Alert System, hitting every television, coming to every computer and smartphone.

I nod, straighten up, feel unexpected emotion rise within me. I look out the window of Marine One into a sky of rainbow sherbet as the sun sets on Saturday.

We didn't lose our country.

The financial markets, people's savings and

401(k)s, insurance records, hospitals, public utilities will be spared. The lights will stay on. Mutual-fund balances and savings accounts will still reflect people's life savings. Welfare and pension payments will not be interrupted. Escalators and elevators will work. Planes won't be grounded. Food won't spoil. Water will remain potable. No major economic depression. No chaos. No looting and rioting.

We've avoided Dark Ages.

I walk into the main cabin, where I find Alex.

"Mr. President," he says, "we're approaching the White House."

My phone buzzes. Liz. *"Mr. President, they found it in the vice president's office."*

"The phone," I say.

"Yes, sir, the companion phone to Nina's."

"Thank you, Liz. Meet me at the White House. And Liz?"

"Yes, sir."

"Bring your handcuffs," I say.

CHAPTER
113

❖

S uliman Cindoruk sits in the small safe
house they put him in, at the base of Mount
Medvednica, staring at his phone, as if staring at
it will make it change.

Virus disabled

First the "virus suspended" message he got,
only moments after congratulating himself on
decimating the United States while riding in the
Jeep. And less than half an hour later, this. He
continues to stare at it, as if doing so will prompt
it to change once more.

How? The virus was bulletproof. They were
sure of it. Augie—Augie was just a hacker in the
end. He couldn't have figured this out.

Nina, he decides. Nina must have done something to sabotage it—

A brisk knock on the door, and it opens. One of the soldiers walks in, holding a basket of food— a baguette, cheese, a large bottle of water.

"How long am I here?" Suli asks.

The man looks at him. "I am told four more hours."

Four more hours. That would equate roughly with midnight, Eastern Standard Time—the moment the virus was timed to go off if the Americans hadn't prompted an early activation.

They're waiting for the virus to succeed before they transport him to his destination. He glances at his phone again.

Virus disabled

"There is…problem?" the soldier asks.

"No, no," he says. "No problem."

CHAPTER
114

❖

I take the stairs down from Marine One, saluting the Marine. Holding my salute longer than usual. God bless the Marines.

Carolyn is standing there, awaiting me. "Congratulations, Mr. President," she says.

"You, too, Carrie. We have a lot to discuss, but I need a minute."

"Of course, sir."

I break into a jog, something close to a full sprint, until I reach my destination.

"Dad, oh, my God..."

Lilly springs off her bed, the book in her lap spilling to the floor of her room. She is in my arms before she can finish the sentence.

"You're okay," she whispers into my shoulder

as I stroke her hair. "I was so worried, Dad. I was so sure that something bad was going to happen. I thought I was going to lose you, too…"

Her body trembles as I hold her, as I tell her, "I'm here, I'm fine," over and over again, smelling her unique smell, feeling her warmth. I am here, and I'm finer than I've been in a very long time. So grateful, so full of love.

Everything else washes away. There is so much more to do, but right this moment, everything else is nothing, blurring into a fog, and all that matters is my beautiful, talented, sweet girl.

"I still miss her," she whispers. "I miss her more than ever."

I do, too. So much it feels like I'll burst. I want her here right now, to celebrate, to hold me close, to crack a joke and knock me down a few pegs before I get too big a head.

"She's always with us," I say. "She was with me today."

I draw back, hold her away from me, wipe a tear from her face. The face looking back at me looks more like Rachel than ever.

"I have to go be president now," I say.

CHAPTER
115

❖

I sit, relieved and exhausted, on the couch in the Oval Office. I still can't believe it's over.

Of course, it's not really over. In some ways, the hardest part is yet to come.

Sitting next to me is Danny, who brought me a glass of bourbon—the drink he owes me after he failed the coin check. He's not saying much, knowing that I need to decelerate from everything. He's just here to be here.

The vice president is still in the operations center, still inside that room under guard. She doesn't know why. Nobody's told her why. She's probably sweating right now.

That's okay. Let her sweat.

Sam Haber has been updating me constantly. The adage "no news is good news" has never felt truer. The virus is disabled. No surprises, no dramatic, sudden restarting of the virus. But we have people watching for it, hovering over computers like protective parents.

The cable news networks are talking about nothing but the Suliman virus. They're all running a banner at the top of the screen saying KEYWORD: SUKHUMI.

"I have some unfinished business," I say to Danny. "I need to kick you out."

"Sure." He pushes himself off the couch. "By the way, I plan to take full credit for all of this. That pep talk I gave you was the difference."

"No question."

"That's how I'm going to remember it, anyway."

"You do that, Daniel. You do that."

I let my smile linger as Danny takes his exit. Then I push the button on my phone and tell my secretary, JoAnn, that I'll see Carolyn.

Carolyn pops in. She looks frazzled, but then again, we all do. Nobody slept last night, and the stress of the last twenty-four hours…all things considered, Carolyn looks better than most of us.

"Director Greenfield's out there," she says.

"I know. I asked her to wait. I wanted to talk to you first."

"All right, sir."

She walks in and takes a seat in one of the chairs opposite the couch.

"You did it, Carrie," I say. "You're the one who solved it."

"You did this, Mr. President, not me."

Well, that's the way this works. The buck stops with the president both ways, for better or worse. If my team scores a victory, it's the president who gets the credit. But we both know who figured out the keyword.

I blow out air, my nerves still jangled.

"I screwed up, Carrie," I say. "Picking Kathy Brandt for a running mate."

She doesn't rush to disagree. "The politics made sense, sir."

"That's why I did it. For political reasons. I shouldn't have."

Again, she doesn't fight me.

"I should have picked a running mate based on merit. And I think we both know who I would have picked if it were based on merit. The smartest person I've ever met. The most disciplined. The most talented."

Her face blushes. Always deflecting the credit, the attention.

"Instead I gave you the toughest job in Washington. The most thankless."

She waves me off, uncomfortable with the

praise, her blush deepening. "It's an honor to serve you, Mr. President, in whatever capacity you decide."

I take one last sip, a healthy gulp, of the bourbon remaining in my glass and set down the tumbler.

"May I ask, sir—what are you going to do with the vice president?"

"What do *you* think I should do with her?"

She kicks that around, her head bobbing from side to side.

"For the good of the country," she says, "I wouldn't prosecute her. I'd find a quiet way out. I'd demand her resignation, let her make some excuse, and I wouldn't tell anybody what she did. I'd close the whole thing quietly. Right now, the American people are hearing that a talented national security team, at your direction, saved us from a massive disaster. No one's talking about a traitor or betrayal. It's a positive story, a cautionary tale, but with a happy ending. We should keep it that way."

I've considered that. "The thing is," I say, "before I do that, I want to know why."

"Why she did it, sir?"

"She wasn't bribed. She wasn't being extorted. She didn't want to destroy our country. It wasn't even her idea. It was Nina's and Augie's idea."

"How do we know that for certain?" she asks.

"Oh, right," I say. "You don't know about the phone."

"The phone, sir?"

"Yeah, in the chaos of it all at the end, the FBI unlocked the second phone they found in Nina's van. They unearthed a bunch of text messages. Texts exchanged between Nina and our Benedict Arnold."

"Oh, God," she says. "No, I didn't know."

I wave my hand. "Nina and Augie got caught up in something bigger than they ever intended it to be. When they realized the massive devastation they were about to unleash, they split away from Suliman. They sent us the peekaboo to wake us up to the problem and then came here to make a deal: if we get amnesty from the Georgian republic for Nina, she disarms the virus.

"Our traitor—our Benedict Arnold? She was just the intermediary. She's just the one they contacted. This wasn't some plot she cooked up. She was trying to persuade Nina to surrender to an American embassy. She was asking Nina how to disable the virus."

"But she didn't tell the rest of us," says Carolyn.

"Right. I think, from what I've read, she felt like the longer she communicated with Nina and didn't tell anyone else, the deeper a hole she dug.

So she wanted to be left out of the direct line of communication. She gave Nina the code word 'Dark Ages' so Nina could get in touch with me directly—through Lilly—and I'd take her seriously."

"That…makes some amount of sense, I suppose," Carolyn offers.

"But that's the thing—it *doesn't* make sense," I say. "Because the moment Nina communicates 'Dark Ages' to me, I know that I have a Judas in my inner circle. She has to know I'll move heaven and earth to find the traitor. She was one of eight suspects."

Carolyn nods, thinking it over.

"Why would she do that, Carrie? Why would she invite that kind of suspicion? Kathy Brandt is a lot of things, but she ain't dumb."

Carolyn opens her hands. "Sometimes…smart people do dumb things?"

Truer words were never spoken.

"Let me show you something," I say.

I reach for a folder bearing the insignia FBI. I had Liz Greenfield print out two copies of the transcript of the text messages. I hand Carolyn the transcript of the first three days—last Friday, Saturday, and Sunday, the first days that I read.

"Read those," I say, "and tell me how 'dumb' our traitor is."

CHAPTER
116

❖

Y ou're right." Carolyn's chin rises, having read all three days' worth of transcripts. "This wasn't something she cooked up on her own. But...this can't be all the transcripts. This ends on Sunday, with her promising to give Nina the code word."

"Right, there's more." I hand her the next sheet. "Here's Monday, May 7. Just six days ago. The day Nina whispered 'Dark Ages' into Lilly's ear."

Carolyn takes the transcript and starts to read it. I read along with my copy.

Monday, May 7
U/C: 1600 Pennsylvania Avenue
Nina: Location unknown

** All times Eastern Standard Time **

Nina (7:43 AM): I made it to Paris. I came here even though you still haven't given me the code word!! R U going to or not? I think someone was following me last night. Suli's trying to kill me u know

U/C (7:58 AM): I've thought about this a lot overnight, and I think if we're going to trust each other, we have to really trust each other. And that means you have to tell me how to stop the virus.

Nina (7:59 AM): Been there, done that. Uh…NO!!! how many times do I have to say it?? Can u spell leverage?!?

U/C (8:06 AM): You said yourself you're in danger. What if you don't make it here? What if something happens to you? Then we can't stop this virus.

Nina (8:11 AM): The minute I tell you how to stop the virus, I'm nothing to you. It's my only leverage.

U/C (8:15 AM): Don't you understand this by now? I can't reveal that we've talked. How could I explain that I know how to stop the virus without revealing that I've been talking with you the last few days? The moment I reveal that, I'm toast. I have to resign. Prison, probably.

Nina (8:17 AM): If that's true then why do u need to know? If u will never use it??

U/C (8:22 AM): Because if something happens to you and there's no other way to stop the virus, then I'll do it. To save our country. I couldn't live with myself otherwise. But that's a last, last, last-case scenario. I'd much rather that you just come in and meet with POTUS and handle it yourself and leave me out of it.

Nina (8:25 AM): No way not gonna do it

U/C (8:28 AM): Then good bye and good luck. Trust me or forget it.

A long pause follows, a good three hours. Then:

Nina (11:43 AM): I'm here at Sorbonne. I see POTUS's daughter. Tell me the code word or I walk away 4ever

U/C (11:49 AM): Tell me how to stop the virus

and I'll give you the code word. Otherwise, don't contact me again.

Nina (12:09 PM): There will be chance to type in keyword before detonation. Window of 30 minutes. Type in that word and virus goes bye bye. If you screw me on this lady I will tell everyone who you are I swear to god

U/C (12:13 PM): I'm not going to screw you over. I want you to succeed! We want the same thing.

U/C (12:16 PM): Look, I know you're taking a big risk. So am I. I know how scared you are. I'm terrified! We're in this together, kiddo.

Carrot and stick. She manipulated Nina. She realized that Nina was feeling serious pressure and needed her more than she needed Nina. Nina was a highly skilled cyberterrorist, an elite code writer, but she was no match for someone accustomed to high-level negotiations on the world stage. It came nearly ten minutes later:

Nina (12:25 PM): The keyword is Sukhumi.

U/C (12:26 PM): The code word is Dark Ages.

Carolyn looks up from the page.

"She knew," she says. "She's known the key-word since Monday."

I don't say anything. I wish I had more bour-bon, but Dr. Lane would probably scold me for having even one glass.

"But—hang on. When did you read this, Mr. President?"

"That page—the Monday page? I didn't read that until I got on Marine One, after the Marines got my phone back."

She looks away, putting it together. "So…that last conference we did, when you were on Ma-rine One, when we got everyone together to brainstorm over the keyword, as the clock was ticking down…"

"Oh, yeah," I say. "I already knew the keyword. Devin had already typed it in. The crisis was al-ready over. Devin and Casey were half passed out from exhaustion and relief while I was in the rear compartment with Augie, talking to all of you."

Carolyn stares at me.

"You'd already disabled the virus?"

"Yes, Carrie."

"So that whole thing with the ticking clock, and everyone throwing out suggestions for the keyword…that was a ruse?"

"Something like that." I push myself off the couch, my legs unsteady, the heat rising to my face. For the last several hours, I've been on a roller coaster of worry, relief, and gratitude.

But right now, I'm just pissed off.

I walk over to the *Resolute* desk, looking at the photos of Rachel, of Lilly, of my parents, of the Duncan family and the Brock family at Camp David, Carolyn's kids wearing goofy sailor hats.

I pour myself two more fingers of bourbon and throw the liquor down like a shot.

"Are you okay, sir?"

I set down the tumbler harder than I intended. "I'm pretty far from okay, Carrie. I couldn't see 'okay' with a telescope right now. See, here's the thing."

My jaw clenched, I come around the desk and lean against it.

"You're right that smart people do dumb things," I say. "But Kathy would have to be certifiably *insane* to leak 'Dark Ages' to Nina and blow suspicion back in her direction. Her odds of being caught were way too high. She could have figured out another way to get Nina access to me. Something. Something better than *that*."

Carolyn's eyebrows rise. She thinks it over but doesn't seem to come to a resolution. "So…what is your point, sir?"

"My point," I say, "is that whoever leaked 'Dark Ages' to Nina *wanted* suspicion to blow back on my inner circle."

Carolyn's face twists in confusion. "But who…would want suspicion thrown on them?" she asks. "And why?"

CHAPTER
117

❖

O h, the *why* part isn't that hard to grasp, is it? Or maybe it is." I gesture with my hands, pacing around the Oval Office now. "I sure missed it. Who knows? Maybe I'm the dumbest son of a bitch to ever hold this office."

Or maybe the one thing I believe is in shortest supply in our capital—trust—is something that I have in too great a supply. Trust can blind. It blinded me.

I pass the table by the couch, where Nina stood yesterday, looking at that picture of Lilly and me on the White House lawn, walking from Marine One.

Carolyn, her brow furrowed, says, "I'm…not following, sir. I can't imagine why anyone would want you to know there was a traitor."

Next to that picture, a photo of Carolyn and

me on the night I was elected president, mugging for the camera, arms around each other. I pick up that photo and remember how giddy we felt, how overwhelmed, how blessed.

Then I smash the picture down on the table, shattering the glass, splintering the frame.

Carolyn nearly jumps out of her chair.

"Then follow this," I say as I stare into the splintered image of my chief of staff and me. "The leak blows suspicion back on the national security team. One person in the inner circle, someone with a particularly high rank—let's say, vice president of the United States—gets blamed for it. She's an easy target. She's been disloyal. She's been a pain in my ass, frankly. So of course she's out. Gone. Resigned in disgrace. Maybe prosecuted, maybe not—but gone, that's the point. Someone needs to take her place, though, right? *Right?*" I snap.

"Yes, sir," Carolyn whispers.

"Right! So who's going to replace her? Well, how about the hero in the story? The person who came up with the keyword as the clock wound down? Someone who surely thinks she should have been vice president all along?"

Carolyn Brock rises from her chair, staring at me, a deer in the headlights, her mouth open. No words, though. There are no words for this.

"That last conference with the national security team as the clock wound down," I say. "The ruse, you called it? It was a test. I wanted to see who would come up with the keyword. I knew one of you would."

I bring a hand to my face, pinch the bridge of my nose. "I prayed to God. I swear to you, on my wife's grave, I prayed to *God*. Anybody but Carrie, I prayed."

Alex Trimble walks into the room with his deputy, Jacobson, standing at attention by the wall. The FBI director, Elizabeth Greenfield, enters the room next.

"You were smart to the very end, Carrie," I say. "You pushed us right to Nina's hometown, all but delivering it to us without saying it yourself."

Carolyn's wounded expression breaks. She blinks hard, looks off in memory. "You misspelled it on purpose," she whispers.

"And there you were to correct us," I say. "Sukhumi with two *u*'s."

Carolyn's eyes close.

I nod at Liz Greenfield.

"Carolyn Brock," she says, "you're under arrest for suspicion of violating the Espionage Act and conspiracy to commit treason. You have the right to remain silent. Anything you say can and will be used against you..."

CHAPTER
118

❖

W ait a second! Just wait!"
Director Greenfield's formality, her
mention of arrest and reading of the Miranda
rights, snaps a defense mechanism in Carolyn,
who holds out her hands in a "stop" gesture.

She turns to me. "Nina wanted to go home. It
was logical. So I know how to spell the capital
of an eastern European city and suddenly I'm a
traitor? You can't be...really, Mr. President, after
everything we've been through—"

"Don't you dare," I bark. "Nothing we've 'been
through' gives you the right to do what you did."

"Please, Mr. President. Can we...can we just—
the two of us talk? Two minutes. Can I at least
have two minutes? Don't I deserve at least *that*
much?"

Liz Greenfield starts to move toward Carolyn, but I raise a hand.

"Give us two minutes. Count it out, Liz. One hundred and twenty seconds. That's all she gets."

Liz looks at me. "Mr. President, that isn't a good—"

"One hundred and twenty seconds." I point to the door. "Leave us. All of you."

I watch Carolyn as the Secret Service and FBI director walk out of the Oval Office. I can only imagine what's racing through her mind. Her kids; her husband, Morty. A criminal prosecution. Disgrace. A way out of this somehow.

"Go," I say once we're alone.

Carolyn takes a deep breath, holding out her hands, as if framing a solution. "Think about what's happened today. You saved our country. You've totally eliminated impeachment as a threat. Lester Rhodes will be sucking his thumb in a corner. Your poll numbers are going to soar through the roof now. You'll have a mandate like you've never had. Think of what you can do over the next year and a half—the next *five* and a half years. Think of your place in history."

I nod. "But…"

"But imagine what happens if you do this, sir. If you accuse me of this. If you publicly ruin me. You think I'll just take my medicine like a compliant little girl?" She puts a hand on her chest, cocks her head, makes a face. "You think I won't fight back? The search of the vice president's office—how'd that turn out? Find anything good?"

Well, the sorrowful, deer-in-the-headlights look is long gone. The gloves have come off. She's thought all this through. Of course she has. She's considered every angle. Carolyn Brock is nothing if not formidable.

"You had twenty opportunities to plant that phone in her office," I say. "Kathy wouldn't have been so stupid as to leave that phone behind a bookcase, for Christ's sake. She would've broken it into a hundred pieces."

"Says you," she responds. "My lawyers say something different. You put me on trial for treason, I put *her* on trial for treason. Look at what you have the chance to do right now, Mr. President."

"I don't care," I say.

"Ohhh, yes, you do," she responds, coming around the desk. "Because you want to do good things in this job. You don't want what could be your greatest triumph to turn into a scandal. 'Treason in the White House.' Who was the traitor—the president's closest adviser or the sitting vice president? Who cares? You picked both of us. Your judgment will be called into question. This tremendous, unprecedented success will turn into the worst thing that ever happened to you. Your feelings are hurt, *Jon?* Well, get the hell over it."

She walks up to me, her hands together as if in prayer. "Think of the country. Think of the people out there who *need* you to be a good president—hell, a great president."

I don't say anything.

"You do this to me," she says, "your presidency is over."

Liz Greenfield enters the room again and looks at me.

I look at Carolyn.

"Give us another two minutes, Liz," I say.

CHAPTER
119

❖

My turn.

"You're going to plead guilty," I tell Carolyn when we're alone again. "My judgment will be criticized, as it should be, for hiring you. I'll deal with that. That's a political problem. I will *not* sweep this under the rug and have you step away quietly. And you *will* plead guilty."

"Mr. Pres—"

"Secret Service agents *died*, Carrie. Nina is dead. I could have easily been killed. That's not something we sweep under the rug in this country."

"Sir—"

"You want to go to trial? Then you can explain how Nina could possibly have gotten that first note into Kathy Brandt's hands when Nina was in Europe and Kathy was here in Washington. What, she sent it by e-mail? Dropped it in a FedEx package? None of that would get past our security. But you, a chief of staff, on the last leg of our European trip, in Seville? Nina could have walked into that hotel and handed it to you. You don't think we have the CCTV footage? The Spanish government sent it over. That last day in Spain, a few hours before we left. Nina entering the hotel and leaving an hour later."

The flare in her eyes seems to dim.

"And how long before we manage to intercept and decrypt the message you sent to Suliman Cindoruk?"

She looks up at me with horror.

"The FBI and Mossad are looking for it right now. You tipped him off, didn't you? None of your plan would have worked if Nina had survived. If she lived, if Augie and I got in her van at the baseball stadium, she and I would have worked out a deal. I would've persuaded the Georgians to take her back, she would have given me the keyword, you wouldn't have gotten to be the hero, and Kathy wouldn't have gotten to be the goat. And who knows? Maybe Nina would've given you up after all."

Carolyn brings a hand to her face, her worst nightmare realized.

"You'd know better than anyone how to get hold of Suliman. You're the one who orchestrated that first call through our intermediaries in Turkey. You could've done it again. She told you everything, Carrie. I read the rest of the text messages. She laid out her whole timeline. Augie, the baseball stadium, the midnight detonation of the virus. She trusted you. She trusted you, Carrie, and you killed her."

That seems to be the poke in the wall that breaks the dam. Carolyn loses all composure, bursting into sobs, her entire body quaking.

And I find myself, in the end, more sad than angry. She and I had been through so much together. She charted my path to the presidency, helped me navigate the land mines of Washington, sacrificed countless hours of sleep and time with her family to ensure that the Oval Office ran with maximum efficiency. She is the best chief of staff I could have ever dreamed of having.

After a time, the tears stop. She shudders and wipes at her face. But her head still hangs low, shrouded by her hand. She can't look me in the eye.

"Stop acting like some garden-variety criminal suspect," I say. "And do the right thing. This isn't a courtroom. This is the Oval Office. How could you do this, Carrie?"

"Says the man who gets to be president."

The words come from a voice I don't recognize, a voice I've never heard, a part of Carolyn that has managed to elude me during our years together. Her head rises from her hands, and she looks at me squarely, her face twisted up in agony and bitterness in a way I've never seen before. "Says the *man* who didn't see *his* political career tanked just for saying a dirty word on a live mike."

I never saw this. I missed the envy, the resentment, the bitterness building up inside her. It's one of the hazards of this thing, running for president and then being president. It's all about you. Every minute of every hour of every day, it's what's best for the candidate, what does the candidate need, how can we help the candidate, the only person whose name is on the ballot. Then, when you actually become president, it's the same thing every day on steroids. Sure, we socialized. I got to know her family. But I missed this completely. She was good at her job. I actually thought she was proud of the good things we did, found the challenges exciting, enjoyed the work, and was fulfilled by it.

"I don't suppose…" She hiccups a bitter laugh. "I don't suppose that offer of a pardon stands." She seems embarrassed to even suggest it.

How quickly she has plummeted. Walking into this room, expecting to be tapped as the new vice president, the hero of the hour, and now just praying that she can avoid prison.

Liz Greenfield returns. This time, I wave her in.

Carolyn offers no resistance as the FBI takes her into custody.

Carolyn looks back in my direction as she is led out of the Oval Office, but she can't quite bring herself to make eye contact with me.

CHAPTER
120

❖

N o. No."
Suliman Cindoruk stares at his phone,
reading the "breaking news" across website after
website, variations of a single headline.

"IT WOULD HAVE DESTROYED AMERICA"
UNITED STATES THWARTS LETHAL CYBERATTACK
UNITED STATES STOPS MAJOR CYBER VIRUS
"SONS OF JIHAD" VIRUS TARGETING UNITED
STATES FOILED

Every one of the articles blasting news of a
keyword—"Sukhumi"—that will stop the virus
from activating.

Sukhumi. No doubt now. It was Nina. She installed a password override.

His head whips around to the window in the safe house. He sees the two soldiers, still sitting in their Jeep outside, awaiting their next instructions.

But the people who brought him here won't be waiting until midnight Eastern Standard Time to confirm the success or failure of the virus. Not if they're reading the news.

He removes his handgun, stuffed into his sock, still loaded with the single bullet.

Then he finds a door leading to the backyard and the mountain. He tries the handle, but it's bolted shut. He pulls on the single window, but it's bolted closed, too. He looks around the sparsely furnished room and finds a small glass table. He hurls it against the window. He uses his gun to knock out the remaining jagged shards of glass.

He hears the front door burst open. He jumps headfirst through the window, clutching his gun as a lifeline. He runs toward some trees, some foliage, that will provide cover in the predawn darkness.

They call out after him, but he doesn't stop. His foot hits something—a tree root—and he tumbles forward, losing his breath as he smacks the ground, stars dancing in his eyelids, the gun bouncing out of his hand.

He yelps in pain as a bullet pierces the bottom of his shoe. He crawls forward to his right, and another bullet sprays leaves by his armpit. He pats his hand around but can't find his gun.

Their voices growing closer, shouting to him in a language he doesn't know, warning him.

He can't find the gun with the single bullet that will end this. He knows now that he does have the courage to do it. He won't be taken by them.

But he can't reach, or can't locate, the weapon.

He takes a breath and decides.

He lifts himself up, spins around to face them, his empty hands together, aimed at the two men.

They unload their rifles into his chest.

CHAPTER
121

❖

In the subbasement, I open the door and stand at the threshold of the room where the vice president has been waiting. When she sees me, she gets to her feet.

"Mr. President," she says with uncertainty more than anything else. Her eyes are ringed. She looks tired and stressed. She picks up a remote and mutes the flat-screen television on the wall. "I've been watching..."

Yes, the cable news. She's been watching it not as the second-ranked official in the country but as an ordinary citizen. She seems diminished by that fact.

"Congratulations," she says to me.

I don't answer, just nod my head.

"It wasn't me, sir," she says.

I look over at the TV again, the constant up-dates on the Suliman virus and the keyword we discovered.

"I know," I say.

She deflates with relief.

"Is your offer of resignation still good?" I ask.

She bows her head. "If you'd like my resigna-tion, Mr. President, you'll have it whenever you wish."

"Is that what you want? To resign?"

"No, sir, it isn't." She looks up at me. "But if you don't trust me…"

"What would you do if the roles were re-versed?" I ask.

"I'd accept the resignation."

Not what I expected. I fold my arms, lean against the threshold.

"I said no, Mr. President. I think you would al-ready know that if you bugged my limousine."

We didn't. The FBI couldn't get to it without tipping off her Secret Service detail. But she doesn't know that.

"I want to hear it from you anyway," I say.

"I told Lester I wouldn't round up the twelve votes he needed in the Senate from our side. I said whatever else, that was simply a line I couldn't cross. I…I learned something about myself, honestly."

"That's super, Kathy. But this isn't a *Dr. Phil* episode. You were disloyal just taking that meeting."

"Agreed, agreed." She puts her hands together, then looks at me. "They didn't ask me about Lester when I was polygraphed."

"Because politics didn't matter. Not then. Now that the crisis has passed, it matters very much to me whether I can trust my vice president."

There's nothing else she can say. She opens her hands. "Do you accept my resignation?"

"You'd stay until I could replace you?"

"Yes, sir, of course." Her shoulders drop.

"Whom should I appoint?" I ask.

She takes a deep breath. "There are a few people who come to mind. But one above everyone else. It pains me to say it, actually. It pains me quite a lot. But if I were you, Mr. President, and if I could pick anyone…I'd choose Carolyn Brock."

I shake my head. At least I wasn't the only one.

"Kathy, your resignation is not accepted. Now get back to work."

CHAPTER
122

❖

Bach sways as she listens to the *Saint Matthew Passion*. She has no music or head-phones—they have been confiscated—only her memories of the complementing choruses, the soprano solo with which she used to sing along. She imagines herself in the church in the eigh-teenth century, hearing it for the first time.

She is interrupted when the door to her cell opens.

The man who walks in is young, with sandy hair, dressed informally in a button-down shirt and jeans. He brings in a chair with him, places it near her bed, and sits down.

Bach sits up, back against the wall, feet dan-gling down. The chains remain around her wrists.

"My name is Randy," he says. "I'm the guy who asks nicely. There are others who won't."

"I am…familiar with the tactic," she says.

"And you're…Catharina."

She isn't sure how they figured out her identity—probably the DNA sample they took. Maybe facial-recognition software, though she doubts it.

"That *is* your name, right? Catharina Dorothea Ninkovic. Catharina Dorothea—that was Johann Sebastian's first daughter, right?"

She doesn't respond. She picks up the paper cup and drinks the last of the water she's been given.

"Let me ask you a question, Catharina. Do you think we'll go easy on you because you're pregnant?"

She shifts in her bed, a sheet of unforgiving steel.

"You tried to assassinate a president," he says.

Her eyes narrow. "If I had wanted to assassinate a president," she says, "he would be assassinated."

Randy holds most of the cards here, and he enjoys it. He nods along, almost amused. "There are a lot of other countries that would like to have a conversation with you," he says. "Some of them don't have such a progressive view of human rights. Maybe we'll transfer you to one of them. They can always send you back later—if there's anything left of you to send back. How does that sound, Bach? You wanna roll the dice with the Ugandans? How about Nicaragua? The Jordanians are pretty hyped up to speak with you. They seem to think you put a bullet between the eyes of their security chief last year."

She waits until he's finished. Then she waits longer still.

"I will tell you whatever you want to know," she says. "I have only a single demand."

"You think you're in a position to demand anything?"

"Whatever your name is—"

"Randy."

"—you should be asking me what it is I want."

He sits back in his chair. "Okay, Catharina. What do you want?"

"I know that I will remain in custody for the remainder of my life. I am under no…illusions about this."

"That's a good start."

"I want my baby born healthy. I want her born in America, and I want her adopted by my brother."

"Your brother," says Randy.

He appeared from behind the house next door as

she stood near the rubble of their home, as she touched the face of her beaten, slashed, dead mother tied to the tree.

"Is it true?" he said as he approached, his face tear-streaked, his body shivering. He took one look at her, at the rifle she held, at the sidearm tucked in her pants. "It is true, isn't it? You killed them. You killed those soldiers!"

"I killed the soldiers who killed Papa."

"And now they killed Mama!" he cried. "How could you do that?"

"I didn't...I'm sorry...I—" She started toward him, her older brother, but he backed away, as if repelled.

"No," he said. "Do not come near me. Ever. Ever!"

He turned and ran. He was faster. She chased after him, begging him to come back, calling out his name, but he disappeared.

She never saw him again.

For a time, she thought he hadn't survived. But then she learned that the orphanage was able to transfer him out of Sarajevo. Boys had it easier than girls.

So many times she wanted to visit him. To speak to him. To hold him. She had to settle for listening to him.

"Wilhelm Friedemann Herzog," says Randy. "A violinist living in Vienna. Took his adoptive Austrian family's last name but kept his given first and middle names. He was named after Johann Sebastian's first son. I'm sensing a pattern."

She stares at him, in no particular hurry herself.

"Okay, you want your brother, Wilhelm, to adopt your kid."

"And I want to transfer all my financial assets to him. And I want a lawyer who will draw up and approve all the necessary documents."

"Uh-huh. You think your brother's going to want your kid?"

She feels her eyes moisten at the question, one she has asked herself many times. This will be a jolt for Wil, no doubt. But he is a good man. Her child will be Wil's blood, and Wil would not blame his infant niece for the sins of her mother. The fifteen million dollars will ensure that Delilah, and her new family, will be financially secure, too.

But most important, Delilah will never be alone.

Randy shakes his head. "See, the problem here is that you're talking to me as if you have leverage—"

"I can give you information on dozens of international incidents over the last decade. Assassinations of numerous public officials. I can tell you who hired me for each job. I will assist your investigations. I will testify before whatever tribunals. I will do all this as long as my child is born in America and adopted by my brother. I will tell you about every job I've ever carried out."

Randy is still playing his role as the man with the upper hand, but she can see a change in his expression.

"Including *this* job," she says.

CHAPTER
123

❖

I walk through the east door of the Oval Office into the Rose Garden, Augie alongside me. It's muggy outside at this late hour, a threat of rain in the air.

Rachel and I used to stroll through the garden every night after dinner. It was on one of those strolls that she told me that the cancer had returned.

"I'm not sure I ever properly thanked you," I tell him.

"No need," he says.

"What are you going to do now, Augie?"

His shoulders rise. "This I do not know. We— Nina and I—we talked of nothing but returning to Sukhumi."

That word again. That word is *trending*, as they

say, on the Internet right now. I will see that word in my nightmares.

"The thing that is funny," he says, "is that we knew our plan might be unsuccessful. We knew Suliman would send someone after us. We didn't know what you would do. There were so many…"

"Variables."

"Yes, variables. And yet we always spoke as if it was going to happen. She talked of the home she wanted to purchase, a half mile from her parents, not far from the sea. She talked of the names she would give our children someday."

I hear the emotion in his voice. His eyes shine with tears.

I put my hand on his shoulder. "You could stay here," I say. "Work for us."

His mouth twists. "I have no…immigration status. I've not…"

I stop and turn to him. "I might be able to help out with that part," I say. "I know a few people."

He smiles. "Yes, of course, but—"

"Augie, I can't let this happen again. We got lucky this time. We need more than luck going forward. We need to be far more prepared than we were. I need people like you. I need *you*."

He looks away, out over the garden, the roses and daffodils and hyacinths. Rachel knew every kind of flower in this garden by name. I only know them as beautiful. More beautiful, right now, than ever.

"America," he says, as if considering it. "I did rather enjoy the baseball contest."

It's the first real laugh I've had in a very long time. "Baseball *game*," I say.

SUNDAY

CHAPTER
124

❖

Your Highness," I say into the phone to King Saad ibn Saud of Saudi Arabia as I sit at my desk in the Oval Office. I raise a mug of coffee to my lips. I don't ordinarily drink coffee in the afternoon, but after two hours of sleep and the Friday and Saturday we just had, ordinary is long gone.

"*Mr. President,*" he says. "*It seems as if you've had an eventful few days.*"

"As have you. How are you doing?"

"*I suppose an American would say that I escaped by the skin of my teeth. But in my case, it is almost literally true. I am fortunate that the plot was uncovered before they could carry out an attempt on my life. I am blessed. Order has been restored in our kingdom.*"

"Ordinarily," I say, "I would have called you

directly after hearing of the plot. Under the circumstances—"

"There is no need to explain, Mr. President. I fully understand. You've been briefed, I take it, about my reason for calling."

"My CIA director told me, yes."

"Yes. As you know, Mr. President, the Saudi royal family is a large and diverse one."

That's an understatement. The House of Saud numbers in the thousands and has many branches. Most family members have little or no influence and simply receive fat checks from oil revenue. But even among the core group of leaders, numbering somewhere around two thousand, there are branches and hierarchies. And, as there is in any family and any political hierarchy, there is plenty of resentment and jealousy. When Saad ibn Saud jumped over a lot of heads to become the next king, there was more than enough of both to fuel and fund the scheme that brought us all to the edge of disaster.

"The members who attempted the coup have been…discontented with my rule."

"Congratulations, Your Majesty, for your massive understatement and for catching the conspirators."

"It is to my great embarrassment that such plans were

able to blossom and flourish without my knowledge. Right under my nose, as you would say, and I was unaware of it. It was a lapse in our intelligence that, I can assure you, will be corrected."

I know the feeling of missing something that's right under your nose. "What exactly was their plan? What did they want?"

"A return to a different time," he says. *"A world without a dominant America and thus a dominant Israel. They wanted to rule the Saudi kingdom and rule the Middle East. Their intent, as I understand it, was not to destroy America so much as weaken it to the point where it was no longer a superpower. A return to different times, as I said. Regional dominance. No global superpower."*

"We'd have so many of our own problems that we wouldn't bother with the Middle East—that was the thinking?"

"However unrealistic, yes. This is an accurate description of their motives."

I'm not sure how unrealistic it was. It almost happened. I keep thinking the unthinkable— what would have happened had Nina not installed the stopper, the keyword to disable the virus? Or, for that matter, if she hadn't given us the peekaboo to tip us off in advance? What if there hadn't been a Nina and an Augie? We would never have known it was coming. Dark

Ages would have become a reality. We would have been crippled.

Crippled, not killed. But crippled would have been enough, from their perspective. We would have been far too concerned with our troubles at home to worry much about the rest of the world.

They didn't want to destroy us. They didn't want to wipe us off the face of the earth. They just wanted to knock us down enough to force our withdrawal from their part of the world.

"We have been successful in our interrogation of the subjects," says the king.

The Saudis permit a little more leeway in their "interrogation" techniques than we do. "They're talking?"

"Of course," he says, as if it were obvious. *"And naturally we will make all this information available to you."*

"I appreciate that."

"In summary, Mr. President, the members of this splinter group in the royal family paid the terrorist organization, the Sons of Jihad, a tremendous sum of money to destroy the American infrastructure. This included, apparently, hiring an assassin to eliminate members of the Sons of Jihad who had defected from the group."

"Yes. We have the assassin in custody."

"And is she cooperating with the investigation?"

"Yes," I say. "We've reached an understanding with her."

"Then you may know what I am going to say next."

"Perhaps so, Your Highness. But I'd like to hear it from you anyway."

CHAPTER
125

❖

"Have a seat," I say inside the Roosevelt Room. Ordinarily we'd do this in the Oval Office. But I'm not having this conversation in the Oval Office.

He unbuttons his suit jacket and takes a seat. I sit at the head of the table.

"Needless to say, Mr. President, we were elated with the results from yesterday. And we were grateful that we could be a small part of your success."

"Yes, Mr. Ambassador."

"Andrei, please."

Andrei Ivanenko looks like he could play someone's grandfather in a cereal commercial—the crown of his head bald and spotted, wispy white hair along the sides, an overall frumpy appearance.

The look works well for him. Because beneath that harmless-seeming exterior is a career spy, a product of Russia's charm school and one of the elites in the former KGB, shipped off later in life to the diplomatic arena and sent here as ambassador to the United States.

"You could have been an even bigger part of our success," I say, "if you'd warned us about this computer virus in advance."

"In…advance?" He opens his hands. "I do not understand."

"Russia knew, Andrei. You knew what those Saudi royals were up to. You wanted the same thing they wanted. Not to destroy us per se but to diminish us to the point where we no longer had influence. We would no longer be a check on your ambitions. While we were licking our wounds, you could reconstruct the Soviet empire."

"Mr. President," he says, almost like a southern drawl, thick with incredulity. This man could look you in the eye and tell you that the world is flat, the sun rises in the west, and the moon is made of blue cheese, and he'd probably pass a polygraph test while doing so.

"The Saudi royals gave you up," I say.

"People who are desperate, Mr. President," he says without missing a beat, "will say just about—"

"The assassin you hired tells us the same thing," I say. "The consistencies in their stories are…well, they're too similar to be false. We tracked the money, too—the money that Russia transferred to the mercenaries—the Ratnici. And to Bach."

"Ratnici?" he says. "Bach?"

"Funny," I say, "how Bach and the mercenaries waited until the Russian delegation left before attacking our cabin."

"This is…this is not credible, this accusation."

I nod, even give him a cold smile. "You used cutouts, of course. Russia's not stupid. You have plausible deniability. But not with me."

From everything the Saudis in custody told us, we figured out that Suliman shopped them the idea, and they paid richly for his services. The Russians didn't start this. But they knew about it. The Saudis were terrified of moving their own money, so they reached out to Russian intermediaries, realizing that Russia would want to bring the United States to its knees as much as they did. Besides moving the money, Russia provided the mercenaries and the assassin, Bach.

I stand up. "Andrei, it's time for you to leave."

He shakes his head as he gets to his feet. "Mr. President, as soon as I return to the embassy, I will be in touch with President Chernokev, and I am confi—"

"You'll be having that conversation in person, Andrei."

He freezes.

"You're expelled," I say. "I'm putting you on a plane to Moscow right now. The rest of the embassy has until sundown to clear out."

His mouth drops open. It's the first sign of sweat on the man. "You are...closing the Russian embassy in the United States? Severing diplomatic—"

"That's just the start," I say. "When you see the package of sanctions we have planned, you're going to rue the day you cut that deal with those Saudi dissidents. Oh, and those antimissile defense systems Latvia and Lithuania have requested? The ones you've asked us not to sell them? Don't worry, Andrei, we won't sell them."

He swallows hard, his expression relenting. "Well, at least, Mr. Pres—"

"We're going to hand them out free of charge," I say.

"I...Mr. President, I must...I cannot..."

I step close to him, so close that a whisper is all it takes. But I keep my voice up, regardless.

"Tell Chernokev he's lucky we stopped that virus before it did any damage," I say. "Or Russia would be at war with NATO. And Russia would lose."

"Do not ever test me again, Andrei," I say. "Oh, and stay out of our elections. After I speak tomorrow, you'll have all you can handle to keep rigging your own. Now get the hell out of my country."

CHAPTER
126

❖

JoAnn steps into the Oval Office, where I sit with Sam Haber, going over Homeland Security's after-action report, its assessment of the fallout from the Suliman virus.

"Mr. President, the Speaker of the House is on the phone."

I look at Sam, then at JoAnn. "Not now," I say.

"He's canceling the select committee hearing tomorrow, sir. He's requesting that you address the joint session of Congress tomorrow night."

Not surprising. Lester Rhodes, publicly, has sure changed his tune since we stopped this virus.

"Tell him I wouldn't miss it for the world," I say.

MONDAY

CHAPTER
127

❖

"M r. Speaker," says the sergeant at arms, "the president of the United States!"

Members of the House and Senate are on their feet as I enter the House chamber with my escort delegation. I've always enjoyed the chance to address a joint session of Congress. As I walk down the aisle, I enjoy the pageantry and the political small talk even more than usual. A week ago, this is the last place I would have expected to be tonight. And the last people whose hands I'd be expecting to shake are the very two whose hands I grasp at the podium, Vice President Brandt and Speaker Rhodes.

I stand before Congress, my teleprompter ready, and take a moment to drink it all in. The opportunity I have now. The good fortune of our nation.

We did it, I think to myself. *And if we can do this, there's nothing we can't do.*

CHAPTER
128

❖

Madam Vice President, Mr. Speaker, members of Congress, my fellow Americans:

Last night a dedicated team of American public servants, with the help of two close allies and one brave noncitizen, foiled the most dangerous cyberattack ever launched against the United States or any nation.

If fully successful, it would have crippled our military, erased all our financial records and backups, destroyed our electrical grid and transmission networks, broken our water and water-purification systems, disabled our cell phones, and more. The attack's likely consequences would have included massive loss of life, damage to the health of millions of Americans of every age, an economic crash greater than the Depression, and violent anarchy in the streets of communities large and small throughout our country. The effects would have reverberated across the world. The wreckage would have taken years to repair, and our economic, political, and military standing would have needed a decade or more to recover.

We now know that the person who organized and triggered this attack was Suliman Cindoruk, a Turkish terrorist but not a religious man, who did it for a staggering sum of money and apparently for the thrill of hurting the United States. The money was provided by a relatively small number of very wealthy Saudi princes who have no influence with their current government. They intended to use America's absence from the world scene to overthrow the Saudi king, expropriate the wealth of his branch of the royal family and its supporters, reconcile with Iran and Syria, and establish a modern technocratic caliphate using science and technology to raise the standing of the Muslim world to heights not seen in a thousand years.

Sadly, there is also another villain in the tale: Russia. On Saturday, I invited the Russian president, the German chancellor, and the Israeli prime minister to a base of operations I set up not far from here in rural Virginia because of their proven capabilities in cybersecurity—and, in Russia's case, in cyberattacks. The latter two came and were supportive and helpful. Every American owes Germany and Israel a debt of gratitude.

The Russian president did not come but sent the prime minister to act sympathetic. We now know what they had already done to support the attack and why. First, they knew all about it well in advance and refused to tell us, even when I asked. Then, to help the Saudi princes keep their identities secret, they handled the fund transfers Suliman required to pay for the plot and even hired mercenaries and an assassin to support it. They wanted to use our weakness not to finish us off with nuclear weapons but to cripple us so badly that they would be free to increase their stranglehold on their neighbors and assert their power and influence in every other region of the world. As he was leaving Saturday night, I told the prime minister what we suspected and assured him that there would be an appropriate response. Yesterday I took step 1, expelling the Russian ambassador and all Russian employees of its embassy in the United States. This is step 2—making sure the whole world knows they are the world's worst bagmen.

The Saudis have been fully briefed on the plan. They are dealing with their traitors.

And Suliman, religious or not, has gone to meet his Maker.

Saturday, none of this was certain. For in the final frantic hours, when we were racing the clock, our headquarters was attacked by well-trained professional killers, the third such attack since I left the White House to work on this. Many of the assailants were killed, but so were two brave Secret Service agents who died to save my life and to save our country when both were in peril. They are heroes.

Another person was also killed, a remarkable young woman who was the brains behind the cyberbomb but who, along with her partner, a young man who loved her very much, decided she couldn't go through with it. They escaped from Suliman's operation and took unusual steps to warn us about and help prevent the attack while doing their best to survive Suliman's wrath and long reach. Only the young man survived. If they hadn't found their humanity in time, the outcome we applaud today would likely have been very different.

In a clever, roundabout way, the woman made the first contact with us, gave us enough information about the plan for us to take it seriously, and made it clear that only she and her partner could stop it. In return, they wanted to be free of prosecution and to be returned safely to her homeland.

Her partner, who was highly suspicious of our government, made his way here separately, then contacted us to say that the two of them would only deal with me and demanded that I meet him, completely alone, in a highly public place.

That is why your president went missing.

Given the stakes, I decided I had to take the risky, very nearly fatal step of going to that meeting in disguise, alone. I still believe it was the right decision, but I pray that no future crisis will force another president to do anything like it again.

A lot has happened in the last couple of days. We will release more details as we can. There are still loose ends to be tied up and security concerns to consider.

While I was gone, the press went into overdrive, and for good reason—where was I? Why was I off the grid? What was I doing? Earlier, I had agreed, against the advice of my advisers, to appear before a special committee of the House that had been set up to decide whether to start impeachment proceedings against me.

In the vacuum I left, there was a firestorm of

speculation. Friendly media outlets suggested I went off the grid because I was dying of my well-known blood disease or having a breakdown from job stress, declining popularity, and the still raw wound of my wife's death. Less friendly outlets jumped immediately to darker thoughts: I was on the run, with lots of money in secret accounts, having betrayed my country to the world's most notorious terrorist and the country most committed to corrupting our democracy.

In fairness, I invited that response by not telling anyone but my former chief of staff what I was doing and why. I didn't even tell Vice President Brandt, who would have succeeded me had I died last night.

I didn't tell the congressional leaders because I didn't trust them to keep it secret. If the story had broken, it would have caused a national panic and undermined our efforts to stop the attack. Even worse, we suspected a traitor among the small circle of people who were aware that an attack of some kind was looming. Besides my former chief of staff and me, only seven other people, including Vice President Brandt, could have known about it. We hadn't figured out who it was by the time I had to go, so I left even the vice president in the dark.

After I left, the Speaker contacted her to say

that he had the votes to impeach me in the House but needed a few more votes from our side to get the two-thirds necessary to convict me in the Senate. He asked her to help get those votes, saying he didn't care if she became president because engineering my removal would give him control of the House and the national legislative agenda for a long time.

To her everlasting credit, the vice president refused to go along.

I say this not to reopen my long-standing feud with the Speaker but to clear the air so we can make a new beginning. *We should have been fighting this threat together,* across party lines.

Our democracy cannot survive its current downward drift into tribalism, extremism, and seething resentment. Today it's "us versus them" in America. Politics is little more than blood sport. As a result, our willingness to believe the worst about everyone outside our own bubble is growing, and our ability to solve problems and seize opportunities is shrinking.

We have to do better. We have honest differences. We need vigorous debates. Healthy skepticism is good. It saves us from being too naive or too cynical. But it is impossible to preserve democracy when the well of trust runs completely dry.

The freedoms enshrined in the Bill of Rights and the checks and balances in our Constitution were designed to prevent the self-inflicted wounds we face today. But as our long history reveals, those written words must be applied by people charged with giving life to them in each new era. That's how African Americans moved from being slaves to being equal under the law and how they set off on the long journey to be equal in fact, a journey we know is not over. The same story can be told of women's rights, workers' rights, immigrants' rights, the rights of the disabled, the struggle to define and protect religious liberty, and to guarantee equality to people without regard to their sexual orientation or gender identity.

These have been hard-fought battles, waged on uncertain, shifting terrain. Each advance has sparked a strong reaction from those whose interests and beliefs are threatened.

Today the changes are happening so fast, in an environment so covered in a blizzard of information and misinformation, that our very identities are being challenged.

What does it mean to be an American today? It's a question that will answer itself if we get back to what's brought us this far: widening the circle of opportunity, deepening the meaning of freedom, and strengthening bonds of community. Shrinking the definition of *them* and expanding the definition of *us*. Leaving no one behind, left out, looked down on.

We must get back to that mission. And do it with both energy and humility, knowing that our time is fleeting and our power is not an end in itself but a means to achieve more noble and necessary ends.

The American dream works when our common humanity matters more than our interesting differences and when together they create endless possibilities.

That's an America worth fighting—even dying—for. And, more important, it's an America worth living and working for.

I did not betray our country and my sworn duty to protect and defend it when I went missing to battle what we came to call Dark Ages for the same reason that I didn't betray it when I was being tortured as a prisoner of war in Iraq. I didn't because I couldn't. I love my country too much, and I want the United States to be free and prosperous, peaceful and secure, and constantly improving for all generations to come.

I say this not to boast. I believe most of you, were you in my place, would have done the same thing. I hope that's enough trust for us to make a new beginning.

My fellow Americans, we just dodged the biggest bullet we've faced since World War II. America's been given a second chance. We musn't blow it. And we can only make the most of it together.

I believe we should start by reforming and protecting our elections. Everyone eligible to vote should be able to do so without unnecessary inconvenience, fear of being purged from voting rolls, or concern that machines that can be hacked in five or six minutes won't count their votes correctly. And wherever possible, state and national legislative districts should be drawn by nonpartisan bodies to more fully represent the diversity of opinion and interests that is one of the greatest assets of our nation.

Think about how different it would be if we reached beyond our base to represent a broader spectrum of opinions and interests. We'd learn to listen to one another more and defame one another less. That would help build the trust necessary to find more common ground. On that foundation, we could bring small-town and rural America, people in depressed urban areas, and Native American communities into the modern economy: with affordable broadband and lead-free water for all our families; more clean power with jobs more evenly spread across America; a tax code that rewards investment in left-behind areas, allowing corporate executives and big investors to help everyone, not just themselves.

We could have real immigration reform, with better border security but without closing our borders to those who come here searching for safety or for a better future for themselves and their families. Our native-born birthrate is barely at replacement levels. We need the Dreamers and the workers, the professionals and the entrepreneurs who form new businesses at twice the national average.

We could have serious training and support programs for police and community leaders to prevent wrongful civilian deaths, increase police officer safety, and reduce crime. And gun safety laws that keep guns away from those who shouldn't have them, reduce the almost inconceivable number of mass killings, and still protect the right to own guns for hunting, sport shooting, and self-defense.

We could have a real climate-change debate. Who has the best ideas for reducing the threat most quickly while creating the most new businesses and good jobs? With the coming advances in automation and artificial intelligence, we will need many more of them.

We could do so much more to stem the opioid crisis, to destigmatize it, to educate the extremely high number of people who still don't know they can kill themselves, and to make sure every American is within driving distance of affordable, effective treatment.

And we could reorder our defense spending to reflect the enormous and constantly evolving threat of cyberattacks so that our defenses are second to none and we have the standing to persuade other nations to work with us to reduce the dangers everywhere before we face another apocalypse. The next time, we won't be so lucky as to have two alienated young geniuses riding to our rescue.

Think how much more rewarding it would be if we all came to work every day asking, "Whom can we help today and how can we do it?" instead of "Whom can I hurt and how much coverage can I get for it?"

Our founders left us an eternal charge: to form a more perfect union. And they left us a government sturdy enough to preserve our liberties and flexible enough to meet the challenges of each new age. Those two gifts have brought us a mighty long way. We must stop taking them for granted, even putting them at risk, for fleeting advantage. Before last night, most of our wounds, including falling behind in cyberdefense, were self-inflicted.

Thank God we still face a future full of possibilities, not the grim duty to claw our way out of ruin.

We owe it to our children, ourselves, and billions of decent people throughout the world who still want us to be an inspiration, an example, and a friend to make the most of this second chance.

Let this night be remembered as a celebration of disaster avoided and a rededication of *our* lives, *our* fortunes, and *our* sacred honor to form *our* more perfect union.

May God bless the United States of America and *all* who call it home.

Thank you. Sleep well.

EPILOGUE

After the speech, my approval ratings rose from less than 30 percent to more than 80 percent. I knew it wouldn't last, but it felt good to be out of the dungeon.

I got some criticism for using the speech to advance my agenda, but I wanted Americans to know what I wanted to do for them and still leave plenty of opportunities for working with the other side.

The Speaker has been grudgingly helpful. Within two weeks, Congress had passed, with bipartisan majorities, a bill calling for more honest, inclusive, accountable elections and providing some funds to transition to nonhackable voting, beginning with old-fashioned paper ballots. The rest of the agenda is still pending, but I am hopeful that with the right compromises and incentives, we can get more done. There's even been some movement on the assault-weapons ban and a bill to enact truly comprehensive background checks.

The Speaker's still deciding his next move. He was mad at me for calling him out but relieved that I hadn't gone all the way by telling America he wanted Vice President Brandt to appoint his daughter to the Supreme Court in return for making her president.

Carolyn Brock was hit with a twenty-count indictment, accusing her in various ways of treason, acts of terrorism, misuse of classified information, murder, conspiracy to commit murder, and obstruction of justice. Her lawyers are negotiating a guilty plea, hoping to avoid a life sentence. It is heartbreaking in so many ways— her betrayal of everything we worked so hard to accomplish, the bright future she could have had if she hadn't surrendered to reckless ambition, but most of all, the impact on her family. There are still times, when I am lost in thought on a tough question, that I will catch myself calling out her name.

Meanwhile, I finally let Dr. Deb give me the protein treatment along with a steroid infusion. My platelet count is comfortably in the six figures. I feel better, and I don't have to worry about dropping dead if I'm a little late taking my pills. Also, not being shot at is nice.

And thank God my daughter's back to her own life, breathing easier.

The mainstream media coverage, from right to left, has become more straightforward, not so much because of my speech but because, at least for now, Americans are moving away from extreme media toward outlets that offer more explanation and fewer personal attacks.

I did send someone to see the homeless veteran I met on the street after I went missing. He's now in group treatment and getting help with finding a decent job and affordable housing. And it looks like Congress will fund an effort to reduce the killing of unarmed citizens, increase police officers' safety, and set up neighborhood councils to work with the police.

I don't know what the future holds. All I know is that the country I love has a new lease on life.

At the end of the Constitutional Convention, a citizen asked Benjamin Franklin what kind of government our founders had given us. He replied, "A republic, if you can keep it." That's a job no president can do alone. It's up to all of us to keep it. And to make the most of it.

ACKNOWLEDGMENTS

For their invaluable assistance in technical matters, special thanks to John Melton, who served in the 75th Ranger Regiment from 1992 to 1994; to James Wagner; to Thomas Kinzler; and to Richard Clarke, who served four presidents as a security and counterterrorism adviser.

ABOUT THE AUTHORS

BILL CLINTON was elected president of the United States in 1992, and he served until 2001. After leaving the White House, he established the Clinton Foundation, which helps improve global health, increase opportunity for girls and women, reduce childhood obesity and preventable diseases, create economic opportunity and growth, and address the effects of climate change. He is the author of a number of nonfiction works, including *My Life*, which was a #1 international bestseller. This is his first novel.

JAMES PATTERSON received the Literarian Award for Outstanding Service to the American Literary Community from the National Book Foundation. He holds the Guinness World Record for the most #1 *New York*

Times bestsellers, and his books have sold more than 375 million copies worldwide. A tireless champion of the power of books and reading, Patterson created a new children's book imprint, JIMMY Patterson, whose mission is simple: "We want every kid who finishes a JIMMY Book to say, 'PLEASE GIVE ME ANOTHER BOOK.'"